Praise for
Midnight Secrets

"Simultaneously building suspense and passion, [St. Giles] brings the classic gothic to a new sensual level without missing a step, combining dark atmosphere and the twisted plot of a great mystery. She hooks you and never lets you go."

—*Romantic Times* (four stars)

"Jennifer St. Giles is quickly proving herself the new queen of the gothic romance." —*Romance Reviews Today*

"Readers, rejoice, the gothic is alive and well . . . a spine-tingling read." —*The Romance Reader's Connection*

Praise for
His Dark Desires

"A sexually charged romance that satisfies whether . . . seeking suspense or passion." —*Romantic Times*

"With its dark, dangerous hero and sexy story line this historical romance will appeal to contemporary romantic suspense fans who enjoy danger and intrigue."

—*True Romance Magazine*

continued . . .

Berkley Sensation titles
by Jennifer St. Giles

DARKEST DREAMS
MIDNIGHT SECRETS

Darkest Dreams

JENNIFER ST. GILES

BERKLEY SENSATION, NEW YORK

THE BERKLEY PUBLISHING GROUP
Published by the Penguin Group
Penguin Group (USA) Inc.
375 Hudson Street, New York, New York 10014, USA

Penguin Group (Canada), 90 Eglinton Avenue East, Suite 700, Toronto, Ontario M4P 2Y3, Canada
(a division of Pearson Penguin Canada Inc.)
Penguin Books Ltd., 80 Strand, London WC2R 0RL, England
Penguin Group Ireland, 25 St. Stephen's Green, Dublin 2, Ireland (a division of Penguin Books Ltd.)
Penguin Group (Australia), 250 Camberwell Road, Camberwell, Victoria 3124, Australia
(a division of Pearson Australia Group Pty. Ltd.)
Penguin Books India Pvt. Ltd., 11 Community Centre, Panchsheel Park, New Delhi—110 017, India
Penguin Group (NZ), Cnr. Airborne and Rosedale Roads, Albany, Auckland 1310, New Zealand
(a division of Pearson New Zealand Ltd.)
Penguin Books (South Africa) (Pty.) Ltd., 24 Sturdee Avenue, Rosebank, Johannesburg 2196,
South Africa

Penguin Books Ltd., Registered Offices: 80 Strand, London WC2R 0RL, England

This is a work of fiction. Names, characters, places, and incidents either are the product of the author's
imagination or are used fictitiously, and any resemblance to actual persons, living or dead, business establishments, events, or locales is entirely coincidental. The publisher does not have any control over
and does not assume any responsibility for author or third-party websites or their content.

DARKEST DREAMS

A Berkley Sensation Book / published by arrangement with the author

PRINTING HISTORY
Berkley Sensation mass-market edition / December 2006

Copyright © 2006 by Jenni Leigh Grizzle.
Excerpt of *Silken Shadows* © 2007 by Jenni Leigh Grizzle.
Cover art by Franco Accornero.
Cover design by George Long.
Interior text design by Stacy Irwin.

ISBN: 0-425-21303-X

BERKLEY SENSATION®
Berkley Sensation Books are published by The Berkley Publishing Group,
a division of Penguin Group (USA) Inc.,
375 Hudson Street, New York, New York 10014.
BERKLEY SENSATION is a registered trademark of Penguin Group (USA) Inc.
The "B" design is a trademark belonging to Penguin Group (USA) Inc.

PRINTED IN THE UNITED STATES OF AMERICA

10 9 8 7 6 5 4 3 2 1

One word frees us of all the weight and pain of life:
That word is love.

—SOPHOCLES (496–406 B.C.)

1

Dartmoor's End, England
1879

The distant cry, pitched perfectly to my roiling feelings, drew my gaze toward the sea, where a lone gull hovered over the terns and pelicans, looking as I felt, adrift and alone. People rushed to and fro upon the busy port's dock while sailors loaded and unloaded cargo and fishermen shouted over the bounty of their morning catch. I stood in the center of it all, trapped within my family's loving circle, yet more alone and lost than I had ever been in my life. In many ways I was like my namesake, Andromeda, chained to the rocks in the sea, waiting to be devoured by a lurking monster. Except, I knew no Perseus would come swooping down to rescue me from my fate, and my monster didn't lie within the sea, but within myself.

The tangy breeze did little to refresh me, and the bright day did little to warm me, for I felt it was only a matter of time before I would have to leave my family because hiding the truth of what I had become from them grew more and more difficult. The looming void left me cold inside.

Death had brought me and my sisters to Dartmoor's End and the wilds of the Cornish coast, but love had kept us here, as my sister Cassie, in her search for the truth about our cousin Mary's disappearance, had met and married Sean Killdaren.

Unfortunately, the bizarre unfolding of events over the past two months had unleashed a disquiet within me that I couldn't seem to lay to rest with the soothing balm of Mary's funeral and Cassie's quiet marriage, as other Andrews family members had. I'd moved beyond the safe confines of artifacts and the past to interact with more people than I had in years and had discovered my gift of "seeing" into people's minds had honed itself to an unbearable point. And just as disturbing were my highly improper thoughts about Sean's twin brother, Lord Alexander Killdaren, Viscount Blackmoor.

Besides being the most dynamic person I'd ever met, Lord Alexander was also the most intriguing. In our short association, I'd touched him several times and had yet to "see" into his mind. I wasn't sure if it was the man or if it was fate. My ability to see into people's minds was fickle in that I never knew if I would receive an image, a thought, an emotion, or a feeling; but I always saw something besides the dark, obscure cloud I got from Lord Alexander.

Nearby, a horse neighed, snatching my attention. My heart sped before I realized Lord Alexander wouldn't be racing his thunderous horse onto the docks. The sound had come from the deck of a ship where sailors were attempting to calm a fiercely wild, and very pregnant, black mare.

Sighing, I forced a smile in place and turned my attention back to my family's bantering goodbyes to my parents. They'd returned from Greece in time for Mary's funeral and were thrilled to be here for Cassie's wedding, but now had to finish their archaeological expedition before their expected return to Oxford.

"Are you all right, Andrie?" Cassie asked, touching my hand in concern.

I nodded and braced myself for her thoughts. Instead of the

thrill of her trysting with Sean, I felt nausea and a knot of worry about the future roiling inside her.

"You're ill. You shouldn't have come," I whispered. She snatched her hand back from mine. I reached for her again, concerned, and she immediately stepped away. Pain squeezed my heart as I dropped my hand.

Cassie was the closest of my family to me, not that I didn't dearly love my sister Gemini, my parents, and all of their chaotic affections. But Cassie with her dreams and I with my "sight" had always been a little set apart from everyone, and we had learned at an early age to hide our "gifts" from others. Since coming to Killdaren's Castle and since her marriage, Cassie and I had grown apart in some ways, and I'd yet to divulge to her the change in my gift, how much more I could see into a person's mind now than I could before. It was too embarrassing and disturbing. I didn't want everyone I knew questioning what I could see of their secret thoughts every time I touched them.

She sighed. "I'm sorry, Andrie. I didn't mean to hurt your feelings."

"No, I'm sorry. I shouldn't have intruded."

"You didn't. I'll explain later," Cassie whispered just before our mother approached, enveloping us in a big hug, and knocking her bonnet awry.

Cassie adjusted our mother's bonnet with a loving pat. "Don't worry about us. We'll be fine."

"I'm here, dears!" Aunt Lavinia called out. I glanced over to where Gemini was helping our aunt carry her satchel of "emergency" necessities. With the way they were struggling, I had to wonder if the bag weighed more than Aunt Lavinia. There was no doubt that it outweighed Gemini.

I squeezed my mother's shoulder, reading her thoughts. Phoebe Andrews lived her life torn between being with her husband and with her children. For the first ten years of motherhood she stayed with us and pined for our father. Now, she traveled with him, but fretted about us. "Stop worrying," I told her. "You're doing the right thing by insisting Aunt

Lavinia accompany you to Greece. Being with us here is too painful for her right now." My aunt would never say so, but the loss of Mary, her only child, had taken the very heart out of life for her. I hoped that by traveling to a new land, Aunt Lavinia would discover something more for her life than her sorrow and her sudden interest in wine. "We'll be perfectly fine staying with Cassie until you return. My only request is that you send the next shipment of artifacts to me here. I don't want to have to wait so long before I can catalogue more treasures."

Laughing, my mother kissed my cheek. "I'll talk to your father."

"About what?" my father said, joining us with a frown, trying to appear as fierce as an ancient warrior might have looked going into battle, and failing. He'd always be the lost professor, with his rumpled cravat and dreamer's blue eyes. Currently, my parents were on a quest to locate a golden temple that Alexander the Great had built to Apollo.

My mother patted my father's sleeve. "Why, dear, to convince you to put some artifacts in Andrie's hands as soon as possible rather than make her wait until we all return to Oxford."

"That's my girl. You love archaeology as much as I do," he said, wrapping his arm around my shoulders, imbuing me with a keen sense of his pride. Part of me wanted to lean into him and revel in his approval, while at the same time part of me wanted to hide, for it wasn't a love of archaeology, but rather desperation that drove me.

My father reached into his pocket. "In fact, I've an artifact I brought with me this morning."

The ring sparkled like green fire as the sun glinted off the emeralds lining the golden serpent's spine and dotting its eyes. Immediately, I called to mind Lord Alexander Killdaren's eyes. "It's beautiful."

"It is for you," my father said softly.

"Me?"

"Yes."

Reverently, I took the ring from my father, my fingers tingling when I touched his hand. Tears misted my eyes at the contact, because for the very first time the depth of his love for me was apparent. I thought I knew my father well. I had read his emotions and thoughts many times over the years, but I'd never seen into his heart as clearly as I did at that moment. His passion for archaeology, which was usually the topic of most of our conversations, had blurred my vision from seeing the truth of his emotions. The revelation stunned me.

I stood there, staring at the ring with wonder, prompting my father to laugh. "Here, let me put it on your finger. Your mother and I thought this would be the perfect way to let you know how much we appreciate all your help."

"Thank you," I whispered past the lump of emotion in my throat as he took my lace-gloved hand and slid the ring on my finger.

"The ring is thought to be over two thousand years old, belonging to a woman known only as Aphrodite during Alexander the Great's reign."

"Oh, thank you, thank you," I said, giving him a big hug, thrilled to have thousands of years of history on my finger.

My father patted my back, blinking quickly behind his spectacles. "Darned wind is drying my eyes," he said, taking off his glasses and rubbing them on his coat sleeve. I blinked at my own tears, holding out my hand to look at the ring.

"Oh, Andrie," Cassie squealed with delight. "It is so beautiful."

"Most beautiful," my mother said. "And so well deserved. You should be paid for all the work you do cataloguing artifacts for us."

"Nonsense. I love doing it." Would be truly lost without it.

"Nevertheless, we feel as if we're taking advantage of your good heart. I hope this conveys both our appreciation and our love."

"It's too much, but I'll not give it up." Smiling, I stared at the serpent's green eyes. I'd not only be able to carry a part of the past with me, but I'd always have a reminder of Lord

Alexander Killdaren. The vibrant emeralds matched his eyes so perfectly, they could have been mined directly from them.

Aunt Lavinia and Gemini lumbered to our side, wrestling with the satchel. A suspicious clink sounded as the satchel fell to the dock.

Flushed, Aunt Lavinia fanned her face and peered down at the case. "Oh, dear."

Gemini dotted her brow with the scented handkerchief she pulled from her pocket. "It feels as if she has half a castle in there."

"Half?" I said. "From your struggle, I'd wager my new dress that she has a whole castle in there."

Gemini laughed. "It would be wise, dear sister, to never wager the clothes on your back. You might find yourself naked on the street one day."

"Let's pray not," my father commented with a scowl. "Whatever do you have in there, Lavinia?"

"Just emergency supplies, Thomas." Aunt Lavinia leaned over and whispered something to my mother. A scarlet blush graced my mother's cheeks.

My father cleared his throat and tugged the front of his tweed jacket into place. "Well, I'm certainly not going to carry that bag by hand all the way to Greece. Let the steward handle it with the rest of our trunks."

"I can't do that. They surely would break something," Aunt Lavinia declared.

Cassie knelt beside the bag. "I think something did break. There's a stain on the side."

I joined her, planning to help her with the satchel, for I was worried about her. She appeared pale and a fine sheen of perspiration dotted her cheeks. Then I noticed the smell of sweet spice, so at odds with the salty breeze and the fish-laden boats.

Cassie sniffed the air then frowned. "It can't be," she whispered, reaching for the satchel's buckles.

I sighed. "I think it is."

Aunt Lavinia waved her hand at us. "I'm sure everything

is just fine, dears. I'll check inside the bag just a soon as I am settled in my stateroom."

But she spoke a fraction too late. Cassie popped open the bag. Inside was surely a dozen bottles of wine, if not more. Spiced wine. A Killdaren family recipe and a wine that brought back keen memories of the last evening I'd seen Lord Alexander. The night I'd almost felt normal for the first time in my life. Lord Alexander had had an elegant dinner party at Seafarer's Inn and had invited me, Gemini, and Aunt Lavinia. It had been the most exciting night of my life. The wine, the music, and the intimate conversation with him still filled my daydreams.

"Aunt Lavinia!" Cassie exclaimed.

"Good heavens, dear," Aunt Lavinia gasped at Cassie. "Close that bag before you give everyone the wrong impression. It's for medicinal purposes I assure you. Mr. Killdaren agreed with my assessment of the wine's properties and gave me an adequate supply."

"Oh, might I have just one bottle, Auntie?" Gemini batted her lashes.

"Certainly not," Cassie exclaimed. She caught my shoulder to balance herself as she quickly stood. Her slight dizziness shocked me as much as the word steaming in her mind. *Aphrodisiac.* Whatever did such an outrageous idea have to do with the wine?

Cassie stood, her hands settling on her hips as a glint sparked in her narrowed eyes. "Sean gave you a supply?"

"Most certainly. Very nice of him, indeed." Aunt Lavinia nodded, answering Cassie. "Its effects on the circulation are phenomenal."

"I'm sure," Cassie said. She didn't sound happy with her husband.

I closed Aunt Lavinia's bag, thinking there might be a grain of truth to the notion, and wondered about her recent affinity for wine. I clearly recalled the heated flush that had filled me the evening I'd imbibed the spiced wine. Details of Lord Alexander that night were unforgettable—his full

mouth, the way he so deftly handled the cards, the smooth-
ness of his voice, the lure of his scent, and the fact that I had
touched him several times, read nothing, and felt normal. I'd
wondered ever since if my desire for him had blinded my
gift. It was a very nice thought.

My father's scowl deepened. "Well, I'm not carrying a
bag of wine around Greece, Lavinia. The establishments we
will be visiting have a supply from the world's best vine-
yards."

"Thomas, might I have a word with you?" My mother
caught my father's arm and tugged him to the side. "Remember last night . . ." The rest of her words died to a whisper. I watched as my father's eyes widened.

He cleared his throat and picked up the heavy bag. "Since
you feel this is necessary, Lavinia, I'll assure its safety during the trip."

The ship's horn sounded, calling all last-minute passen-
gers to board.

"Thomas!" Aunt Lavinia gasped. "I believe I can carry
the bag now."

He walked off toward the gangplank, a very odd smile
on his face. "Nonsense, Lavinia. Phoebe and I will take
care of it."

My mother followed my father, smiling oddly as well.
Realization dawned on me about what that smile meant as
Aunt Lavinia went after them in a huff. I was just glad there
weren't any last-minute hugs from my parents. Cassie's
thoughts about Sean were bad enough. My parents and my
aunt boarded the ship safely and waved one last time before
disappearing belowdecks. My mother could never stand to
stay on deck and watch us slowly fade into the distance. She
always wanted her last memory of us to be sharp and clear in
her mind. I understood her desire, but wondered if it was
possible. Over time, everyone faded.

"Whatever was that about?" Gemini asked as she turned
from the ship.

"Nothing, Gemmi," Cassie said firmly before I could

respond. "You'd best adjust your bonnet or you'll get sun-burned."

Gemini gasped and squashed her bonnet around her face so that she could barely peep out.

I laughed at how quickly Cassie had distracted Gemini from being too curious over the situation with the spiced wine and its unusual properties. Gemini was currently trying to catch the attention of Sean Killdaren's friend, Lord Ashton, but thus far had had no luck. To have her complexion marred by the sun even for a day would have her swooning.

My voice caught in my throat as I was about to comment that Gemini's nose was already irrevocably red, even though it wasn't. The sound of horses' hooves on the shore along with the act of everyone around me turning and gasping in awe and fear told me that *he* had arrived at the docks. Lord Alexander Killdaren.

Though the mystery surrounding Mary's death had been solved, the murder of Lady Helen Kennedy eight years ago had not been. Since Sean Killdaren and Lord Alexander Killdaren were the last ones to see her alive and a witness had seen one of them leaving the scene of the murder, a dark cloud of suspicion hung over their lives. To this day the villagers gave the Killdaren twins a wide berth. Neither Cassie nor I believed the rumors. She was sure Sean was innocent and I was convinced Lord Alexander was, too.

Lord Alexander leapt from the saddle and strode down the dock, a commanding figure to be reckoned with. Shockingly dressed in only snug black pants, a loose white shirt, and knee-high boots, he could have easily been a swash-buckling pirate from a reckless age. His dark hair framed his strong features, and lay wildly windblown well over the collar of his shirt. His thick muscles strained against his clothes as he walked. His charismatic aura jarred the world around him like a stiff wind from the dark sea and blasted me as he neared.

He must have felt my regard, for he suddenly gazed right at me. I stared directly at him as if possessed by a need and will greater than any rule of propriety I'd ever learned. "Lord Alexander is great indeed," I murmured.

"What?" Cassie asked, following my gaze with hers. She gasped and grabbed my hand. I heard the *Sean* that rang through her mind before her pulse steadied and she whispered, "Lord Alexander." All of that pent-up worry I'd felt in her earlier escaped in his name.

As we stared at him, he nodded his head politely, then passed by without offering a cordial greeting before going to the ship where I'd seen the wild horse being gentled.

"What is it?" I asked Cassie, wanting to know about the angst I still felt inside her. "What is wrong?"

"Andrie. I don't know what I am going to do."

I couldn't stop myself. At the note of despair in her voice, I tightened my grip on her hand and focused my whole gift on seeing into her.

"Oh, dear," I said, reeling beneath the revelation. "I mean what wonderful news, but oh, dear."

"That doesn't half convey my sentiments. I don't know why I didn't foresee this fear. I never dreamed I would be afraid to tell Sean that we are going to have a child."

"Surely *you* don't believe Sean and Lord Alexander are truly cursed, that one will kill the other."

Cassie sighed. "It's hard to refute a thousand years of history that shows when twins are born into the Killdaren family, one has killed the other. It doesn't matter if I believe in the Dragon's Curse or not, though, Sean does. Lord Alexander does. Somehow, if we are ever to be free of it, I have to find a way to break the curse. But as long as none of us ever see or speak to Lord Alexander, I don't see any hope of things changing. They've spent eight years avoiding each other."

"I've heard Bridget rail about how blind men are, and I'm beginning to believe her." I drew an exasperated breath, feeling very much like saying a word ladies weren't supposed to use; a word Bridget, Cassie's friend who made an unforgettable lady's companion at Killdaren's Castle, frequently uttered. "Lord Alexander didn't kill Lady Helen and he didn't try to kill Sean either. I know it as surely as I know my own name."

Still, I felt strange making the declaration, for though I believed in Lord Alexander's innocence with every fiber of my being, I'd not been able to read Lord Alexander's thoughts and emotions to *know* it was true.

"Sean didn't kill Lady Helen either, nor did he want his brother to die during their fight. But I don't think Sean will let himself admit that. If he did, he'd have to forgive himself and for some reason he can't. It's easier to blame the Dragon's Curse for what happened eight years ago."

"The whole situation gives me a headache." I sighed. "There has to be a way to manipulate both of them into admitting they are wrong."

"Not as long as the viscount stays locked in his castle and Sean in his," Gemini added, having overheard the last of our conversation. "Oh look, there's Lord Ashton and Mr. Drayson at the market with the Earl of Dartraven and Sir Warwick. Why, they're nearly standing next to our carriage. I will wait for you two there," she said, taking off before Cassie or I could say a word.

As the carriage was only a short distance away, and the Earl of Dartraven, Sean and Lord Alexander's father, would be chaperone enough for Gemini, I turned my gaze back to Lord Alexander. He stood surveying the wild horse on the deck of the ship, managing to look like an impregnable fortress.

"How can we get past Sean and his brother's defenses?" Cassie murmured.

"Trojan horse," I whispered softly as an utterly intriguing idea flared inside me: Weeks ago, long before Cassie and Sean announced their intention to marry, Lord Alexander had mentioned that the generations of artifacts at his castle needed to be catalogued. We'd even spoken at length over dinner the last time I'd seen him about his possibly hiring me to do some cataloguing.

I was desperate to escape being in close quarters with Cassie and Sean. It wasn't that I resented the happy couple, but more that I felt as though I was intruding on their privacy. Too often, when I inadvertently touched Cassie, I felt her private emotions or thoughts. Cataloguing would provide me with a way to spend time on my own, to regain the inner peace I'd lost over the last few months.

The burden of being able to see so much from the minds of those around me grew larger despite my efforts to escape knowing.

"Trojan horse? Andrie, you're not making sense." Cassie peered at me as if I'd spoken in Greek. "You've spent entirely too much time with antiquities."

I squeezed her hand. "We need a Trojan horse to get inside Lord Alexander's castle."

Cassie paused, then slowly nodded as realization dawned. "I see. And wherever are we going to find one?"

I smiled. "You're looking at it. Me. It's time for the Killdaren family to catalogue their treasures, don't you think?"

"You're a genius." Cassie laughed and a ray of hope lit her troubled gaze. Then her smile faltered. "I'm not so sure that it's a good idea after all."

"Why? Surely you don't still think he had anything to do with Lady Helen's death?"

"No. Not since you read Lord Alexander's thoughts on the matter. I'm just worried about you."

I hadn't read Lord Alexander's thoughts. Cassie had just assumed that I had when we'd argued about which brother could have been responsible for Lady Helen's death. I'd yet to tell Cassie that I couldn't read Lord Alexander's thoughts because I didn't want her to doubt his innocence. "What do you mean?"

"You developed feelings for Lord Alexander when we were searching for the truth about Mary. Am I wrong?"

"Was it that obvious?"

"Only to me. You usually go to great lengths to avoid contact with strangers. You didn't with him. That he's treated us like the plague since learning of my engagement and marriage to Sean has to have hurt your feelings. I know something has had you out of sorts lately."

"With so much time on my hands, I've been restless," I said, hoping she wouldn't press for more. "Cataloguing will be just the thing to set me back to rights. Come on," I said, pulling her toward Lord Alexander. "The viscount won't be able to refuse to speak to us. Not in so public a place."

"I'm not so sure about that," Cassie muttered.

I wasn't sure how Lord Alexander would greet us, either. My nerves fluttered more than his dark hair did in the sea breeze. Seeing him coatless and daring in public made me readily believe many of the rumors about him. The Killdaren family was noted for flaunting traditions and living well outside society's strictures, and the gossip I'd heard about Lord Alexander Killdaren indicated he was the boldest of the lot.

He stood at the end of the loading ramp with his back to us, apparently watching the spirited horse prancing on the deck of the ship. The magnificence of the beast had captured almost everyone's attention, and would have had mine as well were it not for the man before me and the way the cloth of his shirt stretched tautly across his broad shoulders, barely masking the supple grace and power of his body beneath. The tailored fit of his breeches followed the line of his body along his trim hips and down the sinewy length of his legs, leaving little to the imagination.

My cheeks flamed more hotly than the sun, a condition that worsened when Lord Alexander turned my way. His gaze slid slowly over me and all thought left my mind.

"Ladies." He nodded his head at my sister, his manner cordial and respectful, if reserved. "I hear you're Mrs. Killdaren now."

"Happily so," Cassie replied, notably relieved he didn't publicly ignore us. "A beautiful day, my lord."

"Yes," he replied, then fell silent, as if either at a loss over what to say, or perhaps hoping we'd continue on our way. After an awkward moment, he added, "The sea air appears to agree with you both. You're looking well since I last saw you."

My voice was tangled up with my pounding heart, but I forced myself to speak, fearing this opportunity would be lost before any significant connection could be made. "Thank you, my lord. Oxford can get intolerably hot this time of the year and we've found the climate here at Dartmoor's End refreshing." The horse on the ship let out a shrill whinny and I glanced at the commotion it caused as the beast reared up from those trying to gentle it. "Unfortunately the sea doesn't seem to have agreed with that one. Is she yours?"

"Yes, and very special. You're looking at my legacy. She's from the Netherlands and carries the seed of the last living Friesian stallion within her. They're a dying breed that I hope to save from extinction." His voice deepened with a haunting emotion as he spoke, vibrating a chord within me so strongly that I almost missed that he'd said *my* legacy as opposed to *a* legacy. The nuance seemed significant to me, but his expression remained casual, revealing little. "I'm about to go on board and welcome her to her new home."

"She's so beautiful," Cassie said.

"She's exquisite," I murmured. I'd never seen a more beautiful horse, sleek and black with an impossibly long mane and tail. Tufts of glistening hair covered each of her hooves, giving her a majestic appearance worthy of any legend. She appeared as if she were made of the greatest elements of earth imbued with the spirit of the heavens. It was also clear to me that Lord Alexander was about to depart from our company. I motioned to the ship and boldly stepped past any rules on manners or propriety I'd been taught. "We'd love to go aboard to join you in welcoming her to her new home."

I barely bit back my groan as Cassie shook her head. "I don't think I care to venture over the gangplank. But why don't you go with the viscount, Andrie, then meet Gemini and me at the shops near the carriage."

Lord Alexander frowned. "The gangplank can be a bit unsteady with the wind as gusty as it is today."

"I've remarkable balance, and would love to meet your legacy, Lord Alexander."

"Enjoy yourself then," Cassie said, with a smile and a wink, before she turned for the carriage where I could see Gemini in conversation with Lord Ashton and Mr. Drayson, mutual friends of Sean and Lord Alexander.

Having little choice, Lord Alexander offered me his arm and I set my gloved hand on him. Once again, I sensed none of his emotions or feelings. His mind was like a gray mist where I could see nothing beyond dark shadows; no thoughts and no images, just strong, nebulous emotions. Being next to him sent little jolts of fire through me though, wreaking havoc on all of my senses. It was no wonder my sight was rendered useless with him.

He stiffly led the way to the ship, taking care that we didn't step too close to the edge of the rocking gangplank, and my heart sank at his reserved manner. It was so different than before. When we first met this summer, I had felt such intense interest from him, so much so that were he a pirate I had no doubt he would have kidnapped me and taken me captive aboard his ship.

"What's her name? It must be something special, I should think."

"I don't know her name yet," he replied. "What would you name her, Miss Andrews?"

I didn't hesitate to answer. "A name is very important and must have a great history behind it. Which of the world's legends or myths do you find heart in? The Druids, the Norse, the Greeks from ages past, or the more recent tales of King Arthur and his knights?"

"Since I'm in the company of Andromeda, I'll be the gentleman and say Greek."

His choice secretly pleased me, despite his diplomatic reasoning. "Iris," I said softly as the name for the dark horse came quickly to me. "The goddess of the rainbow, a symbol of the union of earth and sky, for the horse looks as if she could fly when she runs."

"Interesting," he said. We'd reached the top of the gang-plank. He moved to the starboard deck first, then, surpris-ingly, reached for me, placing both hands at my sides to help lift me over the rail and cargo. I was aware of every sizzling inch of his fingers and palms pressed so firmly against my waist. Heat flashed through me as he set me on my feet, much closer to his person than I should be in public or in private.

"And according to some the mother of Eros as well," he replied, gazing directly into my eyes before releasing me. His heated gaze left no question that he was still attracted to me. I gasped at the connection and the sensations sliding through me as I realized his reserved manner was but an act. "Excellent choice, Miss Andrews. Iris it is, and I'll hope to name the foal Eros."

The seductive tone of his voice went straight to my head with dizzying force. I wasn't sure how I navigated my way across the deck.

Suddenly, before we had quite reached her, the mare reared up again and broke free of her handlers, charging right at us.

"Damn," Lord Alexander said as he scooped me up. In that moment, I saw into his mind as he jumped onto the bags of rice waiting on the deck. The image of a naked blond woman, bound in his bed, flashed before my eyes. My breath caught then flew away with the vision as he deposited me out of harm's way and grabbed one of the ropes trailing behind the mare. She instantly reared up, pawing the air, but he held on, tugging gently on the rope and whispering soothing words to the frightened animal. She pranced nervously in place be-fore butting him with her head. When she appeared to be qui-eting, Lord Alexander grasped her halter, continuing to gentle her with his voice. I had no idea what he whispered in her ear, but I did know one thing.

The bound woman in his bed had been me.

2

The image Lord Alexander had of me in his mind dazed me. Surely it was his thought I'd seen and not mine, for though I'd had the pirate with his captive notion on the gangplank, I'd never imagined myself bound and naked before. I stared up at him, watching him calm the frightened mare with a velvet but iron hand, wondering what to make of the situation.

I couldn't go into an outrage, for I wasn't supposed to be reading his mind and I didn't want him to know that I had. Yet, how could I ignore something so . . . so . . . outrageous? And why wasn't I running from the ship screaming as if the devil were at my heels?

Shutting my eyes, I recalled the image again, realizing that I had been smiling in it, as if welcoming the situation! Impossible. I popped my eyes open and slowly moved closer to Lord Alexander's side. He'd calmed the mare adeptly. That the horse hadn't suffered any injury I counted as much a testimony to the man's persuasive skills as a miracle.

My response to him was thankfully delayed by the arrival

of several sailors who'd been in charge of the horse. They approached slowly, taking great care to keep from frightening the horse again. One ruddy sailor with legs as bowed as his girth had an awed look on his face; he clearly worshipped Lord Alexander. The mare nuzzled Lord Alexander as if he were sugar, or a sweet apple of temptation. She clearly welcomed her capture and his control. The whole incident had been mesmerizing to watch. His deep-toned voice was so soothing, his movements so slow, so patient, his touch so tender and caressing that one would have to be made out of stone to stand against him.

Both the horse and I were made of flesh and blood, but unlike the horse, I'd found Lord Alexander's touch inflaming rather than calming. I had a difficult time reconciling the man before me with the naked image he'd had of me, so much so that I truly began to wonder if *I* had imagined it myself.

"We're right sorry, Captain Black," one of the sailors muttered, poking his hat back onto the empty crow's nest on his balding head. "She's a tightly strung one for sure."

I glanced about, wondering to whom the man thought he was speaking. Surprisingly, Lord Alexander answered.

"You'd be high strung as well, Davey, if someone set you a-sea with a babe in your belly. But you'll settle, won't you girl?" Lord Alexander said, running his palm down the mare's neck. She snorted and flicked her tail, a mild protest that had very little bite behind it. "You can all go back to your docking duties. I'll take charge of her. And tell Captain Jansen there's to be an extra round of rum for you all tonight."

The men let out a rowdy cheer before dispersing on the deck.

"Captain Black?" I blurted out the question with very little finesse the moment we were relatively alone. I think my mouth even hung open a bit, for the name sounded so . . . so . . . pirate-like?

"It's my ship," he said. "On occasion I take her for a sail.

There's nothing like the sea and the stars to fill a lonely n— horizon."

There's nothing like the sea and the stars to fill a lonely night. Was that what he'd been about to say? I was sure of it.

What about a lonely life? I found myself wondering, then shook off the thought. Considering the misery that many less fortunate than my family suffered, I'd no right to this morning's grumblings. I straightened my shoulders and smoothed the skirt of my striped satin day dress only to feel my finger catch on the pocket. Glancing down, I found Aphrodite's ring caught upon the material. The serpent's emerald eyes winked up at me as I freed it, reminding me of exactly my purpose in seeking out Lord Alexander today— *Trojan horse.*

He brought his horse a few steps closer to me. "Iris, meet Miss Andrews and thank her for your name."

"Hello, beauty." I moved to the now-docile horse, slipped off my lace glove, and brushed my fingertips along her soft mane. "Welcome to your new home. My name is Androm-eda, but you and your master can call me Andrie."

"I'm not sure how wise that would be," Lord Alexander said.

Looking up, I found he'd moved in closer, to the point that my skirts brushed his thigh and his heat touched my skin despite the cloth and space separating us. A sharp tingle took that heat deeper inside me to places that made my cheeks burn. He was so close that were I to turn his way, my breasts would press . . . I shook my head.

Whatever was wrong with me? My thoughts kept running down wildly improper paths.

"And why would that not be wise, Lord Alexander?" I shifted enough to meet his gaze, noting that the shadows lurking beneath the vibrant green depths of his eyes had grown darker than they'd been earlier this summer.

His focus dropped to my lips for a long moment before he stepped away, taking my breath with him as he looked out over the sea.

"Blackmoor! You devil! You didn't say a word about buying a Friesian! Mrs. Killdaren just told us. The beauty must have cost you a king's fortune." Shouting up from the docks was Lord Ashton with Mr. Drayson, friends from the Killdaren brothers' university days who spent their summers in Dartmoor's End. Lord Ashton, pale of complexion with golden hair and lively blue eyes, embraced fashion in the same manner that Lord Alexander thwarted it. Mr. Drayson, more subdued, had a strong jaw and serious features that were softened by his curly brown hair and warm brown eyes. Behind them came the entourage of my sisters; the Earl of Dartraven, a watered-down version of his sons; and Sir Warwick, a gray-haired, gray-eyed gentleman with a barbed wit, who lived on a neighboring estate. He used a monocle and walked with a cane, but only for decoration. Unlike Sean, whose injury required a cane for balance and mobility.

Lord Alexander waved back. "Stay there. We'll be down in a minute and you'll see just how much of a beauty she is." Our time of relative privacy had ended and the expression of relief on his face was far from flattering.

He had no intention of explaining his remark and my opportunity to speak to him about cataloguing artifacts had passed. Once we reached the docks, the hustling activity was too disruptive for Iris, and Lord Alexander immediately suggested that everyone move to a quieter spot, just past the town, on the road to Killdaren's Castle and Dragon's Cove.

Cassie and Gemini wanted to stroll by the shops lining the way, so we decided to send the footmen ahead with the carriage and the gentlemen's horses, except for Iris. Lord Alexander apparently didn't want anyone but himself to touch her. He protectively led his new mare over the cobblestones, speaking to her gently as he strode past the streetside vendors. Here the salty breeze of the sea mingled with the pleasant and unpleasant scents of fish, fresh meat pies, sweaty bodies, and perfumed candles. The sound of our booted steps upon the boardwalk grew louder as those we passed lowered their voices to whisper. Cassie, Gemini, and I drew as many curious looks from the owners and the patrons of the shops we peered into as Lord Alexander and Iris were getting from those on the street. The town, ever in awe of the cursed Killdaren twins, didn't quite know what to make of the fact that the mysterious Sean Killdaren had abruptly wed—to a parlor maid no less. Many had yet to grasp the fact that Cassie, a journalist in her own right, had only taken a position as a parlor maid to investigate Mary's death. And I had no doubt that seeing her now in the company of Sean's estranged brother would give wing to even more rampant rumors. None of them particularly kind.

"Look at this new store, Andrie! It's full of antiquities." Gemini rushed ahead, letting out a squeal of delight. With my eyes focused on her, I bumped into a rumpled and soiled man who was exiting the cigar shop. Tobacco from the unlit pipe he held spilled onto my shoulder.

"Are you blind?" he said, brushing at the flakes on my dress as if I had offended him and he had a right to touch me! The minute his hand connected with my shoulder, I saw her dying, a dark haired woman, and this man had his hands around her throat. They were in a small boat and she was struggling, her doe eyes begging for her life.

"You killed her! Strangled her!" I cried.

The man stared at me in horror for a second then whispered in a choked voice, "Who are you? How did you know?" Crying out as if struck, he turned from me and ran.

"Wait!" I shouted, stumbling after him. He dashed ahead of me and into the street just as a carriage came rushing by. The driver swerved, but it was too late. The man went down beneath trampling hooves and spinning wheels. He lay in the dirt, unmoving.

"Good God!" Lord Alexander, who stood nearby me on the street, grabbed my arm, but I couldn't "see" anything. My whole spirit was shuddering from what had happened.

"Andrie!" The roar in my ears made Cassie's cry seem as if it had come from a long way off though I knew she'd left the boardwalk and stood right next to me. I heard every-thing, saw everything, but it was as if I were frozen. "Andrie, talk to me. What happened?"

I saw Gemini approach with the other men behind her. "Whatever is the matt—" She glanced to where the people on the street were shouting. "Dear Lord!" Then she reached out for Cassie and promptly fainted.

Cassie caught Gemini with Lord Ashton's help. I couldn't speak past the lump of horror lodged in my throat. It seemed as if I couldn't even blink. My eyes burned. The man, who now lay twisted and bleeding on the cobblestones, had been so filled with anger that he'd strangled his wife to death. I'd seen it all and felt it all in a single touch, in a single image.

"She spoke to the man after he bumped into her and he ran into the street," Lord Alexander said to Cassie. "Did she know him?"

"Bloody hell of an accident," Sir Warwick muttered, stirred from his habitual ennui. "The chap didn't even have a chance to dodge. I saw it, too."

"There are ladies present, Warwick," the Earl of Dartra-ven admonished. "Has someone sent for the doctor?"

"I'm afraid there is nothing a doctor can do. Looks as if the man has broken his neck," Lord Ashton said, his expres-sion one of offense that anyone would intrude so upon his day. "I see Constable Poole headed this way."

"Drayson, take care of Iris for me." Lord Alexander handed the mare's reins to his friend, then grabbed my hand, squeezing my fingers with concern. "Miss Andrews, did you know the man? I heard you cry out something like Lou Tiller or Miller or something. Can you tell us?" He spoke as sooth-ingly as he had to Iris when she'd panicked on the ship. His hand slid to my back, urging me a little closer to him. The comfort and the heat broke the icy fear that had been freez-ing me.

"Oh, God," I whispered, feeling dizzier by the minute. I didn't want anyone to know what had happened and I didn't want to speak to the authorities either.

If the man was dead, then justice had been served, and I wouldn't have to reveal to the world what I knew and how I'd learned of it. I prayed Lord Ashton wasn't mistaken and that the man really was dead. It was the first time in my life that I'd prayed for such a horrible thing.

A shadow fell over me. Glancing up, I found Constable Poole peering down at me from beneath dark, puzzled brows. "Miss Andrews, what happened? A woman just told me that you chased a man to his death."

I gasped. "No, no, I didn't."

"Who said such a thing?" Cassie demanded, having left Gemini in Lord Ashton's care.

Lord Alexander tightened his hold on my hand and spoke. "Constable Poole, surely you are not accusing Miss Andrews of anything so horrendous? I can assure you that was not the case." Lord Alexander's voice was as sharp as a steel blade. "I distinctly heard Miss Andrews shout at the man to wait as if she were trying to keep him from running."

"My apologies, Viscount Blackmoor. The woman who told me was quite upset, and most likely confused the details."

"Understandable. My daughter-in-law and her sisters are shaken by the incident themselves," the Earl of Dartraven quickly interjected.

"Your lordship." The constable nodded politely to the earl then turned to Cassie, giving her a respectful bow. "Mrs. Killdaren."

"Constable Poole," Cassie said stiffly. I knew my sister was still bristling over the fact that the constable had barely given her the time of day when we'd first arrived in Dartmoor's End at the beginning of the summer.

"Miss Andrews, since you spoke with the man, I assume you were acquainted with him?" The constable furrowed his brow, peering sharply at me.

"No!" I spoke more vehemently than I meant to and everyone looked at me strangely. Drawing a deep breath, I cleared my throat and tried to steady my nerves. "I don't know the man at all. He exited the shop, ran into me, and spilt tobacco on my dress. Then he had the audacity to accuse me of being blind. My shout for him to wait was one of outrage. I didn't see the carriage coming at him, either."

I thought perhaps I knew just how Pheidippides felt after running from Marathon to Athens. My heart raced painfully in my breast, I couldn't seem to breathe, and I felt I would expire at any moment. Telling lies has a way of scaring the soul. My only consolation was that I had essentially told the truth to the authorities.

"You're absolutely sure you don't know anything about him, Miss Andrews?"

I stared at the constable for a moment, watching his nose twitch and his mustache ends flap in the wind. Hysterically, I wanted to laugh and had to grit my teeth. "Constable, I've never in my life seen this man before."

"Miss Andrews, then why—"

Lord Alexander's gaze searched mine with a doubting question lingering in his eyes. He knew something more than what I had described had happened, but he didn't press for an answer. Instead, he stepped forward, coming between me and the constable. "I think Miss Andrews has told you everything she knows for now. The earl and I would both like to be informed of the man's identity so that we can send our condolences to his family. You will notify us of the results of your investigation, of course?"

"I'll send word as soon as I know," Constable Poole said, then, excusing himself from the group in general, he turned to the street and the crowd gathered there. I kept my gaze from following him. My stomach still roiled from having witnessed the man's death and I shivered. I couldn't help but feel my encounter with him was more than a random incident. It was an omen of darkness that seemed to threaten all I held dear.

The ride to Killdaren's Castle passed in a strained silence, with gazes full of questions that tongues were too hesitant to speak. Gemini sat between me and Cassie, facing the earl and Sir Warwick, while Lord Ashton and Mr. Drayson rode their horses. Lord Alexander was astride, too. He rode one horse with Iris trailing behind. Everyone felt as if they needed to accompany me home, a totally unnecessary gesture that I didn't understand. It left me feeling as conspicuous as a queen during her coronation.

Gemini, still pale, had yet to recover from the shock of seeing a violent death. Though eighteen, she'd lived behind the combined fortress of mine and Cassie's protection, and thus had been largely sheltered. She currently had her head resting back against the squabs, ruining her elaborate coiffure of gold curls. Her china blue eyes were shut and her arms were tightly crossed, as if she needed every ounce of warmth that she could keep. She hadn't once glanced out the window of the carriage to watch Lord Ashton, nor had she mentioned his name in the last twenty minutes—a record for the entire summer.

Cassie, grim-faced and straight-shouldered, sat with her hands tightly clasped, clearly counting off the minutes to reach home with her tapping finger. I knew that she, like Lord Alexander, suspected I hadn't told everything, and it was only a matter of time before they demanded the truth from me.

Neither of us had commented on the fact that if Lord Alexander accompanied the carriage all the way to Kill-daren's Castle, he would see Sean. We'd wanted to bridge the gap between the two brothers, but hadn't imagined it would be under the shadow of another death. I shivered again.

An occasional glance from the earl my way showed a mixture of concern in his misty green eyes and something that I could only describe as irritation. I mirrored that feeling, for Sir Warwick incessantly tapped his walking stick on the carriage floor. I itched to snatch it away from him and . . . well, toss both it and his monocle into the vibrant blue sea just visible between the drifting dunes of sand and sea oats outside the carriage window. That I even entertained such an uncharitable act for so minor an irritation took me totally aback and made me wonder if my gift was making it impossible for me to tolerate any intrusion into my world.

The road stretching from the town to Killdaren's Castle stood between the sea and the summer-lush maritime forest, a place I'd recently discovered held dark secrets from the past, both recent and distant. For among the trees lay the Circle of Stone Virgins, Druid-carved images of seven virgins surrounding a huge statue of Daghdha, the High King of the *Tuatha de Danaan*. Local legend was that Daghdha took the beautiful virgins captive, ravaged their virginity, and then claimed their lives. It was in the burial chamber beneath the image of this Celtic faery god that my cousin Mary's body had been found. She'd died in a senseless fall while arguing with the housekeeper of Killdaren's Castle, Mrs. Frye. Fearing reprisal, Mrs. Frye and her mentally feeble son, Jamie, had hid Mary's body and pretended she'd been swept out to sea. While under the guise of a parlor maid, Cassie had uncovered their lie, allowing our family to find some measure of peace in our loss of Mary. None of us had believed the story that Mary had been swept out to sea as she waded in the surf.

Mary had disappeared from the castle while working for Sean Killdaren, and at first my family and I had thought him responsible because of the rumors over his involvement in the death of another woman. Lady Helen Kennedy had been murdered on the night of October 31, eight years ago. Sean and Lord Alexander had been the last to see her alive, and an eyewitness, Mr. Drayson—Sean and Lord Alexander's close friend—had seen a man matching the twins' description leave the maze just before her body had been discovered there.

Over the course of the summer my sisters and I had wholeheartedly come to the conclusion that Sean and Lord Alexander were innocent. And, as Cassie pointed out when she discovered the tunnel in the center of the maze that led to the sea and to the burial chamber beneath the stone virgins, anyone could have killed Lady Helen Kennedy. They could have exited through the tunnels and no one would have ever known they'd been on the Killdaren estate that night.

"Hold just a minute, Dickens," I heard Lord Alexander shout to the driver of the carriage. From the open window, I watched him expertly dismount. We were but a stone's throw from Sean Killdaren's land. Already, Killdaren's Castle's sun-washed walls and towering turrets loomed large against the pristine dunes and deep blue sea. Thanks to Cassie, what used to be a silent-as-a-tomb, gloomy place was now a home of warmth and cheer.

Lord Alexander opened the carriage door, directing his gaze toward his father. "I'll leave off here. Should the constable send any news, have the messenger ride on to Dragon's Cove and inform me as well."

"Of course," the earl replied. "You and Sean have to—"

"Do nothing. He made his wishes crystal clear just a short time ago. I'm content he has recovered enough to find some measure of happiness in life. The very least that I owe him is to respect his wishes." Lord Alexander glanced my way. "Please send word to me tomorrow on your recovery as well, Miss Andrews. I realize what happened today was a shock even if you *weren't* acquainted with the man." He narrowed his eyes slightly as he spoke the last, sharpening his gaze to a razor's edge strong enough to cut the truth from even the most calloused soul.

Unable to trust my voice, I only nodded.

"Please. Why don't you come to the castle for a few moments?" said Cassie. "I'm sure—"

"Mrs. Killdaren, while your good intentions are noted, I've known my brother much longer than you have. I can assure you, he will not easily forgive a betrayal of his wishes. I'd advise you not to jeopardize your happiness with him by trying to repair that which cannot ever be fixed. Good day." He shut the carriage door before anyone could speak.

By the way Cassie flung her hands up in disgust I knew she was close to screaming with frustration. "I think I would have better reception as an English diplomat to the African natives during the recent Zulu Wars than I've had in trying to speak to Sean or Lord Alexander about each other. How two intelligent men can—"

"It's the curse," the earl interjected. "Sean and Alex were born that way."

The carriage started forward and Sir Warwick leaned back, shaking his head. "The boys came out of the womb with their hands about each other's throats, Alex feet first and Sean headfirst. They're fated to die that way as well."

"That, Sir Warwick, is a philosophy I will never accept," Cassie said. "People determine their fate by the choices they make."

"Do they?" I asked softly. "There are some things in life from which one . . . cannot escape." As soon as I spoke, I wished that I hadn't, for both Sir Warwick and the earl gave me a strange look. I couldn't blame them; even to my own ears my voice had sounded haunted, as if I had dark secrets to hide. The problem was that I did.

"Andrie? Surely you don't believe Sean and his twin are cursed with no hope of a different future than one cruelly delivered at birth."

I wanted to reassure her, to tell her that fate was nonsense, and I would have said so just a short while ago. But after the incident in town and the man's death, I wasn't sure myself. My fate seemed to loom over me with no escape. "I don't know," I whispered. "I just don't know."

"I agree with Andrie," Gemini whispered. "Some things you just can't escape."

3

"Turn yet, Miss Andrie?" asked little Rebecca James, Sean Killdaren's beloved but officially unacknowledged half sister.

"Say, 'Is it my turn yet?' " I encouraged her. Rebecca was still recovering from the trauma of Mary's death and being left on the castle's roof by someone. Neither Cassie nor I thought it was Jamie and refused to blame him. Her stuttering had eased, but she still shortened her sentences, perhaps thinking the fewer words she spoke the less she could say wrong. The odd thing was that she could sing beautifully without stuttering.

"Is it . . . my turn?"

"Almost, poppet. I'm hurrying," I said. Gazing down at the special embroidered checkerboard, I once again marveled at Rebecca's mother's ingenious ways of broadening the world of her blind child. The squares on the gameboard had a distinctive pattern for red and another pattern for black, so Rebecca could move her game piece to the appropriate square by feeling the stitches. "There," I told her. "It's your turn now."

She smiled brightly and began to gently run her fingers over the gameboard and its pieces in an effort to discover the move I had made. It took her but a moment. At only seven years of age, Rebecca was the most intelligent child I'd ever encountered, which, coming from a woman who'd grown up in Oxford and known the company of a number of children from highly respected scholars, was saying something.

She and her mother, Prudence, lived with Cassie and Sean. It was a strange and scandalous situation for the son to take care of his father's indiscretions within his own home, but that was the nature of Sean Killdaren. He'd also seen to the formal education of his half brother, Stuart Frye. Sean's care for others went far and deep and his regard for society's dictates was akin to Lord Alexander's—nonexistent.

I hadn't quite determined what to think about the gray-templed, melancholy earl, and I glanced his way a moment. Just past the settee where Cassie, Gemini, and Prudence whispered like court conspirators, the earl sat playing backgammon with Sir Warwick while Sean hovered to devour the winner. Every now and then, I'd see the earl glance—almost beneath his lashes—at Prudence and Rebecca.

When Cassie and Sean had first married, there had been no family gatherings or celebrations or even shared meals. Sean had kept to his wing, sleeping during the day and exploring the stars at night. Prudence and Rebecca had taken their meals in their rooms, and the earl, accompanied more often than not by Sir Warwick, usually ate his meals with a great deal of whiskey in the gentlemen's den. Two days after marrying Sean, Cassie had put her foot down. She'd set a time for dinner, ordered everyone to be there, and then insisted that for the two hours following the meal, the family would gather in the drawing room.

The earl had grumbled about it the most, but a certain spring to his step and twinkle in his eyes during the evening told me that he secretly liked the changes Cassie had brought about. Cassie had told me that during a conversation with the earl, he'd declared he'd vowed to stop loving anyone ever, because everyone he loved either lived under a curse of death or had already died. His glances made me suspect that he regretted his vow.

"Crown me," Rebecca said. Glancing down, I found to my surprise that Rebecca had captured three of my men and stood ready to be crowned.

I capped off her piece. "You make a beautiful queen, my dear."

"Not queen. I'm princess," she said softly.

"Yes, you are. A beautiful and loved princess. And a smart one, too." I tried to focus on the game then, but within two moves my mind wandered again as I played. This time my thoughts went in a darker direction.

With dinner over and the heat of a low-burning fire at my back, I should have been able to partially relax within the open warmth of those closest to my heart, but I couldn't. In that brief moment on the boardwalk, the stranger had brought me face to face with not only the monster lurking within him, but the one within me, and my monster was more frightening than I'd imagined.

Upon our return from town earlier, I'd immediately claimed the need to rest and requested to be left alone. Cassie had to soothe and tend to Gemini, and didn't have a chance to question me then; and later, when I'd heard Cassie knocking on my door and peeping into my room, I feigned sleep. A tactic that her determined glare across the drawing room told me would not work again. The only thing that currently saved me from an interrogation was Rebecca's presence both during dinner and now. We were all hesitant to bring up the subject of death, hesitant to remind Rebecca about the loss of Mary, who'd been Rebecca's teacher and beloved friend.

I would meet up with Cassie's questions before the night was over though, and I would have to explain what happened on the boardwalk. Yet, if I shared with her how much I had seen of the man's mind and actions, Cassie would realize how much my gift had grown and that would lead to more questions.

Cassie had enough things to worry about without adding me to the list. And now that she was with child, those problems were magnified. I was glad for her, glad that there would be another priceless treasure to fill Killdaren's Castle. Yet, I couldn't help but wish my sister had had more time as a married woman before becoming a mother. Despite the infectious cheer Cassie spread to every stone corner and into everyone's heart, there were still so many unsettled and upsetting troubles within the Killdarens' world.

Eight years ago, in a brutal fight with Lord Alexander over Lady Helen's death, Sean had fallen from a cliff into the sea, damaging his leg and receiving a head injury that gave him excruciating pain when exposed to bright light.

For that reason, black velvet curtains covered the castle windows during the day and candles were used instead of gas lighting. The darkness did little to dampen spirits, for everyone welcomed Sean's presence during the daytime hours and hoped that one day he'd make a full recovery.

Since his marriage to Cassie, Sean was up during the day more than he had been in years, but he was still a man of the night. So much so that I wondered how Cassie had the energy to stay up late stargazing through Sean's gigantic telescope or racing horses down the shore with him and still take care of all her daily responsibilities. Thankfully the loud screeching noise, produced by the hoisting of Sean's telescope up and down was barely heard from the wing where I slept. Cassie said that it had given her nightmares until she'd found out what the screeching noise meant.

Other than being identical twins in regards to their features and their charisma, Sean and Lord Alexander were very different. To me, Sean was more like the moon, subdued and darkly gentle, where Lord Alexander was like the sun, bold and blazingly hot—

"Miss Andrie, do you have any men left?" Rebecca giggled.

I stared down at the board to find only Rebbeca's kings in place and mine all captured. It was rather disconcerting since I rarely lost at the game. "I think you've won, poppet."

At Rebecca's joyful laugh, Gemini left Cassie and Prudence and joined Rebecca and me. Gemini still appeared haunted by the day's events. Her rosy cheeks had paled and dark shadows brewed beneath her china blue eyes. It was almost the first time that I could remember seeing Gemini so serious. She normally bubbled with talk of fashion or the peerage. As usual for the evenings we spent in the drawing room, she was wrapped in a cloak for warmth, claiming the draft chilled her. I didn't remember Gemini being chilled often in Oxford, where the climate was much cooler.

"I see the smart princess has managed to do something I've yet to do and beat my sister," Gemini said.

"I'm not even sure how she did it." I stood to let Gemini have my seat.

"I doubt I'll be much of a challenge either." Gemini shuddered. "I'm having a difficult time—"

"Remembering your name," I interjected before Gemini could mention the accident in town.

Gemini winced at what she'd almost said before the child. "Yes, that's right. I keep thinking my name is Georgie Porgie."

Rebecca laughed and sang. "Georgie Porgie, pudding and pie . . . kissed the plums and made them cry."

"Girls, poppet," I said smiling. "He kissed the girls and made them cry."

"No," Rebecca said. "I don't want the girls to cry." Her face clouded with angst and she tightly clutched her rag doll that had been in the seat beside her.

My heart squeezed. The seriousness of her tone told me it was very important to her that the girls weren't made to cry. I touched her shoulder, reading her thoughts from the day Mary died. They were the same as before, reaffirming to me that, at least from Rebecca's perspective, what Mrs. Frye claimed happened to Mary and what Rebecca interpreted as happening didn't match.

"Then plums it is," I said. "The plums can cry until they turn to prunes."

Gemini and Rebecca laughed. The sound I so needed to hear eased into my soul a bit.

Sean Killdaren moved from where he watched the earl and Sir Warwick and joined us. "I'm giving up my turn at the backgammon board tonight. In the last thirty minutes my father and Warwick have made five moves. It'll be past midnight before they're done complaining about which one of them is more onerous than the other and finish the game. Cassie and I have plans to search the stars tonight." When he glanced at my sister, the love filling his gaze caught my breath and somehow made me ache inside.

Sean playfully tugged on a tress of Rebecca's dark hair. "How is little Becca doing with checkers?"

"Gave me a trouncing." I stepped back from the group, needing space from the many thoughts of Lord Alexander that the gleam in Sean's eyes had incited.

"I made lots of princesses," Rebecca added, describing all the crowned game pieces.

"Glad to hear it," Sean said. "Soon we'll have you playing chess as well. Stuart and I are carving the pieces now."

A knock on the drawing room door brought a startled silence to the room. I fisted my hand, knowing this intrusion had to be about what happened in town today. The butler, Mr. Murphy, opened the door. He and his wife, the cook, reminded me of fresh bread, warm and plump and inviting.

"Begging your pardon, Mr. Sean, Constable Poole is here to see you and the earl. Shall I show him in?"

Sean turned sharply, a frown creasing his brow. "Constable Poole? Show him to the library, Murphy." The butler gave a slight bow and left.

Cassie stood. "Sean, I didn't have the chance to tell you what happened in town earlier—"

"Rebecca, it's time for bed," Prudence interrupted. Worry that Rebecca might hear something to trigger a bad memory from Mary's passing rang in Prudence's voice.

Rebecca shook her head. "Play game with Georgie Porgie," she said.

"Who?" Prudence asked, moving swiftly toward us. Deep lines of concern marred the china doll perfection of her face and shadowed her eyes.

"Me." Gemini, who longed for the title of Lady, groaned at the undignified moniker she'd just saddled herself with. She took Rebecca's hand. "Would it be all right to save our game for tomorrow and for us to read a story with Bridget before bedtime tonight?" She asked the little girl.

Holding her doll tight, Rebecca solemnly nodded, sensing something was wrong.

"Wonderful," Prudence said with relief.

The three of them quit the room, and I tried to edge out in their wake as Cassie told Sean about the incident. I wanted to hear what the constable had to report even though I already knew the grisly details, but I didn't want to face another interrogation over the matter. That meant I had to find a good place for eavesdropping before Sean and the earl and Warwick went to the library to meet with the constable.

"Wait for me, Andrie," Cassie said, stopping me before I made it through the door. Her request surprised me. Knowing my sister as well as I did, I had expected her to insist on accompanying Sean and earl to the library.

"Mrs. Killdaren, not so fast," Sean said as Cassie hurried my way. "What is it that you are *not* telling me?"

Cassie's gaze met mine and she lifted one brow before turning to Sean. "I think I remembered everything," she said, giving him a brilliant smile.

He narrowed his eyes to a "we'll talk later" glare as I grabbed Cassie's hand and pulled her out the door.

"Hurry," I hissed under my breath, dragging her along the corridor toward the library. At the center hall, I ducked behind a statue of a David-like man, except for the strategic placement of leafs—an example of the castle's more conservative art.

"Take off your shoes," she whispered.

"Whatever for?" I asked.

"The marble. It's the best way to sneak across it and not be heard." A very telling statement of Cassie's time investigating Mary's death. I almost envied my sister of the adventure she'd had.

Mr. Murphy shut the library door, apparently having just seen Constable Poole into the room, and headed toward the kitchens. The second he passed our hiding spot, we flew across the marbled entryway, down the corridor, and slipped into the room adjoining the library. Slightly breathless, I stood inside the door, my heart thumping.

A sliver of pale moonlight cut an eerie path through the objets d'art, many of which were statues of Greek gods, making a person wonder if she'd suddenly stepped into the middle of Zeus's decadent court.

"Why eavesdrop when you could have requested to see the constable?" Cassie asked in a whisper as we moved closer to the wall separating us from the library.

"I didn't want to have to answer more questions about today. Besides, men tend to tell more and speak more freely when women aren't present. I discovered that you can hear a conversation going on in the library rather well from this wall when I was examining the statues not long ago."

Cassie slid into place beside me. "I feel like I'm seven years old again and we're trying to discover our Christmas surprises with our ears to our parents' door. Who did you overhear in the library?"

"You and Bridget talking about a vampire book, about lovers no less." Cassie's mouth fell open in shock, one that matched what mine had been to discover what my most proper sister and her newfound friend were reading. "Shh," I said, as I heard Sean greet the constable in the library.

"Did you learn the identity of the poor fellow?" the earl asked.

"I did. Wouldn't be calling the gentleman poor, though, nor let any sympathies rest upon him. His name was Prichard,

Miles Prichard. Lived north of here, between Dartmoor's End and Falmouth."

"The chap was a bad sort then?" This from Sir Warwick.

"Quite possibly," the constable said. "I found his wife strangled to death, propped up all prettily in her bed. It's likely he killed her. The neighbors say they kept to themselves and that he was a mean chap, yelling and ordering his wife around. I'll have to investigate further, but I'd wager he killed her."

Cassie gasped and I shivered, my stomach wrapping into a quick knot.

"Damnation," Sean said. "What madness could drive a man to kill the very woman he's sworn to protect?"

"Betrayal would be my guess. Seen it more times than I care to say," replied the constable.

"Nothing will send a man to anger quicker than an unfaithful wife," Sir Warwick added.

"You all sound as if you're worthy enough to cast stones," the earl said. "I for one won't be throwing any, gentlemen. Let's get back to topic. Constable Poole, are you saying there is no family we need to make condolences to, then?"

"Quite right. I'll let you know if we learn differently. Odd thing, you know," the constable added.

"And what's that?" Sean asked.

"The woman who claimed that Miss Andrews chased the man to his death thought she overheard what Miss Andrews initially said when the man accosted her."

The men were silent and I thought they could surely hear the pounding of my heart through the wall.

"She said Miss Andrews cried out 'killer,' " the constable reported.

"Andromeda chased the man into the street shouting he was a killer?" Sean's incredulous demand drowned out any other response there was to the constable's revelation, except Cassie's.

She clutched my arm, her eyes wide with horror. "You should have told me; told someone."

I bit back a groan, and tried to minimize what I'd seen. I didn't want her to know how bad it had been. "I wasn't sure. I could have been wrong."

The constable drew our attention back to their conversation. "Ahem, I beg your pardon, Mr. Killdaren, I didn't mean to imply that at all. In fact, I have it on good authority from your brother that Miss Andrews tried to stop the man from running into the street. As for what the woman overheard, she must have mistaken the incident. I just thought the account strange."

"Alex was there?" If possible, Sean's voice grew even louder and more incredulous. Cassie and I both winced. Considering all that stood between Sean and Lord Alexander, we'd stand a better chance conquering the whole of the British Empire than the brothers.

"Yes. He received a delivery of a prized horse at the same time that Mr. and Mrs. Andrews's ship set sail and took a moment to exchange a few pleasantries."

"Indeed," Sean said. "I'll trust, Father, that you'll let him know his efforts to associate with my wife and her sisters are *unnecessary* and *unappreciated*."

Cassie sighed, a soft whisper of despair that tugged at the very center of my heart. She had her hand pressed to her stomach, as if she could already feel the babe within. Concerned, I set my fingers upon the back of her hand and heard the cry in her heart.

Twins. Dear God, what if I have twins?

"Hush," I whispered. "Don't borrow tomorrow's worries. The Killdaren stubbornness has yet to encounter the Andrews sisters' force combined as one. The Trojan Horse Plan begins tomorrow."

"He agreed to let you catalogue the antiquities then?"

I only nodded, unable to give breath to my lie. She clasped my hand in hers and drew comfort from my words. Comfort that I couldn't find for myself later that night, for I dreamed of myself unclothed and bound, a prisoner of Captain Black's on the high seas where he ruled as a pirate king.

4

At first light, I sent a footman to Dragon's Cove, informing Lord Alexander that I would be arriving at his castle mid-morning, for I needed to speak with him about a matter of importance. His return message said that he would await my visit.

I then spent the next two hours pacing, trying to determine how to best approach Lord Alexander. Any other time I'd seen him, we'd always been accompanied by a number of people, which afforded very little opportunity for conversations—exactly what I didn't want to occur today. I had things to say that I knew my family would not understand, and would only be hurt by. For the Trojan Horse Plan now not only had meaning for my sister Cassie, but for me, too.

In light of the incident with the man on the boardwalk, I desperately needed to face the reality of my situation. After my sensual thoughts of Lord Alexander and pirates, my dreams had turned ugly, to a scene so nightmarish I'd awakened early, drenched in perspiration and shivering. I'd had a vision of myself trapped within a cage where strangers came, constantly touching me, drowning me in their thoughts. I became completely lost, no longer knowing who I was, or who anyone else was either.

Had the dream portended that madness was to be my fate if I didn't find a way to shelter myself? I shuddered.

I had to live alone and I had to support myself. The only thing I knew of life was antiquities and how to catalogue them, which meant I would need to seek employment in a museum or, as Lord Alexander had suggested earlier this summer and as my father had alluded to by the gift of Aphrodite's ring, I could be paid to catalogue individual art collections in private homes. Employment in a museum would most likely put me in a position of having to interact with more people on a daily basis than working in a private home. By living alone and frugally, it was possible I would not have to take many assignments to survive.

To this end, I would need references, thus I *needed* a job. And that was exactly what I planned to ask Lord Alexander for today. He'd offered before, so it wasn't too outrageous for me to approach him about the matter. Still, my heart fluttered at the idea of going to meet him alone, even if he was, in fact, now family. Working for him could be the path to my independence.

Living in the wilds of Cornwall, far from the eagle-eyed confines of Oxford's proper society, afforded both Gemini and me more freedom than we'd ever known, and now having a married sister had in a number of ways expanded those strictures. I knew Lord Alexander had a housekeeper, a widowed sister of Mrs. Murphy's, who lived at the castle. I knew he had a number of servants as well. So, in truth, I wouldn't exactly be alone with him. It wasn't as if I was a society miss with a reputation to keep sterling, either. Marriage was not in my future. Besides, a woman employed did not have need of a chaperone. Cassie herself had come alone to Killdaren's Castle months ago to work as a maid and *she* didn't bring a chaperone along. I could do the same.

With my mind made up, I hurriedly finished dressing. The family usually gathered for a late breakfast, and I wanted to be gone before they started to head downstairs for that meal. Careful not to wake Gemini, Prudence, Rebecca, or Bridget, all of whom slept in the same wing as me, I slipped quietly from my room and went down the servant's staircase that led directly to the kitchens and the back door leading to the stables. My chances of encountering Cassie were limited that way.

The huge hearth blazed with a welcoming fire as the rich aroma of kidney pies and fresh scones filled the air. Maids scurryed to follow Mrs. Murphy's jovial instructions, and she turned my way as I exited the stairs.

"You're up a bit early, lass."

"Yes," I said, pasting a confident smile on my face. "I've a number of important errands to attend to and I'm not exactly sure when I'll be back."

Mrs. Murphy's brows arched. "Then you'll be missing the morning meal?"

"Unfortunately. And most sorry I am. It smells delicious."

"No, need to worry. I'll wrap a few scones for you to carry with you." She told a maid to ready a basket for me, then turned back. "Will Miss Gemini or Mrs. Killdaren be joining you?"

"No."

Her brows lifted again before she stepped a little closer to me and studied my face. "Not to be intruding where I shouldn't, lass, but is everything all right with you? I heard about the events in town yesterday. I can imagine ye'd be a mite upset over it." Her warm eyes were just as inviting as the kitchen and almost tempted me to spill everything that I had locked up inside of me. But I also knew Mrs. Murphy would then feel compelled to tell Cassie, and the last thing my sister needed now was to shoulder my burdens.

"I'm fine, but thank you for your concern. And when you see Cassie, tell her I've gone to see about the errand we spoke of, will you?"

"I'll be sure to." Mrs. Murphy stepped back and the maid handed me the warm package of scones that smelled wonderfully, but I was too nervous to eat. Smiling and waving my thanks, I hurried from the kitchen to make my way to the stables, a little unsure of what to do next.

In Oxford, my family and I most often walked the short distances we needed to go, or if there was need of a carriage, we'd send a servant to hire one for the event. We hadn't the funds nor the space to afford horses. Since coming to Killdaren's Castle, we'd always had the carriage brought to the house. I'd ridden a horse once or twice in a ring, but was nowhere near comfortable enough on horseback to attempt riding along the roads.

The best I could do was go to the stables and make my need known. Stepping into the bright sun of the morning, I drank in the tangy scent of the sea and fresh scents of forest and flowers. Morning always dispelled the darkest dreams of the night, but it seemed to me that here on the coast that was truer than anywhere else on earth. The salty air washed the day to a brighter shine, and the pulse of life beat in tandem to the constant music of the sea. A flock of pelicans swooped overhead, going out to find their morning meal amid the energetic blue waves.

Edging along Killdaren's rich gardens and the dark shadow of the maze, whose legacy I deliberately ignored anytime I was alone, I hurried to the stables. Blinded by the sun, I stepped into the open door unable to see and ran right into Bridget. The words in her mind shouted at me, shocking me. *Bloody, stubborn arse of a man! It'd serve him right if I found myself another man. A vampire lover!*

Bridget was Miss Prudence and Miss Rebecca's lady's maid and my sister Cassie's dear friend. She'd been an unfailing ally for my sister when Cassie had come to Killdaren's Castle as a maid at the beginning of the summer. The turmoil in Bridget's mind jolted mine. She warred between elation and despair, happy that she loved Stuart Frye and that her brother and her mother now lived at the castle since her mother had been declared consumption free, and yet hurt and saddened over Stuart's noble rejection of their love and the continued silence from her sister Flora. Flora had left in the spring for a new performing career in London and had yet to write.

With both his mother and brother under arrest for Mary's death, Stuart refused to allow Bridget to involve herself with him. Bridget also wondered if Stuart would be so quick to reject her if he found her naked in his bed.

I immediately backed away before I could see more.

She blinked. "Miss Andrie, forgive me. I didn't see you."

"Nor I you, Bridget. I've some errands to attend to. Who should I see about a carriage?"

"That would be me." The deep voice came from just a few feet away. Stuart Frye stood with his back against a stall and his arms crossed tightly, as if in the midst of weathering a storm. I didn't doubt that Bridget's red-haired fury was a force to be reckoned with, but cut from the same cloth as Sean and Lord Alexander, Stuart had the appearance of a man who could withstand anything life chose to burden his broad shoulders with.

"I don't mean to intrude, but if you could have someone ready a small conveyance and a footman to drive me, I would be grateful."

"You're not interrupting at all, Miss Andrews. Bridget and I are *through*." His emphasis on the word *through* carried a wealth of meaning, and Bridget gasped in response.

I bit my lip at the sudden sheen of tears I saw in her shadowed blue eyes. Stuart's jaw clenched much as a doctor's would when administering a painful but necessary treatment. I noted he fisted his hands tightly as if he was trying to keep himself from reaching out, and his dark eyes were full of mixed emotions.

After a moment or two of silence, Bridget left without saying a word.

Stuart cleared his throat, making me think that he had trouble finding his voice. "It'll take just a minute. Where will you be going? Just the short distance to Dartmoor's End or farther?"

I swallowed my lump of apprehension, realizing this was my first step to a life alone, one that would likely defy many notions of propriety. "Just a short distance, but I won't be going to Dartmoor's End. I'm going to Dragon's Cove."

Stuart froze in midstep then turned to me. "You're going to Lord Alexander's?"

"Yes."

He glanced at the castle, clearly wondering who else would be going with me.

"I am traveling alone," I said. "And I would appreciate as little attention as possible be given to this."

"In other words, the fewer who know the better?"

"Exactly." Even though I saw concern rather than judgment darken his gaze, my insides still twisted as tightly as my lace-gloved fingers.

"Very well, Miss Andrews. I hope you know what you are doing."

"I do."

He shook his head. "I wonder. Tread carefully, Miss Andrews. Alex isn't a man to be trusted in some ways."

I met his gaze and resisted the temptation to ask exactly what he meant. After a moment he nodded and went to secure my transportation. By responding to Stuart's warning, I would have opened the door for more conversation, which I wanted to avoid. Whatever he was cautioning me against, I didn't want know. I didn't want anything to deter me from the course I had set upon.

Twenty minutes later, I questioned my wisdom; perhaps I needed know everything that I could. The dark castle spires on Dragon's Cove came into view and I shivered at how their sharp points stabbed at the heavens, at how black the stone of the walls were against the bright beauty of the distant sea. Unlike Sean's castle, which nestled cozily along the open coast, Lord Alexander's domain rose amid cliffs of jagged rock where the sea could be heard crashing violently against the earth rather than lapping at the shore.

More fortress-like than any structure I'd seen before, with fanged dragons carved menacingly upon its battlements, the castle loomed over the cove like a preying beast, ready to devour all who dared to enter its lair. As the buggy drove up the long stretch of road, I could readily see why the rumors about the Killdaren brothers were so rampant. The castle was not a vision of wealth from a family blessed, but an outward warning of a family cursed beyond redemption.

More than a few doubts about the success of my venture burned in my mind, as if the dragons encircling the rooftop had set fire to them. I couldn't fail, I told myself, refusing to give in to the worry. Instead, I focused on the heat I'd seen sparking in Lord Alexander's gaze yesterday. On some level I interested him, and I needed to use that to my advantage.

The road between Killdaren's Castle and Dragon's Cove was rough from disuse, giving me a rather bumpy ride. Just before the carriage pulled up to the entrance of the castle, I tugged my dress and fichu into proper place. Only my lace fichu caught on Aphrodite's ring and jerked from its nesting place, leaving the décolletage of my lavender tea gown scandalously low. The emerald eyes of the serpent ring glinted in the sunlight, as if laughing at my predicament. Exasperated, I tried to inconspicuously stuff it back, but gave up as the driver halted.

I managed to shove the lace into my pocket before the driver reached to help me exit. Wild thoughts ran through my mind as I stood at the top of the stairs with my basket of scones and studied the black doors to the castle. They were carved with images, as was the custom with most impressive buildings, but somehow the dragons on these glass-like obsidian doors looked startlingly real. A great attention to detail had been given to each rough scale and needle-point fang. Even a starburst etched the pupils of each of their dark eyes, but the most shocking fact was that each dragon had stabbed the other in the heart with a forked spear. I snapped my eyes closed, somehow feeling the pain roaring from the dragons' wide mouths.

"Lass, I believe you've come to the wrong establishment. Where is it yer looking to be?"

Opening my eyes, I saw a taller, thinner version of Mrs. Murphy, a woman whose motherly appearance was as inviting as her eyes were warm and kind.

"This is the Viscount Blackmoor's residence is it not?"

"Yes," she said cautiously with a hint of cool reserve to her tone.

I forced a smile. "Then I am at the right place. Would you inform Lord Alexander that Miss Andrews is here to see him? He is expecting me."

Here eyes widened and she peered closer at me. "You're the sister of Master Sean's new wife."

It had been a long time since Sean could be referred to as 'master,' but then I knew this woman and her sister, Mrs. Murphy, had looked after Sean and Lord Alexander since they were little. "Yes . . . Mrs. . . ."

"Lynds. Mrs. Lynds," she said, stepping to the side. "Come in. I'll show you to the parlor and let Lord Alex know you are here."

Moving inside, I immediately became lost in the immense collection of art filling every available nook. Greek statues, Chinese silk screens, Spanish armor, and African masks all tried to out-display large portraits of men and women dressed as ornately as kings and queens. Polished to a high gleam, the rich cherry panelling on the walls served as backdrop for the eclectic menagerie of art. It surprised me to find little evidence of the castle's sinisterly dark facade in the inner decor. This same cluttering of art was everywhere I looked.

Mrs. Lynds sniffed the air, calling my attention to the fresh scent of beeswax and cinnamon. "I smell my sister's scones. Not a soul in Cornwall can bake them as delicately as she does," she said.

I held up the basket and she laughed. "Martha should have sent more. It'll take Lord Alex less than a minute to finish those off. Have a seat. I'll be but a moment."

She left, and rather than sitting, I placed the scones on the tea table and wandered about the room to examine some of the art more closely. It was utterly fascinating to have so much beauty within my grasp that I couldn't resist touching. I brushed a lace-covered fingertip over the smooth, vibrant red porcelain of a Chinese vase with a black dragon curling around its surface. The treasure had to be older than Britain.

I needed more. Sliding off Aphrodite's ring, I removed my gloves and placed my entire palm upon the cool vase. Nothing forced its way into my mind, no emotions of anger or joy, no images of murder or indiscretions. My mind was free to take flight and let my imagination flow.

I imagined that I stood next to Marco Polo, seeing the secrets of the orient for the first time, and the emperor, Kubla Kahn, had just made a gift of this priceless ruby vase to me, asking me to make a record of his vast collection of treasures.

"You came alone?"

Turning, I found Lord Alexander, frowning fiercely as he stood just inside the parlor door. He wore slim black breeches tucked into leather boots and a loose white shirt with full sleeves, a style reminiscent of a time when a man needed to wield a sword to live. Oddly, there was a black dragon embroidered over his left breast. He appeared as if he'd been exerting himself, and indeed had a long, thin bladed sword in his hand, which he set carefully upon a nearby table. His ebony hair was a bit mussed, his darkly tanned skin had a sheen of perspiration on it, and his eyes were alight with a challenging fire along with an edge of irritation. He clearly did not welcome my intrusion.

I had to swallow in order to speak. "Yes, the matter I wish to discuss with you is private and I thought it best." I desperately searched about for reasons he needed me to catalogue his menagerie of artifacts.

Much to my relief, he left the door open and crossed the room. As he drew closer, his gaze slid down my lavender dress slowly, then snapped back to a point below my chin where he stared for a moment before lifting a questioning brow as he met my gaze. "A private matter? Very interesting."

I didn't know if his seductive tone was a deliberate attempt to make me uncomfortable, or if he was truly that intrigued by me despite his frowning countenance, but I wasn't about to go fleeing from his liar. Still, the room became hotter, my pulse beat faster, my skin grew damper—everywhere—and the fire burning my cheeks sucked my breath away.

Joining me next to the vase, he slid his fingertip over the smooth enamel, slowly tracing the figure of the black dragon on the porcelain. I found his hands as fascinating as the perfectly sculpted art, with one difference—his hands weren't cold, nor was he. The heat of his body pressed against mine.

"Did you know that the Chinese think they descended from dragons?" he asked softly. "That the emperors believe they *are* dragons. Their clothes are called dragon's robes, their throne is the dragon's seat, and their beds are known as the dragon's beds."

The dragon's bed. Fire breathed down my spine. I glanced at the emblem on his breast, wondering just what sort of bed he slept in, before I snatched my mind back from that precipice and stiffened my shoulders. If I didn't take charge of the situation, I would be lost.

I cleared my throat. "Thankfully no one has such delusions in England, do they, Lord Alexander?" Lifting my brow in return, I hoped to imbue an added challenge to my voice. I didn't doubt that he was deliberately trying to unnerve me.

A smile tugged the corners of his frown before he turned away and moved to the tea table and its neighboring settee. He invited me to sit upon its cushiony white and gold brocade while he sat opposite in a darker, sterner wing chair.

"You appear well. So, I assume you're not here to speak

of yesterday's incident, for it was a rather fitting end for the man if he was guilty of what the constable reports."

I shuddered. "It was horrible, and I have to confess that I have deliberately refused to think about it. As you say, justice was served. The reason for my visit this morning concerns a different matter—I have come to see you about an employment opportunity."

"You wish to hire me?" The devilish gleam in his green eyes deepened; his gaze dropped to the V of my dress.

Lace gloves made for a sorry fan for my heated cheeks and Aphrodite's ring pricked my palm as I tightened my fist around it.

"No, my lord. You need to hire me, assuming that you haven't already engaged someone, to catalogue your antiquities. You mentioned the need earlier this summer, and from the chaotic state of your artifacts I cannot be more in agreement."

"Chaotic?"

"From what I have seen in the grand entry hall, the corridor, and the parlor here, there appears to be very little rhyme or reason to their placement in your home, a situation that detracts from the beauty of the art."

"No one can accuse you of mincing words, Miss Andrews." He leaned back in the burgundy silk wing chair and glanced about the room before adding, "Tell me, since you couldn't have been aware of the ugly and disordered state of my art before arriving, what exactly were your reasons for employment before coming?" The underlying steel in his green gaze wasn't going to bend.

I sighed, fearing that I would have to tell him more than I wanted anyone to know. Setting my gloves and ring on the table, I drew a deep breath and straightened the skirt of my dress that I realized had oddly bunched across my lap. Then I looked him directly in the eye. "If I tell you, you have to promise not to tell anyone else."

Oddly, he paled as if shocked, then clenched his fist. "I see. Well, you have my word as a gentleman then."

"I will soon have to live alone and support myself. So, in truth, I need a job. I know antiquities well and am very adept at organization and art. To secure a living cataloguing private collections will require sterling references. And since you did mention your need of such services before, I thought we could come to a mutually beneficial agreement."

He rose suddenly, as if he couldn't sit a moment more. His clipped steps to the window were angry, and jerked the knots in my stomach taut. At the window, he stared out at the bright day, his expression a dark cloud that eclipsed any hope I had of success. Tears stung my eyes. I hadn't realized how much I had been counting on him, nor how desperately I needed the hope of some acceptable future for myself.

"I deeply regret that you find yourself in such circumstances, but—"

I stood, unable to hear more and not about to beg. "Mrs. Murphy's scones are in the basket. I apologize for intruding and wish you well, Lord Alexander." Then I turned and quit the room. Three steps down the corridor, I realized two things. I didn't have my gloves nor did I have Aphrodite's ring. Panicked, I swung back around and ran directly into an embroidered black dragon on a white shirt with the hard body of Lord Alexander behind it. He exhaled sharply, and the heat of his breath was what I imagined a dragon's fire would feel like against my skin.

5

"Oh," I said, taken completely by surprise. His heat registered first, then the hard feel of him, so solid beneath my bare palms that had somehow landed against his chest. Then the scent of him enveloped me, exotic and alluring, unlike any aroma I'd ever experienced.

He brought his hands up to grab my waist as if seeking—unnecessarily—to steady me. I had to draw in another breath as my body tingled in an utterly shameless manner. The sensations grew as his gazed settled directly upon my rising bosom.

More frightening than that was the fact that whatever he was thinking or imagining was obscured from my mind by what I could only describe as a dark cloud, an angry one, roiling with such emotion that I had to quickly step back.

Lord Alexander dropped his hands from my sides and his gaze shifted to mine. Anger flashed in the vibrant green depths of his eyes, as well as something else, something equally as potent and hot and mesmerizing.

"Are you always so rudely rash?"

Air flew from my lungs. "Me, rude?" Accusation rang high in my voice, along with a healthy dose of outrage.

Amazingly, a half smile quirked the left corner of his mouth and a dimple flashed on his cheek. "Well, just rash then," he amended. "You didn't even give me a chance to finish my sentence before you ran as if the devil himself had set fire to your skirts."

It wasn't the least bit of a stretch to see him as the devil, and he'd sparked more heat in me than I'd every felt in my life before. Not just from his touch, either. I had acted "rash" as he put it.

"I only sought to save you from the embarrassment of having to supply a number of excuses, my lord. Your tone conveyed your sentiments rather well."

"Then you are not very adept at reading tones or sentiments, lass. So I will thank you to at least let a man finish speaking for himself before you speak for him."

Had I been able to think of a reply I wouldn't have been able to utter it; my jaw had dropped so low speech was impossible. I wasn't adept at reading people?

After a long moment he spoke. "Shall we return to the parlor?"

I nodded.

His lip quirked again and he stepped aside, motioning me ahead. The weight of his gaze slid warmly down my back as I returned to the settee and immediately donned my gloves and ring lest I forget them again.

He chose to pace across the room rather than sit. "As I was saying, I deeply regret that you are in such circumstances, but do you realize how extensive the task you're proposing is? My home here is by no means modest and the estate near Hampton Court is larger. Both of them are," he glanced around the room, "what was the word you used? Chaotic?

"It would seem several generations thought only of collecting artifacts, not storing or exhibiting them. To do a proper job of cataloguing the Killdaren's collection would take some time."

My mind boggled at the very idea even as excitement pulsed through me. So many treasures that needed noting and caring for! I cleared my throat. "While I understand your need to caution me, let me assure you, I in no way find the enormity of the task a deterrent. The challenge you present is more than enticing."

He shifted abruptly, his regard direct and searching. My response seemed to surprise him. I met his gaze with assurance and what I hoped was a wealth of interest. The very thought of being able to touch and organize a multitude of treasures from all over the world such as the porcelain vase and the African masks set my pulse racing.

"I see that it is," he replied strangely.

I blinked, wondering at his tone. "Quite frankly, I am extremely enamored of artifacts. It has been that way for me all of my life. I do not come to you without a great deal of experience."

He coughed, but I continued, too enthusiastic to plead my case to heed his odd behavior.

"I believe I mentioned earlier this summer that I have catalogued and organized my father's vast archaeological collections for the Museum of Worldwide Antiquities in Oxford since I was a child."

Clearing his throat, he nodded. "Yes, I do remember our conversation. So, the length of time required for this task isn't going to be a problem for you?"

I firmed my lips with determination. "No. As I said, I would prefer it to be kept as a private matter, but I find myself in the position of needing to earn a living."

He studied me again, seemingly more serious than ever. I didn't let my gaze waver. "One last thing. Is my brother aware of your employment interest here?"

I stiffened my back. "What is the point of your question? I don't see that my future has anything to do with my brother-in-law. He carries no authority or guardianship over me."

"The point is, I am fairly certain your continued association with me will be unacceptable to him and will likely cause strife."

"If that proves to be the case, then as I said, my intent is to support myself. I will secure accommodations in Dartmoor's End if necessary."

His brows lifted. "You surprise me, Miss Andrews. From what I recall, you are very close to your sisters. Yet, you appear determined to separate yourself from them. Why?"

I had to blink back the tears that burned my eyes. "Unfortunately, Lord Alexander, whether we will it or not, sometimes circumstances dictate that our lives take unforeseen and sometimes painful directions."

"That I do know," he said softly, in a tone of voice I'd yet to hear him use. By the time my eyes cleared enough to see, he'd turned his back to me and was once again staring out of the window. His profile cut a sharp, dark silhouette against the sunlight streaming into the room. "I'll expect you to begin tomorrow morning then. Mrs. Lynds will be here and available for any of your needs. As my butler is currently indisposed and I keep only a modicum of servants, please leave a list of supplies you'll require with her and let her know if you need any assistance. Some of the artifacts can be heavy and bulky. Also, the last time I looked, there were a number of unopened crates stored in the Queen's Room. I've no idea what is inside of them."

I couldn't fathom such a sacrilege. "You mean you've never opened them? Why ever not?"

"I choose to dwell as little as possible upon anything from the past," he said.

"Well then, I will see you tomorrow." I stood, deciding that I had best take my leave before Lord Alexander changed his mind about allowing me to meddle with his things from the past.

"Unfortunately, I won't be about," he replied, turning to face me.

"Oh?"

"Right now, I'm spending the majority of my day training

Iris to respond to my touch. She's an exceptionally intelligent horse."

"I see," I said, feeling slightly deflated. Though my main focus this morning had been employment for my future good, I hadn't lost sight of the importance of my sister's situation. Developing a more than passing acquaintance with Lord Alexander was essential. "Might I see her again sometime soon? She was very beautiful and graceful. I would enjoy watching her run."

"We'll have to arrange that sometime then." His voice trailed off as if that might not happen anytime soon. Then he surprised me. "Do you ride, Miss Andrews?"

"Some, when I can. We'd had little need and no opportunity for the pastime in Oxford." I thought for a moment he would offer to take me riding, but he didn't.

"Tell Mrs. Murphy that I thank her for the scones."

"I'll be sure to." Were my stomach not so knotted and his tone not one of such dismissal, I would have ventured to share *my* scones with him. As it was, I walked to the door. "Thank you for your time today. I know you are a busy man and I apparently interrupted your swordplay, so I'll see myself out."

Moving swiftly, he caught up to me at the door of the parlor. "Fencing," he said correcting my nervous words and taking hold of my elbow. "I haven't engaged in 'swordplay' since Sean and I were in knappers. And though I have my rough edges, Miss Andrews, I am gentleman enough to escort a lady to her conveyance."

One would think that the more time I spent in his presence the more immune I would become to the effects of it. That was not the case. By the time we crossed the grand entry hall to the ebony doors, my pulse raced with the tingles his touch sent shooting though me.

It was disturbing that his mind remained so closed to me. Was it because he really did have something deep and dark to hide? Something worse than anyone else I'd ever known? The idea shocked me and I gasped.

He looked at me strangely.

I nodded at the huge ebony doors, seeing they were carved with the same images on the inside as the outside. "The craftsmanship on the entry doors is impressive," I said, sounding odd even to my own ears.

"I thought so. I commissioned a man in China to make them for me. He did a remarkable job with the design I gave him."

I nearly came to a stop, would have if he hadn't had a hold on me. *He'd* designed the dragons in the throes of death? Somehow that fact sat coldly inside me, making me very thankful to feel the bright sun and see my driver waiting with the buggy. Killdaren's Castle and the warmth of my sisters was just a short ride away, and I suddenly yearned to be there, wishing everything were different, wishing I were normal. The thought of my family comforted as well as defeated, for it wasn't a very independent yearning.

"Tell me everything quickly. Mrs. Murphy will bring us tea shortly, and I'm sure the others will join us then. You weren't there very long today," Cassie said as she pulled me into the parlor, shut the door, and opened the black curtains that covered the windows to let sunlight fill the room. With Sean sleeping, she didn't have to worry about him accidentally walking into what would be a painfully blinding light for him and triggering a migraine.

"There isn't much to tell. I'll begin cataloguing tomorrow. The place is in an awful state though." I told her about the overstuffed menagerie of artifacts, about the priceless red dragon-marked vase, about the castle itself and the savagery of its architecture, then about the doors. "The dragons are in horrible pain; they leap from the carving and grab your heart. Do you know he designed them himself?" I shuddered again. "Why would a man want such a scene to be the first thing everyone sees at his door?"

"It's them," Cassie said softly.

"Pardon?"

"I'd wager you almost anything that the dragons on the

doors are Sean and Lord Alexander. Oh, this is very good news, Andrie."

I bit my lip at the hope shinning in my sister's eyes. How she could determine such a thing as good escaped me. I feared she wanted things to be a certain way so badly she'd interpret anything in such a way as to give her hope. "You're going to have to explain yourself."

"Don't you see?" She pressed a palm to her stomach. "It's symbolizing the Dragon's Curse, but though the dragons are in pain, and they've been wounded dreadfully, they're still on their feet."

"A devil's fork through their hearts isn't just a dreadful wound, it is a mortal wound. But you could be right," I said, but that wasn't what I was thinking. Given the carving, if what Cassie supposed was true and the dragons did represent Lord Alexander and Sean, then the message was that neither of them would survive the curse.

A knock on the door produced Bridget pushing a tea cart, with Prudence and Gemini following close behind.

"Tea is served, my queen," Bridget said with her pretty nose in the air. She did a good impersonation of a stuffy, self-important lady's maid.

Cassie laughed and Bridget gave her a saucy grin. "Whot? Ya think'n I'm not prop'r-like?"

I immediately recalled Bridget's scandalous thoughts earlier, a memory that heated my cheeks and made me avert my gaze from her greeting, but not before I saw a questioning hurt in her eyes, as if I didn't think she were proper.

My stomach knotted. I'd have to find a way to apologize. When Cassie had first come to Killdaren's Castle, she'd taught Bridget how to read and write, and now she and Cassie held weekly classes for all of the servants. Bridget sometimes tended to be self-conscious about her education around anyone other than Cassie.

"I hope your errands went well this morning, Andrie," Bridget said, seeking to amend or smooth whatever gaffe she felt she made.

"Very well." I forced the "vampire lover" and the "naked in Stuart's bed" memory to the back of my mind and smiled warmly at her. I don't know why it embarrassed me to know her mind. My thoughts of Lord Alexander hadn't been any different. But then I would be mortified if anyone knew, even more mortified if anyone knew and I didn't know that they knew. My head ached at the circles my mind ran in.

"What errands?" Gemini asked, snitching a scone from the tea cart before she settled on the peacock-blue damask sofa. The rich color against her pink lace tea dress, creamy complexion, and sunny hair, made her shine like a jewel and turned her blue eyes vibrant, though I could still see the shadow of yesterday's tragic accident in them.

"Our Andrie has secured herself a post," Cassie said abruptly.

Gemini coughed on her scone as Prudence's and Bridget's mouths formed perfect *O*s.

"You didn't even tell me you were looking for a position!" Gemini gasped, clearly upset. "Where? Doing what? You two never tell me any of the important things."

"I went to Dragon's Cove. Lord Alexander has hired me to catalogue the Killdaren family's antiquities. Remember?" I looked at Gemini, trying to soothe her feelings. "It was a position he mentioned earlier this summer. I have been desperate to busy my hands with artifacts and this seemed like a mutually beneficial arrangement."

"Oh dear." Prudence gracefully dropped onto a bronze-colored wing chair with lion-pawed feet. "I don't think you should let The Killdaren know about this."

She referred to Sean. Though not titled, Sean's presence left an impression that Mister didn't cover.

Cassie furrowed her brow. "Why do you think Andrie working will disturb Sean?"

Prudence sighed. "I've fought to work a number of times over the years and Sean refuses to have it. He has the means to provide everything Rebecca and I could ever possibly need and he doesn't see the point."

"What?" Cassie asked, her shoulders straightening like a soldier's.

"I thought that was why you resigned from your newspaper column." Prudence delicately poured tea for us all, her deportment enviable.

"No . . . I." Cassie frowned. "Since I was no longer living in Oxford, I thought it best."

Having spoken to Cassie at length about the matter, I knew it was more because she'd gone against almost every word of advice she'd given over the years when she'd taken a position as a maid. She didn't feel qualified to advise ladies on being proper. More important things had filled her life now, too.

"Then Sean didn't ask you to resign?" Prudence handed Cassie a cup of tea, fixed perfectly to my sister's taste.

Cassie sipped and sighed with appreciation. "He did ask, but . . ." Her voice fell lower, heavy with doubt.

"Honestly, Cassie," Gemini rolled her eyes. "Ladies—women of wealth and influence—aren't employed. They expend their efforts for charities to benefit those less fortunate, and to entertain acquaintances and peers in order to keep faith with the family's reputation and increase its influence."

It surprised me to discover Gemini had given a great deal of thought to the responsibilities of being a titled lady. I'd assumed her repeated interest in titled gentlemen over others had been merely her desire for the prestige and a want for a life of frivolity and ease. Fashion and parties and such were always on the tip of her tongue. I loved her dearly, but Gemini had never taken much of life seriously. She always skimmed its surface, almost deliberately so.

"Gemini is right," Prudence said. "Sean is subtle, but in the end the results will be the same for you as for me. In Andrie's case though, I fear it is another matter altogether. One a great deal more serious."

"How?" I asked, taking my own teacup and a scone. I'd not eaten all day and was suddenly very hungry.

"He'll see it as a betrayal," Bridget said firmly as she joined Gemini on the sofa. "Though I've not spoken to The

Killdaren often, I know how most men think. He'll feel as if you've joined the enemy camp."

"Interesting," I said. "Lord Alexander said the same thing, and it's entirely a bunch of poppycock." I set my teacup on the table hard enough to rattle the saucer. "Lord Ashton and Mr. Drayson travel willy-nilly between here and Dragon's Cove, as do Sir Warwick and the earl, and I haven't heard a word about betrayal of loyalties said to any of them. Besides, the point of a woman working is one of prerogative. If it is what she chooses to do then she should be allowed to do so."

"Very well put, Andrie," Cassie said. "Sean can't really say anything about the matter."

I clenched my hand. The last thing I wanted was to cause any discord between Cassie and Sean, but considering the weight of her worry about the future of the child or children growing within her, we didn't have a choice but to do something about the matter. I slipped another scone from the plate along with an orange-flavored tea cake. Prudence poured me a second cup of tea.

"Do you have any arguments I can smack over Stuart Frye's stubborn head?" Bridget asked, changing the subject. "Nothing I say seems to get through to him. As long as his mother and brother are under charges in Mary's death, accidental or not, Stuart won't have anything to do with me. He will barely even speak to me."

"Give him time," Cassie said. "He is only seeking to protect you from having the villagers think badly of you."

"I don't care what the villagers think. My mum and brother are here, safe from harm's way. If he really loved me then it wouldn't matter."

"I went through the same thing with Sean," Cassie said. "In trying to protect me, he rejected me, and that hurt me the most."

"Try living eight years that way," Prudence said quietly, shocking us all. It wasn't a secret that the earl had had a relationship with Prudence when she was an upstairs maid younger than Gemini's tender eighteen, but Prudence had never spoken of it.

Cassie recovered from the shock quicker than anyone else. "My father-in-law or not, the man is a fool for not marrying you. His vow not to love anyone because those he does love either die or live under a curse is ridiculous."

"Marry me?" Prudence shook her head, distressed. "Cassie, he's an earl. Earls don't marry cropper's daughters." She set her teacup down and stood. "I shouldn't have said anything. Forgive me. I'm going to go check on Rebecca." She started to leave the room.

"Prudence," Cassie said. "I'm sorry. What is it? What is wrong? I didn't mean to upset you."

Prudence turned to face everyone. She drew a deep breath. Tears filled her golden eyes. She was breathtakingly beautiful in a very delicate way, like a porcelain china doll; petite, with luxurious dark hair swept into an elegant coiffure, a perfect creamy complexion, and always dressed romantically in satin and lace. "Don't apologize, please. What is wrong is that I don't belong here with all of you, Cassie. You and your sisters have embraced me, befriended me, and have graciously refrained from mentioning the fact that I am but a low-born woman with an illegitimate child. But nothing will ever bridge the gap between the realities of my life and those of yours."

Gemini stood. "But none of that is your—"

"It is my fault. The earl didn't force me. He didn't even chase after me," Prudence said, cutting Gemini off. "He is very handsome man and that attracted me to him, more so than his wealth. I deliberately caught his eye. I put myself in his way and became involved with him, hoping he would make me his mistress. After we were together I fell in love with him. That you believe he would ever marry me shows how very different we are. My only hope, my dream, is that one day he will make me his mistress and I would gladly live that way just to be able to love him. I'm not worthy to be your friend." Turning, she moved quickly to the door.

"Wait," I said, upsetting my teacup to jump up and stop

Prudence from leaving. She paused with her hand on the door handle, but didn't turn. "You can't leave us, Prudence. By going, you're inferring that we're casting stones, that we're condemning you for being who you are and for believing your life is unlike ours. We all have things that . . . that are different from each other, things that isolate us."

"Andrie's right, Prudence," Cassie said softly. "You cannot leave us."

I knew Cassie was thinking as I was, for we both were burdened by gifts. Cassie dreamed a person's death and I saw into their minds.

"Were it not for the fact that I had my sisters and my family to consider, if my choice had been to either be with Sean as his mistress or to never love him, I would have chosen to love him," Cassie said, shocking me completely.

Gemini gasped. Prudence swung around, her gold eyes wide and blinking at even more tears.

Bridget spoke up. "I daresay this is a most scandalous parlor conversation to embark upon, but I would bloody well do the same with Stuart, if that were my only choice."

I shouldn't have been surprised by everyone's admission, for I had already seen enough of their thoughts to know it. It was the admission of it that stunned me. Women really did choose to live improperly sometimes for the reason of love.

"But that's wrong," Gemini said.

"In society's eyes, yes," Cassie said softly. "But then in society's eyes it is wrong for a woman to have much of a say in how her life is lived. No one is speaking of loving a man who has committed himself to another woman. If you think about it, in God's eyes, Adam and Eve never had their banns posted in a church or obtained a special license. They loved and cared for one another and that was all that mattered."

Prudence slowly returned to her seat. "Wanting to be the earl's mistress is my darkest secret," she said in shock. "I can't believe you don't think I'm horrible."

"No," I said. "There are much worse things." Like my secret. I wanted to reach out and touch her, but I didn't.

6

"You're killing her," I shouted at the man whose beefy hands were wrapped around a woman's slender throat. The woman struggled, her dark eyes pleading, her mouth open in a soundless scream.

My heart pounding, I grabbed at the man's shoulder, trying to pull him away. I couldn't move him. Reaching for his hands, I attempted to pry them from the woman's throat. Her skin was icy cold, her complexion a blue tinged milky white. I hit at the man's arms, doing anything I could to stop him. He only laughed. Frustration and rage filled me. "Stop," I screamed at him. "Stop!"

I ran at him from the side, planning to hit him with my whole body and knock him off the poor woman, but at the moment of impact, everything disappeared and I went plunging into a dark abyss where I floundered helplessly. Falling . . . falling.

I awoke drenched, breathing so harshly that my lungs hurt. My heart thudded painfully in my breast, and a high-pitched scream pierced my ears. The scream of a child. Rebecca!

Struggling against the covers, I ran from my room, not even bothering to gather my robe or my slippers. A short distance down the corridor, I reached the quarters where Rebbeca and Bridget slept next to Prudence's room. The door was open and both Bridget and Prudence were with the child. Poor little Rebecca was wrapped in her mother's arms, but was screaming. "Mary! Mary! Horseman take my Mary. Horseman hurt my Mary and make her cry!"

I didn't hesitate; I ran to Rebecca, grabbed her hand, and closed my eyes, plunging myself into her dark world, into her nightmare. I read what Rebecca heard in her mind and instinctively felt that she was reliving the last time she saw Mary.

"Stay away from her. You've compromised her."

"She's sinned, Mary, and now she must pay for her sins."

"What? Are you mad? You seduced her!"

"Only because she asked for it. Just like you. I know what goes on between you and The Killdaren at night."

"You're insane! Stop it! What are you doing?"

"Only what The Killdaren does to you. Scream and the child dies."

"Run Rebecca! God! Run!"

My cousin's scream ripped through me, doubling me over in pain, and I fell to the floor as a black void wrapped around me and sucked me under.

"Andrie? Please wake up, Andrie."

My eyes fluttered open to see Cassie leaning over me. She had my hand clasped in hers. I was shuddering so badly that both her and the curtains on the four-poster bed were shaking.

"What is it?" she whispered. "What did you see?"

I could hear others in the room. Bridget and Gemini were

talking about me in hushed tones. Since I didn't hear Rebecca screaming anymore, I knew she had quieted for now, and that Prudence would be with her. The evil of what I felt I'd learned tonight sickened me horribly.

Oh, God, Mary! What did you suffer? How much more had Rebecca heard of what had happened to Mary? Though Rebecca was blind and couldn't have seen Mary being attacked and worse, the trauma of hearing it was still just as shattering. No wonder the child screamed uncontrollably. I wanted to do the same no matter how irrational it was. Inside, I already felt as if I were screaming.

There was more than just Mary involved in the portent of the words. The man had intended to harm another, and I had a sickening suspicion that person was Flora, Bridget's sister who'd left here after Mary's death to seek fortune on the stage with a man known only as Jack. I had no proof that all I was supposing was true and no real way to communicate it either.

"Nothing," I croaked in answer to Cassie's question. "I . . . I can't remember. My head hurts."

Cassie just looked at me and I tried to meet her gaze but failed. I had to look away. How could I tell her what I'd heard from Rebecca's mind? Cassie was pregnant with Sean's baby and already upset. It would only worsen her situation. And to hear that Mary and Sean might have been involved . . . Oh, God. I didn't want to know these things. They were too painful. It was too hard to accept the dark secrets and dreams hidden inside of everyone.

Tears filled my eyes and spilled over. "Rest," I whispered to Cassie. "Please let me rest."

She sighed. "Rest for now, Andrie. I'm here. I won't leave you."

I saw in her mind, memories of our childhood when we'd climbed into a dark closet together and whispered about our gifts that we weren't supposed to let anyone know about. Having her to share it with had made the secret bearable then. But her thoughts drifted to Sean and I slipped my hand from her grasp and turned over, seemingly trying to make myself more comfortable.

Unbelievably, exhaustion pulled me into a deep, dreamless sleep. But it was my only reprieve. When I woke, it was to find a breakfast tray being pushed at me.

"What time is it?" I asked, sitting up. Cassie stuffed a thick pillow behind my back. She looked as ragged as I felt and made me feel guilty for what I said next. "I need to be at Dragon's Cove by nine."

"You've plenty of time," Cassie said firmly. "The maids are readying your bath water as we speak. What happened last night? What did you see in Rebecca's mind that devastated you so?"

"It's as I said. I don't know. Maybe I just felt her pain and terror so deeply that I fainted. I'm sorry." I'd decided to wait before I tried to tell anyone exactly what I'd heard. I needed more proof of my suppositions before I caused additional pain for everyone, especially Cassie and Bridget.

"Heavens, don't you dare apologize, Andrie. We just need to figure out how to explain things to Bridget and Prudence."

"Tell them I had a bad dream and when I heard Rebecca, I rushed to her so quickly I fainted."

"Are you sure that's all?" Cassie sat back against the stuffed cushion of the chair she'd pulled next to my bed. "I'm sorry, but I was so hoping that you'd be able to see into Rebecca's mind and tell us what happened to Mary."

"I do see into Rebecca's mind, but it is very difficult. Because she is blind I don't 'see' anything. Her thoughts and memories are a collage of her interpretation of the sounds and sensations around her, like a very dark dream. Mostly her thoughts about the day Mary died are a wild odyssey beginning with happiness and songs, of sun-warmed sand and comfort that abruptly changes with the sounds of horse's hooves and Mary's frightened cries, then Rebecca's frantic terror to get help for her and Mary."

Taking time to spread jam on my toast, I contemplated my next sentence. Perhaps I didn't need to be completely silent but subtly steer things in a certain direction. "The impression of those sounds and sensations lead me to the conclusion that we need to be asking questions about Mrs. Frye and Jamie's story."

"I've been asking questions since Mary disappeared and I'm still dissatisfied with Constable Poole's investigation," Cassie said.

"The sensations I glean from Rebecca's thoughts, don't match up to what Jamie and Mrs. Frye claim happened. Mary and Rebecca went on a picnic and then hours later Rebecca was found wet from the cold sea, and screaming for Mary. Later we learned a bad horseman had taken Mary."

Cassie nodded. "Which in no way concurs with Mrs. Frye's claim that she argued with Mary and caused our cousin to trip, roll down the sand dune, and strike her head on a sharp rock. It gets worse when Mrs. Frye claims Rebecca wasn't anywhere in sight and didn't know Rebecca was with Mary."

I set down my teacup. "I can't imagine Mary wouldn't have had Rebecca right next to her. For Mrs. Frye to claim she didn't when Rebecca was always with Mary at that time of the day is ridiculous. And no one has come up with a real explanation as to how Rebecca ended up on the roof either."

"Even if Jamie's knife was in the tower, I don't see him doing that to Rebecca. So why is Mrs. Frye lying about what happened?"

"I don't know," I said, unwilling to suggest anything else until I had time to think about what I'd learned. A knock on the door rescued me from saying more.

"Come in," Cassie called out.

Gemini entered. "I'm sorry," she said, glancing from me to Cassie and looking hurt. You two are talking again. I'll come back later." She whipped around and shut the door behind her, rather firmly.

"What's wrong with her?" I asked.

"It would seem she is feeling excluded again. Remember right after Grandfather died and how badly I felt that I couldn't help him? You spent hours consoling me and Mother kept hovering over me."

"And Gemini decided she was going to run away since she really wasn't part of the family at all."

"And Mother decided to tell her about our 'problem.' Gemini went around for a week predicting the future. Mother nearly had an apoplectic fit when she said it was going to storm and it did."

"Gemini danced all over the house, ecstatic."

"And Mother forbade her to ever play around like that again."

Our sighs seemed to escape at the same moment. I pushed my breakfast tray away. The kidney porridge wasn't very appetizing anyway.

"What are you going to tell her?" I asked Cassie as I slipped on my robe.

"That I'm pregnant and worried the Dragon's Curse will continue. What about you?"

"The truth, as well." As much of it as I was going to reveal to anyone. "That I'm having dark dreams in the night and Rebecca's screaming badly frightened me." There was enough truth in that statement to keep me from going to perdition for lying, but it did little to change the living hell I was in, or keep it from getting worse by the day.

I shuddered. *Dear God, Mary. I'm sorry*. Nothing that I was going through could compare to what she must have suffered.

My first day on the job and I was late. Though I think my nine o'clock arrival time had been more my suggestion than Lord Alexander's and my schedule was completely up to me, it still bothered me.

Each week, or each month, I was to submit a tally of my work hours to Mrs. Lynds and she would see to my payment. Lord Alexander had arranged everything so that he would not have to suffer my presence at all. I should have been elated to be venturing upon my first step toward independence. But between Rebecca's nightmare and Lord Alexander's planned absence, a dark cloud as ominous and threatening as the deadly beasts depicted on the entrance to Dragon's Cove hovered over me.

The buggy drew up to the front and I instructed the driver to return for me at five as I exited with my bag of cataloguing supplies. I firmed my shoulders, stiffened my back, and marched up the stairs. Halfway to the dark doors I came to a halt, checked my appearance, then chastised myself for doing so. I'd worn a simple but elegant high-necked forest green gown with cream lace at the neck, one that I considered extremely proper.

Since I planned to work, I'd left off wearing gloves, but couldn't leave Aphrodite's ring behind. The serpent eyes winked at me again as I drew a deep breath, and had me wishing I'd see Lord Alexander again soon.

I expected Mrs. Lynds to answer the door; instead, an elderly man wearing a patch over his left eye presented himself. "Ye must be the lass the Captain Black mentioned. Blimey but you're a welcome sight. I'm Brighty Smith, his butler. Come on in with ye." He motioned as he stepped aside.

I had to bite off my surprise and force my feet into motion. It was odd to have a formally dressed butler look and talk like a pirate. "Is Lord Alexander here?"

He shook his head, bringing my attention to the matted wig he wore that somehow made him just a little bit endearing. "Knowing 'im as I do, 'e's likely out racing 'is 'orse Devil about this time of day. Which room do ye want to get started in? I'll let Mrs. Lynds know that you're here."

That Lord Alexander rode with the devil fit his character perfectly.

I wasn't familiar enough with the castle to know many of the rooms, or even the most logical place to begin, so I chose the room I was in. "I'll start here, in the grand entry hall."

"Don't be afeared to call if you need anything," he said.

I nodded and he left. First, I made a list of everything in

the room and described each item in detail, giving it a catalogue number and a category notation. Later I would go back
to this master list and create smaller lists so that all pictures
would be together, and all statues, and so on. Before I could
set my eye on what artifacts needed to be removed from the
grand entry hall to make the room more aesthetically palat-
able, Mrs. Lynds appeared.

"Hope you're ready for a bite to eat, lass. You've been
working for hours."

"Yes, I am hungry." A fact that surprised me. Last night
had not only drained my energy but had also stolen my appetite. Glancing at the grandfather clock, I saw that it was already after one and I sighed with relief. I'd actually had
several hours free of troubling thoughts and problems—
mine or other people's. It felt amazingly wonderful.

"I can serve you outside on the terrace or in the family
dining room."

"The terrace would be lovely, Mrs. Lynds."

"You'll find what you need to freshen up in the water
closet at the end of the corridor down this way. I'll escort
you to the terrace when you're ready."

"Thank you." I returned my supplies to my bag and set it
next to the dragon doors on a marble table with a golden ele-
phant pedestal. After refreshing myself, I followed Mrs.
Lynds through a series of rooms and corridors. Lord Alexander's domain was as richly appointed as Killdaren's Castle,
if not more so, and it was dauntingly twice as big. I had the
feeling I could wander inside its treasures my whole life and
never have to see a soul.

Except Lord Alexander. How could I ever begin to help
repair his relationship with Sean if I never saw him to develop any sort of rapport?

After crossing a long, golden, mirrored ballroom, Mrs.
Lynds showed me through French doors that opened to a magnificent terrace. I barely took note of the umbrella-covered
table she led me to, or the resplendent meal set upon its

linen-covered surface, for off in the distance was a man and a beautiful black horse. Both were familiar.

"Will you be wanting to be served, lass?'

I dragged my gaze to Mrs. Lynds and shook my head. "No. Thank you. I'll be fine."

"Very well," she said. If I hadn't been looking at her, I would have missed her glance toward Lord Alexander and the slight smile that lit her kind face before she left.

Heat brushed my cheeks. She'd deliberately set me up so that I could see Lord Alexander. A slight smile touched my lips and my mind drifted back to yesterday's conversation in the parlor with the women about their feelings in regards to men.

I'd always considered a normal relationship with a man out of the question for me. What man wanted a woman who read his thoughts every time he touched her?

Even I, myself, shuddered at the idea of a man reading my every thought. I'd accepted that I would be alone for all of my life. It was the price I was forced to pay for my gift.

Iris neighed loudly, bringing my attention back to Lord Alexander. Though it was hard to discern the details of his actions, I could tell Iris was unfettered in any way and Lord Alexander worked alone with her in the training ring. Amazingly the mare walked beside him, keeping pace with his every move.

He accomplished the deed by soft touches and quiet words, because every time the mare strayed, he brought his hand up and caressed the horse's muzzle until she drew closer to him. His manner reminded me of the quiet way he'd spoken to Iris on the ship's deck. I became so engrossed in watching that I quite forgot about my meal and didn't remember it until he and Iris left the ring, disappearing behind a cluster of buildings.

Blushing, I hurriedly dished out a serving from several appetizing concoctions, slid a delicately cut sandwich onto my plate, and sugared myself a cup of tea before I set about eating. Four bites into the delicious fare, I glanced back at the riding ring and nearly choked on chunk of soft, custard-like cheese.

Lord Alexander hadn't returned to the ring; he was racing toward me on a huge black horse. He was coatless, wearing only a loose white shirt, breeches, and boots, like before. His dark hair streamed in the wind and power churned from both man and horse. Power that seemingly grew with every inch of ground they covered.

7

Lord Alexander had hitched the horse to a railing and started up the curving steps before I found the wherewithal to swallow.

"Miss Andrews." He nodded slightly as he approached.

"My lord," I replied, congratulating myself on the calmness of my voice. Considering the pace of my pulse, it was miracle.

"I trust the meal is to your liking?"

"Extremely so. But there's more here than I could ever eat. I don't know what Mrs. Lynds was thinking."

"It would seem she intended for us to share a meal together, as it is my custom to eat at this time in this very spot every day."

"Oh." Glancing across the table again, I saw the second place setting for the first time. "I apologize. I had no idea. I mean she didn't mention it. I mean I didn't notice the plate." How utterly rude of me! "Lord Alexander, to be quite honest, watching you in the ring with Iris mesmerized me so completely that I've been oblivious to everything else."

"Don't apologize. I would not have kept a lady waiting had I known she was to be expected. I too was very much engrossed with Iris and didn't notice you were here for some time."

"Oh." I bit my lip and his gaze dropped to watch me.

I swallowed again, fighting the need to ease the sudden tingling of my lips with my tongue. He moved abruptly and joined me at the table.

"Would you care for a glass of wine?" he asked, uncorking a bottle.

My gaze drifted from his face to the bottle. Was it the spiced wine? Did it really have aphrodisiac-like properties? I didn't dare ask. "Yes, please."

He poured a small serving into a goblet and handed it to me. The liquid was almost clear, with a tart aroma. It was not the spiced wine, and I felt a bit disappointed.

"Either you've had an exhausting morning or you didn't sleep very well last night. You've shadows beneath your eyes."

"I have?"

"You do." He served several dishes onto his plate and took three of the sandwiches. "So which is it?"

"A little of both."

"What happened last night?"

"The moon must have been full or something. I had a bad dream and woke from that to hear Rebecca screaming. She had a nightmare, too."

"Was your dream related to the incident in town?"

"In a way."

"Visions of what happened?" he asked.

"Of the carriage accident? Not really. I keep thinking about his poor wife."

"A terrible tragedy. Did the man say something more to you on the boardwalk?"

"No," I said quickly. "Why?"

"For him to rush away as frightened as he seemed, I wondered if perhaps you resembled his wife and he'd thought he'd seen a ghost."

"I don't but I wish I did," I said, remembering the woman's dark hair. At Lord Alexander's odd look, I quickly tried to cover and explained. "He deserves to have been frightened. As for the work this morning, I found it refreshing." I wisely opted to change the subject. "I've catalogued and fully described every antiquity in the grand entry hall and feel as if I have accomplished a good amount already. Losing myself in things from the past, seeing them organized and displayed properly so that others can enjoy them, is invigorating."

He quirked a brow. "I've never considered artifacts invigorating. They're a burdensome inheritance to be tolerated."

"Good heavens! That's tantamount to a sacrilege. Each and every piece is a part of history, an intimate reflection of someone's life from the past. Artifacts are a mystery to be discovered, a challenge in some cases, like the pyramids, or a recounting of lives and tragedies, like in Pompeii."

"It's rather amazing—"

"It's more than amazing. It's utterly fascinating what we can learn."

"I'm sure. But what I was going to say is that it is rather amazing to find a young woman so very passionate about such things. Most ladies would much rather spend their time shopping and attending soirees than dusting pottery and bones."

"Sorry. I do get carried away with the subject."

"Quite all right. I'm sure I sound just as enthusiastic when I speak of horses."

"As well you should. What were you doing with Iris in the ring? I've never seen a horse follow a man's movements so perfectly."

"It's a special art of horse training known to my Irish ancestors. Before a man ever rides or trains his horse, he teaches her to respond to his every touch, to his every word."

"It was . . . beautiful. It was like seeing man and nature as one," I said for lack of a better way to describe the gentle mastery he'd exhibited.

He stopped eating a moment and studied me until my cheeks warmed yet again. I took another sip of the tart wine. Several in fact.

"Thank you," he finally said. "That has to be the greatest compliment I've ever gotten."

"You're welcome," I replied.

We ate in silence for a while. He filled my wineglass again.

"My brother was in agreement with your working here then?"

Fueled by my discussion yesterday with the ladies, I leaned back and folded my arms. "I don't know if Cassie has had the opportunity to tell Sean or not. With his intense astronomy studies, he keeps odd hours, tending to sleep during the day. But why should he have a problem with it? Do not Lord Ashton, Mr. Drayson, Sir Warwick, and your father travel frequently between Dragon's Cove and Killdaren's Castle?"

His brows lifted. "Of course."

"Then why should it be any different for me to do so?"

A smile curved his full lips, dimpling his cheeks. "It would seem it shouldn't. Tell me, are you a suffragette?"

"Depends on what you're referring to. If believing a woman shouldn't be condemned for doing the same thing as a man, then yes, I would be an advocate for women's rights." I waved my hand for emphasis as I spoke.

He caught my hand in his. The unexpected contact sent a trail of fire right to my center, disrupting everything inside me. Angling my hand toward the sunlight, he examined my ring. "A unique piece of jewelry," he said. "Any significance to the symbol of the serpent?"

"I'm not sure. My father gave it to me before they left for Greece as a thank-you for the work I've done for them over the years. Supposedly, it dates back to Alexander the Great's time, belonging to a woman known only as Aphrodite. I call it Aphrodite's ring."

Without relinquishing his hold on my hand, he lifted his gaze to mine. Intensely green with golden flecks sparkling from their centers and framed by thick dark lashes, his eyes were mesmerizing, with a soul-baring directness that left me feeling . . . naked. He slid his finger across my palm before he released my hand.

I had to breathe, but couldn't seem to remember how.

"The golden goddess of love, beauty, and . . . extraordinary rapture of a certain nature," he said. "Your father chose well."

I don't think anything conveyed by Lord Alexander's deep-toned, heady words were what my father even remotely considered when purchasing the ring for me. And I didn't dare ask what "certain nature" the rapture pertained to. Oh, my!

"You, uh, leave me speechless, my lord." And breathless. I still could barely breathe, my hand tingled, and my heart raced.

He smiled, flashing dimples that rode just above the shadow of his jaw. "Your ring tempts me to discover if there is truth behind the legend. I imagine with a name like Aphrodite a woman would have to possess an ethereal spirit and be at least as beautiful as you." His gaze dropped from my eyes to my mouth, then went lower.

Desperation finally drove me to gulp in air and my dress stretched to a near seam-bursting point. It required no mind-reading abilities to see just exactly what the focus of his gaze was. My breasts grew heavier and suddenly ached, demanding to be soothed in some way.

Perhaps all wine was an aphrodisiac, for I was truly flushed with a fever that only he could quench. "Well, I wish you luck in locating Aphrodite. Since she was born from the foam of the sea, perhaps you'll encounter her the next time you venture the seas as Captain Black. But if I'm going to rearrange your grand entry hall, I need to get back to work. You don't mind, do you?"

His brow furrowed and his gaze shot up. "What do you mean by rearrange?"

"Well, as I said yesterday, and mentioned today, you do not do the beauty and wonder of artifacts any justice when they are not displayed properly. I see it as part of my job to assure that your things are shown in the best way possible."

He scooted his chair back. "Why don't I accompany you, and you can show me what you are talking about. I'll have a groomsman see to the horse and take my customary ride later."

Bringing the devil with me while I was desperately trying to flee from temptation wasn't what I had in mind, but then I really couldn't deny an owner anything.

Anything in regards to their property, I amended, as he escorted me back to the entry hall. The grand room and its immense size immediately paled and shrank in his presence.

"What would be your first suggestion?" he asked.

My thinking abilities did the same thing as the room. They shrank. It seemed like an entire minute passed as I stood blinking at the room, my mind completely blank.

"We need to go out the door and then walk back in. It is the best way to determine where your eyes focus when you first enter a room. You want your best, most impressive asset displayed there."

"Indeed," he said, his voice sounding strange. "I can see the merit of that philosophy. What if you have more than one outstanding . . . asset?"

"Then you have a choice to make as to what you wish to have seen first," I replied, refusing to look his way. I made a beeline for the dragon doors. His tone matched exactly to when he'd rumbled, "The golden goddess of love, beauty, and . . . extraordinary rapture of a certain nature" at lunch.

Before I could open the doors, he leaned from behind me and placed his hand on the door handle. His warm breath caressed my ear and his enticing scent teased my senses.

"There are a number of things I would love to see first. To have them displayed to their utmost magnificence, so I'll let you decide for me, Miss Andrews."

Not a single artifact came to mind as his words caressed their way through me. I kept thinking of the hunger in his eyes. If he'd hesitated at all upon opening the dragon door, I would have fallen back against him. I burned . . . everywhere.

The fresh air from outside hit my face as the door swung open and came as a welcome relief. I bolted like a rabbit fleeing from the fire of a dragon, but a bit too late. My nerves were so crispy it seemed they would shatter at any moment.

He must have sensed my nervousness, because for the next two hours he kept his distance and his voice didn't deepen to the point that it stole my breath. Or it could be that he had to call the butler and two footmen to help make the adjustments to the room, which left us very little privacy. In the middle of the grand entry hall, I placed a collection of statues. The center one was an elegantly draped, tall woman with one breast exposed. Surrounding her I situated four dancing nymphs that were half her size. Each held their own Maypole. The way the woman's arms were curved, she needed to have a something nestled in them, but I'd worry about that later. The entry hall could change depending on what other treasures I unearthed, but this would do for now.

"There," I said, as Lord Alexander and I walked through the front doors again. "You're immediately swept away into a world of beauty and a celebration of life." A completely opposite impression given by the dying dragons on the entry doors. I smiled in satisfaction. Perhaps this Trojan Horse Plan would bear fruit after all.

"Very well done," he said.

"It only needs one thing to be perfect," I mumbled, almost to myself.

"Which would be?"

"The woman needs to have something in her arms, something colorful like a spray of flowers or—"

"What about glass grapes?"

"Glass grapes?"

"Follow me. I'll show you." He led me down a corridor in a different direction from the ballroom. The room was filled with cabinets displaying all manner of glasswork.

"Good Lord! Look at all this."

"That's most likely why I spend most of my time outdoors, in the stables, on a horse, or on a ship. So I don't have to look at all of this." He moved to a cabinet across the room where a cluster of purple glass grapes was set amid emerald glass leaves and strung together by delicate silver chains.

Unable to stop myself, I ran my fingertips over the cool, smooth surface, marveling in the craftsmanship. As I moved closer, I accidentally brushed against Lord Alexander.

"It is perfection," I whispered. "You can almost taste the fruit."

"I agree, Miss Andrews."

The urgency in his voice made me turn abruptly his way. He stood so close to me that my breasts brushed his chest. His hands settled on my hips, pulling me flush against his chest. "Forgive me," he whispered as he leaned down, bringing his mouth to mine but not touching my lips yet. "But I must taste the fruit."

I blessedly couldn't read a hint of what was in his mind. But I had no question what was in mine. Rather than speaking, I parted my lips and pressed my mouth to his. He groaned, wrapping his arms around me, crushing me against the hard length of his body.

His lips moved against mine, then his tongue caressed my bottom lip. I gasped at the tingling sensation and his tongue delved farther into my mouth, tangling hotly with my tongue. For a brief second I was shocked, but then the passion in him set me on fire and my entire being ached for more of his consuming heat.

I slid my hands up the hard planes of his chest, leaning

into him more as I threaded my fingers into the black silk of his hair. I followed the lead of his tongue, moving with him and against him, feeling the magic and the power of desire sweep over me. The pressure and heat of his hands moved down my back then up my sides to settle against the swell of my breasts.

Groaning, I arched my back, searching to soothe the pulsing ache inside me. He broke off the kiss, breathing heavily. But I wanted more, needed more.

"Please," I said, leaning into him, looking deeply into his drugging gaze.

His features seemed harsh, fiercely intense with his passion. His voice was rough, strangely unsteady, and vulnerable. "Please do or please don't touch you as I so desperately need to do. Have so desperately needed to do for too long."

"Please do," I said.

He cupped my breasts, lifting their fullness as his thumbs brushed roughly over the aching tips through the silk of my dress. I cried out, my hips shifting against him as pleasure rippled over my whole being.

"God help us both." Stepping toward me, he slipped one arm behind my back, bending me so that he could bring his mouth to my breast. Through the silk he suckled me. I writhed against the intense pleasure, latching on to his shoulders as my head fell back in surrender to the sensations driving me beyond reason.

His other hand slid down my stomach to slip between my legs and rub firmly against my most intimate places. Somewhere in the recesses of my mind I knew I had gone from innocence to far past the point of ever returning to it. I knew the mysterious curiosity in me about passion and what he made me feel had grown instantly into an intense hunger. I knew that by all things proper and right I should push him away and recover what little sense I had left.

And I surely would have done that except for one very shocking thing. I didn't want to.

Lord Alexander moved again, abandoning my aching

feminine flesh to lean me farther back as he went to one knee. Then he lay me upon the carpet and stared down at me intently, his eyes burning, his chest heaving.

I might have said stop even then, but he planted his hands on the floor next to either side of my head and his mouth claimed mine in another searing kiss, one that brought the full length of his body and the hard press of his sex intimately against mine.

8

"Good Lord, what am I doing?" Lord Alexander said harshly as he pushed up from me. His arms trembled with the force of his emotions.

My whole body shook from the explosion of our passion. I stared up at him, blinking at him in amazement. "I believe you're very adeptly seducing me, my lord."

He cursed. "No. I am not." He sat, moving farther away from me.

I rose unsteadily to my elbows. "You're not?"

"No, Miss Andrews. What I was doing without a single thought to the consequences was taking serious advantage of a young woman who is not only under my employ, but also a respectable member of my family!"

I couldn't very well argue with him, for I was under his employ and it was essential for my future well being to stay that way. I was a member of the family in that my sister was married to his brother. And though I hadn't behaved in a respectable manner, I was nowhere near ready to abandon my

respectability, at least the concept of it. So I took umbrage
with the only thing I could. With as much grace as I could
possibly muster, I rolled to my side and gained my feet.
"Taking serious advantage implies that I wasn't a willing
participant. And I do believe I kissed you first, Lord Alexander. But you are correct in that we were rash and gave little
forethought to our actions. Is that something one gains with
experience in these matters?" I asked. Heaven help me, but I
didn't think myself capable of much rational thought where
he was concerned.

He stood, stared at me a moment, then burst into laughter.

"Captain Black? The lass's buggy is at the door." The butler's voice reached us before the seaman-turned-servant did.

Lord Alexander whipped around and none too gently
gathered the glass grapes. He shoved them my way. "Carry
these against your heart, my dear." Then he raised his voice.
"We'll be right there, Brighty! Tell the driver to wait."

The seaman appeared in the doorway. "Aye, aye, captain."
Before he left, he nodded eagerly enough to make me wonder if he would lose the bird's nest wig on his head. But I had
more important things to worry about at the moment.

When I looked down at the grapes in my arms I was
shocked to find a large, dark, wet circle stained my left breast.
The breast Lord Alexander had taken in his mouth and done
amazing things to. My stomach clenched and my pulsed raced
again. Oh my!

I shot my gaze to him and found him staring at my
breasts as if he was a heartbeat a way from repeating his earlier actions. I crushed the grapes to me; their hard glass balls
made my nipple tingle even more. "How will I ever get
home?" I groaned.

"I've a cloak I will lend you. Perhaps you can say you accidentally spilled your drink. I will meet you in the entry
hall," he said, then quit the room.

I stood stunned a moment, feeling as if I'd been swept
away from anything and everything I'd ever known by a
wild storm. It was very disconcerting. Forcing my feet into

motion, I found my way back to the entry hall where, less than a few moments later, Lord Alexander came dashing into the room from a completely opposite direction. I truly had to wonder if he were not some dark man of magic.

"Hold this." He handed me the cloak and grabbed the grapes, sliding one hand on top of them and one beneath. "The sweetest fruit God ever made," he murmured.

His brushing of my breast as he lifted the grapes away from me was far from an accidental caress, and let me know exactly what fruit he was speaking of. He turned and securely placed the glass grapes within the woman's arms, creating the dénouement to my day's hard work. It was perfect, a vision of beauty and grace enriched by a dazzling cluster of sparkling jewel-like color.

"Perfect," I said.

He took his cloak from me and slid it over my shoulders, but didn't let his hands linger. His scent and delicious warmth enveloped me.

"I have to agree, perfect. And I won't ruin it," he said, then stepped away from me. "So, in light of that, there will be no need to wait for my opinion regarding any changes you wish to make, Miss Andrews. I have a number of business matters to attend to up the coast and fear I won't be available. I do sincerely thank you for . . . sharing such treasures and your expertise with me today though. Brighty will see you out, lass."

"Aye, captain. Should I send word for Captain Jansen to ready the ship?"

"Yes." Lord Alexander strode from the room, leaving me to feel more alone than ever before.

Upon arriving at Killdaren's Castle, I hid Lord Alexander's cloak under my pillow, "accidentally" spilled an entire ewer of water down the front of my dress, then called for a bath. As the maid helped me undo the row of buttons, I expressed my desire to give the gown away.

She was ecstatic, saying she would have the perfect use for it. I watched the dress disappear from my sight with mixed feelings. I wanted to both remember and forget the feel of Lord Alexander's mouth and hands. Placing Aphrodite's ring in a special box upon my vanity, I sank, deflated, into the heated bathwater. The more I considered my uninhibited response to Lord Alexander, the more depressed I became. Why, I was like Iris in the training ring, responding to his every move, his every word, his every touch like a nymph in the forest.

The man was abandoning his castle and his new horse to escape having to encounter me, a situation that would in no way help repair the Killdaren brothers' estrangement. If anything, I'd added to it.

At dinner, I discovered that Cassie and Sean were at odds and received the impression it had to do with my employment at Dragon's Cove. Prudence's golden eyes were shadowed with worry. After last night's nightmare, Rebecca had relapsed into stuttering badly with her every word, setting her back months in the healing process. The earl and Sir Warwick were absent, but Lord Ashton and Mr. Drayson had joined us for dinner. I knew that the entire Killdaren household was on edge, but it seemed to me that Mr. Drayson was particularly unsettled, or more accurately, distracted. I finally had to ask. "Is something wrong, Mr. Drayson?"

He exhaled, his poet's eyes troubled. "It's the strangest thing. A rather terse note was left for me at the hotel's desk this morning, demanding that if I had compromised anyone of late to make full restitution or pay the consequences. I swear upon my honor that I've never done such a thing. I'm extremely troubled over it."

Lord Ashton cleared his throat. "Egad, Drayson. The same for me. I didn't mention it because I was taken aback by what it inferred. I've done nothing to compromise anyone as I see it. And of course you haven't either. The first thing that came to my mind is someone is trying to set up some sort of blackmail scam. I sent the offending thing on to my lawyers with strict instructions for them to investigate the matter thoroughly. A man could take the missive as a threat of bodily harm for some undisclosed, and believe me, completely unknown transgression."

"What?" Sean asked, stirred from his brown study.

Both Mr. Drayson and Lord Ashton repeated themselves.

My mind raced at the news and ran through Rebecca's nightmare last night. Mary had accused some man of compromising a woman. Could that man have been Mr. Drayson or Lord Ashton? Could either of them been the horseman that had attacked Mary? I dropped my fork and it clattered noisily onto my plate. Everyone looked at me.

"Pardon me. I must be more exhausted than I thought." No! I told myself. I'd spent the summer going on a number of outings with both of these men and never once did I have any doubts about their kindness and respectability. They'd kept gentlemanly distances at all times and never made a move or a suggestion toward anything improper. In fact, the only man in Dartmoor's End who'd ever been improper in any way had been . . . Lord Alexander today.

"You do appear rather pale," Mr. Drayson said. He sat to my right. "Maybe you've taken on a task you shouldn't have."

"I agree," Lord Ashton chimed in. "I must admit that I was more than surprised to learn from Gemini today that you've taken a post. Even if it is only listing artifacts for Blackmoor, it's too much. Women of quality aren't meant to work." He sounded as if the very act of doing so lowered a woman's worth and respectability.

I stiffened my back and drew my brows together, unbelieving of his attitude. "Forgive me for saying, Lord Ashton, but that school of thought is changing."

Cassie leaned forward and narrowed her eyes. "Lord Ashton, can you not see that attitudes such as yours completely demean a woman. Why should she not be allowed to apply her skill and intelligence toward any profitable endeavor just as a man can?"

Lord Ashton's brows arched as he gasped for air. He

looked at Sean before addressing Cassie. "I mean no disrespect. Men are more adept than women at certain tasks and women should accept that as fact, just as I lay no claims to womanly duties. Besides, for a woman of quality to work, it reflects badly upon those who are in a position of responsibility to provide for her."

"I'm in agreement with you, Ashton," Sean said softly.

Cassie turned a wide-eyed hurt gaze toward Sean. "So you're of the opinion that a woman has no identity apart from her 'provider'?"

Sean sighed. "I did not say that."

"Yes, you did," Cassie replied, emotion thick in her throat. I knew tears were only moments behind. She looked at her plate for a long moment, paled, and stood. "Forgive me," she said to the table at large. "I'm feeling a little unwell at the moment." She quickly left the room. Sean stood, as did the other gentlemen. I rose as well and went to follow after Cassie but Prudence grabbed my arm, pulling me back. I read her mind before her whispered words escaped. "She's his now. They must work things out alone."

Sean excused himself curtly and quit the room.

I bit my lip, blinking back my tears and concern. Cassie had enough to worry about right now; she didn't need to be arguing with Sean. Why couldn't he just accept her for the gifted and giving woman that she was?

"Perhaps you shouldn't have stated your opinion so strongly, Ashton," Mr. Drayson said.

Lord Ashton turned his shocked eyes my way. "Please accept my apologies and convey them to your sister, Miss Andrews. It was not my intent to upset her."

"I will let her know, meanwhile gentlemen, let's continue with our meal." Though it was the last thing I wanted to do, I reseated myself and steered the conversation to less treacherous waters by mentioning my parents' return to their archaeological expedition in Greece and their search for the ruins of the temple Alexander the Great built for Apollo.

"Speaking of ruins," Mr. Drayson said. "I chanced by the

old Kennedy Mansion today. The site made my skin crawl. I've no doubt the place is haunted."

Prudence gasped and grabbed my arm. From the images whirling in her mind. I instantly knew everything about the place, and it scared me to death. Mr. Drayson referred to what was once Lady Helen Kennedy's ancestral home. She was the woman Sean and Lord Alexander fell in love with, fought over, and were under the vague suspicion of murdering eight years ago. A week after Lady Helen was killed, her father committed suicide in the home. It had been empty ever since.

"A haunted mansion close enough to explore? Really? I've heard nothing about this rumor. You must tell me." Gemini's enthusiasm nearly made me faint.

"Good God! Miss Andrews. You completely misunderstood me. Don't ever consider doing such a thing. I'm not a man who scares easily and I must tell you the sense of evil lurking within the broken and abandoned ruins is overwhelming. Most likely Lady Helen's father is still wandering the halls, crazed over his daughter's death. No telling what a spirit like that will do."

"Lady Helen?" Gemini squeaked. "Oh! Good heavens. I didn't make the connection."

The dinner had gone from bad to worse and everyone's appetite lagged. At the first opportunity Lord Ashton and Mr. Drayson begged off any evening entertainment to return to Seafarer's Inn. Prudence went immediately to see to Rebecca, who was in the competent and loving care of Bridget. Bridget had even brought her younger brother, Timmy, to play with Rebecca. I hoped having a child her own age with her would help, and thought I would check before retiring. I could then question Bridget to see if she'd had any news from Flora, though I knew she hadn't. If she had, everyone would be giddy with relief and I would have sensed it.

We climbed the stairs to our rooms and Gemini sighed heavily. "I knew it was too good to last."

"What, Gemmi?"

"The happiness."

"Life isn't that way," I said.

"No, but is isn't this dark either. And I fear things are going to get much darker. Do you want me to sleep in your room tonight? In case you have another dream like last night?"

All I wanted to do was to pull the covers over my head and forget the world existed, but I could hear the loneliness in Gemini's voice, and I realized she was just as unhappy and unsettled as I was. "Your company would be most welcome," I told her.

"Really?" she asked, clearly surprised.

"Absolutely." I set my arm across her shoulders, hugging her to me. In her mind I read a swirl of thoughts and confusion going from what she felt about Lord Ashton, imagining being kissed for the first time by him—which in no way matched the wild attraction Lord Alexander stirred in me— to a niggling curiosity about the haunted mansion. I shuddered, wanting to pull her close and protect her from all harm. It seemed the safe little circle we had known in Oxford had disappeared forever.

Tensions had flamed high in just a few days and then hovered at that level for the rest of the week. Gemini, who'd been at loose ends, came with me to Dragon's Cove for two of the days, but quickly lost interest in cataloguing the antiquities. The enormity of what had to be accomplished overwhelmed her, and the dreadful scene upon the entry doors disturbed her greatly. She decided to spend the rest of the week at Killdaren's Castle.

I'd ascertained the day after the dinner fiasco that Bridget had yet to hear from Flora. Cassie had been upset and withdrawn since the dinner, only saying that she and Sean were trying to come to terms with a difference of philosophy. I offered to secure rooms in town if my employment at Dragon's Cove was a difficulty, and not only did she refuse to hear of such a thing, but she'd gone off crying.

Sean appeared shortly afterward, harried and unshaven,

and informed me curtly that while he disapproved of my employment, I had to immediately discard any notion of ever considering not being a guest in his house.

He also informed me—and I was absolutely under no circumstances to tell Cassie this—that he was seeking to relocate everyone far from Dartmoor's End, Killdaren's Castle, and Dragon's Cove. He feared the curse between him and his brother was reaching out to steal away his one chance at happiness with Cassie and he wasn't going to let it happen.

By the end of the week I reeled from how much our lives had unraveled in so short a time. And deep inside of myself, I longed for Lord Alexander to return. Every night I slept wrapped in his cloak, smelling him, remembering him . . . aching to know more of the passion he'd ignited inside of me.

When Friday, the day Lord Alexander was expected back, passed, and he failed to show, I left Dragon's Cove in my own brown study. I would have taken a tray in my room instead of joining the family for dinner, except it was Sir Warwick's birthday and Cassie had planned a special meal for him, which said a lot for her determination to be the perfect hostess. Sir Warwick's prickly wit often served to increase tensions rather than ease them.

As it turned out, Sir Warwick was on his best behavior and dinner was the most pleasant it had been in a week. He seemed genuinely touched by the gesture, and had softened his barbs enough to laugh. We'd just entered the drawing room for our evening's entertainment when the sounds of a disturbance in the center hall alerted everyone to a problem.

"Father! Where are you!"

My pulse raced at the sound of Lord Alexander's angry voice. He was back.

"Bloody hell!" Sean yelled, standing so quickly that he overturned the chess set and sent the pieces scattering upon the floor. Lord Alexander appeared in the doorway at that moment, making my heart tumble. His tan had deepened and he was unshaven, looking as wild and dangerous as any fabled king of the sea.

Frightened and clutching her rag doll, Rebecca screamed and frantically searched for her mother. She tripped and fell after just one step. Amazingly, the earl, who was the closest to the child, reached down and picked her up. I believe he did it without thinking, because he just looked at the girl, wondering what to do. But when she wrapped her arms around his neck and buried her tear-streamed face into his snowy cravat, crying harder, he held her closer to him and told her not to be frightened. It was the first time I'd ever seen the earl interact in any way with his daughter. Prudence, who'd been rushing to Rebecca, grabbed her heart and I think would have fallen had not Bridget been right beside her to steady her. The way Prudence stared at the earl holding their daughter ripped into my heart; her every hope, her every desire was shimmering in her eyes.

Cassie stood and took control. The undercurrents between everyone had reached an explosive point. "Gemini, help Prudence and Bridget get Rebecca up the stairs and settled down. I'll be up as soon as I can."

Gemini gave her warm cloak to Bridget and then caught Prudence's hand. Bridget wrapped the cloak around Rebecca's shoulders and gathered the child from the earl. As they passed by Sean, he reached out and gently touched Rebecca's head. "Sorry, Becca," he said softly.

The minute they left the room, Sean faced his brother. Two men exactly alike, one pale from a life spent indoors, one dark from a life spent in the sun, and both deadly, two dragons breathing fire at each other. "You are not welcome here, Alex! Leave now!"

Lord Alexander crossed his arms and widened his stance to an I-will-not-be-moved position. "I will after I get a bloody explanation from our father! There are things more important than you, or me, and they take precedence over our individual feelings."

Sean stepped toward Lord Alexander with one hand clutching his cane for balance and one hand fisted. "What?"

I could tell the effort to restrain his anger cost him. The room seethed with a hellish tension so intense it almost burned my mind.

"Are you ready to tell Sean what you told me, Dr. Luden?"

"Yes," came a voice from behind Lord Alexander.

Lord Alexander stepped aside and Cassie and I gasped to see the kindly town doctor.

"Christ," the earl said and sank quickly into a chair. "What's the point in telling now, William?"

"Unfortunately, it has become essential. Another woman died with the same marking."

"What's going on?" Sean demanded. Cassie moved to Sean's side, giving him her silent support.

I wanted to go to Lord Alexander. I could feel his pain and anger. His face twisted with disgust as he glared at the earl. "Our father has . . . God I can't even begin to describe it."

Dr. Luden stepped farther into the room. "I'm sorry, Seamus," he said to the earl before he faced Sean. "Eight years ago, I was called to a woman's murder scene in the gazebo here at Killdaren's Castle. Her name was Lady Helen Kennedy. I'd determined at the scene that the cause of her death had resulted from multiple blows to the head and chest by a blunt object. It wasn't until later, when it was necessary to examine her completely for my report, that I discovered a symbol carved upon—" He coughed, looking uncomfortably at Cassie and then at me. "Let's just say it was carved over her heart and had been done crudely with the blade of a knife. There was so much village unrest against you and Alex over the murder that I kept this bit of information private, only telling the earl and Constable Poole. By that time Lady Helen's father had already killed himself and there were no other relatives."

Lord Alexander made an impatient movement. "What he's trying to tell you, Sean is that—"

"I paid the doctor and the constable to keep that secret," said the earl, almost shouting out his confession.

Sean looked stricken. He swung to face his father.

"Why?" Lord Alexander demanded, moving closer to Sean to face the earl. "Did you think Sean or I would do such a thing?"

"No! But I damn well wasn't going to leave your futures up to fate! The villagers would have thought markings over the heart pointed to a scorned lover being the murderer," the earl said bitterly. He stood and ran an agitated hand through his hair as he paced across the room. "Do either of you know what it is like to have someone you desperately love die! To have fate snatch away your very heart? Your mother's greatest wish on this earth was to give me a son and she died doing it. For a long, long time I couldn't face that, nor accept the fact that twins had been born to me. The precious sons she'd left for me to love were cursed. One of you was destined to kill the other.

"I took great hope at the closeness you shared as you two grew. It seemed as if your affection for each other would conquer any darkness from the past. The pact that you both took vowing to never hurt the other made me the happiest I'd been since your mother died. Then before I even realized it was happening the wheels had been set in motion for the Dragon's Curse to take over. You were both in love with the same woman."

"You might as well tell them everything, Seamus," Sir Warwick said firmly, seemingly peering down through his monocle with great wisdom. When I glanced his way, I didn't see a tremendous amount of empathy toward the earl or toward Sean and Lord Alexander. Sir Warwick had an air of detachment that I didn't like, but that suited his ennui well. He was very much a fatalist.

"I paid Lady Helen to tell you both that she didn't love either of you. Her father had amassed a huge gambling debt in London. I offered to cover his debt and pay Lady Helen enough money to live comfortably in her home for the rest of her life."

"Good God!" Sean said, reeling on his feet. Cassie grasped his arm, moving closer to him.

Lord Alexander stood stoically. "Is there no end to your deceit?" The deadly calm of his voice made me shiver.

"No!" the earl shouted. "The chit didn't truly love either of you and I could have killed her for what she was doing to you, pitting you against each other, playing you for fools."

"Did you kill her?" Lord Alexander demanded. "Did she change her mind and you killed her?"

The earl paled, like he'd been given a death blow. "Good God, no! Listen, the woman's only interest in either of you was your wealth. She wanted to save her father and to have a life of ease. If she had loved either of you, she would have thrown my offer in my face. As for paying off the doctor and the constable? I'd do it again. You were both under heavy suspicion in Lady Helen's death, and I wasn't going to let the villagers or the law get anywhere near you. The details of how Lady Helen died weren't important. I would and will do anything to keep from losing my sons, no matter what the price."

Lord Alexander gave a bitter laugh. "Unfortunately, the price you paid was the one thing that has cost you this son. Don't come back to Dragon's Cove. Tell them the rest, Dr. Luden."

Dr. Luden cleared his voice. "I put this in my report and had expected it be common knowledge at this point. I've been away since the young woman's funeral and only just returned today."

"Enough!" Lord Alexander interrupted. "Just say it!"

"What?" Sean demanded.

"Your wife's cousin, Mary, had the same carving over her heart as Lady Helen."

9

"Do you hear that, father?" Lord Alexander asked. "By suppressing the facts you've harbored a murderer for eight years! Your actions have cost another woman her life!"

"No," the earl said, shaking his head, reeling as if he would faint. "No! That can't be! I didn't . . ."

Cassie and Sean were keeping each other upright. She turned to the doctor, a hint of anger in her voice. "Why weren't we, as Mary's family, told about this?"

"Because Constable Poole insisted that we keep this quiet while he made his investigation. He didn't want to jeopardize his chances of getting the truth. I was present when the constable showed a drawing of the carving to Mrs. Frye and she didn't know what it was, didn't react to it at all."

"Why are you just coming forth now?"

"As I said, I've been away. As soon as I discovered that Mrs. Frye was still being held for Mary's murder, I felt it imperative to speak up. It is my personal belief Mrs. Frye might try and hide someone's accidental death if she felt she'd be blamed, but I've known her for a long time and do not believe she would carve a woman up. After repeated questioning, her story has never wavered from that of Mary hitting her head and Jamie carrying Mary into the tunnel."

"Could Jaime have cut Mary then?" I asked, finally entering the conversation.

Dr. Luden winced. "That means that at fifteen Jamie would have murdered and carved up Helen Kennedy. I don't know. It's possible, but in the very least, no matter that she's confessed to the crime, Mrs. Frye is not responsible."

I shut my eyes a moment, realizing more than ever that Rebecca's nightmare was true. A killer lurked in Dartmoor's End, and I might be the only person who could put the pieces of the puzzle together.

"Can you draw the symbol for us, Dr. Luden," Sean asked. "Maybe we could glean a clue as to what happened to Lady Helen and to Mary and why."

"Yes, it's crudely simple but distinct."

"You can use my desk in the library. I've another question or two for you as well."

"I will join you," Lord Alexander said firmly to Sean. "I demand to speak to you and Dr. Luden privately."

"This doesn't change anything between us." Sean's voice was like jagged glass, sharp and cutting.

"I didn't expect it to," Lord Alexander replied, jaw clenched. "But you will accord me the respect of hearing me out."

Sean nodded and turned to Cassie. "Settle Rebecca and your sisters. I'll be with you shortly. Dr. Luden, Alex, this way." Sean motioned them to follow him.

The earl moved to join them and Sean stopped him at the door. "You're not a welcomed party to this discussion, Father. I'll speak to you tomorrow after I've had time to think."

The earl stood stunned as Sean quit the room.

Sir Warwick leisurely rose to his feet and clapped the earl on the shoulder. "I think I could use a drink. Ladies, please excuse us," he said as he led the earl out the door.

I looked at Cassie at the same moment she looked at me. We both discarded our shoes without saying a word. With any luck the library door would be shut and we'd make it to the adjoining room to eavesdrop without being seen.

This time there was no sense of naughtiness nipping at us as we sneaked to listen. The gravity of the situation was too dire, and everyone's emotions had been ripped bare.

"There's no need to discuss anything, Alex," came Sean's voice. "I'm making arrangements to leave Killdaren's Castle and Dartmoor's End forever."

"Damn it. That isn't necessary. In eight years I've never intruded into your space."

"That's because I've stayed a prisoner in my own home."

"Christ, Sean. Is there no bloody forgiveness? It was an accident. I didn't realize we were so close to the edge of the cliffs. I didn't push you over."

"I don't know that. And you were so crazed that you don't know that either."

"Gentlemen. I tended both of your wounds after the accident. I was there when you were born, and have taken care of your cuts and fevers and whatever else ailed you through the years. And quite frankly, you are both being dunderheads and have been for quite some time now. Sean, a man who pushes another man over a cliff does not risk his life by jumping over the cliff after him. In my opinion, Alex was damned lucky he didn't hit rocks like you did. He only broke his leg minimally from the impact rather than shattering his bones. Still, he managed to get himself and you to the shore."

"You weren't there for the fight," said Sean.

"No, but I've heard about the curse all of my life, and I've watched it destroy you two and your father. So what if there had been a real curse? So what if both of you were crazed with drink that night? So what that Alex almost killed you? He didn't. He saved you. Now, do either of you recognize this symbol?"

"No," said Sean.

"Not at the moment. But you can bet I'm going to do some searching about," Lord Alexander replied.

"I've had no luck in determining what it means," said Dr. Luden. "If either of you learn anything, please let me know."

"I'll have your word first that from now on you'll give a full report and not be accepting bribes to suppress evidence. I won't hesitate to make this whole sordid affair public if need be," Lord Alexander said.

"If I thought for one moment that either of you were guilty of the crime, even the crown jewels couldn't have swayed me from making a fact public and assuring you paid for the crime. I gave the money to the Church. I knew neither of you were at fault, but no other viable suspect appeared, so I kept it quiet and kept my eyes open," said Dr. Luden.

"Before you go," Sean said, "I must ask because we need to know what kind of monster we are dealing with here. Were either of the women assaulted in another manner as well?"

"You mean in a sexual way?" asked the doctor.

"Yes."

"I can't answer that. Lady Helen had been beaten. Whoever killed her, undressed her enough to carve up her left breast and then redressed her. Mary's body decomposed enough to make any such determinations impossible."

"Before or after?" Lord Alexander asked harshly.

"What?" asked Dr. Luden.

"Were their breasts cut before or after he killed them?"

"I don't know. I pray to God it was after," the doctor replied.

Cassie lurched away from the wall, holding one hand to her stomach and one to her mouth. I knew instantly she was ill. I rushed to the French doors and swung it open and pulled her outside into the fresh air. We knocked over a statue on the way out.

"Oh God," she said. "Poor Mary."

I wrapped my arm around her shoulder. "I know. But you found her and she's safe now, resting in just the place where she loved to paint."

"What is going on out here?" Sean asked, pushing open the French doors from the library.

"Just getting some fresh air," I told him, looking back.

Both Sean and Lord Alexander stepped outside.

"My stomach," Cassie cried, doubling over. I caught her from falling and read the thought reverberating through her mind. *My babies. I'm losing my babies.*

"Cassie!" Sean yelled, rushing toward us, moving swiftly despite his need of a cane.

"Get the doctor," I shouted at Lord Alexander.

Sean swung Cassie up in his arms and struggled to balance her. "What is it? What's wrong?" Cassie burst into tears.

Lord Alexander rushed back out of the house with the doctor in tow.

I prayed my sister would forgive me, but everyone had to know. "She's pregnant, Sean. And she's worried sick that she's going to have twins. If the babies' father and uncle aren't speaking and believe the family is cursed, what hope does she have for their future?"

"Better get her in bed so I can examine her," said the doctor. "Have someone get my medical bag from your carriage, Lord Alexander."

"I'll get it myself," said Lord Alexander. "It will be quicker that way."

Sean just stood there, holding Cassie in his arms, staring at her. She cried harder.

I grabbed his arm. "Let's get her to bed, Sean."

"Hold my neck tightly, Cassie," he said. Using his cane, Sean gracefully maneuvered them both. His only hindrance was that his pace was slower. I had to snatch my hand away, once he was completely balanced. The emotional storm swirling within him was so intense that when I touched him I felt as if my whole being was being sucked away into a deep pit of angry despair.

The doctor and I followed Sean as he carried Cassie across the castle to his wing, a wing I'd never been in before. Dragons were the theme of the décor here in Sean's domain, but with an ominous flair. Weapons of all kinds lined the corridor, from medieval maces, axes, and shields to dueling sets and swords. We reached the bedroom and I took one look at the biggest bed I have ever seen and immediately backed up from the thoughts that ran through my mind. I knew the intimacies Cassie and Sean shared there and I had sudden images of Lord Alexander with me on a bed of that size. It wasn't a bed one climbed into to sleep. It was a bed of decadence made for . . . play.

I backed directly into a hot hard body. Lord Alexander.

"What's wrong?" he said, catching my side as he peered into the room over my shoulder to where Sean was laying Cassie in the bed. "Very interesting," Lord Alexander murmured, and with the words came a very clear picture of the two of us naked, his hands on me, touching and rubbing my feminine sex. His mouth devouring my breasts. My eyes went wide with shock as he knelt between my legs, grabbed my hips and impaled me with his shockingly large male sex.

"Wait here," Lord Alexander said as he moved past me. The moment he released me, the image faded and I gasped for air. He handed the doctor a black bag and turned back to me.

Dr. Luden cleared his throat. "Give me and Mrs. Killdaren a few moments of privacy and I'll be able to determine the problem."

"I'm not leaving her side," Sean said. "She's pregnant."

"I should have told you," Cassie said. "I'm sorry. I just wanted to make things right before you found out so that you could be happy about it. I'm not hurting like I was just a few minutes ago."

"You're sorry! Good God, woman! Have you no idea how I feel about you? How I will feel about holding our child? Don't you know that I am doing everything within my power to see that the Dragon's Curse never touches us or our children? We're leaving here. We'll move across the world. Move to America. Anywhere. Our children will never hear the word *cursed* from anyone, ever. I'll break it, do you hear me? I love you and nothing will ever stop that!"

The room rang from the fervor of his declaration.

Cassie stared at Sean, all of her love shining in her eyes. Lord Alexander backed from the room and quietly closed the door.

"Come on," he said roughly. I was surprised to find him moving down the corridor with angry steps.

"What's wrong?" I said hurrying after him.

"My brother is a fool," he said. He popped open a door on the left and entered the room. It was a study, lit by only a small dim oil lamp on the desk. He crossed immediately to a sideboard and uncorked a bottle of wine.

"How can you say that? That was the most beautiful thing I have ever heard in my life."

"All the declarations of love in the world aren't going to change the seed of doubt in Sean's mind and it will eventually poison his life wherever he goes, no matter how far he runs." Lord Alexander turned from the sideboard and brought me a glass. I immediately recognized the aroma of spiced wine. My fingers tingled as I took the glass from him. He'd filled it to the brim.

"What do you mean?" I drank several large sips, feeling my insides heat to the elixir. I'd barely eaten dinner and the warmth soothed the ache in my stomach. Aphrodite's ring on my finger reminded me what properties the spiced wine was supposed to have—an aphrodisiac.

"The Dragon's Curse will find a way. Don't you see? It's a sickness in the Killdaren blood. From birth Sean and I heard about it, were told we were destined to end as we had been born, hands around each other's throats. You heard my father. We didn't believe it; we made a pact against it. Sean and I fought the night I discovered Lady Helen murdered. We were both crazed by guilt and drink. But here's the difference. I never thought Sean was trying to kill me that night. He is convinced I was trying to kill him, though. What happened was a foolish accident, but now that Sean feels as he does, the trust is gone and I have no doubt that he will kill me the moment he perceives me as a threat to him and his.

Even staying as far from him as I could for eight years hasn't lessened it. He believes in the curse."

I took another long sip. "Then he's doing the right thing. If his children never hear of the Dragon's Curse it can't hurt them."

"It can't? What if they have twins? What happens the first time they have a fight and he finds one of them has hurt the other? How will he react? What happens if there is an accident and one is at fault and has hurt the other? What will he say? What will he think? The only way for Sean ever to be free is to no longer believe in the curse."

The wine swirled though my body and mind as wildly as Lord Alexander's reasoning. "Then we have to break the curse," I said. "If any one can be cursed then they can be uncursed."

"I've read the tome backward and forward. There is no cure."

"What tome?"

"The book that chronicles the Dragon's Curse upon the Killdaren clan since the beginning of history. I'm sure Sean has it here. He always keeps it near." Lord Alexander went over to the bookcases, searching through the books. How he could read in this light escaped me.

"Where did the curse come from?" I asked. "Why was your family cursed?"

"Legend has it that back in the age of dragons, when magic ruled the earth, the queen of the *Tuatha de Danaan* was very disillusioned with her king's unfaithfulness and sought comfort in the arms of a mortal. That man, my ancestor, was keeper of her dragons and would take her on long dragon rides and showed her every earthly pleasure."

"And?" I whispered, thinking about those pleasures, wondering what it would be to experience them.

"She pledged her heart and her love to this man, but there was only one problem."

"What?" I demanded, impatient to hear the end.

"My ancestor had an identical twin. That twin wanted to

bed the queen, too, so they took turns with her. When she found out that she had been fooled, she cursed all identical twins born in our family, and cursed all dragons, too. The dragons killed each other into extinction and of the identical twins born in this family, one of them has always killed the other."

"So, she was a woman scorned not only by her husband, but then by her lover as well. Or lovers, I should say, because neither of your ancestors loved her."

"True," Lord Alexander said, squatting to another shelf.

To break the curse of a woman scorned one would have to do what? I shook my head. Everything suddenly seemed too complicated to think about. I drained my glass of the sweet, nectar-like liquid, enjoying its smooth feel upon my tongue and the heady scent of spices. "Can I have more, please?"

Turning from the shelves with a huge book in hand, Lord Alexander lifted his brows. "You've already drank that glass?"

"Yes, you've been talking quite awhile, you know."

"Not that long. Just a little more for you. You seem to be very fond of spiced wine," he said. He plunked the book down on a nearby table. "You find a cure in that, I'll be your slave for life," he said. As he slipped the glass from my hand, his fingers brushed over mine, bringing back all of the sensations he'd wrought within me. My breasts swelled, my lips parted, my insides quivered.

"There you are," Dr. Luden said, entering the room with his black bag.

"A glass of wine, sir?" Lord Alexander asked as he handed me mine.

"Yes. It's been quite an evening."

"Cassie?" I said, almost afraid to ask.

"Is fine. As I understand it, she stays up most of the night helping Sean with his astronomy and then is up most the day with everyone else. She needs to rest, eat more, and worry less. It's too early to know if she is carrying twins, and I see no indication of any serious complications at this point. I will of course be back to see her in the morning."

Lord Alexander handed the doctor his wine. I took a relieved sip from mine, welcoming the soothing relaxing of muscles that had been too tense for too long.

"I'll take you home just as soon as you've refreshed yourself," Lord Alexander said to the doctor. A sense of disappointment slid over me. Somehow, though he'd given me every reason not to, I expected something more from him, given our last encounter and the vision on the bed that I'm sure had to have come from him. I'd never imagined a man between my legs before, impaling me with his sex. Though I knew such were the goings on of relations between men and women, I'd never fantasized about them.

"No, need. Since we live in opposite directions, Mr. Killdaren has ordered a carriage for me." The doctor drank the wine in one gulp. "I've always told Seamus this Killdaren recipe could double your fortune if sold. Very . . . invigorating. I expect I'll be speaking to both of you tomorrow at some point, so I'll take my leave now."

"Thank you," I said. The doctor smiled warmly.

Lord Alexander only nodded.

Moving to the door, I shut it. I didn't want any more interruptions. I wanted a few minutes alone with Lord Alexander. "So, were your business endeavors successful this week?"

His brows lifted and his eyes raked down my body, leaving a trail of heat.

Feeling very bold, I moved toward him, making sure that my back was arched enough to press my breasts firmly against the bodice of my dress. That his gaze dropped as I approached gave me a heady feeling.

"Business?" he said, blinking.

"Did you not take your ship up the coast to conduct business this week?"

"Um, yes. I did. Business was . . . fine." He drank some wine. "I haven't been home yet but I trust I will recognize where I live. You've continued on with the antiquities?"

I nodded, taking a slow sip of wine, noting from my lowered lashes how he watched me. "The entry hall, parlor, and
the glass room have all been catalogued. I've only partially
arranged the parlor. I want to see what other treasures you
have before I determine exactly how it should look."

"The glass room?"

"The room where the grapes were," I said, heat flushing
my cheeks. I'd abandoned my tasks in the parlor, just to
spend time in the room where the memory of his touch was
so fresh.

"Yes, the grapes." He drank more wine, but his gaze was
firmly fixed on my breasts. I drew another step closer, able
to feel the heat of him, able to smell the sunshine and leather
and salt of the sea on him.

"Enjoying the sweetest fruit God ever made?" I asked
him softly.

He choked on his wine and moved his arm so jerkily to
catch his breath that the liquid splashed from the glass and
splattered my chest.

"Oh!" I gasped as the cool liquid slid between my hot
breasts. Shoving my glass into his hand, I snatched out my
fichu and began dabbing at the liquid.

"Bloody hell, woman! What are you trying to do to me?"

"Me to you? You're not the one with wine trickling . . ."
I shivered. "Everywhere."

"Not everywhere yet," he said, his voice so dangerously
low that warning signals fired in my somewhat inebriated
brain. Before I could fathom what he was about, he held up
both glasses of wine and poured them down the front of my
dress!

"Oh!"

"There's more." He gripped my hips and lifted me up. I
had no choice but to latch my hands onto his shoulders. He
backed me up to the door and pressed me against it as he slid
his hands down and grabbed the backs of my thighs, pulling
my feet out from under me. He inserted himself between my
legs, pinning me intimately against the door.

"Don't fall," he said softly, hooking my legs that were wrapped in my skirts over his hips before he released them.

He locked the door and my heart hammered wildly.

My wine-soaked breasts were at the level of his mouth. He began licking the wine. Long, hot strokes of his tongue lapped over the tops of my breasts, sending burning shivers of pleasure to the very place where he pressed against me. I wiggled, gasping from the sensations.

He unbuttoned my bodice and camisole and my aching breasts spilled from their confines. He groaned, cupping them with his hands. He took one nipple in his mouth and sucked hard in a demanding, rhythmic motion that had my whole body dancing to his beat. I wanted that pulsing to consume me, to touch every part of my body and to shake the very center of my intimate being.

"Oh, God," I said as my head fell back against the door.

He moved to the other breast, doing the same. Then leaving my aching tips, he licked his way around the fullness of them, driving me even wilder with the want of more until he gave it to me. Suckling me past reason, until my hips thrust to his rhythm, until I knew nothing but his touch.

Suddenly, he stopped, and stepped back a little as he eased my shaking legs from his hips. Damp with wine, I was on fire everywhere. When my feet settled on the floor and I braced my hand on the door handle to stay upright, he moved back even farther.

I blinked at him.

His hair was wildly mussed, his eyes were burning coals of green fire. His chest heaved from his exertions, or was it his restraint? Wine stained his white shirt in patches. And the bulge that pressed against his breeches made it appear as if the buttons would pop free at any second.

"The next time you seduce me, I won't stop, Andromeda. So make very sure you want everything, all the way. I can't marry you either. I'll leave no legitimate heirs. When I die, my title will go to Sean and his heirs. It is the least I can do for crippling him for life."

Then he turned and let himself out the French door.

I stood there stunned, bare breasts heaving and aching. My whole body on fire for a man who'd just coldly walked away. Well, maybe not coldly, but it sure did bloody feel like it. I suddenly knew Bridget's exact sentiments when she'd thought it would serve Stuart right for her to find another lover. Right that minute, I'd even take a vampire, just as long as he could rid me of the blood throbbing painfully to every part of me. I refastened the bodice of my ruined dress, thinking that, at this rate, any more encounters with Lord Alexander and I just might have to start walking around naked.

Stumbling over to the sofa, I gathered the afghan from its back and wrapped myself in it. Just as I was about to leave, I spied the large book Lord Alexander had pulled from Sean's shelf. The book on the Dragon's Curse. I decided to tuck that beneath the afghan to read later, when I could think . . . if such a day ever came.

A quick look out the door showed me the corridor was clear, and I dashed as fast as I could from Sean's wing, completely ignoring any and all dragons that I passed. I'd had enough of them and their fire for the moment. Maybe for life. The more I thought about it the more I realized that Lord Alexander had done it on purpose. The man hadn't even kissed me!

10

I awoke late Saturday morning, after a horrible night of restless, dark dreams. I saw Mary. She chased me, decaying hands reaching for me as she screamed for me to touch her, to "see" what had been done to her. The gown she wore was bloodstained over her heart. There were two women immediately behind her, one white blond, the other reddish blond, and they were doing the same as Mary, screaming for me to touch them and to know what had been done to them. Behind them were even more women.

I ran.

I ran so hard and fast to the town that I couldn't breathe, couldn't move another step, and I fell in the street, gasping for help.

The villagers all came out. They stared at me. Someone told them who I was, what I was, and they gathered around me like I was an animal to be reviled. They poked at me with sticks that turned to swords and left me bleeding. Then the rocks came, bruising, bone-crushing rocks that left no part of me whole.

Cold, despite the bright sun and warm temperature, I rose and washed my face. My skin was icy and appeared to have a bluish tinge in the mirror. Dark shadows made my eyes look bruised and haunted. I turned away, afraid to see more, just as I was afraid to face what Lord Alexander had said last night. I, who didn't believe marriage possible for myself, had been wrenched inside by his declaration that he'd never marry and why. He was sacrificing his life to atone for causing his brother harm. A fact that seemed to dispel the validity of the Dragon's Curse in my mind, but was also completely unnecessary. Sean had built a wonderful and full life for himself, despite his injuries.

I felt as compelled to help Lord Alexander understand the error in his thinking as I was to have him carry through with his threat. *The next time you seduce me, I won't stop, Andromeda. So make very sure you want everything, all the way.*

I kept tossing the words out of my mind, but they kept returning, so I dressed, bent on finding anything or doing anything to distract myself from thinking an affair with Lord Alexander was a fine thing.

Determined to forget, I set my mind on the Killdaren household. After last night's unraveling, I knew everyone within the household would be on edge. I was. The fact that Lady Helen and Mary's deaths were connected stripped away any semblance of normalcy. I wondered what would happen now with Stuart Frye's mother.

Before leaving my room, I hid the Dragon's Curse book in my armoire to read later and went in search of the others. I found that Gemini, Bridget, Prudence, and Rebecca had all left their rooms, and I went downstairs to the kitchens. Tiptoes and whispers were somehow what I expected. Instead, I found the fires were ablaze, everyone was rushing around as if their life depended on finishing their tasks within the next minute. With all of the scrubbing and polishing going on everywhere I passed, it surely seemed to me that the Queen herself was expected.

"What is it?" I asked one of the passing maids. She gave a furtive glance about, making sure no one could see her pause, then she whispered. "It's The Killdaren. The missus is going to have a baby, and while she's resting today, he's ordered that the entire castle be scrubbed and put to rights so that when she's feeling better, there won't be a thing that needs doing." The maid then dashed off, scurrying like a squirrel with but a moment to prepare for a life-long winter.

I located Gemini, Prudence, Bridget, and Rebecca in the dining room.

"Has anyone spoken to Cassie this morning?" I asked as I moved to the sideboard for toast and tea.

"Only to Sean, a few minutes ago," Gemini said. "Cassie is fine, but Sean is a mess. He's quite beside himself on how to keep Cassie in bed. She keeps remembering something that needs to be taken care of and he keeps assuring her that it is being done. Then he wanted to know what Cassie did for leisure and I couldn't tell him a thing."

"Why not? Why, she . . ." My mind drew a blank. "She always . . ."

Bridget nodded her fiery head. "See, I was right about it. She's always doing everything for everyone else and doesn't do anything for herself. Been that way ever since coming to the castle."

"She reads," I said, sitting down to the table slowly, somewhat stunned that I couldn't list a few things Cassie did for enjoyment.

"She's teaching others to read, but she doesn't take the time to do it for fun anymore," Gemini said.

"M-miss Cass, p-play . . . p-piano," Rebecca said, her pale cheeks turning bright red. This was the first time she'd involved herself in a conversation since her nightmare at the beginning of the week.

"Rebecca's right," I said. "Cassie loves music, and she

plays the piano so well. She used to play for hours before she began Cassiopeia's Corner."

Gemini sighed. "I remember. After that she was so busy giving advice and taking care of us that she rarely played anymore. Never really did anything for fun anymore."

"Then we're all just going to have to take charge of Cassie and help her have fun. We have to get her to stop doing for others and to do for herself," Prudence added.

We all stared at each other, and I knew what they were thinking, for I had the same feeling. It would be easier to clean Killdaren's Castle from top to bottom *alone* than it would be to stop Cassie from being Cassie.

"She might not enjoy playing the piano here because the music room is so blimey spooky," Bridget said, and visibly shivered.

"What do you mean? We've a ghost in Killdaren's Castle?" Gemini's eyes lit up as they did with Mr. Drayson's mention of the haunted mansion. I wondered at her sudden interest in specters and why she would ever find things of that nature appealing. Given my recent dreams, anything related to the dead speaking from beyond the grave made me shudder.

"We might as well; dozens of them. Have you not read about the instruments in the glass cases? The last time I dusted them off was more than enough for me."

"No," I said. "I've never been to the music room, but then this place is so big I've only seen just a part of it and haven't done any exploring."

"I've never been to the music room either, ladies," said Gemini. "Why don't we go there after breakfast and see what we can do to make it sunnier for Cassie. Fresh flowers always help."

"Not if you're decorating a tomb," Bridget added.

I thought she was grossly exaggerating until a short while after breakfast when we all ventured to the music room, which had an eerie, tomb-like feel to it. The sensation was different from the eeriness of the nearby archaeological sites like the Circle of Stone Virgins, and of course, the Merry

Maids, the ancient Druid ceremony place that Lord Alexander, Lord Ashton, and Mr. Drayson had taken Gemini and me to earlier this summer. In those places a sense of magical history filled the air. Here, in the music room, something darker hovered, despite the abundance of white and gold decor.

Surprisingly Rebecca exhibited more independence than I had seen before. She used her cane to help guide her down the center aisle and up the stage stairs. She went immediately to the white-and-gold grand piano on the left side of the stage and sat down. After placing her rag doll on the bench next to her she pressed upon the keys. The notes tinkled life into the silence. It was as if she knew exactly how many steps to take and in which direction to move. She was obviously very familiar with the room.

"That is pretty," I said to her. "Can you play the piano?"

"No."

"Then you should learn," I said.

Rebecca played the notes over again and smiled as if she liked the idea.

Prudence moved closer to me and whispered. "Cassie discovered Rebecca didn't stutter when she sang, and so your sister brought her here, played for her, and taught her songs. It was the biggest help in healing Rebecca. Mary used to bring Rebecca here too when she gave Bridget's sister, Flora, singing lessons."

At the mention of Flora's name, goose bumps marched over my skin. I hadn't examined my dream from last night too closely because I didn't want to think about who the two women behind Mary were. Deep inside, I suspected the women were Lady Helen and Flora.

"I've never really thought about this place being like a cemetery, but I guess it is," Prudence said quietly.

"Because of the musty air and the quietness?"

"It's rarely been used since Sean's mother died over thirty years ago. She entertained frequently, had performers from all over the world come, and Sir Warwick's wife would perform every month. She had an angelic voice that Queen

Victoria praised and often requested to hear." Prudence lowered her voice. "It's why Queen Victoria knighted Sir Warwick. The earl told me one . . . uh . . . evening."

"Blimey, I didn't know that," Bridget said, moving closer. Her eyes were wide with wonder. "You mean if Flora is in London and if the Queen were to hear Flora sing and liked it, she could make Flora a real lady?"

"I don't know how it works, just that Sir Warwick was knighted," Prudence said.

"I wasn't even aware he'd ever been married," I said. "Nobody's mentioned her."

"She died on the stage," Prudence added.

I gasped, looking to where Rebecca experimented with the piano.

"Not here," Prudence said waving her hand. "It was in London."

"Good heavens!" Gemini cried out. She turned from a glass case, looking stunned.

"What is it?" I asked, moving toward her.

"Forgive me for saying, but she must have read the bloody card," Bridget said.

"It's horrible." Gemini shivered. "Are they all like that?"

"Yes," Prudence and Bridget answered together.

"Like what?" I asked, moving over to the glass display.

"Read for yourself," Gemini said, stepping aside. "You'll fast lose your appetite for history and artifacts."

In the glass case I found a beautiful gold flute decorated with fiery rubies, giving it a rich flair, much as I imagined the Crown Jewels would have. My gaze reluctantly moved to the accompanying card. The flute had belonged to Katherine Petrovanich, a Russian princess who'd played her seductive music for one too many Russian princes. She died when one of them poisoned her flute.

"Goodness!"

"Nothing good about any of the instruments in the cases," Bridget said. "Every card tells what part the instruments played in the deaths of the women who used them."

Having spent a great deal of my life immersed in artifacts, it wasn't the first thing I'd seen that had been "instrumental" in someone's death, but it was the first time I'd ever encountered a collection of such things that weren't war weapons. This was very disturbing. "Why ever would someone do this?" How could anyone enjoy hearing music when surrounded by reminders of death? The very thought turned my stomach.

Lady Helen. Mary. Now this! There was entirely too much death about!

Prudence frowned. "It's been this way since I came here to work eleven years ago. I assumed it was Sean's mother. She and the earl where avid collectors of art and novelties from all over the world."

Gemini wrapped her arms around herself. "Well, I can see why Cassie hasn't developed an affinity for playing music here. It's a wonder she hasn't snitched and either hidden or burned the cards."

"Why don't we?" I whispered.

No one said anything for a full minute, then Bridget laughed. "If we did, I don't think The Killdaren would demand that we all leave the castle."

"And if we are able to get Cassie to come here and play then he'll be sure to forgive us."

Not another word was said, but twenty minutes later, every display cabinet now only held the beautiful musical instruments and all references to death had been removed.

"Where should we put the cards?" Prudence asked as we'd gathered around the pile.

"I'll not have the bloody things in my room," said Bridget, stepping back. Prudence and Gemini moved back as well.

"They're almost like ghosts," whispered Gemini.

I glared at the cards. "They're just words. They can't hurt you." I scooped them all into my arms and went toward the door. "I'll be right back. I'll put them in my armoire."

"Don't go that way," Prudence said. "There're stairs from the stage that go directly to the quarters I share with Rebecca."

"A secret passage?" asked Gemini.

Prudence shook her head. "No, not secret. Just never used now. My quarters were for honored guests who'd come to perform and the stairs were for their convenience, enabling them to rest and have privacy until their performance. Come, I'll show you." She gathered Rebecca and her doll and led us up to the second floor. I shivered. Whether it was from stairs I didn't know about or the death cards, I couldn't say, but I felt decidedly cold.

Monday morning came faster than I imagined possible. We didn't get the chance to take Cassie to the music room until Sunday evening when Sean either finally gave up trying to keep her resting in bed, or having all of us women constantly intruding into his quarters put him over the edge. He'd muttered something about having to go sleep with his telescope, whereupon Cassie sweetly told him *that* was unnecessary. All he had to do was let her rest somewhere else besides bed. That we'd all come at her explicit request told me she'd deliberately driven Sean to this breaking point. Cassie was not one to sit idle and confided that she *had* to get out of the bed. It was the only way either she or Sean were going to survive until the next day. He wouldn't even let her fluff a pillow by herself.

Bridget also informed us that Dr. Luden's revelation in regards to the similarity between Lady Helen and Mary's deaths didn't change Constable Poole's opinion about Mrs. Frye and Jamie Frye's guilt. He knew all along Mrs. Frye hadn't killed Mary by accident. That she confessed to it proved she'd helped her son hide the fact that he'd committed the crime, which made her just a culpable.

I rose early Monday morning and tried on three dresses before finding one alluring enough to assure I'd catch Lord Alexander's eye. Not that I'd allow him any further freedoms with my person after the way he'd left me last, but I did want him to desire me and regret he'd left me in such a state on purpose.

Much to my dismay, I discovered my wardrobe rather dismal when it came to flattering attire. I'd given such things little attention, for my main thoughts had always centered on history instead of fashion. The deep blue tea dress I'd settled on made my eyes intensely blue and flattered my figure well with an embroidered bodice and a graceful, flowing skirt.

I left my room with a knot of trepidation inside me that had nothing to do with anything it should have, like what I'd read from Rebecca about Mary or its possible implications in Flora's continued silence. Nor did it have anything to do with the connection between Mary and Lady Helen's deaths. It had everything to do with Lord Alexander and what happened Friday night in Sean's study.

I slipped on my lace gloves and my ring as I hurried down the stairs, determined that I wouldn't quit my post because of the incident. In fact, I was more of the mind to pour wine on him or do something just as outrageous. What exactly does one say to a man who'd done what Lord Alexander had done?

The next time you seduce me, I won't stop, Andromeda. So make very sure you want everything, all the way. I can't marry you either. I'll leave no legitimate heirs. When I die, my title will go to Sean and his heirs. It is the least I can do for crippling him for life.

My attraction to Lord Alexander when I'd first met him at the beginning of the summer had been instant and strong, a situation that had intensified ever since, and now loomed larger because my feelings for him had grown even greater.

I'd never truly been attracted to a man before. Not like this. A man's smile might have been interesting, but never had the power to capture my desire. A man's gaze may have made me search his eyes a moment longer, looking to satisfy my curiosity about his spirit, but never had one set me afire as did Lord Alexander's. And I may have wondered on occasion what a kiss might be like, but I had never wanted, allowed, nor sought intimacy with a man. Now I couldn't escape thoughts of us together as man and woman, and the things he alone seemed to have the power to make me feel. He was there with me, inside my mind.

I didn't know what I would do about any of it yet, but I did know that I wasn't going to hide myself away in antiquities, as was my custom. When I saw him next, I'd not only let him know that I was unhappy with the way he'd left things, but I would . . .

What? I didn't know, but I had to figure it out before I reached Dragon's Cove this morning. Whenever Lord Alexander was around, rational thought escaped me.

Much to my surprise, I found Cassie in the kitchens, dressed for an outing, having a discussion with Mrs. Murphy. Mrs. Murphy did not appear happy.

"Lass, I know ye're fine, but you canna go to town today. The Killdaren will have all of our hides if he finds you gone. Give yourself a few more days rest before yer up and about."

"The doctor says I'm fine. I feel fine. I'm only going to speak to Mrs. Frye and I'll be back before Sean wakes up. I promise there is no need to worry."

"But The Killdaren doesn't *know* that."

"Yes, he does. The doctor has told him and I have told him."

"He may know it in his head, but he doesn't in his heart. He's afraid of losing you, lass. Ye're gonna have to take it easy with him for a bit."

"This is too important. I won't be long," Cassie said, heading for the door.

"Wait," I said, moving from the stair landing to make my presence known. "Mrs. Murphy is right, Cassie. You don't need to be running back and forth between here and town."

Cassie turned and rolled her eyes. "Not you, too, Andrie. You're supposed to be on my side. Friday night upset me and resulted in a stomach cramp. Now suddenly everyone expects me to stop living life. I must hurry so I *can* return before Sean wakes."

"I'll go with you." Crossing the kitchens, I joined her near the door.

"Aren't you on your way to Dragon's Cove?"

"Yes, but I'm early and it won't matter if I'm a little late. So don't argue."

"Fine." Cassie tossed her hands up. "But I can't be coddled forever."

"No, but you can learn to do two things." I firmed my lips and tried to give her a stern look. "You can carry a lighter load and do more activities that relax you and make you happy inside. Things you do for yourself because you like them, like long, warm baths and reading books or walking in the garden. Not the dozens of things you do for others. You haven't even sat down to write since you resigned from Cassiopeia's Corner."

Cassie moved ahead as if she didn't hear me. "If you're joining me, then let's go." After we descended the stairs and edged the elegant gardens, still colorful this time of year with huge, blue blossoms and bright yellow bells that shouted for a soul to stop and look, Cassie finally replied, "Are you and Bridget in league with each other? She said the same thing to me yesterday."

"Well," I hedged, "we have decided that you never take time for yourself. Just like now. Instead of resting you're off to town when you can easily send a message to Mrs. Frye and have a servant deliver whatever it is you're carrying in your basket."

"No," she said. "I can't do that. Because though I will see Mrs. Frye, too, who I really need to see are Constable Poole and Jamie."

We'd reached the stables and my steps slowed. "I don't think seeing Jamie is such a good idea, Cassie. Good Lord. The man tried to hurt you twice. He kidnapped you!"

"Ever since Dr. Luden told us about what had been done to Mary, and that the same thing had been done to Lady Helen, I've had an increasingly harder time believing that Jamie is guilty of what everyone is now supposing he did."

"And why is that?" Stuart Frye asked, exiting the open stable door. His stance was that of an angry man, confrontational and challenging, one that made him just as imposing and as dangerous as his half brothers Lord Alexander and Sean. A carriage had already been made ready and stood waiting for us.

I jumped, startled by his appearance. Cassie only nodded as if she'd expected him and didn't see anything threatening about him at all. She stared hard at Stuart. "Do you think your brother is guilty of killing Lady Helen and Mary?" she asked instead of answering Stuart's question.

"No," he said roughly. "Why don't you?"

"Probably for the same reason you don't," Cassie said. "And Constable Poole is going to hear me say it first. Then I'm going to make sure everyone in the village hears me as well."

"It's not going to change anything," Stuart replied. "Even if Jamie were freed, people would be afraid of him and would seek to destroy him."

Cassie straightened her shoulders. "Then we will do what has to be done to protect him and your mother. Give them a new life in a different place if necessary."

"What do you mean?"

Cassie smiled. "Haven't you heard about Stuart Frye and his family?"

Stuart frowned and I looked at my sister twice, just to make sure she knew what she had just said.

Cassie cocked her head as if Stuart was daft. "Andrie, I know you've heard of Stuart Frye and his family. Why, the man is renowned for breeding and training the best horses available. Everyone in the world comes to Frye. I can't remember where the affluent man lives, America, Ireland, or wherever he decided to make his start. But his hard work, together with the land and horses he inherited from his father, has made him famous."

"Oh," I nodded, my lips twitching with a smile. "Those Fryes. Yes, I do recall them now."

"I've heard from a good source that Mrs. Frye has the most amazing blue eyes and fiery hair that just might be as warm as her heart. She holds classes every week for those too unfortunate to afford an education."

Stuart blinked and stared, his dark eyes bleak. "Fiction belongs in novels, Mrs. Killdaren."

"Then I'll have to write one." Cassie squared her shoulders. "A story that reveals that a man without a dream is no man at all. You strike me as quite a man, Stuart Frye. And did you forget? Family calls me Cassie."

Stuart didn't say a word, he just opened the carriage door and waited for us, but I could tell without touching him that Cassie had him thinking.

Cassie put her hand on his arm as she passed him. "I will make a difference. The Killdarens owe it to you, but more importantly, you deserve it. You have to help, too."

When Stuart still didn't answer, she told him, "You have to believe, Stuart Frye. Few men are strong enough to believe. Are you?"

Joining me on the carriage seat, Cassie sat back with a sigh. "This might not be too difficult of a position after all."

"What?"

"Being the unemployed wife of a wealthy man. Since I'm unable to hold a worthy position and must focus my abilities on helping others, I'm rethinking how I can still be a productive member of society. Do you know how many rights I can wrong, Andrie? It boggles my mind."

I didn't know whether to laugh or to give my brother-in-law a wee warning. Either way, I thought it fortunate that Sean Killdaren was a *very* wealthy man. "Are you going to write that story you just spoke of, Cassie?"

She sighed. "I don't know, Andrie. Where would I find the time?"

"You need to find it, because a woman without a dream is no woman at all as well. Don't let life take away your dreams."

Cassie frowned almost the whole way into town, but I

could tell that dishing her own advice back to her had made an impact.

A short while later, we entered Mrs. Frye's stone cell and I had to brace myself. Not because of her living conditions, which were meager at best, but because of her antipathy toward Cassie. Mrs. Frye was a sour shell of a woman, with haunted dark eyes as sharp as her tongue.

"What are you doing here?" she demanded.

Cassie set down the basket. "I've brought you some things."

Mrs. Frye turned her back. "Take them and leave. They're not wanted. This is all your fault. If you hadn't come here then none of this would have happened."

"It would have. Maybe not this summer, but it would have. Murder has a way of rising from the grave. You're unfortunately just going to have to live with the things in the basket and face a few truths as well," Cassie said sternly. "I understand why you are bitter and see many reasons in your life for you to feel justified in being the harsh, unforgiving, and resentful woman you are. But you've brought most of it on yourself. A woman must be loving and giving before she can be loved and given to, and until you realize that you're never going to be free of the prison you've built around your heart and your soul. There are second chances in life. When it comes, don't waste it." Cassie turned and left the woman alone in the chilly stone room. I followed, amazed by my sister's crusading abilities, sure that if she were given the world to fix, she'd have it spinning right in a day.

The jailor led us to a darker cell, one with heavy locks on the door. It was a very dank and cold place with an unbelievably horrendous stench to it. He didn't open the door, but just beat on the wood with a stick and flapped open a tiny slit. "Ye've visitors, Frye."

There was no response from inside the cell.

I blinked at Cassie in the dimness and saw tears brimming from her eyes. "Jamie," she called.

A shuffle and a moan sounded from inside the cell.

"Jamie?"

"M-m-mary?" came a hoarse whisper. "M-m-mary hurt you."

"I know, Jamie. But it is going to be all right. Be strong for me, please. Can you do that? I need your help. Can you be strong for me so that you can help me?"

"M-m-mary. H-h-help M-mary," Jamie whispered.

"I'll help, too," Cassie cried, covering her mouth with her hand and rushing back down the corridor. I followed, feeling just as sickened.

"I didn't know. I didn't know they were treating him like this. Dear God." Cassie marched directly to Constable Poole's office, located in another building. She didn't even knock but rather sailed through the door on a righteous wind.

Constable Poole barreled up from his chair. "Mrs. Killdaren!"

"What you're doing is cruel and inhumane and you must change it immediately or you will no longer be a constable! I'll use every last pound of the Killdarens' wealth to see that you're the one buried alive in a stone cell if you don't move Jamie to an acceptable cell, now!"

I slid into the constable's office in the wake of my sister's thunder and noticed that Stuart stood near the window. He was staring at Cassie as one might at a terrible storm whirling in front of one's eyes.

"Mrs. Killdaren, calm yourself. The man kidnapped you and by your own account grabbed a knife to murder you. He may have also murdered Mary. I'm still trying to get Mrs. Frye to admit she's lying to protect her son. Jamie deserves worse. You aren't being rational."

"Even if Jamie was guilty, he's not an animal to grovel in the dirt. He's a man with limitations and can in no way understand what is happening. I don't care what it looks like Jamie did. The connection between Lady Helen's and Mary's deaths provides enough doubt that everyone needs to seriously question his guilt. I don't think he did it. Why did you not mention the carved symbol to me and my family? Why did you ask Dr. Luden to keep the fact a secret?"

Constable Poole squared his shoulders and shook his head as if stunned. "Mrs. Killdaren, surely you're not insinuating anything criminal has taken place!" He bristled, agitated enough to cause his curled mustache to flap as he breathed. "I'll have to forgive your ignorance on such matters. It is common practice in murder investigations to keep certain facts secret in order to nab the guilty party. Also, even if that weren't the case, I don't see how this fact has any pertinence to you other than that it traumatizes you and your loved ones more. You and your family have been through enough already. The guilty parties will soon go to trial and this whole terrible ordeal will be over."

"If that were the case then there wouldn't be a problem, Constable. Unfortunately it isn't. Neither Jamie nor Mrs. Frye killed Mary."

"And your reasoning for this would be?"

"Jamie loved Mary."

"That's it?" He laughed hard. "That's your whole reasoning in his defense? Did we not just discover last week the man killed in the street had strangled his wife? I'm sure he thought himself in love with her at one time." He pinched the bridge of his nose. "Not to be rude Mrs. Killdaren, but I've more important things to do with my time than to waste it listening to emotional declarations."

Cassie rolled her eyes. "Constable Poole, you're forgetting the fact that in many ways Jamie is like a child, an innocent child. And as being such, given his size and strength, he could have easily harmed Mary in a moment of anger or hurt by hitting and pushing her, causing her to fall and hit her head. But I don't think he would ever take a knife and carve her up."

"And why is that?" the constable demanded.

"I just told you why," Cassie shot back.

I stepped forward, sensing Cassie was getting much too upset. Sean would have my head if Cassie were to have another episode. "What I think my sister is trying to say, Constable, is that if you have a duck that walks and talks and swims like a duck, and suddenly there is a savage and brutal attack on a swan that was in the water with the duck, do you then blame the duck? Or do you look beneath the surface of the water for a shark?"

"Exactly," Cassie said, glaring at the constable.

"It wouldn't hold up in a court of law, Miss Andrews, but that was extremely well put," Stuart said, speaking up for the first time.

"I suggest you start looking for the shark in Dartmoor's End, Constable Poole," Cassie said. "Because I intend to let my belief in Jamie and Mrs. Frye's innocence be known. This coming from the very woman that Jamie Frye kidnapped won't help your case any."

Constable Poole shook his head sadly. "All of your flowery talk, ladies, doesn't explain why Jamie brought you, Mrs. Killdaren, to the very same underground chamber beneath the Circle of the Stone Virgins that he took Mary to. You both surprise me. Considering Jamie seemed to frequently mistake you for Mary, you stand the most to lose. Are you willing to stake your life on Jamie's innocence?"

At Cassie's pause, the constable smiled triumphantly and Stuart cursed.

Cassie groaned, truly distressed.

"That's not fair," I said. "Cassie shouldn't be expected to prove Jaime's innocence by putting her life on the line. But by the same coin, *you* can't say for sure that Jamie *is* guilty, Constable Poole, so I suggest you make sure you're looking beneath the surface because a shark just may be there, ready to attack."

The constable settled his dark eyes on me for a long, very uncomfortable moment during which I could feel his anger. He did not like being told what to do, and by a woman no less. "Then I suggest, Miss Andrews and Mrs. Killdaren, that you get out of the water and stay out of the water and leave this investigation in the hands of the professionals. Now if you'll excuse me." He motioned to the door.

"Sean will be coming to inspect Jamie's living conditions by the end of the day. Change them or you're going to have more trouble than you can swim through. Good day, Constable," Cassie said curtly. "This matter is no where near settled."

"The courts are more than capable of ruling on this matter, Mrs. Killdaren."

"Not if they're like you," Cassie said under her breath as she sailed past me and out the door. I followed Cassie, realizing that in many ways I had been looking for a shark since Mary's funeral. I had no doubt there was one there.

11

Upon reaching Dragon's Cove, I learned from Brighty that the "captain" was away for the day, a fact that only seemed to tighten the growing knot of tension inside me. I could have worn a potato sack for all of the good an appealing dress would do me if Lord Alexander was set to avoid me.

"Heavens, Miss Andrews, we weren't expecting you back," said Mrs. Lynds as she rushed onto the entry hall. "Lord Alexander said your sister was ill and that you wouldn't be returning for some time, if at all."

"Just a misunderstanding," I said, keeping my smile bright even though I wondered if a desire to get me to resign had motivated his behavior Friday night. "Cassie is fine and the doctor doesn't see any complications to her condition."

"Forgive my nosiness, but what is her condition? Lord Alexander didn't say. I hope it's not something awful, Master Sean deserves a good bit of happiness."

"In about seven months, I will be an aunt and Lord Alexander will be an uncle."

"Mercy me! A baby in the family at last! This is wonderful news. Oh, there is so much to do!" She started to wander from the room then stopped suddenly. "Goodness, I almost forgot. Is there anything you need today?"

"Actually, I thought it would be a good idea for me to tour the castle. That way I would know how many rooms I will need to do and what their general contents and decor are." Now that I'd seen to the entry and dwelled as long as I dared in the glass room with the memory of his kiss, I was ready to explore more of the castle and learn more about Lord Alexander through his home.

"Mercy, that will be a lot. Shall I show you about or do you wish to take a turn yourself?"

"You don't mind if I wander around by myself?" The thought of exploring all of the history at my leisure lifted my spirits.

"Don't see what harm it could do. I'll be in the kitchens if you need anything. Lord Alexander has been in such a melancholy state since returning home, the cook and I are fixing his favorite meal for tonight: beef pie, lamb cutlets, asparagus, and fresh bread."

"Oh, is he not feeling well?"

She sighed. "Not that, lass. He's right fit in his body." She didn't say more and I didn't ask.

"Will you be wanting lunch in the dining room or a tray today?"

"A tray will be fine, Mrs. Lynds."

"Very well, let Brighty know if you need anything moved. I'll have him go through and light the gas lamps. The rooms need airing anyway." She went back the way she came shaking her head and murmuring. "A baby. A baby at last."

Without wasting a minute more, I set about exploring Lord Alexander's castle, bringing my cataloguing notebook so I could make a map and notes. The first floor was an amazing conglomeration of rooms from several parlors and dining rooms, a vast library, a study, a drawing room, and a ballroom to half a dozen more areas whose purpose I couldn't discern. Only the ballroom wasn't filled to over-flowing with antiquities. On the far end of the castle I dis-covered a set of heavy iron and wood doors where two suits of armor holding wicked-looking swords stood sentry. A draft of cool, musty air eased through the open door, mak-ing the dim gas lamps flicker shadows on the stone walls and descending step. Intrigued, I descended the first land-ing, thinking that this part of the castle would have to be underground, which would perhaps make this a wine cellar. The Killdarens' spiced wine had to come from somewhere. Reaching the turn, I did indeed see a number of barrels stacked below and I moved downward. Beyond the oak bar-rels were racks of bottles. I slid my fingers over their dusty necks, surprised to find a smile curving my lips and a deli-cious tingle curl up inside me. Friday night shouldn't be a warm and exciting memory, should it? I should be outraged about it, shouldn't I?

Swinging around, miffed at myself, I froze in midstep. What I thought was a wine cellar opened up to a large room that sent a cold chill down my spine, for I surely was looking at a medieval dungeon or a torture chamber for the Spanish Inquisition. I knew a little of those things from history, and it wasn't hard to recognize the rack and the spiked chair, nor the chains strategically placed upon the opposite wall and the stone slab in the center of the room. On one wall hung dozens of metal implements that I couldn't even bear to look at. The horror of them clawed at me.

I turned and screamed at the huge, hulking shadow of a man against the far wall of the stairs.

"Lass!" Brighty cried. Then I heard a loud *umph* and the butler tumbled into the room, nearly rolling into the wine barrels.

I rushed over to him. "Heavens, are you all right?"

"Get behind me, lass. Let me at the scurvy bastard." He sat up with his fists raised, ready for battle, his good eye blinking. His wig sat askew and dust from the stone floor peppered his formal suit.

He made a completely incongruous but most welcomed knight in dusty armor.

"Forgive me, but you frightened me," I said, forcing a smile. "Have you had a scurvy sort in the cellar before?" I asked, curious over how ready Brighty was to fight.

He grumbled and brushed himself off before rising. "Thought the ghost got you," he said under his breath.

My brows rose to high arches. "What ghost?"

"One of the Killdarens' cursed twins died here, in his own dungeon, mind you. His brother accused him of heresy and that was the end of him, it was. Except his spirit still walks about where they tortured him. Leastways, I swear it does. Whenever the captain's away, I hear the ghost, moaning and rattling chains. I'm about the only soul brave enough to come down here and I don't ever come down here when the captain's at sea, I tell ya. Surprised you did yourself."

"I saw the lit stairwell and the wine. I wasn't expecting such gruesome antiquities." I shuddered, forced to glance at the horrible contraptions again. "I won't be coming back."

"Don't like coming here much at all, myself. I light up the cellar a good long while before I come down, just to let the ghost know that I'm coming. Mrs. Lynds needs more spiced wine. Captain drained the lot we had in the butler's pantry this weekend."

"Does Lord Alexander do that often?" I asked.

"Not much anymore. Not like he did when his brother was first hurt. That was a bad spot of it then, to be sure. Captain Jansen had to kidnap Captain Black and keep him at sea to sober him up. The crew didn't have nary a drop of ale or rum the entire trip either. Thought he was going to run every man through with his sword before he settled down."

I could readily imagine that an angry and devastated Lord Alexander made a deadly foe. "Can I help you collect the wine?" I asked, wanting to hurry out of the cellar. Dungeon, I amended. I might as well call it what it was.

"No, you're a sweet lass, but I'll be fine."

I reached over and straightened his wig. "Then I shall

thank you for coming so readily to my rescue, sir, and take my exploration to the second floor. I believe Lord Alexander mentioned there were unopened crates in a room there."

"Don't be thankin' me for doin' a man's duty," he said, blushing. Then he cleared his throat. "The crates are in the Queen's Room, across from the captain's quarters. I'll come up and open a few of them for you after I take Mrs. Lynds the wine."

"Thank you," I said and quickly made my escape. It would seem there were more than dark dragons lurking beneath the castle's black stone. A ghost of a tortured ancestor? No wonder Sean could believe in the Dragon's Curse. The thought reminded me of the book in my armoire. I needed to read it to find out what Cassie and I were up against.

Surprisingly, and much to my excitement, the Queen's Room was an Egyptian treasure trove. Brighty pried open a number of crates and I immediately and blissfully set to work, deciding to explore the other three floors of the castle another time.

Unfortunately, I soon encountered a very big problem. I couldn't concentrate on the treasures as I should. Brighty's offhand comment, "across *from the captain's quarters*," kept intruding. Instead of seeing the artifacts in my hands, my highly improper curiosity kept wondering what Lord Alexander's personal quarters looked like, because as far as I could tell, he didn't really have his mark on the other rooms I'd explored so far. They all seemed just as he'd indicated, a burden he'd inherited that had to be carried, and one which he avoided at all costs.

Sean had done the same at Killdaren's Castle. Except for his private wing, which he'd made his own lair.

Mrs. Lynds appeared with a lunch tray, and after showing me the water closet at the end of the corridor so I could refresh myself, she left. The room lured me further along in my curiosity of Lord Alexander. Upon a dais before a large paneled window sat an enormous porcelain tub with gold fixtures. To its left was a large fireplace, one that gave me no doubt the room could be kept toasty warm even in the middle of winter. With its green watered silk walls and dark wooden chests filled with plush linens, the room was resplendent. On a shelf next to a mirrored white-and-gold sink sat a number of toiletries. Just as soon as I washed my hands I inspected the items, tickling my nose with the scents of shaving soap and cologne. His heady scent of spice, sandalwood, and something else that was mesmerizing in its lure, lingered beneath my nose long after I'd closed the bottle and set it back on the shelf. On my way back to the Queen's Room, I decided to peek into Lord Alexander's quarters.

I hesitated before opening the double doors. My pulse raced almost as deliciously as it did when the man himself would focus on my mouth. Then I slipped inside and stood stunned as I registered the details before me, or the lack of them. The first room, nearly half a ballroom in size, was decorated with little else than a red carpet with a black dragon adorning its center. The fireplace against the far wall appeared as if it hadn't been used in years. Miffed, and a bit perplexed not to see more, I moved into the room and made my way across the plush carpet to open the door of an adjoining room. Here I found a large four-poster bed, minus any bed curtains, and a single wing chair set before a fireplace. A lamp and one table stacked with newspapers and a book accompanied the chair. Next to the bed stood an armoire; it was the only other furniture besides a large covered desk. No pictures hung on the walls, nor did any other objects sit upon the surfaces of the scant furniture. The only thing indicative of Lord Alexander and his wealth was the black satin counterpane and pillows. The loneliness of the room knotted a lump of emotion in my throat, even as the decadent sensuality of the black satin brought to mind images of Lord Alexander kissing my breasts as passionately as he had in Sean's study. Just looking at the bed made me want him to do everything he'd promised should I entice him again.

My hand itched to touch the shiny black counterpane. Instead I forced myself over to the table next to the wing chair and peered down at the newspapers. Shock at the unexpected subject of the publications hit me in the stomach. "Murdered Woman Found." "She Didn't See Her Killer." The main articles on the front pages of all of the crime publications were about murdered women. I dropped the articles and glanced at the book's title. *The Druids' Sacrificial Rites.*

Then the sound of someone else breathing reached my ears. Fear crawled up my spine, and I whipped around, gasping in relief when I saw Lord Alexander standing in the doorway. He leaned against the jamb with his arms crossed in just such a way as to let me know he was not amused. Fiery heat that had nothing to do with his sensual appeal burned my cheeks.

It appeared as if he'd not shaven nor slept well since I last saw him. His jaw and eyes were darkly shadowed, making the fullness of his mouth so much more noticeable and the loneliness of his soul almost too painful to see. No. I wasn't about to excuse his outrageous response to my innocent flirting Friday. I could still feel the wine and his tongue on me . . .

Hmph. I snatched my shoulders as straight as I could and matched his stance, tapping my foot. "Well, you've not a single artifact in your room!" I said, deciding to brazen it out. "Why do you live like a monk?" I glanced at the papers he'd surely seen me perusing. "Make that a Druid-sacrifice-and-crime-reading monk!"

His brows shot up. "A monk?"

"Well . . . a Spartan then," I amended, hoping not to learn what the flashing gleam in his eye meant. It reminded me too much of the moment just before he dumped both glasses of wine down my dress. I swung around to view the whole room then faced him again. "Why ever do you live so bare?"

Before I could read the emotion in his expression, he turned and went into the carpeted room, as if my presence in his bedroom was too painful to stand. "If you must know, Miss Andrews, I simply don't need things about me. My family has collected more than enough of them, and these rooms are where I meditate, fence, exercise . . . and sleep."

My heart squeezed. He led such a solitary life. Why would a man abstain from collecting any personal belongings besides those which were functional?

Personal? Was that it? Was he so set on not developing any attachment for this life? Was he truly only filling space until he died and left his title to Sean?

You're looking at my legacy. He'd meant it, I realized, recalling his words about Iris on the docks. The only things he let himself care for and build upon were his horses. It would seem that the Friesian breed wasn't the only thing on the verge of disappearing from the earth. My heart twisted and tears stung my eyes as I looked about the room again, seeing it for what it was. Even in my worst imaginings about having to live alone, I never pictured anything as stark as what Lord Alexander had imposed upon himself.

I went to the doorway. He'd walked to the center of the carpeted room, standing upon the black dragon woven into the red carpet.

"Miss Andrews, I must—"

"Andromeda or Andrie," I said. "When you last spoke to me Friday night, you called me Andromeda."

He didn't turn to meet my gaze, but stared at the fireplace as if flames danced there. "For which I owe you my deepest apologies and a new dress. I . . . wasn't myself and I never should have done what I did or said what I said."

I'm not sure what possessed me. I suddenly had to touch him. I crossed to him and set my hand on his shoulder. He stiffened, but didn't pull away. Self-disgust, fevered passion, and a bone-deep loneliness rang in his voice, but I couldn't see that in his mind, just a gray swirling cloud of angry emotions.

"We were both at fault," I said. "It was a difficult night and the wine affected us both."

He swung around to face me and my hand fell from his shoulder, leaving a void his gaze filled. For a moment I saw the truth in his eyes. To blame the wine and the intense emotions were polite excuses for uncontrolled lust. I knew it and he knew it, just as we both knew that lust wasn't going to go away. It had sparked the moment we met earlier this summer and had grown whether we'd seen each other or not.

I wasn't ready to confront the issue of our attraction, nor did I know what I wanted to do about it. I did know for certain that I did not want to walk away and let Lord Alexander live a barren existence. I forced myself to lower my gaze from his and searched for a subject. "Did you say you fenced in here? With whom?"

"Captain Jansen if the ship is docked, Brighty if it is not, or most often just myself."

"Yourself?" I held up a mock sword. "Move a muscle and I'll run you through." Then I lowered the pretend sword, turned to face the opposite direction and lunged. "Think you can get the best of me, do you?"

He stood blinking at me with a pained expression.

I quickly recovered myself. "My apologies, Lord Alexander. I often get carried away with myself. Hand me a Chinese vase and suddenly I'm in Kubla Khan's court."

"I believe it's called being rash, Andromeda. And you must call me Alex," he said as he moved away from me, closer to the fireplace. "After all, if we're going to duel we might as well do so on a first-name basis."

"Duel?" I managed to spit the word out before he left me speechless by pressing on a panel next to the fireplace and causing the wall to move. A whole room opened up, with swords of every kind mounted on the far wall.

"Yes, your form is deplorable. Even if you're going to just pretend to run a foe through, you should at least do so with style. Besides, you trespassed into the dragon's lair. Did you not think there would be a consequence to such an action? You must fight me for your freedom." His sexy, almost devouring grin was exactly what I'd imagine a pirate's to be.

I drew back a step, several in fact. "Uh, Lord Alexander, I mean, Alex. I think a duel is not a good idea. No, I mean I am certain it is not. Since I was only doing my job and thought it most prudent to catalogue the items in your room during your absence, I don't see how I trespassed at all. So consequences aren't necessary." I backed even more to the open doorway.

He crossed toward me, smiling a bit too much like a cat about to pounce a mouse, making me feel like the most delicious morsel ever to cross his path.

"Catch," he said as he tossed a very thin sword straight up into the air above me. With its point toward the ceiling, the guarded hilt fell first.

I yelped but couldn't move back fast enough to avoid the sword and reached out to catch it, amazed to find my fingers had wrapped around the hilt. At least I think they did. It was as light as a feather.

"Excellent," he said. "But it would go better if you didn't close your eyes."

I opened eyes that I hadn't realized I'd shut to find he'd caught the tip of the sword blade he'd tossed at me and had held it in place for me to grasp, something I would have seen if I'd kept my eyes open. He let go, and the sword became slightly heavier, but not as much as I'd expected.

I pushed the sword toward him. "Here. This is ridiculous. I know nothing about swordplay."

"Fencing," he corrected. "You'll learn then. First you need to gain a feel for having a blade in your hand and keeping your balance as you move."

He meant what he said, and after another stunned moment, I realized the notion interested me. I lifted the sword tip higher as I met his gaze and he arched a brow. "How do I accomplish that?"

"Mirror me," he said. "But hilts need to be held just right." Moving in behind me, he held his sword out to the right, so I could see how he held his. At first I saw nothing but a haze, for I think my eyes blurred from the sensations prickling me. All I had to do was to lean just a few inches and I'd know the warmth of his heat and the feel of his hard, sculpted planes pressed intimately to me.

"Here," he said, reaching over and moving my fingers for

me. "Now this is your en guard position." Closing the inches separating us, he used his body to mold mine into place. His arm pressed mine, his leg curved mine, his hand held me so intimately tight against him that the heat of him warmed me everywhere, and the caress of his words were a tantalizing whisper in my ear. "Different parries will require your wrist to be turned up like this, or down like this. Your blade can face to the inside like this or to the outside like this. For example, if your opponent thrusts at you, you respond with a parry using the forte, or lower part of your blade, to block his attack. Then riposte like this to keep your opponent on the offensive. Making him retreat first will give you a psychological edge in the match."

I wasn't sure of anything he showed me except that another minute of his body touching so intimately to mine would surely set my skirts on fire. The heat enveloping me made me burn.

"Now I'm going to face you from the opposite side of the room and I want you to follow my every move. Parry number one is known as prime. Turn your blade down and to the inside with your wrist . . ."

He moved with such slow, controlled grace that I'd often forget to follow and he'd have to repeat the movement. The steps I made and the arcs I swung with the light sword soon took on the feel of a very unique, slow-moving ballet. "This fencing isn't too hard," I said after he'd shown me the seventh parry position.

"Getting to know how your body moves and what a sword feels like to hold is an important step, but you aren't exactly fencing yet." His voice deepened, rumbling over me in an almost mesmerizing way.

"Show me then," I said, taking a step back. "What do you do when you fence by yourself?"

"You really want to know?"

I nodded.

"You'll have to go stand by the door then." I did as he asked and found that he'd gone to the sword room and disappeared for several long moments. When he returned, he'd changed his clothes and now wore loose black pants and a shirt with flowing sleeves. His feet were bare and he'd exchanged the long, thin practice sword for two shorter, heavier, and deadlier blades, one in each hand. Then he moved to the dragon at the center of the carpet and bowed. After that, I forgot there was anything else in the world besides him.

He swirled the blades so fast and adeptly that I could hardly see them. The action would be quite a feat alone, but add to that the fact that he jumped, kicked, dove, flipped, and rolled from one corner of the carpet to the other made what he did impossible. When he finished, he stood with his head bowed in the very place he'd started, his swords clenched tightly in his fists as they crisscrossed his chest. I didn't know what special ritual I had seen, but I did know that it was the most passionate thing I'd ever witnessed, and the deadliest.

"That was beautiful. I now understand why this room is so empty. You fill it with your freedom, your energy, your art."

He didn't respond at first as he sauntered toward me, his every movement one of grace and style. I stood with my back against the door jamb. The raw masculine power of his every movement sent my heart racing. He planted his hand on the wood molding above me and leaned down, bringing his face to a whisper away from mine.

"If you understand that then you'll also understand why the other room is empty and will stay empty." His gaze searched mine then dipped to my mouth, sending shivers of anticipation dancing through me. He wanted to kiss me so badly I could taste it, feel it. Or was it my own desire and need that I couldn't escape? The exercise he'd put his body through had energized him in a very charismatic, sensual way. But instead of kissing me, he met my gaze again. "And you'll understand why I'll never marry, no matter how much I want something. Sean and I began learning to be sword masters together. In my anger, I stole his freedom. I condemned him to a life of darkness and dependency. He'll never move with freedom and grace again. He'll never be free of pain."

"I understand," I said softly, pressing my hand to his cheek, sensing and feeling his pain and his passion, even though I couldn't see into his mind. I had yet to comprehend why my gift vacillated so wildly with him. But I did understand him. He'd put himself in prison for life, to atone for injuring his brother. I could have pointed out that it was an accident, that he hadn't meant to hurt Sean so severely; but I knew he wouldn't hear or understand anything I could have said. Our lives weren't all that different. I let my thumb slide over his lips, to gently soothe the pain inside him. He inhaled sharply, his nostrils flaring, his pupils dilating, turning his vibrant green eyes to nearly black.

"I need to get back to work," I said and ducked under his arm, escaping into the corridor just as he leaned to kiss me. If I had let him, I would have been lost completely. Nothing would have stopped us from consummating our passion. And when I wasn't drugged by the heady pleasure of his touch, there was still a part of me that hesitated. He'd been honest with me about who he was. I had yet to tell him what I was.

He followed me to the Queen's Room and I found I still had the fencing practice sword in my hand. Frowning at the hand wrapped around the hilt—for I'd never imagined that I could hold a sword and forget it was there—I held it out to him. "Take this," I said.

Without realizing it, I'd pressed the blunt tip to the center of his chest.

He held up his hands in surrender.

"I'll do whatever the lady wants." The gleam and sensual pull grabbing at me was stronger than ever. "Within reason," he amended.

I stepped back and directed the hilt his way this time. "Then take this away before I hurt someone."

He quickly set the sword aside instead of returning it to the other room as I'd hoped he would. I could have used the moments to quiet my clamoring senses and either protectively immersed myself in the lunch tray Mrs. Lynds had left for me or another box of artifacts.

Forced to do something before he could follow up on the desire in his eyes, I said, "You've explained your sparse room, but not the rest. Why have you collected so many crime publications about . . . well—"

"About murdered women?"

I gulped. "Yes."

"Since you just handed me your weapon and you're not racing from my home screaming, I gather you don't suspect me of perpetrating such crimes."

"Heavens no!"

"I'm not sure which of us is the bigger fool. You for not suspecting me of murder or me for being relieved that you don't."

"I brought up the subject because I hope you're attempting to investigate the similarity between Lady Helen's murder and my cousin Mary's. Have you learned anything from the book on Druid sacrifices? I don't know that Constable Poole is giving the matter the attention it needs. At least that was my impression after Cassie and I spoke to him this morning."

"You what?"

"I accompanied Cassie into town this morning. She is convinced that Jamie Frye is innocent, and since his attack was against her, she thought it her duty to inform the authorities." I told Alex about our conversation with Constable Poole.

"Andromeda, this is not a game or an adventure for you and your sister to be meddling in. Investigating what happened to Mary understandably brought your family from Oxford to here. At great risk to herself, Cassie uncovered the fact that Mary hadn't been swept out to sea. Now you need to leave it to the authorities and to me. Learning about what was done to Helen and Mary from Dr. Luden has drastically changed everything."

"Have you found any other women who've been murdered and marked?"

"I don't think you heard me," he said.

I tossed my hands up in frustration. "Alex, you can at least discuss the matter with me and let me ask questions."

He sighed. "No. I've contacted all of the authorities along the coast and have not found any similar cases. No symbols carved upon the victims."

"What does the symbol look like? I know a great deal about different symbols in relation to ancient people and their artifacts. I may be able to help."

He hesitated.

"Given the severity of the situation, I don't think any stone should be left unturned or any resource ignored."

"I'll draw it for you as the doctor showed it to Sean and me."

I handed Alex my cataloguing notebook and a pen. "Use one of the blank pages in the back."

He flipped it open and glanced at the work I'd done already in his home. "Good Lord, woman. This is amazing." He scanned several more pages before turning to the blank pages in the back. He spoke as he drew. "You're not only thorough, but you've done more in a week than I'd expected could be done in several."

"As I consider such work my profession, I wouldn't be anything but thorough and timely."

He handed the notebook back to me and I glanced at the drawing. It was simple enough, a circle with a line bisecting it, only at the bottom and at the top, the line branched into three segments. The center line continued straight to the edge of the circle with the right angling to the right and the left angling to the left. A small oval lay in the center of the circle. I studied it for a minute, feeling my stomach turn over when I imagined where this had been carved. "I've never come across this particular symbol before."

"Neither Sean nor I recognize it either."

"It could mean more than one thing."

"For example?"

"The oval in the center looks like an eye."

"Which could mean a number of things. Evil eye. Watching. Is the killer saying he watched Helen and Mary?"

"Maybe." I shivered. Put in that context, it made me wonder if the killer was watching someone else now.

Alex wandered over to the open crates to peer down at some of the things I'd unearthed, not as unconcerned with what might be in the boxes as he'd indicated.

"You have to see these artifacts," I said. "They're amazing." I held up two heavy, gold figurines. "These are most likely worth a fortune. And you won't believe this." I pulled out an alabaster carving of a lotus blossom, running my fingers over the cool, solid smoothness of the stone. "Isn't this magnificent? Look at how gracefully made this flower is."

"Beautifully wrought," he said softly.

I glanced up and he just smiled, making my heart flutter and my cheeks heat. Artifacts. Focus on the artifacts. "Honestly, Alex, these things shouldn't be in a crate. They should be displayed at the very least, better yet if they were put in a museum for others to enjoy. How long did you say they have been like this?"

"I didn't say," he replied, his voice almost like a whisper. "The last trip my parents made together was to Egypt. My mother returned from the trip just before she gave birth to me and Sean. I asked my father one day when I was about seven years old why this room was kept as it was, untouched. Do you know what he said?"

I shook my head, afraid of what was coming.

"Upon returning from Egypt my mother gave strict instructions that no one was to touch her treasures. She'd unpack them herself just as soon as she had her son. These were my mother's quarters. There's an adjoining bedroom and nursery. He told me he was waiting for her to unpack the crates. I don't think my father has ever been back to this room since she died."

Was the earl mad? So grieved that he'd lost touch with

reality? Was there no part of the Killdarens' lives that wasn't touched by such sadness? "Are you going to forgive him," I asked quietly, recalling what Alex had told his father last Friday.

"No," Alex said. "His insecurity and cowardice cost Mary her life. You should be outraged that he'd had important facts about Helen's death deliberately kept quiet. Knowing what had been done to her could have changed things."

"What?" I asked, trying to play devil's advocate, maybe because in some way by not telling what I'd read from Rebecca's mind I was doing the same thing the earl had done. "I'm not attempting to excuse or condone what your father did, but the doctor said he didn't discover the mark on Lady Helen until a day or so after her death. You and Sean had already fought. So learning about it then wouldn't have changed things. If you had known of the mark before, what would you have done differently? Knowing now hasn't led you to the killer's door. How would knowing then have changed things?"

"How could it now? I would have . . ."

"What?"

His hands fisted. "I would have searched harder for Helen's killer."

"Why? Why does knowing about the symbol change things?"

"You want the ugly truth?"

I nodded and he turned away from me. I thought he wasn't going to answer then, but after a long moment, he spoke harshly.

"Because I would have known without a shadow of a doubt that neither I nor Sean had killed her. As it was, we were both so grieved and drunk that neither of us could remember much about what we did between Helen's rejection and Sean going over the cliff. Neither of us could swear upon our innocence. I've done nothing because there has always been a small doubt that either he or I had killed her."

I went to him, took hold of his shoulders, and pressed my

cheek to his back. "I'm sorry," I said. The dark cloud of emotions in him swirled stronger than ever, but I could see more than ever before; anger, pain, regret, passion, and a deep need to turn around and pull me into his embrace, a need that was completely at odds with his self-imposed prison. I'd gotten too close.

He pulled away from me then, stalking from the room, a man in pain and anguish, and part of my heart went with him.

12

I left work early, deliberating about what to do next. How could I get past the barriers Alex had built? Looking down at the emerald-eyed serpent ring on my finger, I wondered what a woman named Aphrodite would do under such circumstances. And just as I saw myself in Kubla Kahn's court with Marco Polo, I saw myself dressed in Grecian robes and draped with gold. I was a goddess, pampered and supreme. A woman whose appeal no man could resist. I very clearly saw Alex march into Aphrodite's private rooms, his dark hair cut shorter, his pirate's air hardened beneath the armored demeanor of a Greek warrior. His skin just as tanned against the stark white of his dress that molded tightly to the supple curve of his taut muscles. He was a man fearless in life and in battle, a man insatiable in passion, a man that Aphrodite had seen from afar and wanted as hers.

"I am Alexander. You wished to see me?" Alexander said.

"Yes," Aphrodite said, rising from her cushioned divan to step into the full light of the sun pouring into the room. The golden light bathed her lush beauty to a dazzling brilliance, and she knew it. Alexander was indeed great, godlike. She watched his eyes slide down her body and saw the hunger in them rise. She noted the slight parting of his lips as if anticipating the taste of her. Arching her back so that her full breasts strained against the almost sheer fabric of her dress, she moved gracefully, pouring two cups of wine and handing him a goblet. "I'm in need of a man."

He lifted a brow. "A warrior? A steward? An advisor?"

"A lover." She drew a long sip from her spiced wine, sliding her tongue over its lingering taste upon her lips.

He arched a brow. "I've always admired directness in my men and my foes."

"Then should a woman be less than a man? Should you value her directness less?"

He closed the gap between them and took the goblet of wine from her. She thought with a thrill that at last the man she'd wanted from afar for so long would be hers, at least for a night. Instead of setting down the wine, he handed her his goblet. Then he drank from hers, placing his mouth exactly where she'd placed hers. "You're obviously not one of my loyal men. Question is, are you friend or foe?"

Aphrodite smiled and drank from his goblet. "Neither. I am your lover."

He laughed. "I determine who my lovers are."

"Then I eagerly await your decision, Alexander," Aphrodite said as she poured the wine she held down her dress. Then, loosening her belt, she slipped off her robes. Moving to the puddle of sunshine warming her large bed, she laid down. She cupped her breasts, lifting them as an offering of headily drenched fruit. "I hope I won't have to wait too long. Wine dries rather quickly."

"Only when there isn't enough," he said, approaching the bed. He dribbled more on her from the goblet he held and followed the action with the heat of his tongue. A fire lit hotly in her loins and burned bright with every lash of his tongue. She purred as the wine slid down to her navel. He drank from her there, not letting a drop escape. He pressed his palm against the fire of her sex, slipping his fingers intimately against her yearning flesh.

Then he stood back and drained his goblet. Aphrodite rose to her elbows, her full breasts aching for more, her body yearning for the hard staff straining against his robe.

"I'll let you know when I decide," he said, then turning, he walked for the door.

Aphrodite didn't even blink. She rolled from the bed and snatched up a sword. "Move another step and suffer the consequences."

He turned, undaunted by the sharp weapon. "And what would those be?"

She laughed. "You'll lose your dress and walk naked through the streets. You may lie to yourself about your desire for me, but I'll not let you lie to the world."

"Then shall we duel?" he said, humor glinting his green eyes.

"With what?" she asked.

"Sword or tongue, lady's choice."

"And for what shall we duel?" she asked

"My choice. To be determined upon the end of the battle.

Aphrodite tossed aside her sword. "I choose tongue."

"A shame," he said stripping of his robes. "My sword was all ready to play."

"Miss . . . Miss . . . can you hear me? We're here."

I shook my head, removing my gaze from Aphrodite's ring, and stared openmouthed at the driver, who stood waiting to help me down from the buggy. Bits of information slowly filtered into my mind. No naked Alexander. No plush bed. No naked me.

The driver waved wildly, but not at me. "Mrs. Murphy," he shouted. "I think Miss Andrews is ill."

I scowled and straightened my shoulders. "I'm just fine, sir." I set my hand in his and climbed down on shaky legs, seeing in his mind an image of him drinking in a pub, singing at the top of his lungs with friends who were even worse off key than he. While I was far from fine, I wasn't going to let anyone else know.

Mrs. Murphy ran down the steps with Bridget and Cassie on her heels.

"Lass, what's ailing you?" Mrs. Murphy asked, peering closely at me. I had no doubt that if Alex had kissed me today as he had before, she would have seen the evidence. As it was now, I greatly feared she could read my scandalous thoughts.

"Andrie? What happened? Why have you returned so early? You look flushed." Cassie set her palm on my forehead, making me thankful for the very first time in my life that it was I who could read thoughts and not she.

I drew a deep breath. "I'm fine, really. Just a number of things on my mind and I lost track of time. It surprised me to find we'd already arrived."

"Still, you're early."

"A—Lord Alexander thinks that I'm working too hard," I explained.

Both Cassie and Bridget gave me an odd look, telling me I wasn't going to get off that easily.

Cassie waved her hand toward the bright blooms and sculpted shrubs sprawling from the graveled path. "Bridget and I were just about to take a stroll through the garden. Why don't you come with us?"

Knowing I'd not escape, I joined them. Considering the wild path my thoughts ran when I was alone, their company was a good thing for the moment. The gardens at Killdaren's Castle were somewhat of an oddity and not just from what one saw at first glance. They were overshadowed on the left by Sean's dark, gargoyle decorated observatory, and literally hedged in at the back by a large, dense maze, a teasing puzzle Sean's mother had spent years planning and had built to please the earl, who at one time had thrived on puzzles.

Now the maze was something Cassie and Sean considered having removed, a place of unpleasant memories for everyone except the earl. Lady Helen had met her death in the gazebo at the center of the maze. Jamie had snatched Cassie from the edge of the garden and dragged her into the maze and then down through tunnels that ran from the gazebo to the ground beneath the Circle of Stone Virgins, and amazingly to the cliffs at Dragon's Cove. I would liked to have seen them for myself, but they were closed off after Cassie's rescue.

No, what made Killdaren's gardens particularly unusual was the collection of statues reining over its glorious dahlias, lush roses, and daffodils, sweet, nectarous beauties that never failed to attract the prettiest butterflies and the fattest bumbling bees. Even the birds seemed to sing louder when amid the collection of gods and goddesses of many myths. From Poseidon and Zeus to Aphrodite and Venus, their creamy marbled nude images were larger than life . . . everywhere. It made for a rather interesting walk. Thankfully, today we went opposite Zeus's direction.

"Where's Gemini?" I asked, hoping to divert the conversation from me.

"Wrapped in a blanket in the drawing room playing checkers with Rebecca while Prudence is embroidering a chessboard, and Sean is asleep. Now let's not waste time. Why are you back so early? Did something untoward happen with Alex?"

"Good heavens, no. He's upset about his father keeping the symbol marking Lady Helen a secret. He blames the earl for Mary's death." Then I bit my lip. What was it about older sisters that seemed to pop the truth out of you even if you didn't want it to? I hadn't planned to tell Cassie everything. She had enough to worry about. "He has been in contact with all of the authorities along the coast, searching to see if any other women have died under similar circumstances."

"So he's of the same mind as we are? Jamie is innocent," Cassie said. "Bridget and I came out here to discuss the matter. Sean insists that I wipe everything from my mind and fill it with plans for the babies. I can't. What did Alex find out?"

I knew the only way to get her to rest at all was if she

thought someone else was taking care of the problem. "No other women who've died have been marked with a symbol."

"What else did Alex have to say, Andrie?" Cassie asked.

"Not much. He did draw me a picture of the symbol that marked Mary and Lady Helen."

"Great day in the morning, Andromeda Andrews, why didn't you say so first thing! What was it? Sean refused to show me."

"It's in my bag in my cataloguing notebook. Which I left in the buggy."

"Come on." Cassie grabbed my hand. "Let's go get it."

"I'm with you two," Bridget said, thankfully taking Cassie's other hand. Stuart would most likely be around the stables, and I had enough sensual thoughts of my own to contend with. Cassie's mind was totally focused on the mystery of Mary and Lady Helen's death and thus safe for the moment.

We dashed to the stables. My driver was still tending the horses he'd unhitched from the buggy and I asked him about my notebook. He promptly retrieved it and we hurried from the stable with Bridget lagging behind.

"He might be in town," Cassie said.

"Most likely," Bridget answered. "It's not like I would have said anything to him if he was here, mind you. But it does get a girl's dander up when he's not even around so she can flaunt herself in front of him and make him regret what he's missing."

I laughed. Not because what Bridget said was so funny, but because Bridget had just expressed very clearly what I'd experienced the whole week Alex had been gone. Even today I'd been miffed to learn he wasn't at home. Stopping a few feet away from the stable, I dug my catalogue out of my bag and opened it up to Alex's drawing.

Cassie exhaled in disappointment as she peered down at it. "I've never seen anything like it before."

Bridget squinted at the book. "The sun's in my eyes. Let me hold the book."

I handed it to her, and she turned so that she could see it better. "I think there's something like this at the Circle of the Stone Virgins," she said.

Cassie gasped and my pulsed skittered.

"Now, I said I *think* there *might* be. I haven't spent a lot of time looking around so I can't swear, but . . ."

"Let's go look," Cassie said. "It's not more than five minutes away, up the trail behind the stables."

The pounding of approaching horses' hooves gave us a fright. Bridget stuffed my notebook behind her back as we looked up to see Stuart almost upon us. He pulled the stallion to a halt and swiftly dismounted. "Ladies," he said, nodding his head politely.

"Hello," we all said in various tones, none of them good.

His dark gaze shot between each of our faces. "You want to tell me what is going on?"

Bridget huffed. "Ye don't want to talk to me when I'm a wanting to talk to you, Stuart Frye. So I'm not talking to you when you're a wanting me to either. Come on, ladies. Let's continue our walk." Bridget then marched on past the stables, heading toward the trail that led to Dartmoor's End.

Cassie and I followed, barely resisting the urge to giggle, but once we were out of sight of the barn, Bridget burst into laughter. "Lawd. I may not like it much when he's dishing it out, but I love it when a man gives me the ammunition to fire back at him when the shoe is on the other foot."

We laughed a bit more, but when we reached the trail leading to the Circle of the Stone Virgins, I halted. "I don't know if this is such a good idea. How do we know it's safe?"

"Andrie?" Cassie looked at me, flabbergasted. "You're shying away from an archaeological site that's less than a few stones' throw from the bed you sleep in? I've been there several times. In fact you insisted on going there the moment you learned of it. You forced me to go, if you remember right. This isn't like you. Do you know more than what you've told Bridget and me?"

I did, but none of it had to do with the old stones at the Circle of the Stone Virgins. "It's just that Mary's body was found in a chamber under the site. And if Bridget thinks that there's a carving at the site that might match what the killer did to her, I don't think we should go there un-armed."

"Blimey, I've been traipsing through those stones since I could walk," Bridget said. "Ya don' think that he's there, do you, Andrie?"

"No." It was ridiculous to think the murderer was sitting in the circle waiting for us. "Let's hurry, though." We started out at a brisk walk, then ran until we reached the carved stone pillars encircling the Druid god. A sense of something otherworldly hung about the clearing, as if the rules that bound earth and humans didn't apply to the spirits that dwelt within the crudely carved stones. The seven virgins surrounding Daghdha had a benevolent feel to their curved smooth-ness, and stood in sharp contrast to the lewd figure of a naked-below-the-waist man with a large belly and even larger unmentionables. I could barely force myself to look at his ugliness or how he gripped the Uaithne, his magical carved harp—the frame of which was a naked woman bent unnatu-rally backward.

I suddenly wished we hadn't come, and from the way Cassie and Bridget stood unmoving next to me I guessed they might feel the same way. The three of us were at the edge of the forest, staring cautiously at the circle.

"Where do you think you saw the symbol?" Cassie asked. That she whispered so softly spoke volumes as to her own fear.

"I'm not sure," Bridget said.

"We should go," I said. "I don't know why, but I have a bad feeling."

"It might just be that she has more sense than the rest of you," Stuart Frye's deep voice interrupted the quiet, making us all jump with fright.

Bridget pressed a hand to her heart. "Don't you dare tell

me you're a worried about me, Stuart, as you've nearly kilt me yourself. What are you a doing here?"

Stuart moved from the trees to join us on the trail. "Finding out what you three are up to. I'd advise none of you to ever gamble over cards. You're lousy liars. I'll ask once more before I alert Sean. What are you three up to?"

"Sean did not become God the day I married him, Stuart," Cassie said, a miffed frown creasing her brow.

Stuart laughed. "I bet he felt like one though. Listen, I'm not your keeper, Cassie, and you more than anyone know that I am inclined to let a woman make up her mind about what's right for her—"

"What?" Bridget cried, outraged. "You've never let me—"

Stuart spoke louder to be heard over Bridget. "BUT when it comes to a woman's physical safety and future, I can't stand back and let her hang herself."

"What's he talking about, Cassie?" Bridget demanded.

I wanted to know, too, but I didn't have to ask. Since I was holding Cassie's hand I saw her flash of memory. I saw her talking to Stuart and then going into Sean's bedroom, finding him in pain; her kissing Sean in his bed . . . I snatched my hand from Cassie's.

"I'll tell you later," Cassie said. "Show Stuart the symbol and what you told us, Bridget."

Stuart looked at the symbol and paled. "It's here," he said. "At least most of it is. Just eliminate the oval from the center of the circle, and you find the rest of it carved inside the sacrificial bowl at Daghdha's feet over there. We need to tell Sean and notify Constable Poole."

"Then it wasn't a poacher this summer, was it?" Cassie whispered.

"What are you talking about, Cassie?" I asked.

"The bowl at Daghdha's feet. Bridget and I walked through the site on our way back from the village one Sunday and found blood in the bowl."

"I don't know if it was a poacher or not," Stuart said. "I found an animal trap in the woods not far away that day.

There was blood on it, but nobody has come and reset it since. I've been checking on it. Now I think we should all leave."

I didn't argue. I didn't need to peek into the sacrificial bowl, not with the story of a sacrifice so fresh in my mind. We returned to the house, sobered by the ominous implications that someone in this modern day and age had taken up the ritual of offering blood to a pagan god. And perhaps offering more than just the blood of animals—offering the lives of women.

13

That night I couldn't sleep, too many things were swirling through my mind, thoughts about Alex and the prison he'd sentenced himself to, remembrances of Aphrodite seducing her Alexander that led me to think about seducing Alex, then the whole discovery about the symbol's connection to the Druid ruins.

Cassie had told me about the legend behind the Circle of the Stone Virgins earlier this summer, when Gemini and I had first come to live at Killdaren's Castle. Daghdha, High King of the famed faery folk the *Tuatha de Danaan*, and a god worshipped by the Druids, was notorious for seducing mortal women, a fact that made his queen very jealous. At the Circle of the Stone Virgins it is said that he played his harp made of living oak, the Uaithne, to seduce seven of the world's most beautiful mortal virgins on the eve of Beltane. Then, after having his pleasure of them, he turned their earthly bodies to stone so that his queen would never learn of his deed. Or, it was rumored that he put the stones there to dupe his queen, and he actually kidnapped the seven virgins and took them to a secret lair to pleasure him for eternity.

Giving up on sleep, I lit my lamp and searched for a warmer robe in my armoire. My hand came in contact with the Dragon's Curse book. I eagerly snatched it up, shuddering as I pushed away the historical fact cards I had stolen from the music room. Daghdha had used music to lure his seven virgins, and music had played a role in each of the women's deaths. I wondered if there was a connection.

It was enough to make me think twice about doing something as simple as singing a song, or listening to an instrument for that matter.

I stretched out on the gold brocade divan in the corner of my room, but the more I read about the Dragon's Curse and how horrifically it had played out in the Killdaren family history, the more chilled I became. I finally had to move to my bed to read, curled up under the thick blue- and gold-tasseled counterpane to keep from shivering. Age after age, time and again, whenever male twins were born, one died at the other's hand. When I reached the year of 1490 and read where one brother in an authoritative position in Cornwall had accused his brother of heresy and saw to not only his public execution but had had his brother's wife burned at the stake for witchcraft as well, I shut the book. When one focused on the history of the Killdaren family twins the Dragon's Curse seemed so real and so hopeless to overcome that it was more than I could absorb. I needed time to think about what I'd read and to get some perspective on it before I could do anything to help Alex or Sean.

And I either needed to find something else to read or forget sleep for the rest of not only the night but my life as well. Dark dreams were sure to plague me. Donning my slippers, I snatched up my lamp and headed for the library. Even Bridget and Cassie's book on vampires would be more conducive to helping me get to sleep than reading or thinking about so much ill intent and death.

The library shelves were ordered by subjects. I started

with the As, passing through an entire case of books on astronomy, and moved quickly to the Es, thinking that a book
on equestrian matters, especially one on the Friesian breed,
would give me something to discuss with Alex, or at least
prompt a few intelligent questions on the subject. Something
needed to bridge the gap that I felt had been made by his
walking away from my touch today. I found an interesting
book on equine dressage. As I slipped it from the shelf another title jumped out at me. *A Gentleman's Treatise Upon
the Art of Fencing*. Looking further, I found *Coup de Temps:
Besting Your Opponent*.

Fingers tingling, I stacked the books in my arms and turned
to leave the library only to come to a startled halt in the middle
of the room. For a moment, in the shadowed light, I thought
Alex stood with his back against the door jamb and his arms
crossed in a familiar way, but it was Sean.

"You're up late," he said.

"I couldn't sleep. I thought you and Cassie would be hard
at work on the stars tonight."

He sighed heavily. "Cassie's not speaking to me and I
can't concentrate. It's a good thing no astronomical events
were predicted for tonight."

"I guess Cassie is still angry then."

"That would be an understatement," he said, pushing from
the doorway to march across the room with a limping stride,
his hands fisted with frustration. He didn't have his cane
with him tonight, so his gait was more marked. "Why won't
she listen to reason?" he demanded.

"All she wanted to do was to ride into town with you, the
earl, and Stuart to report what we discovered to Constable
Poole. Why was her request unreasonable?"

"Because," he said, tossing his hands up in the air to
prove his point. "I can't allow her to involve herself anymore
in this investigation. Don't you understand? Even if it turns
out that Jamie didn't mean Cassie any harm in kidnapping
her, it still happened. Now that she is with child . . . I—"

"It makes loving her even more painful."

"Bloody hell, yes!" Despite his disability he swung around so fast that I stepped back in surprise and had to juggle to keep the books in my arms. "Sorry, that's exactly how I feel," he said, reaching out to help steady the books. "Fencing?"

Heat flagged my cheeks and I cleared my throat. "Well, your brother sort of offered to teach me a little about it."

"He did!" Both of Sean's dark brows shot up. "I thought you were cataloguing the eyesores our ancestors hung about our necks."

I stiffened my back. "I am, and they are most certainly not eyesores. They're an amazingly rich inheritance of history that needs to be properly noted and displayed, not just stuffed into a room and forgotten. Now, let's talk about Cassie. Have you told her how you feel?"

"She knows how much I love her."

"That isn't the same as telling her, now. Also, you're going to have to realize that you married a woman who has never sat idle or docile. I think you should involve her with the investigation on some level."

"No. I won't compromise her safety, but I will make sure she understands how much I love her."

"Well, I guess I'll say good night then." I started from the library.

"Wait, Andromeda. What exactly is Alex showing you about fencing?"

"Very little as of yet. He's extremely good. He mentioned that you both began learning to be sword masters together before . . ."

"You can speak of the fight."

"I was going to say accident. He didn't mean for you to fall from the cliff. It was an accident and both of you need to stop punishing him for it."

"You're talking about something you know nothing of. You weren't there. You don't know what it was like. The anger."

"No. I wasn't there. I don't know what it was like, but I do know that a man doesn't sentence himself to a life of desolation because he meant to kill someone and didn't. Only a man who didn't mean to kill someone and almost did would."

"What do you mean?"

"While your brother wasn't at home, I went to catalogue any pictures, or art, or artifacts in his quarters, figuring that his would be similar to yours. You've a wealth of interesting antiquities, from medieval weaponry to suited armor."

He lifted a skeptical brow that had me blushing from my lie. "And?"

"There was nothing. Not a picture. Not a single item except a desk, a chair, a table, a lamp, and a bed. Your brother lives like a monk in many ways. He denies himself attachment to anything that is not functional for his existence. He goes through the motions of life on the surface. He can be seen riding a horse at breakneck speed, or training one with a magical hand. He goes to town for an occasional event. He entertains Lord Ashton and Mr. Drayson at card games, and can even be a charming host over a meal. But it is all a front, a smokescreen that hides the fact that every day he is just passing time until he dies, alone. And it is such a waste, because *you* don't live the empty, dependent life he feels he condemned you to. You're one of the most remarkable people I know. You've triumphed over tragedy and have carved a very unique existence for yourself. You don't need to have the title he's sacrificing himself to give you. You have more than he ever will." I turned quickly to leave, sadness scorching my heart.

"Andromeda!" Sean set his hand on my shoulder before I reached the door and my knees nearly buckled from the pain inside of him. Pain of loving his brother, of being betrayed, and of fear that the Dragon's Curse would continue. "What are you saying? I dissolved our pact to never marry. He's free."

I stepped from the weight of his hand and faced him without the burden of his pain. "No, you didn't, and you can't free him. Because the pact isn't with you; it's inside himself and what he feels he owes you because of what happened. And don't you dare tell him I said anything. He'll never trust me again. I didn't mean to tell you and I shouldn't have. But no one seems to consider Alex in what happened."

Sean blinked at me a moment, stunned, and I took the opportunity to leave before I could say or do something else I shouldn't, like give in to the tears filling my eyes.

"You're going to need an épeé and a *contre-attaque*," Sean called out to me down the corridor.

"A what?"

"Meet me in the center hall at dawn and I'll show you. And thank you," he said. "Cassie will have to talk to me now."

"Why?" I asked, blinking to bring him into focus.

"Do you think she'll miss out on a fencing lesson?"

I went back to my room, shaking my head. Sean may have found a way to win this battle, but I hated to tell him that it wasn't going to do a thing to solve the war brewing between him and Cassie. The trouble was, I understood both of them, and they were both right and both wrong.

I traveled to Dragon's Cove the next morning sure about only one thing: If the opportunity to spend more time with Alex presented itself, I wasn't going to walk away from it. Alex needed me, and deep inside myself I knew my feelings for him were such that I'd never feel this deeply for another. Would it be right or wrong to allow myself to experience the fullness of our passion before I resigned myself to living a life alone?

No matter what happened to me personally, I had to do what I could to make him see he had needlessly put himself into prison. And I thought I knew a way to force him to listen to me. At sword-point, no less. When I left Killdaren's Castle, Cassie and Sean were at blunted sword points with each other, and Cassie was talking to him, for now. Or at least *at* him.

Seeing Sean in action this morning made me wonder if Alex even knew how well Sean had compensated for his disability. With the help of his cane, Sean moved adeptly and rather deadly as well as he showed us some fencing maneuvers, especially considering the sharp, hooked blade hidden in the tip of his cane.

A slight plan began to form, one that involved Alex, me, a challenge, and I hoped just the right amount of luck to pull off the little trick Sean taught me this morning. I'd done a good bit of reading late into the night and at least intellectually knew what a *contre-attaque* was.

After yesterday, I expected Alex would have escaped to his ship to prowl the coast again, and I'd have to wait another week to see him. So the sight of him charging up on a splendid gelding, with another saddled horse in tow, stole my breath. I'd yet to enter the Dragon doors, and stood on the steps seeing the doors in light of what I'd read about the Dragon's Curse.

Cassie was wrong. The dragons weren't just wounded and standing. They were indeed dead, but had not fallen, and it was hard to imagine that Alex saw himself that way. His charismatic aura was so full of life.

I watched him approach, reveling in him. His dark hair, like rich, black silk, waved back from the strong, sensual lines of his face to a daring length that brushed the top of his broad shoulders. The gleam in his vibrant green gaze matched the unorthodox manner of his coatless attire, for he seemed to be undressing me with his eyes.

"Iris has something to show you down by the stables," he said. "You did say you could ride, didn't you?"

"Yes." I stared warily at the lively brown mare he'd brought. "My experience, though, is somewhat limited to mares of notable age."

"Then Delilah will be perfect. She responds well to a light touch and will follow Samson to the ends of the earth."

He dismounted, bringing his strength, vitality, and heat so close he made me tingle everywhere.

"You must be riding Samson then," I said, managing to sound inane despite my efforts.

"None other," he said. "Do you need help mounting?"

"Well." I glanced cautiously at Delilah. She was larger, younger, and definitely had all four hooves on solid ground and none of them in the grave. Not at all similar to the other horses I'd ridden. "Maybe a little." I swallowed hard. "Are you sure she's gentle? From the way she glared at Samson as you rode up, Samson should be guarding his mane rather than grazing on sweet violets."

He laughed as he set his hands to my waist, unexpectedly picking me up to set me in the sidesaddle. "If she handles a blade as well as you do, then he has nothing to fear."

"What?" I said, grabbing his shoulders even as I stiffened my back in protest of his slight. The result was disastrous in that I didn't quite gain my balance in the sidesaddle before moving, and thus fell forward, burying my bosom in his face before I could push back. He slid his hand up from my waist to cup the sides of my breasts, seemingly pressing them even more firmly to him. I flushed from the tip of my toes to every mentionable and unmentionable place imaginable before I could extricate myself without any help whatsoever. All he did was laugh harder and, considering the dampness between my breasts, he may have licked me.

"You, sir, are no gentleman. That was an accident and you didn't lift a finger."

He cocked a questioning brow, reminding me he'd adeptly lifted ten fingers.

"To help me," I added. "Not yourself." I took Delilah's reins from him and she skittered back a little, making me bite my lip in fear.

"My apologies," he said, not looking the least bit contrite as he mounted Samson.

I set my concentration on staying upright and trying to show a degree of confidence I didn't quite have. Something

I would never have unless I ventured out from the artifacts I buried myself beneath.

"We'll take the long way to the stables so you can see a little of the land," he said, leading us to the left and toward the crash of the waves. After passing through a small barrier of low-lying trees, we came to a high edge of black rocks where the horizon became an endless vision of deep blue.

"I suppose Dragon's Cove was named from the Killdaren curse?" I asked, desperately trying to distract myself from the fact that I was on a horse. Even though the horse seemed to be docilely following Alex's lead at a leisurely pace, I couldn't seem to breathe. Every bumpy step bruised some unmentionable part of me.

"Actually no. The Killdaren who settled here did so because the land seemed to be as cursed as the family. The castle is built on the crest of a high cliff that rises sharply from the sea. From a ship, the cliff and the treacherous rocks below have the appearance of a clawing dragon, with the crashing waves as its continuous roar. Ships sailing along the coast in the fog often wrecked upon the rocks and the survivors swore the sleeping dragon had awakened and attacked their ships."

"It's easy to see how those stories took root," I said, looking out at the dark rocks, hearing the roar, and feeling the deadly energy.

Once past the cliff, he paused at a trail. "If you follow this path, you wind your way down to a cove with a sandy beach." I nodded, biting my lip against my discomfort. How ever did people *enjoy* riding? Moving back through the woods he crossed in front of the castle and down a long stretch of rolling grass, increasing his pace, and I groaned at the sharp pain as I bounced stiffly in the saddle. Everything was so different than trudging along on a piebald mare around a training rink.

He must have heard me because he dropped back to ride beside me. "You don't have to concentrate so hard at riding, you know. You look as if you're trying to solve the world's problems. Relax and let your body flow with the movement of the horse's steps. Use her movements to balance yourself and don't try and fight her sway."

"That's easier said than done," I replied through clenched teeth, dismayed that my inexperience was so apparent, despite my efforts.

"Shut your eyes," he instructed, moving closer to my side. "You'll feel the rhythm."

My eyes widened instead.

"Go ahead," he urged. "Trust me. I won't let anything happen."

I shut my eyes. In the ensuing darkness, I was carried forward with no control over where I was going. It was the strangest feeling I'd ever known, and it gave me a better understanding of what every moment of Rebecca's life was like.

"Yes, that's it," he said softly, easing the timbre of his voice over me like a warm caress. "Loosen your fingers, ease your legs apart a little, and let your boot rest in the stirrup and absorb the brunt of her stride. Relax into her pace."

After a few minutes, I didn't feel as if I would fall anymore, and surprisingly the ride become less painful, almost fun. I opened my eyes, amazed. I had to admit the day itself was glorious. Bright sunshine warmed my back and a fresh, salty breeze cooled my cheeks. The crash of the sea's waves against the cliffs made me feel as if I heard the very heartbeat of the land, or that of the sleeping dragon, if you went by the stories of sailors.

"There," Alex said. "You feel it now, don't you? The ease and the harmony of riding in rhythm. You learn fast. Now look ahead at the terrain and anticipate what Delilah is going to do in response to your lead and you will soon be master over the horse. Fencing is the same in that you let your body flow with the rhythm of the fight, but you have the added uncertainty of only being able to control and anticipate your opponent's moves to a certain point. After that . . . well, things can become difficult and much more interesting."

"It sounds very much like marriage," I said.

"What does?"

"Horse riding and fencing. Unfortunately, Cassie isn't proving to be as predictable as Sean thought she'd be."

"I can't say that I'm surprised, but what do you mean specifically?"

I frowned, trying to reduce Cassie and Sean's conflict over the past few weeks to a simple idea. "The basic problem is that Sean and Cassie's expectations of what the other should do and how they should react to each other isn't matching up to who that other person is. For instance, when I left, Sean was sputtering with outrage because Cassie had likened him to a peacock."

"A peacock! Good God, your sister called my brother a peacock?" Alex roared with laughter that would have had a less skilled rider tumbling from his horse. I had to laugh as well, for it was fairly funny, only I hadn't dared laugh at the time. Alex wiped tears from the corners of his eyes. "What did Sean do to deserve such a fate?"

"Herein lays the problem. Cassie is miffed that Sean refused to let her to go to town with everyone to report what she, Bridget, and I discovered about the symbol. She contends that Constable Poole will never accord women with the necessary intelligence to investigate a crime if the men involved always prance like peacocks into town with the information the women have gathered. Sean doesn't want Cassie involved in any way with the investigation."

Alex brought Samson to a sudden stop. Having moved ahead, I had to turn Delilah to face him. "What's wrong?"

"What was discovered about the symbol?" he said harshly.

"According to Bridget, and verified by Stuart, most of the symbol is carved inside the sacrificial bowl at Daghdha's feet in the Circle of the Stone Virgins. We still don't know its meaning, but it is a start. They didn't send a messenger to let you know?"

"No. I'm obviously not important enough to keep informed." He moved ahead at a faster, tenser pace.

I had to hurry to catch up. "It was just last night and I don't think you were meant to be slighted at all. It was more likely Sean and Stuart were arguing with Cassie and Bridget too much to even think about anything else."

"Sean and Stuart are absolutely right to not want Cassie and Bridget involved. So why is there a problem?"

"What do you mean, 'absolutely right'? How can you say that? Cassie and I were asking questions about this long before any of you were. All of you were so mired in your own worlds that you couldn't see anything else, and still are to a large extent. This investigation is important to all of us. You can't expect women to just turn off their minds like a water faucet. And Sean is partially wrong. He should have let Cassie go to town with him. He should discuss the situation with her and let her do things that she can do without jeopardizing her safety, instead of pigheadedly insisting that she do what he thinks is right in all things. Before this came up, they were already in disagreement about a married woman working."

"I don't see your point? Why should she?"

"Because she wants to. There should be nothing wrong with her using her intelligence and skill for monetary gain," I replied, exasperated. "Perhaps it is a good thing I'll never marry." I spurred Delilah ahead and did so with very little apprehension. I had no room in my mind for fear at the moment. The ease to which I adjusted to Delilah's gallop surprised and pleased me.

He caught up to me and reached over, grasping Delilah's reins, bringing us to a halt. "Why will you never marry?" he asked, his keen gaze searching mine with such concern that I relaxed my stiffening spine until he spoke again. "Are you with child?"

14

I reeled in the saddle, catching Alex's arm for balance "What? How could you think *that*!" My sputtering surpassed Sean's peacock outrage.

"Thank God. Please forgive me," Alex said, shutting his eyes a moment as if he were offering a silent prayer. Then he met my gaze, contrite. "When you came to me saying that you were in need of a job to support yourself, that you would soon not be able to live with your family, I assumed you'd been compromised and left alone to face the consequences."

My cheeks burned. "But how could you—"

"I've known men callous enough, my own father for one. He never took responsibility for his indiscretions. Married Mrs. Frye to his groomsman, which ended in tragedy, and as far as I can tell he's never lifted a finger to help Prudence either."

"I'm not talking about that! How could you think that I would kiss you and let you touch me if I'd been involved with another, especially if I carried another man's child?"

"You're too innocent about the world, Andromeda. Women have been known to—"

"Not this woman!"

"Then it would seem I owe you yet another apology. Now, will you tell me why you are so desperate to support yourself? And in a hurry, mind you. That was something else that influenced my erroneous assumption, for you did say you needed to be able to support yourself very soon." He frowned. "Why the devil can't you remain with your family? I know you love them. They love you. And as far as I've seen and heard, you've no angst, strife, or curses between you and your sisters. So why?"

I hesitated, so tempted to tell him, but I couldn't. The words lodged in my throat. I couldn't take the chance that Alex would reject me, not only because I needed the employment, but also because I wanted more time with him before risking everything. I wanted to see him whole. "I'm sorry. I can't tell you. But I will say that I am not with child." I forced a smile. "Has Iris had her foal? Is that the surprise you mentioned this morning?"

"I'll let her show you," he said after a long moment. I could tell from the set of his shoulders that I'd alienated him. Thankfully he moved past the training ring toward the stables just ahead of us and I followed. We'd ridden beside the long stretch of lawn and pasture sprawling from the back of the castle. Perfectly rounded hedges were backed by lush trees filled with the chatter of birds and the hum of roving bees. In the distance I could see the small table on the terrace where Alex and I had shared lunch. At the time I had assumed the gardens of the estate were located elsewhere, but I didn't see evidence of them today either. "Do you not have a formal garden area?"

"On the trail leading down to the shore there's a gazebo that is surrounded by a garden, but we don't have one adjoining the castle. Good pastureland this close to the coast is difficult to find, so we made the most of it here at Dragon's Cove, even if it meant being highly unconventional. But I gather you've already discovered that the Killdarens are never conventional."

Once at the stables, he dismounted and came to assist me. When I set my hand in his, I couldn't see into his thoughts and his expression was more reserved than usual, making me wonder if I hadn't lost more by not telling him the truth. After all, he'd shared his thoughts and emotions with me to a certain degree. Stepping away as quickly as he could, he tethered the horses and moved on into the stable.

The strong scents of horses and hay mixed with the sunshine and the salt of the sea. I blinked to adjust to the cool dimness inside the stable. Horses neighed and nickered amid the crooning mutterings of several groomsmen who were attending to their chores. I found Alex peering over the door of a stall about halfway down the main earthen corridor. A proud smile sat warmly on his full mouth, dimpling his cheek and softening the harsh angles of his brow and jaw.

Slightly breathless, I joined him and rose to my tiptoes to see over the rough wood. Iris stood near the door, crunching on oats from a bucket next to a feeding shelf of fresh hay. Nestled up against her side, butting her stomach with its head and looking for milk, was a beautiful black foal. Its delicate, long, slender legs weren't quite steady yet, but its tail wagged like a pro. I exhaled, satisfied and relieved. I hadn't even realized in the back of my mind that I'd even worried about how Iris would settle in.

"Meet Eros, Andromeda."

"Oh, he's so perfect, he's almost magical! Can I touch him?"

"Sure. Just move slowly, and let him come to you. Iris is still a bit skittish yet with others." Speaking low, in a language I didn't understand, Alex murmured softly to the horses as he opened the stall door, moving inside first then allowing me to slip in behind him. When he shut the stall door, he slid his arm to my back and urged me in front of him. Heat from his body pressed against me from the backs of my thighs to the nape of my neck. My pulse surged and my breasts tingled. I had to fight to keep my gaze on Eros, for every part of me wanted to turn and wrap my arms around the man behind me, to press my lips to his and taste the excitement vibrating between us.

He seemed to know what I was thinking, for he slid his hand around to my stomach and pressed me tighter to him. His sharp inhale sent a shivering thrill through me. My lips parted and my head fell back against his shoulder.

"What scent do you wear?" he asked, his voice but a whisper as his lips brushed my ear.

"Lavender with a drop of rosemary oil. It never fails to refresh me." I turned my face toward him, feeling as if my world had shrunk to this single moment and all that mattered was to feel his kiss.

"You mean it never fails to seduce." Gaze intent, he angled my way; his full lips softly brushed mine for a moment, then hungrily claimed them. Moaning with pleasure, I opened to him, welcoming the dueling demand of his kiss as I met the stroke of his tongue with my eager response. I slid my hand to his cheek, cupping his clean-shaven jaw in my palm, wanting more from him. He groaned. His other hand wrapped around me and the firm heat of his palm ran deliciously up my stomach to cover my breast. I arched to him, offering more, only to gasp in confusion and surprise from a punch to my stomach.

"Ooh!" I exhaled sharply as a second hit landed. It took a moment for my eyes to focus and to realize that Eros had approached and was playfully jabbing me. "He's strong."

Alex released me, chuckling as I held out my hand to Eros. He sniffed my fingers for a moment then butted his velvety muzzle into my palm and licked. Laughing, I knelt down and brushed my hand down his neck. "He's already looking for treats."

"He must be a ladies' man. He's yet to be that friendly with me. We named him well, I think."

"We?"

"Certainly. The name Eros would have never crossed my mind if you hadn't suggested Iris for his mother." His gaze centered on my mouth, telling me it wasn't my naming Iris that had brought the god of love and sexual desire into his thoughts.

"Alex! Where are you?" I jumped at the sharpness in the Earl of Dartraven's voice. Alex's father was clearly not at all happy.

"Hell," Alex muttered.

Eros skittered to his mother as she backed nervously across the stall, neighing a warning. Remembering her frightened dash on the ship, I quickly gained my feet and backed firmly against Alex, unsure of what Iris would do. Alex spoke softly to her again, and she immediately settled. He opened the stall door and pulled me out with him, then turned to face his father.

"What in the bloody hell are you doing, yelling like that in here?" Alex hissed. "You could have caused Miss Andrews harm as well as my new mare and colt."

The earl blinked with surprise. "Wouldn't have any cause to yell except your butler shut the door in my face. Wouldn't even let me inside to wait for your return. The man is deranged."

"The man is following my orders. You aren't welcome here."

The earl sputtered. "This is ridiculous. No matter what, I am your father and you are my heir. I'll not have this."

"By using your money to manipulate Helen and to hide evidence you're as guilty of murder as if you'd killed the women yourself. I have no father." Alex turned his back on the earl and took my hand. "Come, I'll escort you back to the castle."

I shook my head. "I can find my way back if you need to speak privately."

He tugged me forward. "There's nothing to be said."

Wincing at the earl, who stood white-faced and shaken, I

went with Alex. His movements were fast and agitated as he helped me into the saddle and then mounted Samson. I understood his anger at his father and felt bad for them both. We moved from the stables at a quick pace. I urged Delilah forward, catching up to him. "Aren't you being—"

"Too harsh? Is there too harsh a punishment for murder, Andromeda? You think about what may have happened to your cousin and you tell me. By bribing Helen and then suppressing evidence on her death, God only knows what evil has been done since, and I hold him responsible. My father doesn't deserve to have his life while others have lost theirs."

I shuddered, feeling ill, but would have said more except Alex raced on ahead, his countenance as harsh and unforgiving as the rocky cliffs of Dragon's Cove. After helping me dismount, he rode off without saying another word. The bright promise of the day had dimmed beneath the dark shadow of murder and the fact that a killer lurked amid those living at Dartmoor's End.

Once inside the castle, I returned to the Queen's Room, searching for more treasures to bring to the light of day. I lost myself in my thoughts until I heard the slam of a door from across the corridor and I knew Alex had returned. Some part of me recognized that I should stay with the artifacts; that I should ignore all of the clamoring inside of me that urged me to seek Alex out. But I didn't listen. I left the safety of what I knew and went to his door. I pressed my ear to the crack and heard the soft thud of his movements as he dueled with himself. Without knocking, I quietly opened the door and peeked inside. Alex, wearing only the loose black pants and holding the same two deadly looking swords as the previous day, was putting himself through a grueling exercise of fighting movements. Anger and pain, grace and an almost savage beauty oozed from him. It was mesmerizing; he was mesmerizing. I slowly let the door fall open wider, stepping into the room, letting him know that I watched.

I saw the moment he paused, realizing I was there; and felt a deep thrill and connection to him when he didn't stop but rather continued. His skin, bronzed by the sun, glistened in the light streaming through the windows. Dark hair smattered his chest and tapered into the thin line that bisected the hard planes of his stomach. The danger and the power rippling though his muscles stirred me in a way I had never been touched before. My heart sped, moving in tandem to the beat pulsing at his neck. My skin warmed and my body tingled with the need to touch him, to feel the passion coursing through him.

When he finished and knelt with his head bowed and the sharp blades of his swords resting on his shoulders, I moved toward him, reaching out my hand, aching to touch him.

"You shouldn't be here," he said harshly.

"I cannot *not* be here."

He stood abruptly and moved to the room where he kept his swords. He came back wearing a loose, unbuttoned shirt and carrying two practice swords. This time when he tossed the épeé at me, I caught it, gripping the hilt as he'd shown me. He lifted a brow in surprise and I smiled sweetly and brought my sword up into the dueling position, widening my stance. Between Sean's teaching this morning, the books I had devoured, and my own bravado, I didn't appear as foolish and inept as I had the day before.

"Is that a challenge?" he asked, both brows now arched.

"Most certainly," I replied.

"Exactly what have you been doing since yesterday?"

"I found several books on fencing and read about the sport last night."

"Unexpected and very interesting," he said as he circled me, his own épeé lightly caressing the tip of mine.

"I'll wager you something," I said, my palms growing damp. I matched his movements, turning slowly with him and sliding the blade of my épeé along his, enjoying the hiss of the steel and the sensual curve of his responding smile.

"Surely you don't think that reading a book is going to enable you to match swords with me. There's a great deal of practice involved."

"I know."

"And you still wish to make a wager?"

"Yes," I said, moistening my lips with the tip of my tongue. His gaze dropped a moment.

"What are you willing to lose?" he asked, his voice deepening as he moved in closer.

"Who says I'll lose?"

He just smiled.

"You have to grant me one request if I score a point. If I don't then you get one request of me."

"Only one?"

"Just one, but there's a stipulation."

"And that would be?"

"Considering my inexperience, you can't attack. You can only defend against my advances."

"Done," he said, lowering his sword point to the ground.

Smiling confidently, I moved into an en guard stance. I figured that after one or two inept moves, Alex's guard would be down and I'd try and disarm him with the maneuver Sean had shown me this morning. I lunged forward, aiming for Alex's right shoulder with my sword tip. He didn't lift his blade, but stepped sideways, moving toward me so close that my outstretched arm slid against his chest and his leg pressed to my thigh.

He leaned closer still and brushed a fingertip along the side of my neck to the center of my collarbone, then moved downward to the top of my lace fichu and tugged it loose. I gasped at the heat and pleasure bolting through me as he exposed the tops of my breasts. "My point," he said softly before he pocketed my fichu.

He didn't look as if he would listen to anything I had to say about him and his brother even if I did win the wager. His interest was on something else entirely. Good heavens, this wasn't exactly what I had in mind but . . .

Butterflies and a strange sense of anticipation fluttered deep inside me. I backed away, lifting the épeé to the center of his chest, expecting to tap his chest at the point he'd touched mine, but he moved too quickly out of range. The gleam in his green gaze was akin to a pirate enjoying his stolen treasure and greedy for more.

This time I circled around him, looking for a vulnerable moment. The frustrating trouble was he didn't appear to be on his guard at all. He kept his sword pointed down, his sensual smile curved up, and his gaze centered on my breasts.

After a moment, I feinted to the right but then swung the sword tip down and to the left, hoping to halt his countering advance. He merely ran the blade of his épeé beneath mine as he advanced, forced my sword straight up between us, and popped open the first button of my dress with his fingers.

"My point again, Andromeda."

Another few moves and the man would have me near naked. I'd run out of time and needed to act. Inhaling to the point that my second button gave way, completely drawing his attention there, I didn't retreat, but slid my blade down his until the bell of my hilt wedged beneath his. Then I shoved suddenly upward with all of my might, pulling his épeé from his grasp. Unfortunately my enthusiastic upward thrust sent me plowing into Alex. He was clearly stunned that I'd managed to disarm him. Off balance, we fell. He twisted so that I landed on top of him.

"My point," I said, dropping my sword to the rug.

"Your match," he whispered, sliding me up his body until my mouth was but a breath away from his. "What spoils will you claim?"

"You," I said, pressing my lips to the sensual fullness of his, pushing aside that fact that I'd meant to speak to him about Sean. Talk could come later. Right now I wanted nothing but the feel of this man's pleasuring touch, of his body against mine, of his mouth devouring mine. I wanted to let the fire he stirred in me loose.

He met my kiss with passion, his tongue thrusting to mine as powerfully and as adeptly as he handled a sword. I cupped his face in my palms, feeling the clean-shaven edge of his jaw before I threaded my fingers into the silk of his hair. His hands slid down my back to grip my bottom and press me against the urgent heat of his hard arousal, kissing me harder and longer until I knew nothing but the taste of him and the rhythmic thrust of his need.

I moaned, wanting more, meeting his thrust. Groaning, he rolled until I lay slightly beneath him with most of his weight on his right side, his left leg between mine and his left hand palming my right breast. Pressing my head against the soft carpet, I arched my back, lifting my breasts to him.

Leaving my lips aching and swollen, he kissed his way down my throat, licking the tops of my breasts as he unbuttoned my bodice and chemise until I lay exposed to the waist. He leaned on his right elbow to gaze at me as he circled the tips of my tingling breasts with his finger. "Like Aphrodite must have been, you're so perfectly lush in just the right places, that all I can think about when I am near you is tasting you, touching you, pleasuring you, feeling myself inside you. Is that what you want, Andromeda? Knowing everything about me. Is that what you want from me?"

My heart beat faster than my blood could race, leaving me lightheaded and breathless. We'd reached a point of no return and yet he was still giving me a choice. "Yes," I said, sliding my hand up the sculpted curves of his chest, across the tickling silk of hair until I reached the edge of his shirt. Then I tugged the material back and down, exposing the golden expanse of his broad shoulders and firm, muscled torso.

He helped by shrugging his arm free, then he leaned down, taking my left breast into his mouth, flicking his tongue over the aroused peak until my hips lifted to his demanding rhythm. My eyes closed as waves of pleasure filled every part of my being. He made me want nothing more than to have him taste me, touch me, pleasure me. I wanted him inside me. I wanted impossibly to be inside of him.

"Watch me pleasure you," he said roughly.

I opened my eyes to meet his intent gaze that never left mine as he suckled my breasts until my nipples were hard points of need and so filled with a fire that I'd do anything to assuage the burning want.

"I need all of you." His breathing was as labored as mine as he unbuttoned my skirt and untied my drawers. Sliding to my side, he tugged my skirts down my legs and finished stripping off my bodice and chemise, leaving me wearing only my white silk stockings and my black kid boots. The carpet was soft against my back and buttocks and the sunlight streamed a gleaming path across the room to bathe me in its warm light, turning the burnished gold curls covering my sex a fiery copper color.

"Beautiful," he whispered, kneeling between my legs, spreading them farther apart. I felt more vulnerable and more glorious than I'd ever felt before when he pressed the palm of his hand against the heat of my femininity and shut his eyes if he'd reached heaven. He brushed his thumb over a special place that seemed the very center of my being. I cried out with the sharp pleasure of it. Then he moved so quickly I didn't even realize what he meant to do until his mouth replaced his hand and his tongue found the very spot his thumb had awakened.

Shocked, I rose to my elbows, intending to stop him, but the pleasure was so great I could only gasp as my hips rocked upward for more. Eyes shut, he appeared as if he were dining on ambrosia as his tongue lapped. He opened his dragon-green eyes and met my gaze. The dark hunger burning there was as shocking as the fire he breathed into my loins. My entire being was caught up in the heat and lash of his tongue. White-hot pleasure spread over me in wave after wave, building a knot of unbearable tension inside me. I knew that at any second I was going to breathe my last. Then I felt something new and different and realized after he moved his hand against me that he'd slid his fingers inside, opening me even more to his seeking passion. It left me wanting more.

A fever burned through me and I cried out. "I need . . . I need . . . please."

"You, Andromeda," he said as he rose above me. Scooping me into his arms, he carried me into his bedroom and set me on his black satin counterpane. Untying his silk pants, he shoved them down his hips, freeing his arousal. Then he climbed into bed beside me. "I need you more than I have ever needed anything my entire life," he whispered to me just before he kissed me again, gently and with a tenderness I'd yet to know from him.

"And I you," I said as I wrapped my arms around him, feeling the supple strength of him, the smooth warmth of his skin. The trembling of his body reached deeply inside of me and I thought I saw directly into his mind. He was in such deep emotional and physical need that he was scared to continue and he was concerned for me as well. His desire for me fought desperately against this fear, causing him to tremble.

"Love me," I told him.

Groaning, he deepened his kiss, sliding between my legs, pressing the hard heat of his sex against my weeping, intimate flesh. Looking into my eyes, he slid inside of me a little. I gasped and tensed at the unexpected fullness of him, and at the pain.

"Easy. I'm going to come all the way inside and then I won't move until you say."

"You mean you aren't already there?"

"Not hardly."

"Are you sure? I feel quite a bit of you already."

"I'm sure. Are you changing your mind about this?"

"Certainly not. But—"

He kissed my words away. Then he flicked his tongue over my nipple as he cupped my other breast in his hand and brushed my burgeoning nipple with his thumb. My hips rocked against him and the discomfort I felt eased.

"Relax into the motion of it, let yourself go, feel me," he said softy and drove himself deep. I felt another sharp bite, then the pain eased to an unfamiliar yet strangely fulfilling fullness in the very center of my being. He slid back and thrust again, rippling a hot wave of pleasure through me. I arched to him, asking for more. He moved deeper and faster, catching me up in an escalating, drumming passion that had every part of me focused on moving my body to the demanding rhythm of his and the hot fire he breathed into my soul.

My entire world narrowed to the very points where my body connected to his. Nothing mattered but him and the pleasure he built higher and higher until I cried out and shuddered as white stars burst before my eyes and heaven swept me away.

His body shuddered against mine and I saw his stars, felt his throbbing pleasure so deeply within me that another consuming peak of pleasure rippled through me.

15

Having Alex intimately inside me seemed to open his mind to me, and I knew the minute his pleasure had ebbed and the world began to intrude. His thoughts were a jumbled mass of conflicting desires. More than anything else he wanted to make love to me again. Though thoroughly satisfied, he was strangely hungry for more and saw himself thrusting into me again and again. This intense hunger made him want to get me dressed and out of his home as quickly as he could so that he wouldn't do just what he wanted to do. He'd yet to focus on the worry of pregnancy or if he would allow me to seduce him again, but those thoughts were there. And I wasn't about to lie around and wait until he decided whether or not he was glad he'd made love to me.

I pressed against his chest and he rolled to the side. The minute he slipped from me, his thoughts were gone, but I'd seen enough. "That was quite lovely," I said. Leaning up, I brushed my lips against his cheek and slid from the bed. Since he was lying on the counterpane and scarcely had anything else in his room, I had to pick up his silk pants and wrap them ineptly about my person before I went for my clothes.

"Andromeda! What in the bloody hell was that?" he said.

Turning slightly in the doorway, I found him sitting on the edge of his bed, looking dazed and confused.

"What was what? Surely you know that we just . . . well . . . you know."

"I'm not talking about that. I'm talking about the 'quite lovely' thing."

"Well, it was. Would you feel better if I lied and said it wasn't?"

"No. Hell and damnation, you sounded as if we'd just had tea!"

"It was a bit more than tea, I'd say. Wasn't it lovely for you, too?"

He stood, a thundercloud of frustration darkening his brow. It was the first that I'd seen him from head to toe in all of his naked glory and he was magnificent . . . everywhere. I smiled brightly, still feeling the burn of his thoughts; but my steam of outrage was slowly cooling to misty tears that stung the backs of my eyes. I'd expected his thoughts would have been different after making love to me. I thought that in the very least he would have been awed, or felt stirrings of love, something similar to the emotions consuming me. He hadn't. "Speaking of tea, I promised Cassie I would be home for tea today. So, I'm in a bit of a hurry."

Dashing into the other room, I gathered my clothes, wondering if I could chance running down the corridor to the water closet to make myself presentable.

Alex caught my shoulders from behind and pulled me back against him. "What is it?" he whispered softy. "What did I do to upset you? Did I hurt you in some way?"

Oh, God. I fought back the tears. My seeing into his thoughts in an unguarded moment wasn't fair to him. I didn't ask for promises of love, nor did I give any. He would never marry because of the life sentence he'd given himself, and I would never marry because of what had just happened now.

"No," I whispered. "I'm just overwhelmed. It was so much more than I ever imagined it being and I need time alone to think about what happened."

He wrapped his arms around me and pulled me back against his chest. He kissed the top of my head. "I feel the same way. Do you really need to be home for tea with Cassie?"

I shook my head, unable to speak. He turned me to face him.

"Then why don't you refresh yourself and have tea with me?"

The earnest need in his eyes and in his voice for my company surprised me. It didn't quite fit in with the thoughts I'd read. Confused, I nodded.

"Good." He exhaled softy and bent down, kissing me gently. "You're right, it was a bit more than tea. And it was a bit more than lovely. It was amazing. Unlike anything I've ever experienced before. Just in case you're wondering. There's a back way to the bathroom through my bedroom."

Why did what I saw in his mind not match up to how he was acting now?

I followed him, clutching my clothes against me with one hand and holding the pants I'd wrapped around me in place with the other. Passing through his room, I glanced again at the black silk counterpane, remembering its softness and the feel of being in his bed, wishing I hadn't seen into his thoughts and that I was still blissfully lying there next to him and he was saying that what he'd felt was amazing.

Opening a door, he led me into the water closet. "Would you like a bath? I've hot water that runs through the pipes so there's no need to disturb the servants."

"A bath would be good," I said, finding my voice. This all felt very strange, but as he crossed the room to the resplendent white tub I didn't argue. I looked for a place to set my clothes. Then, locating a towel, I wrapped it around me and set his pants aside as well. At the vanity, I sat down and began unbuttoning my boots. I'd made it half way, when Alex, wearing a towel wrapped around his waist, knelt at my feet and brushed my hands away. "Let me," he said.

He deftly slipped the buttons loose from their moorings and slid off my boot, doing the same to my other foot. After that, he eased his hands up my legs to untie my garters and to slide off my silk stockings. With each movement his touch became more sensual and lingered just a little longer than the last. Already I could feel my desire for him stir again. Glancing down at him, I saw the heat in his gaze had rekindled as well. He stood, holding out his hand to me, and I knew it was more than just a request to lead me to the tub. It was a request to touch him, to trust him to touch me, and I placed my hand in his after hesitating but a moment. I realized in that instant that it didn't matter what he felt or thought. I'd wanted to know him, I'd wanted the opportunity to love a man fully before I spent my life alone, and Alex was that man. I'd chosen him. Fate had chosen him.

He led me to the immense white porcelain tub that was still filling with steamy water and the scent of sandalwood and spice. Loosening the towel from around me, he let it drop to the floor and kissed me, gently at first, then hungrily.

He stepped back, searching my gaze. He must have found what he wanted, for he dropped his own towel and stepped into the tub. Sitting with his back against the smooth, comfortably curved porcelain, he tugged me into his lap. I landed with a splash and a gasp. Wrapping his arm beneath my breasts, he slid me against him so that I sat in his lap with his legs stretched out beneath mine, even though the tub was large enough that we could have sat side by side. He cradled my head between his chin and shoulder and stretched his arm out alongside mine, twining his fingers with my own. Sunlight filled the area, making the room even steamier than the heat rising from the water.

I shut my eyes, enjoying the intimacy of the moment, thinking that if marriage had been in my future, I would have wanted things to be like this. He traced his finger over the serpent ring curling around my finger.

"What's sailing like?" I asked.

He didn't say anything for a long moment and I thought he wasn't going to answer. Then he brushed his lips against my head and spoke. "At the bow of a ship, facing the elements with the sun beating upon your face and the wind at your back? It's like racing over rough terrain on a huge horse one has little control of against a wild wind. A wager with God and nature that a man has no assurance of how the journey will end, but a risk he will take every chance he gets because feeling the power of the wind carrying him across the sea is worth every risk. It makes a man feel more alive and more human than anything else, except for one thing."

"What is that?" I asked, wondering if I had read Alex wrong. What if he raced his horses at breakneck speed not because he was trying to end his life, but to make himself feel alive?

"You just shared that one thing with me. Care to sail again?" he said softly as he slid his fingers over the tips of my breasts and kissed my nape.

I gasped, arching toward him, feeling the press of his hardening arousal against my back. One word, one look, one touch, and I wanted to feel everything I had just felt all over again. "How often do people . . . go sailing?"

He rubbed a bar of fragrant soap between his hands, filling my senses with his heady scent. Dropping the soap in the water, he cupped my breasts and bathed them with excruciatingly pleasurable strokes. "With you, Andromeda, every hour sounds about right to me. I'm an excellent captain, so you can relax. You're in expert hands." He snaked one hand down my stomach and slid a slick finger directly where I tingled the most, magically finding that one single spot that made me ache for more.

"Every hour?" I gasped as he brought his knees up on the insides of mine and spread my legs wide. How did anyone ever do anything else? Why anyone ever did anything else was my last coherent thought, for Alex slid his fingers inside me again and he rubbed that special place until my whole body throbbed to the rhythm of his touch. My head fell back against his shoulder and his lips sought mine in a deep, dueling kiss where every thrust and parry made us both winners. I barely felt his slight lifting of my hips. I only knew the satisfying moment his hot, urgent sex thrust into me and he rocked insistently in and out. He had one hand rubbing over the hardened tips of my breasts and his other hand cupping my sex so that his fingers vibrated with growing intensity directly on that very sensitive place where my whole body and soul became his. Stars exploded, and time disappeared beneath the burning pleasure shuddering through every fiber of my being.

This time when Alex followed me to heaven; his pleasure sent a sharp spasm through me that was so dizzying, the bursting stars blinded me, leaving me dazed. His whole being was caught up in the experience. At that moment nothing else mattered to him. He wanted nothing more than to be inside me and to stay inside me, driving himself into every part of me. I became his whole world in an instant and I decided that was all that mattered. Whatever his thoughts would be a minute from now or a day from now, we'd shared something special, and deep inside him, in his own way, that meant as much to him as it did to me.

I didn't have any regrets, but I did feel awkward as I left Dragon's Cove. It wasn't anything that Alex did or said. He'd been very attentive, the perfect lady's maid in helping me dress. We even shared tea, during which I ate twice as much as I usually did. There were moments that I'd find him looking at me in a puzzled way, and moments when everything became too quiet, like there were things that needed to be said, but neither of us was willing to say them.

And there was nothing to say. We both had to content ourselves with the situation as it was. We had no future.

Still, as the dark towers of Dragon's Cove and its crashing waves disappeared behind me and the sounds of the birds singing and bees searching for nectar unfolded before me, I knew I would be returning to Killdaren's Castle a different woman. A woman who was both more than what she had been when she left that morning, and less, for Alex had opened a whole new world to me, but had taken a part of me captive as well. It wasn't just my heart; I think he'd laid claim to that long before today. It was part of my soul that was missing, a part of me that was still tangled up with him and that moment when his driving force sailed us into an unknown sea.

I didn't have long to dwell on my melancholy state. The buggy pulled up to the castle's rear door, and rather than going inside to face everyone just yet, I took the path into the gardens and accidentally found myself eavesdropping on a very private conversation between Stuart Frye and his mother. She was expressing her outrage over the efforts of Cassie, Bridget, and me to clear her and Jamie of murder charges. I was surprised to find she'd been released from jail. Cassie must have had some impact on Constable Poole after all.

"All of you should have just left well enough alone," she said.

"No," said Stuart. "You shouldn't have confessed to a crime you didn't commit. You shouldn't have made up lies about Mary's death thinking to save Jamie."

"I had to. He's different and they would have killed him on the spot. He's a child inside. I had to protect him. Now they will hang him for sure. There's unrest among the villagers. So much so that Constable Poole had me brought back here. I think he's afraid of a mob and most likely didn't want to have a woman hanged on his watch. I still have to face charges for lying to the authorities."

"Jamie is innocent and I will find a way to prove it," Stuart said. "I'll speak to Sean about hiring more guards to keep him safe, and you need to stay here in the castle."

"How can you be so sure he is innocent?" said Mrs. Frye. "He had Mary's body in the burial ground beneath those cursed stones he was always at."

"If Mary's death had just been an accident, I'd think Jamie at fault," said Stuart. "He might have pushed her or squeezed her too tight when trying to help her, but you know as well as I do that if Jamie's life had depended on him carving Mary with a knife, he would have killed himself first. Besides, he was fifteen when Helen died. There's just no way he did it. He cried for a month when a horse had to be put down."

"It doesn't matter. The only way to save Jamie now is for the real killer to be caught red-handed while Jamie is in jail. I'm sure the killer isn't foolish enough to do that."

"I'll find a way to save my brother no matter what. That I promise."

Stuart's grim pledge had a note of assurance in it that sent a shiver of warning down my spine. I hurried back to the castle and into the warmth of the kitchens. Mrs. Murphy had the staff running about, preparing a special servants' meal in honor of Mrs. Frye's return. She'd been the vigilant house-keeper at Killdaren's Castle for years and now that it was learned she'd lied to protect Jamie, she was being welcomed back with loving arms.

Rather than retreating to my room and my thoughts, I went in search of Cassie to escape them. I also understood for the first time just why I felt as if I had lost my sister in some small way after she'd met and married Sean. Sean had led Cassie to the new and exciting world Alex had opened up to me, and part of her belonged to him in a special way.

I found Cassie, Bridget, Prudence, and Gemini together in the library. Each of them had a book in hand and they were searching through the pages as if the world would end if they didn't find what they were looking for. All except for Cassie, who paced like an angry tigress in front of the fire-place.

"What's wrong?" I asked, stepping into the room.

"What's right?" Cassie demanded, throwing her hands up. "My husband doesn't credit me with any intelligence what-soever. Constable Poole came by today, escorting Mrs. Frye back here. He spent two hours with Sean. Two hours dis-cussing my cousin's murder and Lady Helen's death and my dear husband won't tell me a word of what was said. I'm supposed to knit stockings and not concern myself. I've never knitted a stocking in my life."

"You did learn how to knit scarves, if I remember right," I said.

Cassie glared at me, almost breathing fire like a dragon herself.

"He's only trying to protect you," Prudence said. "You should appreciate the fact that he loves you so much. I'm not sure the earl spared me a glance after he learned I was with child."

"I think the earl feels a great deal more than he lets anyone see," Cassie said. "He's too afraid that he'll curse someone else. I don't mean to be ungrateful about Sean's attention, but . . ." She groaned. "Considering I have plans for a number of children, I'm going to be a prisoner in my own home for the next ten years. The doctor swears that I am fine, and I am, but Sean won't believe it."

"Maybe you should just rest and let the men solve this mystery," I said. My sister was more agitated than I'd ever seen her.

Cassie gaped at me. "Andrie! Whose side are you on?"

"Your side, of course. But Sean is right in that you don't need to do anything dangerous."

"We're not," Bridget said. "But we are going to prove that women are capable and don't need to be coddled. Stuart has the same problem that Sean does." Bridget held up the book in her hands, letting me read the title. *Druid Magic Through the Ages.* "Tonight we're going to scour the library to see if we can discover any significance to the symbol and tomorrow after tea we're going to take a little ride."

"What kind of little ride?" I asked, apprehensive.

"We're going to pay a visit to a haunted mansion," Gemini answered, her blue eyes bright with excitement. "This all started with Lady Helen and we are missing out on important clues by not learning more about her."

I quickly found a seat. "You mean the place that

Mr. Drayson mentioned at dinner? The place that scared even him?"

"I'm sure he was exaggerating," Gemini said.

"I agree that we haven't asked as many questions about Lady Helen as we should, but I don't think going to a haunted mansion is the way to get the answers we want."

"It's the perfect place to go," Bridget said. "From what I hear, not a thing has been touched since the night Lady Helen died. She might have a journal or some letters or something to help us figure out what could have happened that night. Someone hated her enough to kill her. Who?"

"It wasn't the earl," Prudence cried out. "He hated her for what she was doing to his sons but he wouldn't have harmed her. I know him."

Cassie put a comforting hand on Prudence's shoulder.

"Solving her murder will be the only way to let her spirit find peace. Mary's, too," Gemini said.

"Wait a minute," I cried. "All of you are moving too fast here." I felt as if I'd been caught up in a storm that was spinning out of control. "What are you taking about? Putting their spirits to rest?"

Gemini frowned at me. "Wouldn't your spirit be upset if you were murdered?"

"I suppose so, but you sounded as if you had actually heard their spirits."

Gemini shrugged, looking oddly as if she was hiding a lot more than she was saying. "The important thing is that we find out who did this. The men have had eight years and don't have any answers. The matter needs a woman's perspective."

"We'll work together to solve this and prove to the men that we are capable. By staying together we'll be safe as well," Bridget added.

"I'm afraid I'm going to stay here," Prudence said softly. "I don't want to be that far from Rebecca, not since we've learned that Mrs. Frye and Jamie aren't responsible for what happened to Mary. Rebecca could still be in danger. Somebody put her on the roof. If not Jaime, then who?"

Cassie exhaled as if punched. "God, I don't want to ever have to live through what happened before again. You're right to keep Rebecca close, but I think she may be safe now. I think whoever tried to hurt her was afraid that when Rebecca started talking clearly she would say something that might tell us who harmed Mary. Now that she has recovered and hasn't said anything more, she may be safe. But you're right not to leave her."

"Maybe we should all just stay here and ask questions about Helen from people who knew her," I muttered, hoping that I'd get one of the other women to go along with the safer of the two evils. Cassie, Bridget, and Gemini glared at me, and I knew I didn't have a choice.

"I don't suppose a short drive tomorrow for an after-tea excursion will be that hazardous as long as we stay together." I bit my lip and winced, wondering why I felt so very uneasy about everything.

A few minutes after everyone went back to their search for Druid symbology in the library books, I eased over to Cassie's side. "Have you had any dreams?" I whispered.

"No," she said, shaking her head. She set her hand on mine. "No, none at all. You know I would do anything, say anything to keep someone from harm."

"Yes." I also knew that, except for once in the case of Rebecca being left on the roof, Cassie's dreams about a person's death always came too late to do anything to save that person.

The firm knock on the door made me jump guiltily, as if I'd been caught doing something I shouldn't. Cassie did as well. She cleared her throat. "Come in."

One of the downstairs maids stood at the door appearing white-faced, shaken, and crying. "Begging your pardon, Mistress Killdaren, but Sir Warwick wishes to have a word with you. I swear I didn't do anything with the cards in the music room. They were there when I dusted last week, honest. Please ma'am, but it's not my fault. I canna afford to lose my job, ma'am. I promise I didn't do it."

"Heavens! I forgot all about them. There has been so

much happening," Cassie said, crossing the room and setting her arm across the girl's shoulders. "Don't you worry, Nan. I'll take care of this. Tell Mrs. Murphy I said to give you some tea and scones, and you take a short break and gather yourself. Nobody's going to lose their job. I know exactly what happened to the cards."

"Yes, ma'am," the maid said as she curtsied and left sniffling. She didn't appear very reassured. I imagined Sir Warwick had given her quite a fright.

"Odd that Sir Warwick is asking about the cards. I expected it would be the earl. Well, it's time for me to go and face the music, so to speak." Cassie straightened her shoulders as if readying for battle. "You three did the right thing in removing those horrid cards about the women who died. I've wanted to do it since I first came here. I just hadn't had time since Sean and I were married."

"I'll go with you," I said. "The cards are shoved into the back of my armoire."

"No," Cassie said. "As far as anyone is concerned we've burned them. This is my home now and I don't want them here. If you don't take charge of your own life and make it what you want it to be then someone else will choose for you."

"Blimey, Cassie. That has to be the greatest thing I've ever heard said. I am coming with you, then I'm going to stop letting Stuart make my choices." Bridget set down her book firmly on the desktop and tugged her dress into place as she stood.

"And I as well," Prudence said quietly. "But not everyone can choose what they want. Many have to settle for what is given to them."

"Sometimes that is true, Prudence, but then you don't know if something is possible until you try and make it so," Cassie said, looking at Prudence, but somehow the weight of the words settled on me and I couldn't seem to shrug them off.

We entered the music room, bolstering Cassie's wake, surprised to find the Earl of Dartraven pacing in agitation and Sir Warwick staring at the cardless display of Tartoelen

Dragon Shawms where the woman who used them on stage had been burned at the stake as a witch—one of the gruesome stories I recalled reading as I'd removed the card.

The earl looked up at us all with a puzzled expression. "I'm not sure how this has happened but all of the research on these instruments is missing. We need to find the cards. Warwick will be able to tell the maid where they belong."

"I'm afraid that isn't possible, my lord." Cassie replied. "I apologize if I have upset anyone but they were removed because I felt that their content didn't belong in my home. I've a child on the way and those stories of death were nightmares no child ever needs to hear. The cards, unfortunately, met with an untimely end."

"That was my fault," I said, moving to Cassie's side, unable to let her bear the brunt of the gaffe. "I thought destroying the cards would rid them of their ghosts."

"There should be no blame cast here," said Prudence, who took Cassie's other side. "As long as the tragedies involved with the instruments are kept fresh in everyone's minds the beauty of the music they could make can never be heard."

"They were a memorial to Olivia," said the earl.

"My wife," added Sir Warwick at our puzzled looks. "She began collecting the instruments before she died, and after her death, I continued."

The earl sighed. "Sean's mother had Warwick place the instruments here where Olivia loved to sing as a memorial to her. The harp on the stage was hers."

"She was playing it and singing when she collapsed on stage and died. She sang so passionately that her heart literally stopped from exhaustion."

The men were suddenly so melancholy that I thought they were going to cry. I felt stunned to see such emotion from them. Nobody said a word for a few minutes. I could see that Cassie was searching for the right thing to say. For no matter what the content of the cards had been, the music room was apparently a memorial and we'd desecrated it in some way. And to be honest, Cassie and I were the last ones who could actually judge another for their collection of antiquities. Though we didn't have cards delineating who the men were and how they died, my parents had picked up two shrunken heads in their travels and they were sitting on the shelf of the dish cabinet in our Oxford home at that moment.

"I think it is time for all of us to put what happened in the past behind us and find a new life," Prudence said firmly, looking directly at the earl and gaining his attention.

He blinked at her as if he hadn't seen her for some time. "You make that sound like you're about to sail to America." He didn't appear to like the idea at all.

Prudence furrowed her brow. "I just might. Stuart has been urging me to start a new life for myself and Rebecca for a long time. I never thought it possible, but maybe I am wrong."

The earl gaped like a fish out of water.

Though Cassie and Prudence were right, it was time to free many things from the chains of the past, I did feel contrite for upsetting Sir Warwick and the earl. Not so bad that I wanted to return the cards, but I did need to say something. I leaned forward and touched Sir Warwick's sleeve and quickly snatched my hand back. "I'm . . . sorry." I could barely get my words of apology past the sudden lump in my throat. Inside, Sir Warwick was raging with anger. *These imbeciles have destroyed years, years of research! Olivia's memory was more important than these low-class upstarts.*

A clear image of his wife singing on stage, strumming her golden harp, looking like a Greek goddess in white robes and delicate flowers in her upswept hair flashed in my mind and I saw her fall to the ground, clutching her chest as she cried out in pain.

I felt as if I had been punched in the stomach so hard that I couldn't breathe.

16

How could Sir Warwick appear so outwardly calm and composed while such anger raged inside him? Clearly he did not wish to cause a scene. I marveled at his restraint; were I that angry I would be screaming or crying. The hidden thoughts in the minds of those around me, thoughts that only I knew were there, seemed to reach out and wrap their hands around my throat, suffocating me.

Was I becoming mad as I had in my dream? Was I losing sight of where I ended and another's thoughts began. My heart raced and I grew dizzy.

"Forgive me, but I just remembered something very important that I must attend to," I said, and hurried from the room without looking at anyone. By the time I reached my room, I'd yet to escape Sir Warwick's thoughts regarding low-class upstarts, nor the vision of his wife writhing upon the stage.

I went to my bed, climbed in, and pulled the covers over my head, completely overwhelmed by the events of the day.

Tears escaped from the corners of my eyes. How could I live like this? How could I face a future of reading other's private thoughts and emotions?

How could I stop battling the enemy I faced now? A killer was lurking and I had to find him. Alex was wasting his life and I had to save him. I would never be able to walk away from a wrong without trying to make it right. Maybe there was no escape for me, ever. Maybe like my namesake I was chained upon a rock in this seething sea of human thoughts and I would die here as the monster slowly devoured me. And deep down inside me, there was another realization dawning. Not all of my anguish today had come from my gift, but from finally facing how deep my feelings for Alex really were. All of my life I'd known I was different and had resigned myself to the fact that I'd never know marriage. But now that I'd discovered love, that empty future cut me to the core. My gift had never been more of a curse.

Cassie appeared at the door, saving me from the throes of my dilemma.

"Andrie? What's wrong?" She came and sat on the bed. "Did Sir Warwick and the earl upset you? They'll live without the gruesome cards and we'll all be better off."

"I know. It's not that," I said, forcing a wan smile as I peeked out from under the covers. There was no point in telling Cassie what Sir Warwick thought about our presence in the Killdarens' lives, or how painful his wife's death had been.

"Then what is it?"

"Life is changing. We're all changing and nothing will ever be the way it was before. Sometimes that overwhelms me."

"I know. I feel that way, too. Especially when I realize that I will soon have children to care for and what their lives and futures are going to be like with the Dragon's Curse over their heads."

I tossed back the covers, realizing that I was only wasting time that I didn't have to lose. "Though I haven't read every page, I've searched through the Dragon's Curse book. It's in my armoire."

"You've got Sean's book in here? Good Lord, Andrie, Sean will be livid. He's never let me take it out of the study."

I winced. "Sorry. The night you collapsed Alex showed it to me and I just brought it back here, hoping to find a way to break the curse. Too bad it's not as simple as making the macabre cards disappear."

"What do you mean?"

"Well, without the awful stories to remind people of what happened, the instruments will now just be instruments of music and beauty, and perhaps will come to have happy memories attached to them to erase the bad ones."

"Andrie!" Cassie squealed and hugged me hard. "That's it! I can't change the past but I can change what is said about it today and how people see things that happen now. And just what would happen to the legend of the Dragon's Curse if the book disappeared? Keep it hidden for now and we'll see what Sean does when he discovers it missing."

I immediately saw that she thought to dissolve the Dragon's Curse through the power of spreading positive rumors.

"Think about it," she said. "Instead of everyone remembering that Alex nearly killed Sean in a fight eight years ago, why can it not be said that Alex saved Sean's life after a terrible accident?"

"I can't argue with that. Because that is exactly what Alex claims happened."

"I'm sure as close as the earl said Sean and Alex were growing up, that I can get him to tell a few stories about what they were like as boys over dinner tonight after we tell some of our childhood tales. Cassie Andrews is declaring war on the Dragon's Curse. I'm going to go fish a few tales out of Mr. and Mrs. Murphy in case the earl's still upset about the music room."

"Did they say more about it after I left? Sir Warwick was . . ."

"What?"

I shrugged. "I don't know. I don't think he likes us very much."

Cassie shook her head. "He doesn't like anyone very much. Not even the earl."

"Then why are they always together?"

"Unfortunately, I think they use each other to keep from being bored. With Sir Warwick around the earl doesn't have to face the emptiness of his own life."

"Alex won't even let the earl inside Dragon's Cove."

"Good," Cassie replied with a smile.

"Have you a fever? How can something like that be good?"

"Because if the earl has to stay here, he won't be able to escape from seeing Prudence every day, and now that Prudence is changing how she sees her life, I think things are going to get very interesting. Did you see his face when she said she was thinking about starting a new life?"

"He did appear a bit upset by the idea."

"I hope she does. Sometimes people don't realize how much they really do love someone until they are gone."

"Do you think the earl loves Prudence?"

"What matters is that she loves him. But, in an odd way, I think he does love her. Not like Sean loves me, mind you. Sean would have beaten the bedroom door down in eight days, and for them it's been eight years."

Cassie clamped her hand over her mouth. "I shouldn't have said that," she mumbled.

I laughed. "Yes, you should. And I understand." My cheeks flushed hotly as images of Alex and me flashed through my mind. Alex would most likely obliterate the door in eight hours. No, make that eight seconds.

Cassie narrowed her eyes and peered closer at me, setting her hand on my forehead. "Andrie, is everything all right?"

"Certainly," I said, shooing her to the door. "Go get your stories from Mrs. Murphy and I'll see you shortly for dinner.

And it's not just Cassie Andrews who's declaring war on the Dragon's Curse; we both are doing so."

Besides putting the Killdaren family's antiquities in order, the one thing that I could do for Alex would be to free him from the bonds of the past. If there was a real curse, I wasn't sure Cassie and I could ever find a way to break it, but we could do its reputation some serious damage. Enough to make Sean and Alex doubt that the curse ruled over them, and that was all that mattered right now. While I couldn't remain in Alex's life, I would see to it that he could truly live again.

I had the strangest feeling that if Sean and Alex's mother had survived, what happened eight years ago to put them at odds with each other might never have occurred, and maybe having twins live their lives without giving in to the curse would break it. A mother would have done anything to save her sons, because love . . .

It suddenly occurred to me that the only way to end a curse born of scorn would be to cure it with love. But how?

At dinner Sean oozed tension and Cassie's smile was over-bright, making me wonder if this whole situation between them would end in tragedy. Cassie was determined to prove to Sean that he was wrong, and Sean was determined to have Cassie do exactly what he wanted, regardless of what she thought or felt. They needed to compromise, but neither seemed willing to give an inch.

Besides Cassie, Sean, Gemini, Prudence, and me, the Earl of Dartraven, Sir Warwick, Lord Ashton, and Mr. Drayson joined us for the meal. Thus far the conversation centered on the weather, news from Penzance, and the continued success of Gilbert and Sullivan's play *HMS Pinafore*.

"Have you had the opportunity to see the play, gentlemen?" Cassie asked Lord Ashton and Mr. Drayson. "I was just telling Sean about it today, having found the premise of the story extremely interesting."

"Actually, I did see it at the Opera Comique in London when it opened in May of last year," said Mr. Drayson. With an intricately tied cravat and his brown hair, which was usually mussed, perfectly groomed, he seemed especially attentive to Gemini tonight. A situation I wasn't sure Gemini welcomed, even though she didn't seem as enamored with Lord Ashton as she'd been just a short time ago.

"Oh, I remember that night." Lord Ashton shook his head sadly as his blue eyes glanced toward heaven. He was dressed in a cutaway jacket and an elaborate gold-embroidered waist-coat that made him as glittery as a cache of gold. "It was the one and only night in my life that I wished I'd been languishing away at a performance rather than playing cards. I lost a thousand pounds to that dastardly Handerland and I've yet to win it all back."

A thousand pounds. Heavens, I nearly fell from my chair. Lord Ashton had to be extremely well off to wager so much in just one night.

"The play was the most amusing bit I'd ever seen," said Mr. Drayson. "And the women's parts most decorous, considering the risqué situations portrayed in public these days. It's scandalous."

"It was very well done." Cassie gave me the "eye." "I thought the premise was extremely interesting," she repeated.

My mind scrambled for what she wanted. "That a nurse accidentally switched two babies at birth, one low born and one high born?"

Cassie nodded. "Yes. That two men can grow up believing in something because that's what they've been told all their lives, only to find out that what they believed wasn't really true."

"It was delightful," said Gemini. "Here the captain's daughter who is supposed to marry an admiral falls in love with a lowly sailor, but the lowly sailor turns out to be high born and the captain himself low born. The now high-born sailor becomes the captain and marries the captain's daughter, and the low-born captain marries Buttercup, the nurse. Love supposedly levels all ranks."

"Without question," Sean said.

"Only for a time," said Sir Warwick. "Love doesn't last forever and eventually class will show and divide by its very nature."

Winter, I thought. Sir Warwick's gray hair, gray eyes, black outlook, and harsh and barren opinions made him like winter. I wondered if he'd always been this way or if losing his wife so tragically had made him so. Just like the earl in some ways, grief must have changed him. When he was younger, I had to wonder if he'd been as dynamic as Alex and Sean. It didn't seem possible.

"I think you're wrong, Sir Warwick," Prudence said, surprisingly entering into the fray. "I believe you should have said *heart*. Eventually the heart of a person will show and by its nature it will bind or divide."

"Very well said," I added, refusing to believe in Sir Warwick's cynicism. "Class doesn't determine good or evil; heart does."

"Class does divide though. There's no question about it," Lord Ashton said, his nose angling higher. I hadn't realized before how disapproving he was of those less fortunate than himself. "And I fear we are going to see a nasty division right here in Dartmoor's End soon. Drayson and I had to leave the inn and move to Dragon's Cove this evening."

"Did you receive another note demanding you make restitution for compromising someone?" Sean asked, leaning forward interestedly.

Mr. Drayson laughed. "Oddly enough the chap must have realized his mistake. We received two notes delivered to Dragon's Cove just before we left to come here. The man apologized for his erroneous accusation and hoped he didn't cause us any undue discomfort."

Compromised? Make restitution? My cheeks began to burn as I realized that Lord Ashton and Mr. Drayson received their notes after I had gone to Alex asking for employment. Then the very day Alex discovers he'd wrongly assumed the reasons for my need of a position, notes of apology were delivered to the gentlemen whose company I had enjoyed sporadically over the summer. I didn't think the events were coincidental. I tried to focus on what Lord Ashton was saying, but the buzzing of my thoughts made my ears ring.

"The notes have left me more than curious," he said. "I've instructed my attorney to keep investigating where they came from. As for why we left the village, I wanted to be able to sleep at night without worrying about being attacked. Ever since word about the symbols carved . . . well, the connection between Lady Helen and Mary's death, if you know what I mean, I've noted a growing unrest among those in the village. Today I heard one chap ask another if he thought there was witchcraft going on in the castles and if the men, meaning Drayson, me, you, and Alex, weren't warlocks or vampires."

"Surely nobody really gives credence to those idiotic rumors," Sean said.

Cassie coughed. "I, uh, don't think you should dismiss this as total nonsense, Sean. Your nocturnal lifestyle has foddered these people's superstitions for years and you don't do anything to dispel their notions. You know that no mob is rational. Prudence told me what almost happened to her. If you and Stuart hadn't shown up when you did—"

"What almost happened?" the earl demanded, looking from Sean to Prudence.

"Nothing," Prudence said. "I've finished the embroidered chessboard for Rebecca—"

"No, don't change the subject," said Sean. "He should know and I've kept my promise of silence too long. What happened is that the villagers almost stoned Prudence when they learned she was with child."

"No," Prudence cried. "He didn't have to know." Pressing her hand to her mouth to keep back her cries, she ran from the room.

The earl turned pasty white. "When! Where was I? Why wasn't I told?"

"You and Warwick had gone to London," Sean said. "Prudence left, having decided she'd rather not live here considering the circumstances. When Stuart and I arrived the villagers had already caused her bodily harm, and that may be why Rebecca is blind. You weren't told because Prudence doesn't want your pity. I don't think she realized the alternative was having eight years of your indifference. That is all I am going to say on the subject. You will have to get the rest of the story out of her. I apologize to everyone for the serious lapse in our dinner etiquette, but sometimes it is more important that what needs to be said gets said."

"I agree with my husband," said Cassie. "So he won't mind me bringing up the subject of his relationship with Alex."

Sean's jaw dropped. Sir Warwick laughed. Lord Ashton choked on his wine. Mr. Drayson dropped his fork into his plate and Gemini giggled. I bit my lip wondering if Sean would explode or if he would toss Cassie over his shoulder and cart her from the dining room.

"Now history would have us look at their relationship and conclude they were doomed to repeat the past," Cassie continued.

"Cassie," Sean said sharply.

She ignored him. "In speaking to Mr. Murphy just before dinner an interesting fact came to light. Apparently, when they were just seven years old, they escaped their governess and took a boat out in the sea—"

"Cassie!" Sean stood up.

"Do you know what happened? A huge wave came up and flipped the boat."

"That's it!" Sean thundered. He pulled back Cassie's chair and scooped her up, then marched with his hitched gait for the door.

"Alex hit his head and was knocked unconscious," Cassie shouted. "And Sean—"

Whatever she was going to say was silenced by Sean kissing her. Since she wrapped her arms around his neck just as they disappeared through the doorway, she didn't appear to be in distress.

"I could use a drink," said the earl, still looking stunned.

"I'll join you," replied Sir Warwick.

Gemini settled her gaze on Lord Ashton. "Shall we play cards in the drawing room? I'll wager that I can win."

What was my innocent little sister going to wager? I wondered as she retrieved a cloak to keep her warm. The outcome of my little bet with Alex had had some earth-shattering results. Not that I regretted them, but Gemini was a great deal younger than me and nothing marred her prospects of having a wonderful marriage. I shut my eyes, hoping that I'd fallen asleep in my bed and this entire evening was nothing more than my imagination. The world had gone completely mad.

I discovered the situation wasn't as bad as I imagined. Gemini was not betting funds we couldn't afford to lose, but frivolous things like the marzipan Mrs. Murphy had made for dessert. It was perfectly harmless. Besides, Gemini was showing herself to be quite an adept card player. During the start of their gaming, I'd gone upstairs to check on Prudence but didn't get to see her. Bridget said that she'd given Prudence calming tea and that she had already fallen asleep. Two hours after starting their play, the men left for Dragon's Cove looking rather dazed. Gemini had won every hand.

"Where did you learn to play cards so expertly?" I asked as we left the drawing room for our quarters.

Gemini pulled her cloak closer. "I've only played once before. Remember the night that Lord Alexander had the dinner party at Seafarer's Inn? We learned then."

"Either you are a genius at cards or Lord Ashton and Mr. Drayson need to sharpen their skills a bit. Let's hope Lord Ashton doesn't wager more than he can afford to lose. Can you imagine betting a thousand pounds? It makes me shudder to even think of it."

"I didn't know people bet money like that playing cards. Why, a woman could win an entire fortune in a single night if she were lucky."

Something in Gemini's voice sent warning signals through me. "What are you thinking?" I said, reaching for her hand.

She skittered back, laughing happily. "Nothing of note. I'll see you in the morning. Tomorrow is going to be even more interesting than today."

"How so?"

"Don't tell me you've forgotten already? Remember the haunted mansion after tea?"

My eyes popped wide. I had set that to the back of my mind and being reminded of it now let me know a very restless night lay ahead of me. "I'm getting a book from the library. Do you want one, too?"

"No. I'll see you in the morning." She danced up a few steps and I shook my head, walking toward the library. There were no lamps lit and I was forced to run my fingers lightly along the wall of the corridor. I suddenly got the strangest feeling that someone was behind me. I turned quickly but only found the corridor and center hall empty.

"Gemini," I called, wondering if she had changed her mind.

"Andrie, what is it?" came her loud whisper down the stairs.

"Nothing," I said. "Good night." Finding the first door on the left I turned inside the room and tripped over something large. I realized as I fell that it was the body of a man.

17

I ended up buried facedown in the cushion of a wing chair, which muffled my scream. My knees stung as if I'd landed in a nest of angry bees and my heart seesawed with my stomach until I heard a distinct snore from the floor behind me.

Well, at least I hadn't stumbled over a dead body for my grand finale on the strangest day of my life.

Getting shakily to my feet, I felt around for the lamp and lit the wick, then turned to find out who had nearly scared me to death. The Earl of Dartraven lay on the floor and the strong scent of whiskey hovered in the air. His dark, gray at the temple locks were mussed, but not as badly as his cravat. And he wasn't too far gone because when I brought the light closer to his face, he flung an arm over his eyes.

"Careful lass, I've indulged in a wee bit too much and just might set us both on fire if I breathe near that lamp."

"Whatever are you doing sleeping on the floor in the library?"

"Don't think I planned it that way. Last I remember I believe I was looking for Pru."

"Who?"

"That bloody woman who's bewitched me. Prudence."

"Considering the state you are in I'd say it is extremely fortunate that you didn't find her. What do you think you could have said to her as drunk as you are?"

"She has some 'splaining to do."

"Here," I said reaching down to tug on his arm. "Let's get you off the floor and maybe I can hear you better."

The moment I touched him, I gasped and backed away. What the earl was thinking about Prudence told me that Alex and Sean were most definitely their father's sons. Heavens, if people didn't go "sailing" every hour, they at least thought about it. Or at least the Killdaren men did.

"What's wrong, lass? Did I hurt you?" The earl sat up quickly, gaining his feet. He wobbled as if he were at sea in a storm.

I cleared my throat. "No."

"Then what is wrong? Ye look a mite upset."

"I'm fine. What were you saying about Prudence?"

"I said she had some explaining to do. For eight years I've been thinking she deliberately seduced me to have an easy life. But if that was the truth she never would have left the castle and gone to live in the village to her own peril it would seem, right?"

"That's what I would think."

He groaned and sat down on the sofa. I ventured back to the wing chair. "How, in eight years, could either of you not have spoken of this."

"Pride," he muttered. "It's my fault. When Prudence told me she was in a family way, I didn't take the news very well and told her that wasn't supposed to happen. That she was messing everything up. I'd come to care for her, more than I'd cared for any other woman besides my wife, and the thought of losing Prudence in childbirth scared me to death. I told her we'd discuss it when I returned from London in a month and I left. When I returned, Sean informed me that Prudence had gone to a convent and once she had her child she would be returning to live at Killdaren's Castle as an honored guest for the rest of her life at his invitation. Prudence never said anything differently and I assumed that was what she'd wanted all along."

"Sounds to me that you're the one with the explaining to do. I hope it's not too late."

"What do you mean, lass?"

"By not going to her before you found out about what happened in the village, she'll always wonder if you really do care for her or if you are feeling sorry about what happened. I know one thing for sure, though. You go to her like this and she won't believe a word you say. You have to show her that you really do care for her."

"How?"

"That is something you'll have to discover yourself. If I told you then it wouldn't be you caring for her, it would be me." I stood and walked over to the desk where Bridget had put the book on Druid magic she had been reading earlier. Picking up the book, I went to the earl and bravely set my hand on his shoulder. I had to face my demons, but I also wanted to see what the earl really felt for Prudence. Deep down he loved her, but that was buried under a mountain of fear and denial and guilt that he was betraying his first wife by loving again. "I imagine you could make it right with Prudence if you really tried, but first you're going to have to admit that you love her. Loving again doesn't betray another's memory."

I left him then, not really sure if he was capable of doing what it would take to win Prudence.

After a predicted restless night where dreams of Alex and me together failed to keep the darkest dreams from coming, I rose, dressed in my prettiest tea gown of deep rose and ivory lace, and went in search of Prudence. I found her, Bridget, and Cassie enjoying a breakfast of tea and scones with clotted cream and dried fruits.

"Where's Rebecca?" I said, joining them.

"With Mrs. Murphy in the kitchens baking pies." Prudence pushed a teacup into my hand, and as I touched her fingers, I felt her calmness inside, but I also felt despair. She honestly believed that having the earl learn about the village incident would negate any feelings he expressed now.

"I tripped over a body in the library last night," I said, matter of factly.

Teacups clattered amid gasps and cries.

"A ghost?" Gemini oddly asked.

"Don't be ridiculous," Cassie muttered. "There aren't ghosts here."

Gemini bit her lip as if troubled. But I didn't have a chance to study her expression.

"Andromeda Andrews, if you don't immediately explain, you're going to be a body on Prudence's floor," Cassie said, glaring at me.

I focused my attention on Prudence. "Ahem, it was a man in his cups thoroughly lamenting the fact that something he believed to be true for a number of years wasn't true, and nobody had told him differently. Personally, I believe that he shouldn't have had to be told, but unfortunately I have recently discovered how blind men can be to truths dangling in front of their faces."

Bridget rolled her eyes. "Blimey. You'll have to tell us more. That description fits every man we're are up against at the moment." She handed me a plate laden with goodies, which I immediately began enjoying.

"The earl," said Prudence. "Andrie found the earl. He's more likely to drown himself in whiskey than face himself. The others busy themselves with astronomy or horses." She turned to me, her golden eyes delicately sad. "Whatever he said, it doesn't mean anything, not now."

I shook my head. "You don't know that for sure. He knows his pride and false beliefs have wasted eight years. It would be a shame if that continued to happen."

Prudence sighed. "But I will never know if he truly loves and wants me."

"If you never give him a chance to prove himself then that will be true," I said.

Bridget sat back and crossed her arms in irritation. "Well, at least the earl may have seen the light now. Stuart's so mired in the dark I'll be an old woman before he'll see anything but his own foolishness."

Cassie frowned. "Having been married for a month now, I've come to the conclusion that the only thing a man sees aside from his own foolish council is the bedroom."

Prudence gasped and Bridget giggled. I had to bite my tongue from agreeing wholeheartedly with my sister. That would have been too telling. As it was, I found it difficult to believe nobody had seen a change in me since I'd been intimate with Alex, because every part of me felt different. Couldn't they tell how strong my feelings for him had become? I set my teacup down and stood. "On that wise note, I had better go or I'll be late."

"How is the cataloguing coming along?" Cassie asked. "You usually rave on and on about every artifact you list, but you haven't this time."

Turning from the doorway, I knew my cheeks had to be red flags as telling as a scarlet letter stamped upon my person for the whole world to see. I hadn't spoken of artifacts because my thoughts were all of Alex. "That is most likely because my mind is boggled. I found entire crates of antiquities from Egypt that have been sitting packed and unseen for over thirty years."

"Good heavens," Cassie said, surprised. "How did that happen?"

"They're in Alex's mother's room. She and the earl had just returned from Egypt and she went into labor before she could unpack the treasures, and she gave strict instructions that they weren't to be touched until she could take care of them herself."

"So she died in labor and nobody has unpacked them in all these years?" Gemini asked.

"That is correct."

Gemini set her teacup down and stood. "Is the room cold, Andrie?"

"What?"

"Do you ever notice a chill when you're there?"

I shook my head. "No. What would it matter anyway?"

"Just curious," Gemini said. "Rooms sometimes are that way. Like in the drawing room here. I can get so cold. Don't forget we're making an outing today just after teatime."

I studied Gemini a moment, tempted to cross the room and hug her so that I could read what she was thinking. I clenched my fists instead, wondering if I was slipping into a bad habit of deliberately reading people's thoughts. That would make me some sort of monster.

"I'll be back," I said, and ducked from the room, realizing that I was living my life on a very precarious edge and that the least ill wind would send me crashing to ruin, or worse.

Had I expected Alex to be waiting for my arrival as he had yesterday, I would have been sorely disappointed. I learned an hour after I had arrived that he'd left without warning yesterday evening and had yet to return. By noon, I had worked myself into a fine state of agitation so great that I could barely see the artifacts I was supposed to be taking meticulous notes on. Rustic statues became lumps of clay and delicate etchings became chicken scratches with little meaning. I didn't know with whom I was angrier—Alex for his absence or me for being upset by it. At the very least he could have left me a note.

Finding a small box of carved figurines, I carried them to the window to examine their detail by a better light. They were made of jade no bigger than my thumb and packaged in such a way that I had to wonder if they were Egyptian at all. Slipping one from its niche, I held it up to a sunbeam and blinked it into focus, then stared hard, wondering if I was really seeing what I thought I was. Or if my mind had been completely corrupted by Alex yesterday.

The figurine was a carving of a man and a woman to-gether, naked and intimate. The woman was on her hands and knees with the man behind her, pressing into her, his hands cupping her breasts.

"Good heavens!" I exclaimed, looking back at the box. There were thirty-six niches.

"Heavens what?" Alex said from just behind me. He pressed full against my back, slid a hand to my waist, and leaned down, inhaling softly by my ear.

I had to grapple with the box to keep from dropping it and only succeed when he reached around me and grabbed hold of it.

"Uh, nothing," I said, trying to breathe in between the thundering beats of my heart.

"You look a bit too flushed for it to be nothing, Androm-eda," he said, slipping the box from my fingers. I squeezed my eyes shut as he dug out a figurine.

He chuckled. "Interesting and heavenly," he said smoothly. "And to think this little gem has been hidden in a box for years. I'm in thorough agreement with you, Andromeda. These antiq-uities need to be displayed so that all may enjoy them. Where shall we put these? In the grand entry hall?"

Turning to face him, I slit one eye open to find him caress-ing the carved jade breasts of a woman who sat upon a man as if astride a horse. I dampened my lips. "If you want every visitor to go 'sailing' upon your marble floor then I think that would be a fine thing."

He laughed again. "So you've been thinking about sail-ing, have you, lass?"

Before I could find my voice to answer him, he placed the figurine back into the box and inserted his fingers into my closed fist, extracting the one that I still held. After sliding his finger along the woman's back, he returned it to its empty space. Then he held the box out to me. "Pick one," he said.

"What do you mean, pick one?" I squeaked. "You sound as if you are offering me a chocolate to savor."

"Better than chocolate, my dear. If you are daring enough,

I'm offering you the chance to challenge my abilities. Pick one and I'll make it happen now."

My breath escaped in a whoosh of air and I felt light-headed from the racing thud of my heart. A very strange and excitingly hot tingle centered itself between my legs. I should have been outraged, I should have railed at him for being gone, but I was too intrigued. I lifted my finger, deciding that I would choose the second figurine he had fished from the box, the position where I would be in control, or so it seemed. But he pulled the box away. "You have to close your eyes, and I have to spin the box around a bit, so that neither of us will know what it will be. Close your eyes."

I did and he bent down and kissed me first, gently, then more insistently. I leaned into him, breathing deeply of his scent.

"Now choose," he whispered.

This time, my hand shook and my palm dampened as I reached and felt the dividers on the box. I slid my finger across a row and then dipped it into a square.

"Excellent choice," he said.

I popped my eyes open. "What?"

He palmed the figurine and shook his finger at me. "You can't see yet. You're not ready."

Good Lord! What did I pick? "What do you mean I'm not ready?"

"You've got all of your clothes on and you're not in bed. You can't see this until then."

"That's not fair. How do I even know I'll want it?"

"Trust me. You will. Shall we?" he said, holding out his arm. After a sharp glare at him I set my hand on his arm, hoping I'd get a clue from his thoughts, but I felt nothing save the heat of his muscled arm beneath the soft fabric of his linen shirt. By all appearances he was a gentleman leading me to the ballroom, but my insides were tumbling end over end. Yesterday, I hadn't planned to be in Alex's arms, but it had happened. Now I'd made an even bigger step, for I was planning on being in his arms again, and wasn't sure if this was the move that would send me falling over the precipice I wavered on. For I wanted there to be so much more between us than the physical expression of love. I wanted all of the things that I could never have. I wanted him forever. Suddenly, walking into his arms, letting myself become more intimately entwined with him had my heart aching, and part of me knew that being with him again would only make the parting harder. And another part of me wanted to grasp every moment that I could, to savor every experience, to love him just once more.

I halted at his bedroom door, unsure what to do. "Mrs. Lynds is expecting me down for lunch shortly."

"I had her pack a picnic and send it to the stables with Brighty. I'd planned an outing for us this afternoon, so she'll not be expecting you."

"Oh." I moved on into the bedroom with him. He shut and locked the door. I swallowed the lump of nervousness lodged in my throat. "Perhaps we shouldn't let the meal go to waste."

"It'll wait. We'll picnic after and be hungrier for it." He slid his fingers into my hair and expertly eased out the pins until my hair fell down my back and over my breasts.

"I've a concern that needs to be addressed," I said hesitantly.

"Which is?" His fingers settled on my bodice buttons and plucked them free from their moorings, exposing my nearly sheer chemise. He flicked his thumbs over the tips of my breasts and they pebbled to hard tips. My heart fluttered and my intimate flesh dampened with need.

I grabbed his wrists as he palmed my breasts. "I'm sure you're more knowledgeable on these matters, but how exactly can I prevent . . . well—"

He slid his hand up to cup my cheeks and looked seriously into my eyes. "Having a child?"

"Exactly." I exhaled with relief that he understood and thought my concern important.

"That's why I journeyed to Penzance last night. I have

taken care of the matter. We've several options, which I will explain later. Now, if you've run out of excuses, I would very much like to kiss you again."

"I wasn't—"

His lips settled on mine. "You were," he mumbled against my mouth, then slid his tongue inside to gently sweep across the tip of mine before plunging deeper. I ran my hands over the hard planes of his chest up to the broad curve of his shoulders and into the silk of his dark hair, leaning closer to his heat. His scent, so exotic and heady, surrounded me, made me want to bury myself in him and revel in the sensations.

As he thoroughly kissed me, several deft moves left me only in my stockings and boots with my clothes a puddle at my feet. He started to kneel before me and I caught his arm, urging him to stay. I focused on his shirt buttons and managed to loosen three of them before he impatiently jerked the shirt over his head. Sliding to one knee, he untied my garters and pulled down my stockings before easing off my boots. Once I stood naked before him, he ran his hands from the tips of my toes all the way to the aching points of my breasts, seemingly memorizing every dip and curve. He blew his hot breath over the curls of my sex as he cupped my breasts, making me shiver to the very center of my being with anticipation. Scooping me up into his arms, he set me on the silky counterpane of his bed; and I sat up, watching him undress, noticing for the first time that he was sun-bronzed everywhere. His arousal jutted large and thick from a matte of dark black, curly hair. If he hadn't already been inside me before I would have claimed the deed impossible. He was so silky dark to my golden light.

"Do you sail naked?" I asked.

He frowned, puzzled by my question. "Your skin is darkened everywhere," I said.

"I often swim in the cove during the summer and occasionally nap on the beach in the warm sand."

"Outside without your clothes where just anyone could wander by?"

"Considering it's my land, just anyone isn't apt to wander by, and my servants know to give me privacy. But I daresay there are worse things than spying a naked man on the beach, should someone happen to stumble my way."

"Worse things? I was thinking that I hadn't ventured far enough this summer."

Alex laughed and the gleam of desire in his eyes darkened. "For this to work properly we need some pillows," he said.

"For what to work?"

He held up the figurine and I gasped, shaking my head. "That's impossible."

"Trust me," he said softly.

"Trust you?" I glared at the little jade carving. "You aren't the one standing on your head. Just exactly what is the point of being intimate like that? He can't even kiss her if he wanted to."

He laughed, gave me a quick kiss, and climbed onto the bed. Then he began stacking pillows up in the center of it. I was gauging how far it was from my clothes to the bathroom, wondering if I could make a quick escape. I had to have picked the least intriguing, most impossibly uncomfortable . . . Great heavenly day, it wasn't supposed to be like this. He was supposed to gently seduce me, sweep me off my feet with sweet words and soft music and a laughing smile. But maybe that only happened when a man loved a woman rather than just lusted for her, and Alex had made it very clear there was no place in his life for love. Tears burned in my eyes and I drew a deep breath. This is what I had decided as well. There was no place in my life for love, for no man could live with my secret. Knowing all of this didn't take the burn away. Not the burn of wanting things different, nor the burn of knowing they would never be different.

"Andrie." Alex whispered my name as if it were the most sacred of words. "Do you trust me?"

"Yes," I said, turning to him. Seven pillows made a huge wedge in the center of the large bed, but Alex wasn't kneeling or sitting beside them as I expected. He was lying across the bottom of the bed on his back with one hand cupped behind his head. The other hand he held out to me. I knew that by taking his hand, I was committing myself to experience all that I could of his passion before reality would steal everything away. I loved him. I didn't have a choice.

I set my hand in his and he drew me closer, pressing my palm to his chest. The solid thud of his heart thrummed beneath hot, rippling muscle.

"Touch me, feel me, and when you're ready to explore further we can try the pillows. Intimacy is about pleasure for you and for me, and if something doesn't fall within those guidelines then it doesn't belong here and isn't important. You're so arousing, so sensual and responsive, that I forget all of this is new to you. I didn't mean to make you uncomfortable with the challenge and the Kama Sutra figures. All I've been able to think about since you left yesterday is making love to you again, and I found the situation extremely arousing. I've never let myself be around anyone long enough to even play such a game."

Though I still trembled inside as if I were on shaky ground, his words and the loneliness lying starkly beneath them wrapped around me and tugged me impossibly closer to him. I had to be honest as well. "It was arousing. It made my heart beat so hard that I almost became dizzy. I don't know what happened. If you had marched in and swept me off my feet where I didn't have to think then I might not have started feeling so strange. Does everyone talk so much when they are being intimate?"

"Hardly," he said. "If they did maybe there wouldn't be as many mistakes made, because talking requires thought and not just feeling."

"Are we making a mistake?" I asked, afraid for us both.

"Maybe, but not like many that are made. Both of us appear to have made a choice here, am I wrong?"

"No." I slid my finger down the thin path of hair bisecting

his stomach. He sucked in air and his arousal jerked upward. "Did I hurt you?"

"Quite the opposite." He moved his hand over mine and brought it to the burgeoning tip of his sex. He was hot and very hard and so surprisingly soft that I circled my fingertip all the way around his sex and then slipped it down the long length of him. He groaned. "You pleasure me greatly," he said.

Emboldened, I repeated my motions, exploring further. The hard length of his thighs and legs felt so much more powerful than the softness of mine that it was difficult to believe I could make him tremble, but I did. I made him tremble and sweat and grow almost frantically needy when I spread my touch to all of him, then kissed him everywhere, too.

He rolled as he ended the kiss, angling himself above me. "My turn now," he said, his green eyes gleaming dark with desire. The power I had over him awed me, for I realized that he was just as vulnerable and just as needy as I had been yesterday. Between his kisses and his questing tongue plundering my every curve and secret, my breasts soon ached and my sex burned with a fire only he could assuage. I arched my hips against him. "Fill me," I said, writhing with my desire to have him inside me.

He kissed me long and hard. "Gladly."

Scooping me into his arms, he set me on top of the pillows on my back so that my bottom was high and my head low. Blood rushed dizzyingly to my head. I might have protested, but he slid between my legs, leaned down, and kissed my sex thoroughly. My fists gripped the covers and I cried out from the erotic waves sweeping over me.

He rose up, sliding my legs along his body until my heels rested on his shoulders. Then he grabbed my hips and drove himself deep inside of me, going farther than before, going so deep that for a moment I thought I would split apart. But he rubbed his thumb directly on my most sensitive spot, pulling my hips higher into the air as he rocked deeper and deeper into me. My shuddering release was so forceful, so intensely pleasurable that my entire body shook. My lungs spasmed for air and my mind filled with an unbelievable euphoria, obliterating any thoughts but that of the pleasure washing over me in wave after wave.

Then Alex slid my legs from his shoulders so that my knees hugged his hips. He leaned down and over me, pressing himself slowly deeper until he could kiss me by bracing his hands on the bed beside my head. He made one last thrust of his hips as his tongue mated with mine and his release shuddered through us both. I couldn't read any of his thoughts. His mind was filled with the feel of his blood rushing to his head and the pleasure claiming him.

I wrapped my arms around him and pulled him close, wondering what other heavens the figurines in the box would lead to. I knew I was closer to Alex at that moment than I would ever be to another ever again, and I knew our time together wasn't meant to last.

18

❧

"I'll race you back to the picnic," I called as I spurred Delilah past Alex, who was astride Samson. Sand flew and the waves lapped at the horses' legs as we rushed along the shore with the salty wind and the hot sun beating upon our faces.

"On what wager?" he shouted.

"I'm still recovering from your last challenge," I said. "And you've yet to pay up from the duel I won the day before."

He laughed and reached my side. "Yes, I did. You asked for me and got me. I've been meaning to ask where in the devil you learned that trick."

I slowed my pace to lead him into a false sense of security. There was no way Delilah could actually beat Samson all the way back down the beach, but if I timed things just right I could spurt ahead and beat Alex at the last minute. "Your brother," I told him, deciding to give him the truth whether he wanted to hear it or not. "Sean caught me pilfering fencing books from the library and I had to confess that you were teaching me. He decided to give Cassie and me lessons the next morning and thought I needed an ace up my sleeve if I was going to match swords with you. You know, he is almost as good as you are, and probably more deadly. The cane he uses to balance on has a secret dagger on the tip."

"Stop," Alex shouted as if in pain, his expression dark. "I don't want to know or hear any more." He leapt ahead and went thundering down the beach, going faster than I'd ever seen a person race on a horse.

"Wait, Alex," I yelled. "You have to at least listen to me." I sent Delilah after Samson, realizing too late that I didn't quite have the skill to properly hold on while galloping that fast through the surf. Frightened, I jerked back on the reins. Delilah squealed in fear and reared up. I went flying into the sea, landing on my back, slightly stunned by the cold water. Before I could catch my breath or stand a huge wave slammed into me, rolling me over, and sucking me deeper as it washed back into the sea. Water went up my nose, my eyes stung, and my lungs burned with the need to breathe. I fought for a footing, but my skirts weighed me down, making it almost impossible for me to move. Panic that I could die rushed through me and I floundered wildly.

A sense of surreal slowness took over my body. Through my burning vision, I could see the water whoosh around me. I could see my hair floating about me. I could see my arm stretch for the light and my skirts move as I tried to kick my way to it. An inky blackness stole into my mind and I knew that as impossible as it seemed, I was moments away from death.

I wasn't frightened as much as I was angered. I didn't want to die. I hadn't loved everyone enough. Hadn't told them how much they meant to me. I wanted to see Alex laugh again. I wanted to feel his arms around me. I didn't want him to be so alone that he had nothing to tie him to this world. I wanted to love him longer. Shoving with all my might, I surged upward, but another wave crashed against me. I could feel it twisting me even though my vision had gone. Then something jerked my arm and I read Alex's turbulent thoughts of guilt and fear as he pulled me upward. Wrapping his arm around my waist, he surged to the surface. I broke through to the air, and dragged in deep, long breaths. The blackness receded, leaving me dizzy.

"Don't you dare think that! It's not your fault," I said, gasping.

Alex looked at me strangely then shook his head. "Come on," he said, slipping an arm around me and pulling me against him. He swam backward to the shore. I was shocked to realize just how far out the sea had dragged me in so short a time. The moment we hit the beach, he laid me on the sand and kissed me as if the world had really ended.

"I'm sorry," he whispered. "Good God, I'm sorry."

I blinked salt water from my eyes and thought there were tears falling from his. "Shh," I said. "It's not your fault and I'm all right. I panicked and jerked on Delilah's reins so hard I frightened her and I fell off when she reared back. You didn't do that, I did, so you can't blame yourself." I sighed with relief that he didn't bring up the fact that I'd chastised him for blaming himself before he'd verbalized it. The fact that he'd looked at me so strangely in such a dire moment told me that I was right to keep my secret. It would change everything between us were he to find out, and I didn't want that to happen. Not yet. But guilt that I wasn't being honest with him about who I was swamped me as hard as the sea had. I couldn't think about that now. Alex had to understand he wasn't responsible for what had happened.

"I went rushing off and left you," he said grimly.

"Well, you did do that. You should have at least listened to me before you rushed off. But good Lord, Alex. You can't blame yourself for every mishap. I am an adult and I could have very easily dismounted and marched down the beach if I hadn't felt confident enough to ride. And if you remember, *I* challenged *you* to a race. So if anyone is to blame it is myself."

He bent down and kissed me again. "You make a beautiful liar, Andromeda."

"And you make a wonderful Perseus. You do realize that you just saved me from the sea."

He shook his head and I saw the beginnings of a smile curve the grim set of his lips.

Horses' hooves thundered along the beach. Neither Alex nor I looked up. I assumed as he probably did that Samson and Delilah were approaching.

"What have we here? Exploring artifacts on the beach, Miss Andrews?" came a cynical drawl.

Alex rolled to his feet and I managed to sit up and glare at Sir Warwick and Constable Poole.

"I don't like your tone or your insinuation, Warwick. You owe the lady an apology. What we have is a woman who almost drowned when she was thrown from her horse. Since this is my land, perhaps you'd better tell me why you two are running about on it?" Alex had both hands planted on his hips, looking like a pirate ready to run the enemy through at the least provocation, and Sir Warwick's mere presence was just that.

Alex caught hold of my elbow and helped me to stand. I felt like a miserable drowned rat and probably looked that way, too.

"My apologies then," said Warwick. Dressed impeccably as always, he wore his habitual expression of boredom and disdain. By the way he studied my face I felt as though he could see right into my thoughts and knew exactly how intimate Alex and I were.

"We're here looking for you, Viscount Blackmoor," replied the constable. His long mustache whipped in the wind, and one hand held his hat while the other clutched the reins of a horse that appeared as if it had three feet in the grave. "The caves have been opened again. Did you give the order for it to be done?"

"Of course not. It would seem that I'm going to have to put a guard on the cliffs. Any idea who keeps trespassing?"

"No, but it could be we've smugglers about."

Alex shook his head. "I would know if something like that was happening at night in my cove."

"That's what I think," said the constable.

Alex cocked his head, his stance widening just enough that I knew he took the constable's remark as a threat. "Are you insinuating that I am involved in such an activity, Constable Poole? I assure you, any goods I transport on my ship are legally exchanged. Do you doubt that?"

The constable blustered. "Certainly not. I only agree that you would have known if something ill was taking place."

"Then Miss Andrews and I will bid you adieu, gentlemen. It is imperative that I get her back to Killdaren's Castle before she catches a chill. I'll have the caves attended to."

I think my shivering was more from almost drowning than from cold, though the wind did seem cooler now that I was wet.

"Then we'll say goodbye," said Sir Warwick. "Would you like for us to ride to Killdaren's Castle and have one of your sisters come?"

I shook my head, a bit consoled by his consideration. "No, thank you. I'll be fine."

They rode off and Alex turned to me. "Are you sure you aren't injured?"

"Only my pride, I think. I know how to swim, but I couldn't seem to make any headway between the strength of the current and the weight of my skirts."

"Dragon's Cove is known for its treacherous current. Something about the shape of the land pulls everything out to sea even during an incoming tide. It's even worse now with the tide receding." He slid his arm around me and pulled me close against him, holding me tight. "When I think of what almost happened . . . I—"

"Don't," I said, leaning up to brush my lips over his. He kissed me as if I were fragile glass that would break in a soft wind. I wrapped my arms around his neck and demanded more, and he gave me more. Desire flared hotly, making me ache for the feel of him inside me again.

"Another kiss like that and you'll not only be wet, but you will be naked on the beach even if Warwick and the constable are wandering around. We'd better get you back home." He whistled and received an answering neigh. A moment later Samson and Delilah appeared, coming over the top of a large sand dune. "We're halfway between Dragon's Cove and Killdaren's Castle. Do you want me to carry you back to Dragon's Cove, so that you can take a carriage home?"

"No," I said, drawing a deep breath. "I think I can ride home, but just slower than before."

"All right. We'll take the path though the woods. With less wind, it will be warmer than riding along the shore." He helped me remount Delilah and then joined me once he was on Samson. Riding side by side, we entered into the maritime forest and made our way to Killdaren's Castle.

"What upset you before?" I asked after a few minutes. "When I spoke of your brother?"

"Can't you just leave this alone? There're things that you won't tell me. Do I keep probing you for answers?"

"No."

"I want them though. I hope soon you'll trust me enough to tell me everything."

"It isn't a matter of trust, Alex. My situation is different than yours. You're sacrificing your life on an erroneous assumption that Sean's life was forfeited during your fight and all that is left of him is a shell of a man. You couldn't be more wrong. How can I not make you hear the truth at least once?

"He was injured in an accident. He's made adjustments. He lives a full life. He is not crippled. What if the reverse had happened, Alex? What if you had fallen over the cliff during the fight and not Sean? What if he'd saved your life, like he did when you were eight and the boat capsized? Would you want him to do what you are doing?"

"That's not a fair question."

"Why not? Is he any more or less of a man than you are? I don't think so. The only one who thinks Sean is crippled is you, and ironically the only one who was crippled in the accident was you. But you don't have to believe me. You can find out for yourself by making peace with Sean."

"So you've figured everything out and it is as simple as that?"

The exasperated sarcasm underlying his question set my teeth on edge. "No, but I do know that nothing will ever be different unless you make it different. Sean won't see that he is wrong about this whole Dragon's Curse nonsense unless you show him and that can't happen as long as you two sit in your castles like hermits with your fingers stuck in your ears so you can't hear anything but yourselves."

"What makes you think a thousand years of history is nonsense?"

"I didn't say the history of the curse is nonsense. The existence of the curse between you and Sean may just very well be, though. Both of you have proved it false. He saved your life when you were children and you saved his life eight years ago. Why aren't you both shouting that you've managed to break the Dragon's Curse? You can't change the past, but you can direct the future. Start a new book. Title it the Dragon's Curse Undone. A record of the Killdaren twins who saved each other's lives."

"Any other world problems you want to solve?"

"Yes, but I'll wait and speak to someone who is intelligent enough to listen to some simple truths." The towers of Killdaren's Castle appeared over the trees and I urged Delilah ahead. Alex kept close, but silent. I may not have been all right in what I'd said, but I wasn't all wrong either, and I wasn't about to let him make me feel as if I were.

Reaching the back of the castle, I didn't wait for his help. I slid from the saddle and forced my shaky knees to hold me upright as I handed Delilah's reins to Alex. "Thank you for a lovely day," I said primly, and marched away.

"Bloody hell, Andromeda, you can't expect—"

"Andrie! What happened?" Cassie exclaimed, opening the back door and stepping outside.

"I went swimming," I said.

Gemini joined her. "Why did you do that in your dress? You know we're supposed to go to the mansio—ohh."

Cassie jabbed Gemini in the side. "Never mind," she said, looking curiously at Alex. "Hurry inside and we'll ready a bath for you. We were about to have tea."

"I'll take mine in the tub," I said, marching up the stairs.

"Your sister was thrown from her horse and almost drowned. She's more than a little addled at the moment."

Gritting my teeth against the inference that I had no idea what I was talking about, I turned to face him. He looked as if he teetered on the edge of being as wet and wild and angry as a man could get. I didn't hesitate to push him over. "At least I haven't spent the last eight years of my life with my head buried in the sand."

"At least I realize that cataloguing artifacts doesn't qualify one to be an expert in relationships."

"At least I have relationships," I shouted back and then ran inside, bursting into tears.

Cassie came to me and put an arm around my shoulders. "Gemini, go tell Bridget that we'll take our outing another day."

Gemini groaned.

"No," I said, dashing my tears away. "I'm fine. We'll go just as soon as I can bathe and dress. It's just that he can make me so angry. How can he be so smart but so stubbornly stupid?"

Gemini giggled. "Bridget just came storming in from outside and said the same thing. Only she said 'bloody stupid.'"

"Ladies don't say bloody," Cassie said, half-heartedly. "Go get Andrie some tea and some clothes while I help her get in the tub."

Gemini ran off and Cassie hurried me into a room off the kitchens where a number of tubs waited with water already heated in a nearby kettle.

She started to pull down soap and a towel from a nearby shelf as I worked on my buttons. "Sean's going to put in electric lighting and plumbing," she said, sounding odd.

I frowned her way. I already knew that, just as I knew that Sean hadn't bothered with lighting before because light bothered him and that he'd seen no use for plumbing the whole castle since he had a natural hot spring Roman bath in his wing.

"Bloody hell, Andrie. Is he going to marry you?" she blurted as she swung around, looking angry and confused.

"What?" I paused while unbuttoning my skirt.

She flung her hands up in the air. "We don't have time to pretend. Gemini will be back in just a few minutes. I quite understand the Killdarens' devastating appeal. I'm married to Alex's twin, and I know you. The look in both of your eyes says it all. So, is he going to marry you?"

I shut my eyes, praying for strength. This was going to be the hardest battle of all to face. "Cassie. It isn't a question of him marrying me. I won't be marrying anybody."

"Why?"

"Because I can't." Hurriedly undressing, I climbed into the steamy tub and picked up the soap.

She poured water over my head. " 'Because I can't' doesn't work. Why?"

I sudsed up my hair and she rinsed it. "You know why," I said. "No man can live with a woman who goes around reading all of his thoughts."

"What do you mean? I thought you only read thoughts and feelings on occasion."

I drew a deep breath, realizing that I had to tell Cassie. She had to understand what was happening in my life. Not knowing was only going to cause her to worry more. "When we lived in Oxford, I guess I didn't come into contact with others very much. I was accustomed to reading your thoughts and Gemini's and wasn't overly concerned or burdened by my ability, but when we came here everything changed. It's worse now, Cassie. That man on the boardwalk who went running into the street—I saw the image of him murdering his wife when he bumped into me. I accused him of killing her and that was why he ran. It's that way with everyone now.

Even you. If you've an image of something in your mind when I touch your hand, I see it."

"Good Lord!" She sat down on a nearby stool. "Why didn't you say anything?"

"Because nobody can know. Do you know what people would do to me if they found out? I have nightmares about them stoning me, reviling me, burning me at the stake as a witch."

"They don't do things like that now—"

"A mob can do just about anything it wants to do. The villagers almost stoned Prudence for being an unwed mother."

"Sean knows about my dreams and accepts that part of me. I myself didn't think a man would be able to do that. Andrie, Alex wouldn't—"

"Reject me? Think about it, Cassie. What if you lived with someone from whom you could never have a private moment or thought? Do you want Sean to know exactly what you are thinking at any moment, or do you want him to know only what you are comfortable with him knowing? I already erred when Alex pulled me from the water today. He was so filled with guilt and anger at himself for what happened that I shouted at him not to blame himself. That I alone was responsible for my actions. He looked at me very oddly, leaving me little doubt of how horrified he'd be if he knew I could read his thoughts on occasion. It's not as bad with Alex as it is with others. It seems that I can only see directly into his mind during moments of high emotion, but that is bad enough."

"Not that I'm agreeing with you, but if you aren't going to marry him then why are you being with him?"

"Because I love him. I want to see him healed and to go on and live a full life. I don't want him serving a life sentence of loneliness just because he feels he has to leave his brother his title to make restitution for crippling Sean."

"Sean's not crippled."

"In Alex's mind he crippled his brother and there is no dissuading him of the notion."

"We'll discuss that later. So, what you're saying is that you're healing Alex so that he can go on to live a full life without you. He can marry another woman, kiss another woman, touch another woman, make love to another woman, and give that woman his love and his children, and that's wonderful by you."

The more Cassie went on the more my stomach churned and a knot centered itself in my throat. "Yes," I shouted, tears gathering in my eyes.

"You're just as addled as Alex is" Cassie shook her head. "But I'm more worried about you at the moment. I think you're doing him a great disservice by not being honest with him. He might just be a bigger man than you give him credit for."

Gemini came into the room with my clothes and a cup of tea. "We need to hurry or we're not going to have time to properly explore."

Cassie handed me a towel. As I dried off and dressed, I wondered if we all weren't fools dangling from puppet strings controlled by some unknown master whose intent was just as Machiavellian as that of the man responsible for Mary and Lady Helen's deaths.

19

It took some maneuvering, but Bridget managed to arrange for one of the newer groomsmen to drive the buggy, so that with any luck Stuart wouldn't catch wind of our outing. The driver didn't think anything of heading away from the village for our venture, and when Bridget directed him down the road leading to the Kennedy Mansion, which we learned was the estate on the other side Alex's vast holdings, the driver only raised his brows.

I'm not sure what I expected, but the peaceful bucolic drive leading to the mansion didn't quite fit with the word haunted. Sure there were overgrown weeds skirting the road and the grasses in the pasture were high as one would suppose. Yet the shady fullness of the lazy trees along the road and the bright chirp of starlings mixed with the chattering of chipmunks and the buzz of bees dispelled any gloom.

I had to wonder why Mr. Drayson had made such a point

about the evil feel of the place and had cautioned us against coming here. It was almost as if he'd purposely dangled a forbidden carrot in front of Gemini's nose.

"This doesn't seem very haunted," Gemini said, almost reading my thoughts.

"Well," Cassie replied. "You can't expect that you're suddenly going to have barren fields and leafless trees just because no one is living in a house, can you? Not unless there's a ghost that scares all the wildlife away and kills all of the plants."

"What do you think ghosts can do to you?" Gemini asked.

I lifted my brows in surprise.

"Blimey, why would you ask that now?" Bridget asked, her eyes wide as she smoothed back a strand of fiery hair from her face.

Cassie stiffened her spine. "I believe that spirits who have something important to say can say such, but that's it. Any evil perpetrated in this world has a flesh-and-blood hand behind it. Now is not the time for a discussion of the nature of ghosts. We came here to learn what we can about Lady Helen. What do we know so far?"

"Her father gambled badly," said Prudence.

"Sean and Alex were enamored of her," I said.

"She was very beautiful," Bridget said. "Silvery hair, sapphire eyes, and the voice of an angel. Flora sang beautifully, too, but Helen was different. If you could imagine what the morning mists would sound like if they could sing, then you'd know her voice. It was delicate and surrounded you with a mysterious, ancient feeling."

I shivered, remembering the three blond women chasing me in my dream, one of them Mary, one of them silvery blond and the other . . . I forced myself to say what I knew would cause Bridget to be upset. "Helen was blond and she could sing. Mary was, too. They had that in common."

Bridget frowned. "Flora was blond and sang, too."

"The earl paid Helen money to reject Sean and Alex."

Cassie sighed. "I wonder if all of this would have happened if he hadn't done that."

"Alex wonders, too," I said. "Did anyone ever check on the money Lady Helen recieved? It had to be a considerable sum to pay off her father's debts and to keep her comfortable for the rest of her life."

"Excellent question, Andrie," Cassie said. "We should ask the earl. We don't even know when and how he paid her."

The knot of tension inside me wrenched tighter. "We haven't been very good investigators. We should have asked these questions days ago."

The buggy came to a stop and we all turned in surprise to find that we'd arrived. The manor was a large brownstone with a center section and a right and left wing. Its two stories were topped by a high-pitched roof with tiny windows peeking out from its darkness. It almost seemed as if a black cloud hovered over the home. Weeds had overtaken any semblance of civility and vines had strangled the once white porch columns to a sickly green. Whatever wildlife we'd heard before made its absence known now. The silence screamed at me.

Before anyone could say a word, Gemini jumped down from the buggy and started for the door.

"Gemini Andrews! Stop right now," Cassie shouted, scrambling to exit the buggy.

Gemini didn't even turn her head or slow her step; she kept walking decidedly forward and up the stone steps.

"Blimey!" Bridget muttered as she and I followed on Cassie's heels.

Gemini had opened the door and crossed the threshold before we reached her.

Cassie grabbed Gemini's arm. "Stop right now. We will do this slowly and all together or we won't do it at all."

"What?" Gemini shook her head as if dazed.

"Look at me." Cassie set her palm on Gemini's cheek. "Good Lord, you're freezing cold."

"Can't you hear her crying?" Gemini whispered.

Cassie gasped.

"Bloody hell," said Bridget.

I peered closer at Gemini, seeing that her pupils were di-
lated. Touching her icy hand, I heard the faint cry of a woman
in pain echoing in my sister's mind.

Without letting go of Gemini, I grabbed Cassie's arm.
"She hears a woman. It's faint, but it's there. A woman in
pain and crying."

"Let's go home," Cassie said, backing up a step.

"No! We have to help her." Gemini pulled free and ran.

I didn't even blink before I went after her. God only knew
what my sister was hearing, but it had sounded very bad, and
no matter what it was I couldn't let her face it alone. Cassie
and Bridget were right behind me. Running as fast as I could,
I caught Gemini's hand. The cry of the woman had escalated
in volume. Cobwebs danced off pictures and chandeliers, dust
flew from our skirts, and ghostly shrouded furniture passed in
a whir. Reaching a staircase, Gemini turned to go up. A quick
glance upward revealed footprints marring the dust that had
settled on them. Someone had been here—recently. I tried to
pull Gemini to a stop, but she struggled, frantic to help the
woman whose cries grew louder and louder in her head.

Cassie cried for us to stop.

"She can't," I yelled back. "She has to help and I can't
leave her."

Gemini was shivering so badly from cold that she wobbled as she plunged ahead. At the top of the stairs she turned
right and went down the corridor to the first door on the left
and nearly fell into the room.

The screaming in Gemini's head was so deafening that my
head and ears hurt. I barely had the chance to register that we'd
entered a pink-and-gold bedroom when Gemini fell, her mind
going blank. I managed to break her fall enough so that she
eased to the floor and I landed on my knees, half holding her.

"Oh, my dear God." Cassie rushed up and knelt next to
us. "What happened?"

"She's fainted. She's breathing easier, her skin is getting warmer, but her heart is still racing with fear. Thank God she's out of it. I don't think I could have stood hearing the woman's tortured cries another minute."

"You all best better tell me whot's a happenin'!" Bridget cried. "There's no screamin', and if this is a prank it's not bloody funny."

"Gemini heard screaming. I could hear it in her head," I said, so weary and drained that I had to fight to think."

"What does she mean?" asked Bridget.

Cassie sighed and sat back. "Bridget, you know I have dreams about deaths or near deaths. You remember that from the night Sean saved Rebecca, right?"

Bridget nodded.

"Andrie—"

"No, don't," I whispered.

"We can trust her, Andrie. She needs to understand what just happened. Andrie can read people's minds when she touches them."

"Bloody hell, no!" Bridget jumped up, looking totally frightened.

"Bloody hell, yes!" Cassie shouted back.

Bridget blinked at Cassie.

I shut my eyes and spoke. "The day you stormed out of the stables when you were arguing with Stuart and I ran into you, there were two thoughts in your head. You called Stuart a 'bloody, stubborn arse of a man!' And thought that it'd serve him right if you found yourself another man. A vampire lover! Then you wondered if he would be so quick to reject you if he found you naked in his bed." I opened my eyes to see Bridget's mouth fall open.

Cassie frowned. "You've read some of my thoughts that clearly, too?"

Tears filled my eyes and poured down my cheeks. "Not on purpose. It just happens and I can't stop it. I see images, too. I'm sorry."

"Good Lord, Andrie," Cassie wrapped her arms around

me and hugged me unreservedly. There was no rejection in her mind, only love. It completely shocked me. "I'm sorry that you have to live with so burdensome of a gift."

"Gift? It's a curse."

There was a very long silence in the room as Bridget stared at me. I could tell she was having a difficult time accepting what we said. She took a long, shuddering breath. "Blimey," Bridget said, moving closer to me rather than farther away. "I've never had friends as loving and loyal as you both. And just because you have a quirk or two doesn't mean I'm going to stop being your friend either. Seems to me that it'd be a bloody curse to have to put up with everyone's nonsense. Since you both know how I'm planning to corner Stuart, do you think he'd reject me?"

Gemini stirred.

"We'd better get Gemini out of here before she wakes up and hears the screaming again. You'll have to help me carry her, Bridget. I don't want Cassie straining herself."

"I'll get her feet," Bridget said.

Cassie stood. "I can help. Why don't you let me get her feet and you and Bridget—"

The bedroom door slammed shut and we all screamed.

"The wind," I said, swallowing my burgeoning fear. "We left the front door open."

"Right." Cassie moved confidently to the door and grabbed the handle. The door didn't budge. She shook it again, but it was firmly locked.

Cassie backed away from the door. "Andrie?" she whispered.

I reached up and touched her hand. "I'm with you," I whispered back. "Ghosts might make their voices heard, but anything that's physical has to have a flesh-and-blood hand behind it."

Cassie ran for the door on the other side of the room. It was locked as well. The only other way out was through the window.

"Find a weapon, Bridget. You hold Gemini, Andrie. Keep

her quiet if she starts to wake." Cassie went to the fireplace and jerked up a dusty iron poker.

Bridget grabbed a heavy candelabra from the desktop. When she did, something fell and hit the wood floor. The tinkling of breaking glass scraped over my raw nerves. Leaning down, Bridget picked up the little picture frame that had fallen, then gasped in horror.

"Oh, my God, Cassie," Bridget cried and started shaking so badly that she dropped the candelabra.

"Bridget," Cassie hissed. "What are you doing? What's wrong?"

Bridget turned the picture our way. "It's me mum and me brother, Timmy. Flora took this with her when she left."

I groaned, my gaze flying about the room, looking for—"Cassie," I croaked. "The killer. He must . . . he must have come here. He must have brought Flora here."

Bridget fell to her knees with a cry.

"Andrie, how do you know?" Cassie moved to my side.

"Rebecca's nightmare the other night. When I touched her I heard Mary arguing with a man, accusing him of compromising someone. He was awful, saying he was going to punish that someone for their promiscuity. And then . . . then . . . I think he hurt Mary badly . . . and forced her to . . ."

"Jack?" Bridget whispered. "Was his name Jack? Flora went away with a man named Jack."

"I don't know what his name was. Names weren't in Rebecca's head. Not even Flora's name was. That's why I didn't say anything. But Flora's continued silence together with Mary's defense of a woman made me very suspicious. For that picture to be here . . ."

"Means the screams Gemini heard could be those of my sister's ghost. She was here. He hurt her here." Bridget's face turned as red as her hair. "And that bastard is here now!" She grabbed the candelabra up and ran for the door, swinging the heavy brass against the door. "Come and face me you coward!"

Cassie grabbed Bridget's shoulder and pulled her back.

"Wait. We have to think what he would do next and then we have to do exactly what he wouldn't expect for us to do."

"It depends on why he's locked us in here. Is he going to keep us prisoners and do what he did to Mary and Helen and Flora . . . ?"

"Or what?" Cassie asked. "Try and eliminate us all together? We need to get out of here now."

"The windows," I said. "Maybe there's a way we can climb down. But how can we get Gemini down?"

"Try and wake her. Bridget, let's take the sheets off the bed and tie them together." Marching over to the bed, Cassie grabbed the pink satin counterpane and pulled it off the bed. She screamed, backing away in horror. Bridget cried out a deep, keening sound of grief. The sheets were stained with dried blood. Bloody ropes that had to have been used to bind the victim lay on the bed along with some gruesome-looking iron contraptions that reminded me of the medieval torture devices I'd seen in Alex's dungeon. The image of me tied in Alex's bed flashed in my mind. Had I only thought I saw myself . . . what if I'd—

My heart thundered in my ears and my mind screamed. *NO!*

Then I smelled smoke.

Leaving Gemini, I stood and grabbed Bridget's arm. At first her grief was so overwhelming I couldn't think. *Alex*, I screamed in my mind, forcing out Bridget's sorrow. I pushed her toward Gemini. "He's set the house on fire. Drag her to the window."

"The curtains," I yelled to Cassie. "Help me. Rushing over to the heavy pink satin, I pulled hard, nearly having to hang my entire weight on the panel before it broke free. Cassie managed to get her panel down. I shoved mine at her. "Knot these together while I get more."

"He'll expect us to escape through the window," she said.

"I know. He won't be expecting us to be armed and ready to beat him to a bloody pulp though. We don't have a choice, Cassie."

"Then let's do it."

Tying the curtains together, we made a long ladder. Then we wrapped Gemini in a curtain and attached her to one end of our ladder. I went to the window and scanned the area, but didn't see anything but overgrown gardens and the distant spires of Dragon's Cove. My stomach twisted again, but I pushed away the uneasy thoughts and opened the windows. I may not be able to see into Alex's mind at any given moment, but I knew him. He wasn't capable of murdering in cold blood. He'd kill to defend and he might have been rash enough in his youth to have accidentally caused a death, like his fight with his brother. But he wasn't capable of the evil perpetrated here. What I feared was that someone might be trying to make it appear as if Alex were guilty. I knew what I had seen was a medieval torture device, and I seriously doubted it was a common item here in Cornwall.

"Give me the free end. I'm going to put it halfway down and then drop the rest of the way to the ground. Then you and Bridget pull that end back up and tie it to the bedstead. You'll be able to lower Gemini to me and climb down after."

"No. I'll go first," Cassie said.

"Give me the poker, Cassie. We don't have time to argue and I will not allow you to put the life of my future niece or nephew at stake from some foolish sense of responsibility to me. If the killer is down there waiting, throw the candelabra at him and anything else you can find."

As soon as I had the curtains out, I started down. Dear God! The bottom floor was on fire as well, which put Cassie, Bridget, and Gemini in even more danger. Wiggling down with the poker clutched between my neck and shoulder, I reached the bottom of the curtains and dropped. I landed on my feet on the stone below with a thud. The poker clattered to the ground and I fell to my knees. Tears stung my eyes as I scrambled for the poker. Picking it up, I swung around in a circle, looking for lurking danger. I didn't see anything, but I could feel it. I was certain that I could feel him watching.

I motioned to Cassie to hurry. She and Bridget lowered

Gemini to me, and as they climbed down, I untied Gemini from the ladder. She was really beginning to worry me now. She was still unresponsive, her mind an inky mass of darkness. Cassie joined me first, and then Bridget, who had now turned a ghostly white with eyes more haunted than. I imagined a living person's could be.

"He's near," I whispered. "I feel him watching. Let's go to the left. It'll be closer to our driver." I handed Cassie the poker and grabbed one end of Gemini's cocoon. Bridget grabbed the other end and we lifted Gemini. By the time we made it around to the front, I knew Gemini was going to have some painful bruises.

Looking up from the concealing foliage of bushes and weeds at the side of the house, my heart took a dive. The buggy was there, just where we left it. The driver was slumped over in the seat, a heart-stopping sight in itself. But next to the buggy stood a very skittish Samson.

Alex was here.

20

"Andrie? Isn't that Alex's horse?" There was no mistaking the accusation in her voice.

"Yes. It's not him, Cassie. He is not the killer."

"How do you know for sure? You said that you couldn't—"

"It doesn't matter. I'll swear that I can before the whole world if I have to. He's not guilty."

"Then where is he?"

"Oh, God. He must be in there looking for us. I have to go back inside."

"The place is on fire, Andrie."

"I have to." I didn't want to leave my sisters, but I had to go look for Alex.

"You're not going alone."

"You're not coming with me. You and Bridget need to stay with Gemini. I swear I think the killer watched us escape through the window. Both of you need to stay together and protect Gemini. Maybe you should get in the buggy and leave."

"No, we'll all stay together as much as possible." Cassie's tone brooked no argument and I decided she was right.

"There's a gun," Bridget whispered. "In the buggy, hidden in the driver's seat. No one leaves the castle without being protected. I'll get the gun and then Cassie can stay hidden with Gemini while I go with you to search for Lord Alex. We need to hurry."

Before we could say a thing, Bridget broke through the shrubs and ran to the buggy. Keeping her head low, she dove into the front of it. I saw her grapple past the driver, who didn't move at all, and then she came scrambling back out of the buggy.

"He's alive," she said, handing a long-nosed pistol to Cassie. Someone has knocked him a good one over the head, but he's breathing."

My stomach had wound itself into a knot so tight I could hardly breathe. I hated leaving Cassie and Gemini even for a second until we were all safe, but I had to find Alex. "Come on," I said to Bridget. "Let's hurry."

We slid through the bushes and ran up the stone steps. Smoke was starting to billow from the door. The heat hit me the minute I crossed the threshold. A thick blanket of smoke hung low. I ducked down, wanting to avoid the ugly black darkness. Bridget followed right behind me.

"Alex!" I heard no answering call, only the crackle of the devouring fire spreading through the deserted mansion. I wondered if I was on a fool's errand, but I couldn't turn back. I raced ahead, following the same route that Gemini had taken. The heat began to burn my skin, even my skirts seemed as if they were burning my legs. My lungs hurt so much that I had to put my hand over my mouth to breathe. My eyes watered. Bridget coughed and coughed.

Just as I was about to turn back, I saw a man's legs sticking out from a doorway near the staircase we had taken. I grabbed Bridget's arm and dragged her to him. It was Alex. We each gripped a leg and pulled him from the room. There was no time to see how badly he was hurt. We could hardly see at all. The heat was worse in the room where he lay, so I knew the best way out was the way we had come. Bridget and I struggled and pulled and coughed and eventually crawled as we dragged him. But the smoke was getting worse. I couldn't see. I couldn't breathe. I couldn't find the entry hall.

Then Bridget fell, coughing so hard her whole body spasmed. A waved of dizziness washed over me as I coughed and fought for air. We were all flat on the ground with a thick smoke burying us alive. I rolled, pulling on Bridget. She grabbed my hand.

Her mind was crying out for Stuart, for a chance to love, to hold him in her arms just once. I wrapped my arm around Alex and laid my head on his chest. My tears dried before they could spill from my eyes. I'd get us out. I had to. In just a moment.

When someone pulled me up, I thought angels had come until the blurry figure of a hooded ghoul wavered before my eyes. He shoved me aside and I thought I would fall, but someone behind me caught me. I managed to stiffen my knees enough to stand. Then the grim reaper lifted Bridget up and tossed her my way as well. Whoever held me jostled until he caught Bridget and began to drag us, save us. My mind was so addled I couldn't read the man's thoughts. I didn't know who he was.

"Alex!" I cried, but no sound escaped. Then, through the smoke, I saw the black hooded figure loom closer, dragging Alex.

Bright light and cool, fresh air told me that we'd escaped the burning mansion. But I still coughed and my lungs still fought to breathe. Through the haze I could hear Bridget doing the same, and the man holding us was cursing loudly. It was Stuart.

"Where's Sean?" Cassie ran up and pulled me into her arms. She sobbed with joyful relief. All I could do was lean into her and stare at the doorway, praying for Alex. Then I realized I couldn't read Cassie's thoughts either. My mind was too addled to think.

"He's coming," said Stuart as he swung Bridget up into his arms.

Just then a black-hooded man came staggering out of the mansion dragging Alex with him, and relief flooded through me. Sean had just saved Alex from a fiery death, but the blood on Alex's head and shoulders told me he'd been hurt by someone.

I wondered how much more proof the Killdaren brothers would need before they realized they'd either broken the Dragon's Curse or it had missed them completely.

Mr. Drayson appeared, completely disheveled, waving his hands in agitation. "This is all my fault! I never should have mentioned this place! I knew evil lurked here! Good God, why did you come?"

Sean, still hooded—I assumed to protect his eyes as much as possible from the light—turned. "Talk can wait. Take the pistol and get Ashton. Stay on your guard! Bring the doctor to Killdaren's Castle immediately."

Mr. Drayson nodded and I followed him with my gaze as he crossed to the buggy where Lord Ashton stood. I could see the edge of the pink satin curtain hanging from the back seat. Gemini must still be unconscious.

"How . . . did . . . you know to come?" I rasped to Stuart.

"Drayson and Lord Ashton saw smoke on their way back from the village and alerted us. At first we thought it was Dragon's Cove on fire. Thank God they saw it. If we hadn't come immediately, you, Bridget, and Alex would all be dead."

I nodded. Even though I wanted to think I would have gotten up and dragged Alex and Bridget to safety. I doubted I would have been able to save even myself. I glanced at Mr. Drayson and Lord Ashton as they departed on their horses, and wondered if they'd seen the smoke as they'd said, or if they knew a fire had been set because *they'd* set it, and had sounded the alarm to put themselves in the clear. Come to think of it, it was Mr. Drayson's testimony of having seen either Alex or Sean leaving the maze the night Lady Helen had died that had cast suspicion their way. Both men even had access to Alex's home and could have taken the torture device from the dungeon. What if they were the killers? I'd read their thoughts at least once this summer when I'd fallen and pretended my ankle was more hurt than it was. They'd helped me up and touched my ankle. Both of them had been in high spirits from the cocktails they'd introduced to Gemini and me. They'd been more interested in the curve of my leg and what that led to than anything else. I hadn't given their thoughts much notice because my mind had been filled with Alex.

The trouble with reading thoughts was that I could only read what was currently in a person's mind. I could touch the killer, read his thoughts, and never know he was the killer unless he was thinking of the murder. I shivered with a deep cold that refused to leave me despite the heat of the sun and the slightly scorched skin on my hands and face. Even moving to Alex's side and setting my hand on him, seeking to comfort us both, did little to warm me.

On the ride home, we looked like defeated troops returning from battle. Gemini, Alex, and the driver were unconscious and lay on the buggy seats. I held Alex's head in my lap. Bridget and I were shaken and weakened. Cassie, though unharmed, was suffering greatly, and I was sure the grim set of Stuart's features didn't even come close to the thundercloud of Sean's, which were thankfully hidden beneath his dark hood. I feared there was to be a greater price yet to pay for our venture.

"I'm most concerned about your sister," Dr. Luden was telling Cassie when I exited Alex's room. Upon arriving at the castle the doctor had treated the three invalids immediately. The driver had regained consciousness before arriving back at Killdaren's Castle and didn't need more than a cursory examination.

Alex had required stitches for the gash on the back of his head, but had awakened and was becoming more coherent as the minutes passed, though he had a major headache. I'd left Sean and Stuart in the room with him, anxious to find out more about Gemini. Cassie was clearly of the same mind, having left Bridget and Prudence with Gemini, so that she and the doctor could speak privately. Rebecca was safely in the kitchens with Mrs. Murphy.

"What do you think is wrong with Gemini?" Cassie asked the doctor.

"You say you think she fainted from fright?" the doctor asked.

"Yes," I said. "I . . . well . . . she heard something that seriously scared her."

Sean joined us in the corridor.

"Your sister should have come to long before now," the doctor said, his voice filled with concern. "What I fear is she was so traumatized that her mind could not accept what happened and has chosen to close itself off from the pain. I'll leave a sedative should she waken in an agitated state, but this may be a very serious situation."

"What do you mean?" I asked.

"The mind is capable of so much more than we can even begin to understand. She may not wake until she either feels safe again, or is able to accept the fright or pain that put her into this state."

"You sound as if that won't be tonight," Sean said.

"If she doesn't wake up in the next few days, we're going to have to discuss getting her to a treatment facility that can care for her special needs for as long as possible," the doctor replied.

"What sort of a facility?" Cassie asked.

"A hospital where they treat people who have illnesses of the mind," he said gravely.

"No. Gemini will not go to any asylum." Cassie reeled on her feet, grabbing Sean's arm.

"I hope that won't be necessary," the doctor replied.

"It won't," said Sean. "Whatever care she needs will be seen to here, no matter who we have to consult, or what the costs."

"Then, I suggest that someone stay with her and talk to her, let her know she's safe, tell her stories from her childhood. Anything you can think of to make her feel loved and secure. I'll check on her one more time and then I'll be back in the morning."

"Thank you, Dr. Luden," said Sean. After the doctor disappeared back into Gemini's room, Sean caught Cassie's arm. "We need to talk. Now," he said.

Cassie winced and looked toward me. "We have to tell him. He has to know what happened or he can't help or protect us. He needs to know everything."

"Okay," I whispered.

"What's *everything*?" Sean asked, clearly not liking the sound of that word.

"Let me close my curtains and we can talk in my room." After I shut out the fading sunlight, leaving the room in dim shadows, Cassie entered with a grim-faced Sean close behind.

Sean still had to hold up his hand to shield his eyes until he adjusted to the light.

"Are you in pain?" Cassie asked him quietly.

"I'll live. Though whether others will is questionable today," Sean replied curtly, glaring at Cassie.

She bit her lip.

"It's not her fault," I said. "What happened today began eight years ago, not because we decided to drive to a neighboring estate where supposedly nothing bad has ever happened. You can't blame her for today any more than you can blame her for Lady Helen, Mary, or Flora's deaths. The fault rests squarely upon the killer's shoulders. If Cassie was the type of woman to knit in a rocking chair you would have never met or fallen in love with her. So expecting her to do that now is unreasonable. She would have come to you with our idea to search the Kennedy Mansion for clues, but she knew you would object."

Sean narrowed his brows at me, but clearly seemed to be sifting through my words. "What do you mean Flora? Are you speaking of Bridget's sister?"

"Yes," Cassie said, her eyes tearing.

"Let me go back to the beginning," I said, and starting with a description of my unusual "gift," I told him everything, what I'd gleaned from Rebecca's mind, what happened to Gemini at the mansion and our gruesome discovery there, the torture device and its similarity to those in Alex's dungeon and how I thought he was being framed. I even mentioned my suspicions about Mr. Drayson and Lord Ashton, and questioned why they were so conveniently in a position to sound the alarm about the fire. When I finished, Sean just stared at me.

After a long silence, wherein it seemed as if my every nightmare was coming true. I stood. "I'll leave within the hour," I said, moving to the armoire.

Sean exploded from the chair. "What the bloody hell would you do that for?" He turned to Cassie. "What's wrong with your sister?"

"Andrie thinks you'll either stone her to death or burn her as a witch."

Sean's jaw dropped.

"I didn't say *he* would do that!" I cried, for it really did make me sound insane.

"No, but that's how you feel. You really don't think that anyone can accept who you are and love you. I know because I felt that way once."

"My situation is different, Cassie." I looked at Sean. "How comfortable would you be with a woman in your home, or even a wife, who at any moment could read your most private thoughts, even those fleeting ones that nobody is supposed to have?"

Sean raked his hands through his hair and paced across the room. "Good God. This is a mess."

"Sean Killdaren!" Cassie exclaimed, standing up and looking horrified.

"What?"

She shook her head and burst into tears. "You're not the man I thought you were."

"Bloody hell, Cassie. I'm trying to think here. We've a murderer who has killed people I cared for, and came close to killing you, your sisters, and my brother. And we don't know who he is."

"Why didn't you answer Andrie's question?" Cassie demanded.

"What question?"

"About living with someone who could read your thoughts."

"If the woman was you, my wife, it wouldn't be a problem. Even if you didn't have the presence of mind to read my thoughts all the way to their conclusion, as most of my thoughts end up with you, I'd still love you. Since it's my sister-in-law, well, we'll have to work out an arrangement. What I'm worried about is the killer learning about Andromeda's gift before we catch him. Who else here knows about your ability, Andrie?"

"Only Gemini and now Bridget. You're serious," I said staring at him.

"About the killer coming after you? Yes, I'm dead serious."

"I'm not talking about that. I mean you're serious about my reading minds."

"Good Lord, woman, of course, I am."

I stared at him hard, wanting to march across the room and touch his hand to make sure he spoke the truth. Could it be possible? Could I be wrong in what people would think? Was Sean just saying what he had said for Cassie's benefit? She did have to prompt his answer. Yet, he'd accepted her dreams. But dreams were different than thoughts.

"Andrie is right," Sean said. "You can't let everyone know about this. God only knows what possesses people and the insanity they get in their heads about those who are different. And until we catch this killer, you can't tell anyone else. None of you are to leave the castle, either." He zeroed his gaze in on Cassie. "Are we in agreement on that?"

She nodded. "I should have invited you to search the Kennedy Mansion with us. Since you were excluding me from even hearing about your conversations, at the time it was more important for me to prove that I wasn't a nincompoop than it was to include you."

"Whatever made you think that I thought you were a nincompoop— NO!" Sean threw his hands up in the air. "I did not just ask that question and use that asinine word! Cassie Killdaren! If you ever question how highly I regard your . . ."

"Mind," I said.

"Mind," he repeated. "Then you will be a . . ."

"Nincompoop," I said.

"Idiot," he said, and glared at me. "See, you didn't read my mind. I'm going to see the constable just as soon as the sun sets and inform him of what you found at the mansion." I decided not to remind Sean that I could only read the thoughts of people I was touching.

"Don't go alone," Cassie said.

"I'll take Drayson and Ashton with me."

"How do you know you can trust them?" Cassie asked.

"I don't, but I'd rather have them with me than here with you."

"You aren't going to tell the constable about the medieval device, are you?" I had to grip my hands together to keep from touching Sean to see what he really thought. Aphrodite's ring bit into my skin, surprising me, because I'd forgotten it was there.

Sean lifted a brow in just the same way Alex did, and my heart thumped. "Wouldn't that be suppressing important evidence?"

"Do you think your brother's the killer?" I asked.

"No."

"Then I see no reason to let the killer get away with implicating Alex, do you?"

"No," he said slowly.

"Tell me something. If you're so sure Alex isn't the murderer, then why are you so certain that the Dragon's Curse exists between you? As far as I can tell you both keep saving each other's life rather than trying to take it. There's more circumstantial evidence to implicate him in the death of Helen and Flora than there is to convict him of trying to kill you," I reasoned.

Sean furrowed his brow to a sharp angle. "What is this? The Andrews sisters' crusade?"

"Yes," Cassie and I said in unison.

He shook his head and looked at Cassie. "I'll talk to you when I get back." Then he quit the room.

Cassie ran over and gave me a big hug. "You see, Andrie, people won't ostracize you for your gift. I'm sure that Alex will be just as understanding as Sean." In Cassie's mind, Sean's acceptance of my gift had ascended him from a stubborn idiotic male to the most wonderful man in the world. I wondered how long it would take him to fall off his pedestal again.

"I'll think about it," I said as I patted her back and forced a smile.

"You go see Alex for a while and I'm going to go hold Gemini and tell her everything that I can remember from the time she was born."

We exited my room and came to an abrupt stop. Stuart had Bridget up against the corridor wall and was kissing her so passionately that neither of them were aware of anything but each other. We tiptoed right by them and disappeared into Alex and Gemini's rooms. I didn't think Bridget was going to find it necessary to sneak into Stuart's bed naked. In fact, she was going to be hard put to avoid it.

I went directly to the bed where the curtains had been pulled shut, most likely to cut down on the light so Alex could rest. I gently parted one silk panel. Soot dotted his face, which appeared reddened by the sun; he smelled of smoke, and blood crusted his neck. He mumbled restlessly and seemed to be uncomfortable and in pain. I knew I had to look and smell just as badly. Though far from proper, I couldn't let him stay in that state, and I didn't want to call anyone to attend to him, nor have to leave as they did. The doctor hadn't used all of the warm water and cloths and soap that had been sent up to treat Alex's wound, so I gathered them. Placing the supplies on the beside table, I set to work, gently cleaning the chiseled lines of his face, enjoying the sensual fullness of his mouth and the rough brush of his shadowed jaw. From what I could see of his thoughts, they were a whirling wind of ideas and emotions moving so swiftly that I couldn't discern a single concept from the storm.

Unbuttoning his shirt, I tugged the garment down his shoulders and slipped his arms free before sliding it out from under him. By the time, I'd accomplished that I felt flushed and short of breath to the point that my lungs and throat, already raw from the smoke, hurt. I rested a moment by sitting on the side of the bed and leaning over to lay my hand on his chest. The strong, steady beat of his heart thrummed as the sweetest music I could ever hear besides the rumble of his voice. I brushed my lips against him, pressing a small kiss on his chest, and continued bathing him, drinking in the hard, muscled contours of his body, so strong and yet so very vulnerable.

To think that he'd almost died today twisted everything inside me and turned it upside down. I thought that I loved him before, but now I knew without a doubt that I loved him with my whole heart and was so very glad that I would have a few treasured memories of him making love to me to warm my heart forever.

After cleaning his torso as best I could, I moved to his pants. Someone had already removed his shoes and socks. The buttons slipped free with a few deft movements. I tugged his pants open and was met immediately with his sex. He didn't have drawers on, and now that I gave it some thought, I couldn't remember him ever wearing drawers. Heavens, the Killdaren men never did anything according to society's

rules. Without his help, it was no easy task to get his pants
down. I finally had to climb onto the bed and sit between his
legs in order to pull down both sides of his pants at the same
time. I'd made it halfway down his hips when all of a sudden,
his sex sprang to attention, pointing right at me. I sat up
straight and looked at him. "Thank God you're alive," I said.

He lifted a brow. "People usually check for a pulse to determine that, but this is kind of nice." He shifted his hips for
emphasis.

"I'm bathing you, you dolt," I said, tears of relief and humor blurring my vision. "I think you could be dead and that
thing would still work."

"That thing?"

"Well, what do you call it?"

"I call a penis a penis and a spade a spade; though some
men are compelled to name their sex, I'm not."

"What do they call it?"

"John Thomas. Jack. Roger. You and I get into the
damnedest conversations. I don't care what you call it at the
moment. Where in the hell am I, Andromeda? What in the hell
are you doing? Why in the hell do you look so bloody awful
and why does my head feel like it's been shipwrecked?"

"You don't remember?"

"Remember what?"

Good Lord. "Do you remember anything about today?
Your return from Penzance? Our, uh, delayed picnic?"

He shut his eyes and pressed his palm to his head. "The
jade figure," he said softly. "You fell in the ocean . . . Holy
hell . . . The Kennedy mansion!" He attempted to sit up, but
groaned in pain and fell back upon the bed. Even Roger went
flat, or whatever it was called.

"You have to take it easy. You have a concussion." I slid
the sheet over him, deciding I'd continue his bath after we
talked. Climbing off the bed, I sat in the chair that had been
pulled up to the side of the bed. I wet my lips, hoping to ease
the dryness of my mouth. "Why did you come to the mansion, Alex?"

"Why? What was I supposed to do? You go home, having nearly drowned, and then thirty minutes later, I see you, your sisters, and Bridget go breezing past Dragon's Cove when I'm returning to speak to you again? I wondered what was so important that you didn't even rest after such a harrowing experience. I followed you. Found the driver knocked out and went running inside the mansion, looking for you, and someone coshed me from behind. Now tell me what in God's name were you doing?"

"Looking for clues as to who killed Lady Helen."

"Jesus, Andromeda." He groaned. "I told you to stay out of the investigation. What happened next? I don't remember anything after falling to the ground."

"Whoever knocked you over the head set the place on fire. To make a long story short, Sean dragged you out of the burning mansion. You're at Killdaren's Castle, where he insisted you come. You have to be watched closely for the next day to make sure there aren't any ill effects from your concussion."

"Was anyone else hurt? How did you get out?"

I explained how we'd escaped through the window.

"You're not telling me everything. You have soot on your face. You smell like smoke, and your skin looks as if you've spent hours in the sun unprotected."

"When I realized you were in there, Bridget and I went in to find you. We did try and drag you out at first, but we weren't being very successful."

"You both risked your lives to save me? Were you hurt?" His features set to a grim line.

"No, everyone is fine. Well, except Gemini. She became so frightened that she fainted and has yet to recover." Then, I told him about the blood on the bed and the picture of Bridget's mother and brother that her sister, Flora, had with her when she left with a mysterious man named Jack, and how she hasn't been heard from since. "We're sure she was murdered there."

"Will this never end? Good God." He sat up again, this

time forcing himself to stay upright even though his body shuddered from the pain the movement caused. "The killer was there. He set the fire."

"Yes, did you see who hit you? Do you remember anything at all?"

"No. Where's Sean?"

"He's gone to see the constable."

"I want to talk to him when he gets back."

"Under one condition: You lay back and rest until then and let me finish cleaning you up."

Alex fell back with a groan. "That wouldn't be conducive to rest, but it might make my head feel better if we went with position number two."

"You're not making any sense."

"Have you already forgotten the jade figurine, my dear? The one with the woman naked on top, satisfying herself by riding the man? I want to fill my hands with your breasts and I want to feel you slide me inside you."

"Your brain has definitely been addled. The doctor put six stitches in your scalp, and I can promise you that you don't want him to do it again."

"Not a problem. We'll go very slow. I brought the protection with me when we left for the picnic. It's still in my pocket. I had planned to seduce you on the beach."

"Well, it's a good thing you didn't. It was bad enough to have Sir Warwick and Constable Poole find us like they did. I can't imagine how embarrassing it would have been to . . ." I frowned. "What do you mean by protection?"

"A sheath that keeps my seed from spilling into you. You didn't even know I'd put one on and used it when you were propped so prettily on the pillows. That's what I went to Penzance to purchase in such a hurry. I bought three hundred of them, cleaned the apothecary out."

"Three hundred! Good Lord!" I had to fan my face to keep my cheeks from catching fire.

"Well, we needed enough for at least a month."

"That would be . . ."

"Ten times a day. I decided every hour was a bit too much. We do need to eat; speaking of which, you have the most delicious sex. Golden and plump and rosy, a flower that opens for me with the sweetest nectar imaginable. Come here, Andromeda."

My whole body tingled and burned. "Alex! Will you be serious?"

"I am serious. Don't you want to make me feel better?"

"You're insane."

"No, but I will be if you don't come here. You make me that way."

"Never mind. I think we'll finish your bath when you're thinking more clearly."

A knock sounded on the door. "Come in," I said.

The earl entered the room. "Alex, I need to speak with you."

"I'm not interested in speaking to you," Alex replied.

"Well, that's too bad, because you're going to hear what I have to say no matter what."

I stood. "I'll leave you two alone."

"Stay, Andromeda. The earl is leaving now."

"Not unless you're strong enough to toss me out on my ear, and by then I will have said what I came to say anyway."

Alex sat up, looking as if he was going to oust the earl. Then he glared at his lap, and I realized his dilemma. His pants were half way down his hips. It would not be a very dignified move to stand up, and it would be highly improper because I was here. Not that the Killdarens did anything properly, a trait that I feared the Andrews family fit in with all too easily. Alex wobbled a bit and then lay back with a groan. "Make it quick," he said curtly.

I jumped up. "I'll be outside the door." The earl didn't even wait until I'd cleared the room before he started speaking. "I've said this to Sean and now I'm saying it to you. I am sorry." Though I stepped into the corridor, I could still hear his voice. Surprisingly, I found Prudence there, nervously smoothing her skirt. From the hopeful look in her eyes, I realized she'd heard the earl. We both listened.

"I deeply regret what happened eight years ago and the fact that any harm fell to any lass because of my actions. My intent had been to protect me and mine. Someday I hope you will understand that, right or wrong, you will do anything and go to any length to assure that your children are safe, especially when you have already lost so many loved ones. Maybe you will forgive me then. I'll be removing myself from your lives just as soon as this horrific madman has been caught, and I won't be troubling either of you again. Should you have any reason to contact me, you may send word to my estate near Hampton Court."

Prudence gasped, pain struck her features, and she nearly doubled over. It was clear the earl had yet to inform her of his plans and my heart went out to her. I reached for her, but she backed away, shaking her head, and she ran for her quarters. She disappeared before the earl stepped into the corridor. Rather than saying anything, he just nodded sadly in my direction and turned to leave.

"So that's it," I whispered. "You're just going to disappear from everyone's lives? Take the coward's way out?"

He froze in midstep, but didn't turn to face me as he spoke. "Everyone is better off without me in their lives."

The words I'd been about to say wouldn't come, because what the earl said mirrored part of my own reasoning for leaving my family and for eventually leaving Alex. But I couldn't just let him walk away. Prudence deserved more and as flawed as the earl was she loved him.

"Sophocles wrote almost five hundred years before Christ that 'One word frees us of all the weight and pain of life: That word is love.' Your life will always be burdened and you will always burden other people's lives unless you find the courage to love again. You may not have had a choice in losing the woman you first loved, but you are choosing to lose the second woman you loved. And the saddest thing about it is you're making Prudence suffer the same pain that you live with day in and day out."

He turned to face me, his features drawn in pain, his complexion ghostly white.

"She's in her room," I said softly. "She heard you say you were leaving." Turning from him, I started for Alex's room, but went to Gemini's instead. My emotions were too raw to face Alex at that moment. My situation with my family and with Alex was nowhere near similar to the earl's with Prudence.

21

I found Cassie asleep in Gemini's bed, cradling Gemini's head against her shoulder as if she were a fragile child. As I crossed the room, I earnestly prayed that Sophocles's words would prove true. Something needed to remove the weight and pain of what happened to Flora from Gemini's mind, and all Cassie and I really had to fight such a horror was our love.

I set my hand on Gemini's arm, searching for her thoughts, but found nothing but an inky darkness so desolate that tears stung my eyes.

"Nothing yet?" Cassie whispered.

I met her sleepy gaze and shook my head.

She forced a smile. "Don't worry. There's time still."

I sat on the edge of the bed and clasped Gemini's hand in mine. "I keep thinking back, wondering what we could have done differently today. There was no warning in Gemini's thoughts that the screams were hurting her so badly. All I could read from her was that she had to help."

"We never should have gone. My stubbornness and pride let this happen to her," Cassie said.

"No. You're wrong. In fact, it may be a good thing that we all went together. Ever since Mr. Drayson mentioned the haunted mansion at dinner, Gemini has been fascinated and has mentioned her desire to go there more than once. She would have gone alone. I'm sure of it. And her fate then would likely have been . . ."

"The same as Flora's?" Cassie whispered.

"Yes."

Tears fell from Cassie's eyes and I reached for her hand. "We're going to be all right, Cassie. All of us. Me, Gemini, you, Sean, and the babe inside of you. And Alex? Both Alex and Sean are reasonable men . . . Well, mostly reasonable men, and I think we've seeded enough doubt in Sean's mind that the Dragon's Curse doesn't have as much of a hold as it did. The truth is shining through. The fact that Sean brought Alex here is very telling."

"I know. I'm holding that very close to my heart at the moment. What about you? Surely after everything that has happened today you can't still believe that you and Alex have no future."

"I'm not sure," I said slowly. "I have decided that I will tell Alex when the time is right. Then we will see. Do you want me to sit with Gemini for a while?"

"No. I'm not leaving her tonight. If she wakes she's going to need me. And I'm sure Sean will camp out on the divan. Why don't you get a bath and get some rest?"

"First, I'm going to check with Mrs. Murphy about dinner trays for everyone and then get back to Alex. I'm fine for now."

By the time I made the quick trip to the kitchens and returned to Alex's room, he'd fallen asleep. I found his pants and the wet bathing cloths on the floor next to the bed. He'd finished the job himself, it would seem. Unable to keep from touching him, I brushed his hair back from his temple, wishing so much that things between us were different. That I was different. That I was normal.

I then left a maid listening for him and went in search of hot water and soap. When I finished bathing and eating a small bowl of savory chicken soup, I could barely keep my eyes open. Donning one of my simplest house dresses, I headed back to Alex's room. A quick peek into Gemini's room showed Cassie with Gemini, and Sean resting, his long legs dangling over the end of the divan. Empty trays outside the doors told me that everyone had been fed. Night had fallen and dim shadows filled the castle's stone corridor. I thought about tapping on Prudence's door, then changed my mind. Tomorrow would be soon enough to learn if the earl had had the courage to see her. And by not checking, I'd at least have the hope of a future for them to ease the darkest moments of the night.

Slipping into Alex's room, I dismissed the maid and curled up in the wing chair next to his bed. Unorthodox or not, it was the only place I knew I would be able to get any rest tonight; for alone in my room, I feared my darkest dreams would return with a vengeance.

Alex lay sleeping with several freshly plumped pillows behind him. The covers were pulled up to the middle of his stomach, leaving the broad expanse of his tanned chest, shoulders, and arms exposed. I drank my fill of his dark beauty, mentally enjoying all of the pleasurable sensations he'd brought to me. That his life could have been forfeit today wrenched me deeply, made me ache in the very depths of my soul. I loved this man beyond reason, and I had no idea what I would do about it. Was it really my concern for others that had me planning to isolate myself from the world? Or was it my fear of others that had me seeking to escape?

My eyes drifted shut and I eventually found myself carried away on a ship, sailing swiftly across a turquoise sea with the hot sun kissing my naked body and a sensual wind caressing me everywhere—the pirate Alex filling me completely.

I moaned, arching my back to the hot pleasure licking my breasts.

"Wake up, lass. This isn't a dream but a real man a'wanting you like no other."

I slit my eyes open to find Alex kneeling before me. My dress and chemise were unbuttoned completely and his hands were cupping my breasts, tweaking my nipples to hard points.

"Alex. Good heavens!" I tried to close the edges of my dress. "Somebody could walk in at any moment."

"I've locked the door and for the next little while you are all mine." He leaned forward and kissed me, expertly opening my mouth for the sweeping pleasure of his tongue. My heart leapt in pace with the hot rush of desire filling me. "Please," he whispered against my lips. "I need you. I must hold you and feel you. When I think about what almost happened today to you and to me, I . . ."

He shuddered and I clearly read his thoughts. He couldn't face the idea of losing me. Realizing how deeply he cared for me, though he'd never said so, wrenched me inside. I needed to tell him the truth about who I was, but not yet. "Shh," I said then kissed him. "I understand, and I need you, too."

Taking my hand, he stood and tugged me up from the chair. His naked body shook and I knew it wasn't as much from his need of me but that he was still recovering from being injured. He started to press my dress from my shoulders and I stayed his hands.

"Lie down and let me." I urged him to the bed and he fell back on the pillows with a sigh big enough to make me hesitate. "Are you sure you're strong enough for this?"

He gave me an impish grin. "We'll see. I sure as hell know I'm not strong enough to go without being with you."

I wasn't looking for declarations of love and most likely would have rejected any, at least until he knew the whole of who I was, but that came as close to one as any heart could desire. Shedding my clothes and climbing into bed with him felt as natural as turning my face to the heat of the sun.

He pulled me down for a kiss. Teasing me with light brushes of his lips, then dipping to soul-searching duels with my tongue, he brought my burgeoning want of him to a feverish level as he ran his fingers through my hair and down my back.

"Sit up for me," he whispered in my ear. "I want to come inside you and I want to see the pleasure on your face as you make love to me."

I angled up, bending my knees on each side of him, and felt the brush of his hard hot sex against my bottom and lower back. Slipping something from beneath his pillows, he reached behind me.

"What are you doing?" I asked.

"Readying myself to come inside of you."

"Can I help?"

"Next time. I've almost finished. But you can do something else for me."

I lifted a questioning brow and Alex reached back beneath the pillow again. This time he handed me a tiny silver snuff box with a polished shelled top. "You want snuff now?" I asked.

"Open it," he said softly. "But be careful it doesn't spill. We only want it to go on some very special places."

"What is it?"

"Dragon's oil."

"What's that?"

"A very potent aphrodisiac. Originally made exclusively for Chinese emperors. It is very expensive to obtain due to its rarity."

"How expensive?" I popped open the box, which had a unique cork lining about the lid, sealing it like a bottle of wine. There was a mercurial-looking liquid inside that smelled faintly of ginger.

"The small bottle I have at home cost two thousand pounds."

I almost dropped the box.

"Easy." He steadied my hand and dipped a finger into the oil.

My mind boggled as I watched him paint each of my nipples with the oil.

"Raise up on your knees a moment." When I did, he slipped two fingers in the oil and liberally covered my sex.

The oil felt cool and pleasant, but other than the excitement of having him touch me, I didn't experience any other sensations. He took more of the oil and covered his sex.

I frowned. "Did the apothecary in Penzance sell this to you as well? If so, I think you may have traded a fortune away on a pleasantry. I don't feel anything different. Should I?"

"You must have patience. This was a gift from the Emperor of China himself in exchange for a Friesian horse." Taking the silver box from me, he dabbed a bit of the oil on his tongue and lips then shut the lid, sealing it carefully.

"Why on earth would you spend so much money on this?"

"Because your ultimate pleasure is worth any price, Andromeda." He gripped my hips and, angling me back just a little, he surged himself inside of me. Sliding so smoothly into me, he took me by surprise.

"Oh."

He leaned up and kissed me hard, spreading the pleasant tasting oil through my mouth. I expected him to start touching me and rocking himself deeper into me, but he didn't. He leaned back and set his hands on my knees and looked at me.

"Now what do I do?"

"Nothing for the moment. Just sit there and enjoy the feeling of me inside you. I'm going to relax and absorb the pleasure of being there. Then when the time is right the Dragon will move you. Just follow the path of his fire."

I giggled and rolled my eyes. "This is lot of blarney, Alexander Killdaren."

"Ah, lass, are you not believing me when I tell you that there is no price on your pleasure?"

"Yes, but this whole Dragon's oil malarkey goes over the top."

"What do you have to lose? Trust me, the Dragon will move."

Just then I felt him inside of me. He hadn't shifted his hips, but he'd done something that stroked me deep inside. My stomach clenched in response and a sharp pleasure rippled through me. "Oh my." My eyes widened and he smiled.

He moved again and this time an arrow of burning heat went straight to my breasts and I arched my back, needing more.

"Do you feel the Dragon's fire, Andrie?"

"Yes," I gasped as he made another magical stroke. My breasts ached for him.

"Follow the path of the fire. Where do you burn?"

"My breasts. Touch me, Alex, please. Make me yours."

"Mine," he whispered just as he covered my breasts with his hot hands. He grasped my nipples between his thumbs and forefingers and rubbed back and forth, just little, tiny, squeezing strokes that sent my hips jerking hard against his. He didn't stop until I cried out with my need for more.

"Where do you burn?" he said.

"Here!" I grabbed his hand from my breast and shoved it down to my sex. I was so hot that I knew at any minute I would erupt in flames. Every part of me thrust to him and my whole being rose to a pinnacle of pleasure so excruciating that I thought I would explode if he didn't assuage me.

The moment he slid his thumb over my most sensitive spot he surged his hips up from the bed, driving deep inside of me, and I came apart in a shuddering explosion of intense pleasure that overtook every part of me, filling me with heaven. He groaned, his body spasming intensely against mine before he fell back to the bed. I collapsed against his chest, gasping for air as badly as I had when he'd thrust me to the surface of the sea.

For a long time neither of us moved. We held each other with only the sound of our thudding hearts and the rasps of our breaths filling the room like the lulling waves of the sea, rocking us both to sleep.

A piercing scream woke me and I knew it was Gemini. I rolled from Alex and off the bed, landing unsteadily on my feet.

He grunted in pain as he sat up and grabbed his head. "Bloody hell, what's happened?"

"It's Gemini. Oh, God, I have to get to her. Where are my clothes?"

"On the chair."

I grabbed my chemise, shrugged it on, and fumbled with the buttons, managing to get two in place. Then I slid on my dress, belting the skirt to my waist. Patting my fingers through my hair, I rushed to the door.

"Andrie, wait!' Alex hissed.

I turned to look at him and he held up my drawers.

"I don't have time. You hide them." Grappling with the lock, I peeked into the hallway in time to see Bridget and Prudence run into Gemini's room. I opened the bedroom door, and glancing toward the stairwell to make sure no one was coming down the corridor that way, I dashed across to Gemini's room and ran immediately into a hard wall of male flesh.

I didn't have but a second to read Sean's thoughts before he set me quickly back. But that second was devastating enough. It was fear. I gasped in shock. Sean didn't even look my way. His gaze was centered on the room I'd just left. "Cassie needs you," he said curtly.

Tears stinging my eyes, I dashed into the room. He'd lied, my mind cried. He did fear me. The fear in him had been extreme, much as I imagined that of an unreasoning mob would be. I shoved the rejection from my mind and focused on what was happening across the room.

Gemini was no longer in bed. She cowered in a far corner of the room, keening softly. She held a poker in her hand and had it threateningly held aloft as if to hit anyone who came close.

"Good God, what's wrong?" Stunned, I couldn't move.

"Don't make any sudden movements. She woke up screaming and then when she saw Sean, heard Sean, she went wild and ran for a weapon."

"Gemini, it's Andrie and Cassie. What's wrong?"

My sister didn't act as if she even heard me. She continued to cry inconsolably.

"I need to touch her. I need to know what she's thinking."

"How? What do you want to do?"

"Trying to approach her might make it worse," said Prudence.

"What do you mean?" asked Cassie.

"She's threatened and confused and obviously doesn't recognize either you or Andrie, people she should know. With Rebecca there was a time we had to leave her alone and let her cry herself into exhaustion before we could help her."

"I wish Mother and Father were here. Maybe Mother's voice would get through to her," I said.

"Cassie," Sean called softly from the corridor. "Stuart is going to come into the room. There's something I have to know."

"Whatever is the matter with you, Sean?" Cassie asked, backing slowly to the door.

"I have to know if it's my face that has Gemini frightened or if it is just the sight of a man in general," Sean said.

"Why don't you just tell them the bloody truth," came Alex's harsh whisper from the corridor. "You think I've done something to harm the woman. You don't trust me."

"What the hell am I supposed to think when a woman goes mad the second she looks at me and I know she has no reason to fear me? She must have mistaken us, and be afraid of you."

"If it were me in your shoes, I'd look for a different explanation. And if you were any other man, I'd challenge you for the insult."

"Consider it done," Sean said sharply.

Alex didn't reply. Then he spoke to me. "Andrie, I want everyone to back away from your sister. Then I want to try something."

I looked at Cassie; tears fell from her eyes. I didn't have to touch her to know she felt that everything we'd done to dispel the Dragon's Curse had, with a few words, been undone.

"All right, Alex. You can come in," I said. He didn't at first, but he started chanting in a very low voice that was so melodious and soothing it washed over me like a benediction from heaven. Nobody moved; everyone was entranced by his voice. After a few minutes, he slipped into the room. He didn't look at Gemini or move toward her, he went to the corner farthest from her, still chanting softly. Then after a short time, he increased the volume of his voice.

Gemini held the poker higher and Alex lowered his voice until she seemed to ease a bit, or grew tired of holding the poker so high. Then he chanted louder. This time she didn't brandish the poker higher and her crying decreased. Next, Alex moved to the middle of the room and did the same thing. He kept working his way closer and closer to her, never looking her way or advancing directly at her, but crisscrossing the room side to side with his deep voice soothing over her continuously. She stopped crying, but remained huddled.

I watched, too stunned, too mesmerized to feel the least discomfort at having stood for what had been much longer than an hour. This is what he'd done in the training ring with Iris. The beauty and the gentle strength of him filled the room. Alex eventually reached Gemini, but he didn't take the poker away. He kept moving from side to side, never facing her, but now he let the sleeve of his shirt brush against the hand that held the poker. She watched him, moving her gaze back and forth to follow him. On the next pass, he slid his fingers over her hand, then her arm, then her face. Then he took the fisted hand she had clutched against her mouth in his and urged her to stand. He moved back a step at a time, bringing her forward until he reached the divan where he coaxed her to sit down. Only then did he touch the poker, easing it from her grasp and slipping it behind him. Still chanting, he motioned me to move toward him. When I reached his side, he motioned for Cassie.

"Sing softly to her something she knows," he chanted, using English for the first time. "And keep singing quietly as I back from the room. Prudence and Bridget back out with me. I'll stay outside the door until we see what she does. She's slightly hypnotized at the moment, but when she slowly comes to, she should be calmer than before."

As he backed away, I didn't touch Gemini, but continued to sing with Cassie the lullabies we'd sung many times, years ago. Alex's voice got lower and lower until I no longer heard it.

Gemini's eyes began to droop and she wavered on the divan. I caught her shoulder and eased her back, reading her thoughts as I did. Amazingly, she was thinking about the time there'd been an awful thunderstorm and the three of us had huddled under a blanket until the morning sun had risen. I told Cassie.

"Then we'll huddle until dawn," she said, taking a step to ease a blanket from the end of the bed.

"Blimey, what did you do?" I heard Bridget ask outside in the corridor.

Alex didn't answer.

"It's an ancient Druid ritual of mesmerizing to put anything wild at ease," Stuart said.

"Why would they do that?" asked Bridget.

"It's a secret used by the very best horse trainers in the world," Stuart replied.

"You better tell the whole truth now, Stuart. That's what it's used for today," said Alex. "Back then they used it to put their sacrificial victims into a trance. Also, I think I have an idea of what the symbol represents. A crude version of an inverted cross with an eye in the center. Either evil is watching or the killer is watching for evil."

I shivered and nearly groaned with dismay. Why did Alex almost deliberately seem to be setting himself up for blame? His knowledge of the Druid sacrifices and their symbols would surely be incriminating evidence to some.

"Mum, Bridget, Timmy!" Gemini cried out, shocking us all. The voice wasn't Gemini's. "I'm so bloody sorry. I should have never left you. I sinned and he punished me. Jack ripped me from the inside out. Forgive me, please! Forgive me! Please! Forgive me—"

"Flora?" Bridget cried, running into the room.

Gemini stood and fell to her knees, crying. "Forgive me, Briggie, please!"

After a stunned moment Bridget knelt down and wrapped her arms around Gemini. "You're forgiven, Flory. We love you." Bridget burst into tears. "All you did was love. You didn't bloody sin. Jack did. He's evil. Who is he, Flory? He needs to be punished."

"Tell Mum and Timmy I love them. I love you." Gemini fainted in Bridget's arms.

I looked up to find that all three of the Killdaren men had entered the room.

Cassie stood. She was crying and her whole body shook, as did mine. She looked at Sean. "My sister isn't insane. She's not evil. Andrie isn't and I'm not either. We're just different, Sean. Please understand."

Sean looked at Cassie as if she'd shot him through the heart. He crossed the room and pulled her into his arms. "Good God, woman, how could you doubt me? How could you doubt my love?"

"Now you know how I feel," said Alex quietly to Sean before he turned away. "Stuart, help Bridget. I'll get Gemini."

Alex eased Gemini out of Bridget's tight grasp and Stuart swung a weeping Bridget up into his arms.

"I love you, Bridget," Stuart rasped, his dark eyes filled with deep emotion. Bridget turned to him, burying her face against the solid strength of his chest. He pulled her closer as he carried her from the room.

Prudence had already moved to the bed and fixed the pillows and counterpane, readying it for Gemini. Alex laid her gently down, and I pulled the covers up, pressing my palm to her forehead.

Gemini opened her eyes. "Andrie, my head hurts. I'm so tired."

"I know," I said, tears of joy filling my eyes. "You just need to rest and you'll be all right." My sister was back and she was whole.

"No it won't," she said. "Everyone knows that I hear ghosts now. Mum said people would kill me if they found out. I wasn't ever supposed to listen to them. I was supposed to ignore them. I wasn't ever supposed to tell anyone. Remember the day that I said it was going to rain and it did? A ghost told me and I told Mother. It was the first time she ever believed me. And remember when the man was run over by the carriage on the street? I saw his ghost leave his body. He hovered over everyone, looking down at himself. That's why I fainted. He was so angry and flew right at me."

It was surprising to learn about Gemini, but given mine and Cassie's gifts, it wasn't shocking. Some of the pieces of our lives fell into place. An odd comment or two from Gemini every now and then. Her focused obsession with parties and fashion. She kept herself busy and distracted so she didn't have time to listen to ghosts.

"It's all right, Gemmi," Cassie said softly, coming to the side of the bed.

"Oh, Cassie!" Gemini reached for her and Cassie gathered her close.

"Alex!" Sean said sharply.

I turned to find the room empty and I hurried to the door. Sean stood in the middle of the corridor. Alex faced him from the doorway of the bedroom he'd slept in.

"We have to talk," Sean said.

"Maybe," Alex replied. "It will have to wait."

"I'll expect you for dinner tonight, and we'll talk after. Not everybody in this world is as bloody perfect as you are," Sean said, then turned and left.

Alex looked stunned.

Apparently there was more bubbling beneath the rift between Alex and Sean than even Alex knew.

22

The following day simmered with a dark tension that reached the boiling point by dinnertime. After resting most of the day, Gemini seemed to be herself again, though her skin remained pale and dark circles shaded her eyes. Lord Ashton and Mr. Drayson came to see her. I watched both men carefully for any indication that one or both of them could be Jack. We had sat in the drawing room and as usual Gemini wrapped herself up warmly in a blanket.

I was properly grateful that the men had sounded the alarm about the fire at the Kennedy Mansion and told them so, but I still remained suspicious that they were so conveniently placed. They didn't stay long, though, as they were extremely uncomfortable with the fact that Gemini had fainted and had remained unconscious for such an extended time. It wasn't "normal," and Lord Ashton advised Gemini to seek treatment for such a "sensitive" condition. I thanked them for their concern and ushered them from the room, stating that Gemini needed to rest.

Gemini cried then. "Lord Ashton doesn't even know the whole of it and already he's put off. Mother was right."

"Maybe." I thought about how Alex didn't even hesitate to carry Gemini to the bed, and how upset Sean was that Cassie had felt the need to defend us. Was it possible Alex could be as accepting of my gift? I set the thought aside. "Maybe it is that way with most people, but not all."

"How do you know who you can trust and who you can't? One mistake could cost you everything."

"I know," I whispered. "Maybe you know who to trust when you find true love, a man who accepts all of you."

"Cassie is very lucky."

"Yes, she is." I realized just how fragile love was, too. What would happen to Cassie and Sean if Sean never resolved his conflict with Alex, and Cassie had twins and history repeated itself? Would she blame Sean then?

"Well," I said. "I wouldn't feel too upset about Lord Ashton and Mr. Drayson. You play cards much better than they do."

"With a little help," Gemini replied with a giggle.

"What do you mean?" I asked.

"Don't tell Cassie, but there's a ghost at Killdaren's Castle."

I sat back shocked. "Where?"

"Here," she said. "In the drawing room. He likes to play cards. The day I beat Lord Ashton and Mr. Drayson, he told me what they had in their hands."

"Heavens!" I glanced about and didn't see a thing. Then I blinked. "You cheated."

Gemini winced. "Just for the marzipan."

I laughed until I cried and then I hugged my sister. "I think that is one secret that we'll keep just between you and me. You're right. I don't think Cassie is up for a ghost, and what's a little marzipan?"

Gemini smiled brightly and we spent the rest of the day recalling moments from our lives that were filled with warmth and tenderness.

I thought Sean mostly responsible for the antipathy between him and Alex until the dinner hour came and Alex didn't show. Everyone else was there, Lord Ashton, Mr. Drayson, Sir Warwick, the earl, but the conversation never flowed smoothly.

"It's a godsend that place burned to the ground," Mr. Drayson said. His voice rang with relief that seemed to me overdone for a person who had so little connection to the Kennedys. A quick glance at Gemini showed me that she'd fisted her hand upon the table, but otherwise appeared to be able to deal with the traumatic subject.

"Why?" I asked, challenging him.

He flushed. "Well, because it was . . . evil . . . Didn't you feel it when you were there?"

"Evil was done there, but the place itself was very sad. It was someone's home at one time and should have been filled with the love and laughter of those to whose family it belonged. Were their no heirs?"

Mr. Drayson frowned. "I don't know. Ashton? You were distantly related, weren't you? Did Lord Kennedy have an heir?"

Lord Ashton's brows rose. "Not related by blood. Lady Helen's mother was the cousin of the man who married my aunt Louisa. I don't know who would have inherited the estate and the title, though I gather from her father's gambling debts there wasn't much to it."

I set my gaze on the earl. "Didn't you pay her a considerable sum?"

He flushed a deep red. "I, um, I gave her a cache of jewels that night to whet her appetite, but didn't get the chance to pay her the money as she didn't live to collect." My insides twisted. That was convenient for the earl.

"Tell them the rest." Surprisingly, this came from Prudence.

The earl buried his face into his hands. "Days after Helen was murdered, I was too burdened to let my promise to her go. I took the money to her father and told him how much his daughter had loved him, and that he'd better not squander the money."

"Jesus," said Sean. "He killed himself instead."

"That night," the earl whispered.

"What happened to the money?" I asked.

The earl shrugged. "I assumed he'd had his factotum take it and attend his debts."

I wondered if those debts were ever paid. Though Helen's father's suicide was plausible, it also struck me as convenient, too.

Sir Warwick changed the subject, but the political topic was forced and quickly petered out, as did the rest. So a loud disturbance in the center hall toward the end of the meal came as a welcomed relief at first.

Alex appeared in the dining room. He held two deadly looking swords, one in each hand. Sean's chair toppled backward as he stood.

"You accepted my challenge last night." Alex tossed Sean a sword. Sean adeptly caught the blade by the hilt.

"So I did," Sean said with soft menace.

"Shall we," Alex motioned for Sean to precede him from the room.

"Where?" asked Sean.

"Your choice."

"The terrace."

"No." Cassie stood. "This is insane. You two are grown men."

Neither Sean nor Alex looked at her as they left the room. We all followed in a state of silent, surreal shock. I couldn't quite believe that Alex was challenging Sean to a duel. That he'd risk either of their lives like this. I couldn't believe that I could be so wrong about who he was. I refused to believe it.

When we reached the smooth stone of the terrace, Sean and Alex circled each other. Alex holding his sword low, Sean holding his higher and balancing his uneven gait well with his cane. The only light came from the moon. The only sound came from the wind and the sea, and the men. Powerful, charismatic, and deadly, they both looked as if they were breathing fire.

Sean made the first attack, Alex defended, and the night erupted in a duel of sparking steel and hard blows from two sword masters with no equal. They covered the entire length of the terrace. Alex flipped and rolled, but could never gain an edge on Sean, who met his every move with confidence, and drove home a number of impressive attacks that had Alex sweating to defend.

"Just as you've always feared," Alex said. "I'm here to kill you. The Dragon's Curse is real. I'm going to win, and when I do, I'm going place your body at the feet of your wife, because I'm a coldhearted bastard who can't ever be trusted."

My heart wrenched as I realized what Alex was doing. He was deliberately being exactly what Sean feared.

Sean halted mid thrust and stared at Alex hard. The tension was so thick I could barely breathe. To my shock, Sean burst into laughter and tossed his sword aside. Then he started walking toward Alex. Alex brought his sword toward Sean. I expected Sean to block the blow with his cane. He didn't, but stood there as a sacrifice. At the last second, Alex twisted his wrist and hit Sean on the shoulder with the flat of the blade. Then he threw the sword to the ground.

"You fool," Alex said. "You're the one who taught me never to disarm yourself before friend or foe."

"I didn't. I disarmed myself before my brother," Sean said.

Alex stilled and Sean clasped Alex to him. After a moment, Alex returned the embrace. Either it was sweat rolling down Alex and Sean's cheeks, or they'd both shed tears. Cassie, with tears streaming down her face, motioned for everyone to go back inside and leave Alex and Sean alone. Love, it would seem, was the answer to ending the curse.

"Well, Drayson, you were right." Lord Ashton clapped Mr. Drayson on the back.

"About what, my friend?" Mr. Drayson looked puzzled.

Lord Ashton laughed. "You'll find it interesting to know, ladies, "—he motioned to Gemini, Cassie, and myself—" that after meeting you at the inn this summer, he said, the only way to reconcile Alex and Sean was to get them involved with the Andrews sisters."

Mr. Drayson laughed. "I did say that. We had a devil of a time convincing Alex to leave his horses long enough to come to the inn, didn't we?"

"However it came about," the earl said, sounding as if he'd been given a new lease on life, "it's a miracle I'm not going to question."

"How much will you wager me, Dartraven, that the truce won't last out the year?" Sir Warwick said, being his usual cloud of cynical darkness.

The earl swung around from where he walked just ahead and shoved Sir Warwick against the corridor's wall. "Don't even bloody suggest it, you hear me? I hear you even mention the Dragon's Curse and I will . . ."

"What?" Sir Warwick laughed.

Prudence grabbed the earl's arm. "Ignore him, Seamus. He isn't worth the upset."

Surprising us all, the earl released Sir Warwick and moved ahead down corridor at Prudence's side. Sir Warwick shrugged indifferently, but not before I saw a spark of pure disgust in his eyes.

"Well," said Cassie firmly. "I've decided that the first book I am going to pen will be about how the Killdaren brothers broke the Dragon's Curse. From their birth on, I am going to document how these Killdaren twins saved each other instead of killing each other."

The earl looked back from where he walked next to Prudence. "I'd like to add to that book if you'd allow me to," he said. "The only real curse is allowing fear to rule your life."

Cassie smiled warmly. "I think I'll have all the Killdarens write a part and we'll keep passing it on to future generations to continue the story."

"Fools," Sir Warwick muttered.

The earl glared at Sir Warwick. "Not only am I weary of a fool's company, but I'm realizing too late that those who think they're the wisest are the biggest fools of all. Myself included. Take your ridicule home and don't bring it back with you, should you return."

Warwick's monocle popped loose as he gaped at the earl, who'd turned his attention back to Prudence. No one spoke again, for I daresay we were all a bit shocked to hear the earl be that harsh to Warwick. Not that Warwick didn't deserve it, but the usual banter behind their words was gone. Once we reached the center hall, Sir Warwick stalked out the door without saying a word to anyone. Mr. Drayson and Lord Ashton took their leave as well after exchanging a polite good night.

"I think I'll go to bed now," said Gemini. "My head still aches."

Cassie slipped her arm around Gemini. "I'm coming with you. I don't think it will hurt to have someone close by for a day or so, do you?"

Gemini gave a wobbly smile. "I think that would be most welcomed."

"Ahem, Pru," said the earl. "Would you care to enjoy a game of cards in the drawing room before retiring?"

Prudence blinked, so stunned that no words came from her opened mouth.

"Of course she would," I said.

"But Rebecca—"

"Will be just fine with Bridget for another few hours, so don't hurry. In fact, I will run up and check on them, right now."

Cassie, Gemini, and I all left before Prudence could say a word. We ran quickly up the stairs and once we were in the corridor, slightly breathless, we giggled like we did as children up to no good. It made my heart sing to hear Gemini laugh even for a moment.

I left Cassie and Gemini at Gemini's room and went to Prudence's quarters.

Bridget answered the door. She appeared both saddened and strangely at peace. Inside I could hear Rebecca giggling and cocked my head to the side.

"Stuart brought Timmy and my mum up to play with Rebecca. Stuart's been entertaining us all with magic tricks."

"I love magic. I came to tell you that Prudence is going to play cards with the earl and won't be coming immediately back from dinner."

"Good, it's about time they spent an evening together." She leaned in closer to me. "Besides, my mum and brother could use some more time to laugh." She lowered her voice to a whisper. "I haven't told them everything about Flora. I wrote a letter from Flora saying how much she loved them and that she was sick with a fever. Then Stuart wrote an official-looking short note stating that Flora died peacefully in her sleep. I couldn't tell them what happened to her."

"You did the right thing for them. They're lucky to have you."

Her eyes filled with tears. "And I'm lucky to have Stuart."

She dashed at her tears and I forced a smile. "Now go spend time with him and your family." She nodded and shut the door, and I started toward my own room. The thought of being in there all alone was unappealing, though, and I crossed back to the room where Alex had stayed last night. In all of the upset, the maids hadn't been in to clean it and the bed was still mussed.

My heart nearly stopped at the sight of my drawers on the bed. I ran over and snatched them up, quickly folding them into a ball and stuffing them inside my dress.

Looking about, I didn't see anything else to indicate that I'd been here last night, and decided to at least pull up the counterpane. When I leaned over the bed, his scent reached me. I set my hands on the bed and inhaled deeply, already tingling with need.

"Don't move, lass. You're in the perfect position."

I stood up to see Alex entering the bedroom, and then locking the door. "Now, I'll have to get you back into position.

Remember that first figurine, Andrie? Don't you want to feel me every way that you can?"

In three sentences, my insides were melting so badly that my sex was drenched. "What are you doing here?"

He grinned and crossed the room. "I seemed to have misplaced my Dragon's oil: I expect it's on the bed somewhere." He stepped up behind me and pressed himself against me.

I shut my eyes and leaned back against him. He slid his hands around to cup my breasts. Suddenly he urged me forward until my thighs hit the soft mattress.

"Why don't you look for the Dragon's oil while I find some interesting things to give my attention to?"

"I can't reach the bed much less think well enough to see straight when you touch me like this."

Moving a hand to my back, he pressed my upper body to the bed as he moved his arousal against my bottom. We were fully clothed, yet I felt as naked as ever as I braced myself with my palms, smelling his scent again, feeling his insistent need demand more and more of me as he thrust me against the soft mattress.

His hand slipped inside my bodice and he tugged at my skirts. "Did you find the oil, yet?"

"No. I can't see." I gasped.

He laughed. "Just feel then, Andrie. Feel."

I did feel everything, with my skirts and drawers at my feet and my bodice only partially unbuttoned. Alexander was Great indeed. Before dawn, he'd used at least five of the three hundred sheaths he'd bought. When he left, I barely had the strength to make it back to my room and to crawl into bed. I didn't know if there was any real truth to his Dragon's oil tale or not, but I thought he'd made a wise purchase.

I rose late and was in the middle of writing Alex a note, telling him that I would return to work the next day because I thought it best to be with Gemini today, when Cassie burst into the room.

"Andrie!"

In all that we'd been through, I'd never seen her so shaken. "What is it?"

"Alex. Constable Poole has arrested him for murder."

My anger flared. "That is ridiculous. Just because that instrument was in the mansion doesn't mean—"

"No, Andrie. Another woman was murdered last night. A woman from the village. She was killed in the Circle of the Stone Virgins and the symbol that was carved on Mary and Lady Helen was on her as well. Alex's sword from last night was used to kill her. He was found on the beach this morning, naked. He hadn't been home all night."

"It could be anyone who was here last night and witnessed Alex and Sean's duel. Let's go," I said, grabbing her hand. "I have to see the constable."

"Why?" Cassie asked, keeping pace with me.

"Because Alex never left here last night. He was with me all night. Tell the maids not to clean the room he used. Believe me there's enough evidence to convict me as the worst harlot who has ever been born."

"Let's get Sean and Stuart. I have a feeling this is going to get very unpleasant, Andrie."

Unpleasant didn't even come close to describing the next few hours. I truly did become the worst harlot imaginable. Constable Poole questioned me repeatedly with contemptuous disdain about the entire course of my relationship with Alex. When the constable pressed for graphic detail about the previous night, Sean called a halt to the interrogation and demanded Alex's release. We had yet to see Alex.

The constable made us wait until Alex admitted to where he was last night, which he refused to do until he was informed that I was here. Even then, it wasn't until Dr. Luden confirmed that the woman had died long before Alex left me at dawn that the constable released him. Jamie had already been released that morning.

The moment Alex entered the constable's office I went to

him and set my hand on his arm. One clear thought came blazing through his anger. He *had* to marry me.

— I snatched my hand back, but before I could speak, Alex did. "I need either a special or a civil license to marry immediately. Which one can I get faster?" he asked the constable.

He made the declaration before everyone and didn't even look at me. And though I'd never planned to marry, though I knew our time together wasn't a forever joining, I thought I'd meant more to him than to be a burdensome obligation, like a chore that had to be taken care of.

"No, you don't," I said emphatically. "Unless there's a different woman you're marrying. Remember? I'm not marrying anyone, ever." Turning abruptly, I quit the room, amid a crowd full of stunned faces and gasps. The most shocked were Constable Poole's deputy and secretary. I had little doubt that everything that had transpired during the day would spread like a fire through town. I ran from the building. With each step my heart felt as if little pieces shattered off to painfully stab me everywhere. Tears burned my eyes.

Diving into the carriage and snapping the curtains shut, I buried my face in my hands, realizing just how big a fool I really was. I thought I could walk away from Alex and quietly live my life alone in some obscure corner, protected from the demons lurking in the minds of others, the demons that clawed at my peace of mind. What I didn't know was that walking away from love for any reason would rip the very heart of me apart.

That was the real monster hidden beneath the surface of life. The destruction of love. I'd proven to be my own worst enemy, for I'd not only chained myself to love's unrequited rock and unleashed a monster to devour me, but I'd slain Perseus as well.

* * *

"You shouldn't have rejected Alex so thoroughly in front of the whole world," Cassie said as she paced the floor of my room.

I'd spent the remainder of the day in my room. My untouched tray of food sat on my desk and I'd sent away everyone who tried to see me. Cassie hadn't taken no for an answer and had filched a key and intruded into my misery anyway. I'd already prepared for bed, had the lights off, and the covers over my head. I knew Alex wasn't coming. Not tonight, and maybe never again. I felt as if I had a six-foot-two hole in my heart and I couldn't seem to stop the tears.

Cassie had snatched the covers back and started pacing the room. "We have to do something, Andrie!"

I dabbed at my eyes. "Cassie, things are better off left as they are. You didn't read his thoughts about marrying me; I did. I won't marry any man who feels that he *has* to marry me. That's not love."

"Are you sure that's how he felt? When Sean first declared that he was marrying me, I thought he was doing the honorable thing as well, but he loved me."

"A man can lie with his words, and with his actions for a time, but his thoughts will always tell the truth of it. I'm sorry I've brought this upon you. When I involved myself with Alex, I knew I would be impugning my reputation to some degree, and that there would be whispers. But I didn't expect I would be shouting my affair before the entire village."

"Hush, Andrie. I don't give a fig about what people say anymore and you know that. And the Killdarens thrive on controversy, so they'll not be calling any kettles black."

I didn't tell her that once we'd rid Dartmoor's End of the evil stalking and murdering innocent women, I would leave. There would be time enough to cross that bridge in the future. Since I couldn't cower, I too felt the need to pace. Getting out of bed, I walked over to the window to gaze out at the night and the gardens. Alex was so very close. I wanted to just reach out my hand and touch him one last time, to feel the warmth of him, the vitality. I wanted to know the heat of his desire deep inside of me one more time, even though once more would never be enough. Tears blurred my vision again.

Cassie joined me at the window. "It's hard to believe a woman died last night. That she died just beyond the stables while we slept."

I shivered. "I know. Why didn't anyone hear her screams? Surely the groomsmen who slept in the quarters next to the stable should have heard something."

"I don't know," Cassie said. "This time the killer murdered a stranger to us, yet I feel as if the circle of death he is drawing around us is closer than ever."

"Cassie, I hate to say this, but I think that circle is even closer than we've ever realized. Alex was framed with his own sword that he used here last night."

"I know. Sean knows. He sent messages to Lord Ashton, Mr. Drayson, and Sir Warwick, telling them that we wouldn't be receiving callers for the next few weeks. Thinking that the killer is either the earl or Stuart is almost like thinking Sean or Alex guilty." She drew a deep breath. "Right or wrong, I can't do that. Though the weapons were inadvertently left on the terrace last night where anyone could have taken a sword, Sean doesn't want to take any chances. I also overheard him and Alex planning something else as well."

"What?"

"Alex is readying his ship. I expect that in the next day or so we'll be asked to pack a small bag and we'll take a tour of the coast."

"As much as I would dearly love to do that, it won't solve the problem here, only delay it. This murderer hasn't been caught in eight years. He's smart and he's deadly and he bides his time. He'll wait until we are least expecting it and then he'll act."

Cassie shuddered. "Andrie, you scare me. That is not a

very reassuring prediction. I may just suggest to Sean that we take those whom we know we can trust and disappear to America."

Before I could ask just exactly who we could trust, I saw a sudden flash of fire in the darkness outside my window. My heart thudded, remembering the fire at the Kennedy Mansion. Though this light came from the gardens, it still frightened me.

"There's a fire in the gardens."

Cassie gasped, pressing closer to the windowpane. "Oh, no!" She ran over and doused the lamplight, drenching us in darkness.

The flash of fire erupted into five different lights that outlined about a dozen people standing together. Then a huge blaze caught and the image of a woman hanging on a rope from a tall pole came into focus as she was set on fire.

I screamed.

"It's an effigy, Andrie," Cassie said, grabbing my arm. "It's not a real woman."

Half a dozen lantern lights appeared from the direction of the stables and the distinct pop of a pistol sounded.

The torch carriers began to separate.

Cassie gasped. "I hope that's the groomsmen sending a warning. I'm going to get Sean." She ran to the door then turned back. I couldn't seem to do anything but stare at the burning figure, feeling the hot flames sear my soul. "Andrie, see if Prudence and Rebecca are in their quarters. I left them in the drawing room, but that was some time ago. Tell them what's happening and get Gemini. All of you meet me in the drawing room."

She left and I stuck my feet in my slippers and slid my robe on as I ran across the corridor and knocked on Prudence's door. Receiving no answer after my second knock, I opened the door to peek inside and would have left except I saw the flickering light of a lamp from under the door of the adjoining room and thought Prudence and Rebecca might have fallen asleep.

"Prudence," I called, dashing across the darkened sitting room. Getting no response, I opened the door and gasped in shock. Prudence and Rebecca lay bound and gagged on the bed. I took one step and something heavy slammed into the back of my head. Searing pain blinded me. Though I couldn't see, I knew I was falling. Then everything went black.

23

I awoke to a suffocating blackness, gagged, and from the pain at my wrists and ankles, I knew I was tightly bound. My head throbbed so badly that I feared I would be sick. A man carried me over his shoulder, a man who struggled with every step, a man whose pent-up rage screamed through my mind like a gale force wind. It made it very difficult to see the images flashing through him, like trying to see in the blinding rain of a horrific storm.

I didn't struggle, instead I focused on looking into his mind.

The more I saw, the more confused I became. I thought his rage would be directed at me, but it wasn't. At the center of this man's anger was the earl. I didn't see more than that before he dumped me on cold, hard stone. His slow steps and labored breathing disappeared, and I lay in confused darkness, wrapped in a blanket.

I listened for a while longer until I was sure I was alone, then I struggled to sit up, but was too tightly bound. After several frustrating attempts, I decided to roll. My efforts had me falling through the air and landing painfully hard, face-down. I cried out and had to fight the nausea trying to consume me. Once I could focus again, I felt the blanket was looser so I fearfully rolled again. This time I didn't fall and I eventually freed myself from the rough material, but still didn't know where I was. Total blackness surrounded me, one that smelled dank and musty and gnawed at the edges of my memory.

Before I could feel around, the sound of footsteps returned and light filled the room. I blinked with sickening dread at the medieval torture devices in front of me. I was in Alex's dungeon. Whipping my head around, I found Sir Warwick entering the dungeon from a stone door in a far corner nowhere near the stairs leading up to the main castle.

"You harlot. What are you doing?" Scowling angrily at me, he set down the lamp and marched toward me. I flung myself back against the stone floor, lifted my bound legs, and kicked him in the knees. He cried out and fell to the side.

"What in the hell is going on in there?" a man roared. Just as I was trying to place the voice, Constable Poole ran into the dungeon from the same direction as Sir Warwick. Relief flooded me until the constable smiled. "You ready for your punishment, whore? You've dishonored all of mankind and must die." He walked over to the shelves and picked up a deadly looking contraption. "We'll use a number of these tonight, but I think I'm going to enjoy this one the most. It's called a pear, did you know that?" He held up a long bulbous thing with needle-sharp points on the end. He pressed a lever and the bulb snapped outward into four deadly spikes. "And when I'm done, I'm going to rip you open to see just how well your cleansing went. Blood washes away sins, and your sins are great."

Above the thundering of my heart, I already felt an excruciating pain wrench me deeply inside. I'd never encountered such evil. The man was completely insane and Sir Warwick just stared at the constable and his Inquisitional toy with a look of utter fascination on his face.

The constable glanced at Sir Warwick. "You were supposed to have her ready for me." ·

"I was delayed. By trying to frame Blackmoor, you've put their guard up against even me. So while I had the opportunity, I had to take the time to assure the earl will wallow in pain for the rest of his life."

"What do you mean?"

"His whore and his brat will disappear tonight. They're in the caves."

"You imbecile! Now I've even less time. Your vendetta against the earl is ruining everything. Putting that brat on the roof only made them question more. Things haven't been the same since."

"You told me to shut the brat up," Warwick said.

"We'll discuss this later."

The constable grabbed my bound wrists and hauled me to me feet. I screamed and gagged from the horror of his thoughts as they whirled through my mind. Images of women screaming for mercy as he tortured their bodies. He painfully jerked the gag down, cutting my lip against my teeth. Bitter blood filled my mouth.

"Scream for me," he rasped, excited. "I want to hear you scream." He grabbed my thumb and wrenched it back. I cried out at the pain stabbing up my arm and fell to my knees.

An almost orgasmic euphoria filled the constable's mind. It was short-lived. Images of a small boy huddled in a corner watching man after man use a naked, broken woman in every way imaginable and tossing a coin on the floor when they'd finished flashed through his mind. Those images were followed by ones of the boy stabbing that woman over and over again.

"You killed your mother," I said, gasping to hold back my need to scream again with pain. No matter what, I had to keep him from feeding off my pain, even if he killed me in the process. Provoking his rage would be less painful than satisfying his desire.

He let go of me and stepped back.

"Your mother was a helpless prostitute and you stabbed her to death."

"You liar," he screamed at me.

"I can read your thoughts, you bastard. You're unworthy to judge or punish anyone." Though I didn't believe one's birth determined one's worth, he did, and I used it.

"What does she mean? Read your thoughts?" Sir Warwick asked the constable, moving closer.

"She's lying," yelled the constable. Grabbing my hair, he pulled me up and dragged me to the stone table, where chains were anchored to hold victims in place for torture. Tears spilled from my eyes and my scalp felt as if it were on fire. Shoving me down upon the slab, he grabbed my wrists, wrapped a chain around them, and wrenched them over my head. I focused on seeing into his mind. It was a roaring hell unimaginable anywhere but in the depths of the most evil damned souls.

Through the slew of murders marching like grotesque soldiers through his mind I saw Mary's image and his thoughts about her. "Mary was an innocent virgin and you raped her," I cried.

"What?" Sir Warwick asked, his face twisting in surprise.

"She's lying." He squeezed my breast hard.

I wrenched away, screaming at him. His thoughts flooded my mind. "That's why you didn't torture her as you did the others. And Lady Helen, too! She came to you for help because Sir Warwick had stolen the jewels the earl had given her. You beat and raped her and put her in the maze from the tunnels. The symbol means they were virgin sacrifices."

"She knows. She's a witch," said Sir Warwick, shaken.

"See this ring of a serpent on my finger?" I said directing their attention to Aphrodite's ring. "It protects me. I can see the future too, and you're both hanging with the birds feeding on your carcasses. Alex and Sean are almost here."

The constable took a step back. "She wears the mark of

the serpent. She must be burned at the stake. It will be the only way to purge her from Satan's hand. Unchain her," he ordered Sir Warwick.

"Touch me and I'll tell your darkest secrets to the world," I told them, glaring at them as I forced myself not to struggle or show any weakness.

"You do it, you unclean, lying bastard," Sir Warwick sneered to the constable. "The son of a cheap whore."

The constable swung around and slammed his fist into Sir Warwick's face. "Your mother was a whore, too. Just a rich one kept by Dartraven's father. And your wife, as well. Isn't that why you poisoned her? All women eventually become whores."

My mind reeled, but I didn't have a chance to filter through the implications of his words.

"Get her loose now." The constable pulled out a long knife and brandished it at Sir Warwick.

Warwick pulled out a pistol and smiled.

"You don't want to kill me just yet," the constable said. "You've got Dartraven's woman. You've watched her long enough that you want her before you eliminate her, don't you? Just think how much you can torment your half brother if you send photographs of her being used, of *her* being punished."

Sir Warwick gazed at the constable, admiration rekindling in his eyes.

"Drop the knife," Alex demanded in a low and deadly voice as he entered the room, pistol pointed. Sean stood right beside him, armed as well.

Constable Poole laughed and lifted the knife higher. Straining against the chains, I kicked the constable in the back just as Alex fired. Alex and Sean ducked and Sean fired, too. One bullet hit the constable's face, decimating his left cheek. The other dug a furrow along his temple. He fell against the shelves of torture devices, knocking a number of them down on his head. One sharp metal spike pierced his groin and he screamed in pain and passed out. I wanted to chain him in place and leave him just like that until his flesh turned as rotten as his soul.

Turning away, I tried to shove that thought aside. I couldn't let what he was make me like him. I saw Sir Warwick move.

"Watch out," I yelled as Sir Warwick pointed his pistol at Sean's head. Warwick fired. Twisting, Alex knocked Sean aside and the bullet that would have killed him hit Alex.

"Alex!" I screamed.

Sean shot from his position on the floor and Sir Warwick dropped his pistol, grabbing his stomach.

Alex staggered over to me, unleashing the chain wrapping my bound wrists. His face was grim, twisted with pain; blood spread wildly down the front of his shirt. Before he freed me, he keeled over, passing out on top of me, his only discernible thought was that he had to marry me now.

"Sean," I cried. "Alex is hurt badly. Help me!"

Sean rushed over. He cut the rope binding my wrists and the chain fell free. My arms and hands stung horribly and I cried out as I tried to touch Alex.

"Help is coming," Sean said as he cut through the rope at my ankles then lifted Alex into his arms. "Can you walk?" Sean planned to carry Alex upstairs. Sir Warwick groaned from where he twisted with pain in the corner.

I scrambled up, my body shuddering from the effort. I knew that Alex's wound was bleeding too much. "Lay Alex down, Sean. Bring the doctor here. Alex won't make it if you move him."

Sean stared hard at me for a second. Then he set Alex on the stone table. I quickly gathered the hem of my robe and pressed firmly against Alex's wound, digging deep into the soft tissue where his arm and shoulder met. But my arms were shaking so badly that I feared I wasn't doing him any good. "Get the doctor quickly," I cried.

"I can't leave you. Stuart will be here with the doctor soon. Let me do that," said Sean. Pushing my hands aside, he applied deep, steady pressure to Alex's wound. "You aren't going to die! You had bloody well better hear me, Alex! I'll find a way to follow you to the grave and bring you back." Sean cried quietly then and I shut my eyes and prayed that there wouldn't be any more graves dug in Dartmoor's End for a very long time, except for Constable Poole's and Sir Warwick's. But even that seemed too humane for the monsters they were.

The five minutes before the doctor and Stuart appeared seemed like a lifetime. They were accompanied by the earl, Lord Ashton, and Mr. Drayson. I didn't pay any attention to what was happening to Sir Warwick or Constable Poole; my mind was focused on Alex.

The minute Sean released pressure for Dr. Luden to see the wound, blood surged in a flood.

"An artery has been hit," said the doctor urgently. "Press here so hard you think you're going to break his ribs." He shoved Sean's hands to a certain place on Alex's chest. "Stuart, hold Alex down; don't let him move or he'll likely lose his arm." Dr. Luden looked at me. "I'm going to need your help, can you do it?"

"Yes."

The next thirty minutes passed excruciatingly slowly. The doctor liberally poured eye-burning antiseptic over everything. He soaked Alex's bared chest and gaping wound. Then he poured it down his arms and hands, my arms and hands, and into the metal case that contained small surgical instruments. Then he opened the wound wider with a knife, and as I handed him different instruments, he removed the bullet and stitched Alex's wound closed.

"Now all we can do is clean him up and pray he doesn't develop a high fever. If infection sets in, he'll lose his arm anyway. During the Crimean War an injury like that did cost a man his arm. We'd have to amputate and cauterize before—"

The world went completely black and all that I could think was I was falling off the ends of the earth and would disappear forever.

* * *

When I awoke, it was to Cassie and Gemini's concerned faces in my own bedroom in Killdaren's Castle. An entire day had passed.

"Alex," I said, scrambling up from the bed, my head throbbing.

Cassie pressed me back upon the pillows. "Is alive. Now you need to take care of yourself." She looked quickly away and busied herself with the counterpane.

I grabbed her hand.

"Bloody hell, is he insane?" I exclaimed as I read her thoughts. Burning with a fever, a wounded Alex had left Dragon's Cove and was currently sailing along the treacherous coastline, making ever widening circles, dredging a fishing net through the water in his search for a body. Sean had hired an army of men, half of them were guarding Killdaren's Castle, and the other half scoured the shore. While being transported in a cart with his hands bound, Constable Jack Poole had escaped, even though he had been unconscious until that point. His guards chased him to the cliffs of Dragon's Cove where he jumped into the sea. His body had yet to be found.

"Good God. This is awful." I released Cassie's hand and pushed back the covers.

"Andromeda Andrews! Just exactly what do you think you're going to be able to do about anything?" Gemini asked, her face flushing with anger.

"You've already done what you can," Cassie added. "Now it's time to let the men do what they can."

"*You're* saying that?"

She cleared her throat. "This investigative stuff is entirely too dangerous. We've all nearly come close to dying this summer and I'm declaring an end to it. Are there any arguments from either of you?" She looked at Gemini, who shook her head. Then Cassie glared at me.

"I—no." Sighing, I leaned back again. "What about Sir Warwick? Surely he didn't escape as well."

"No. The earl's half brother is hovering on the edge of the very painful death of being gut shot. Dr. Luden, who refused to give the man anything for pain, says that he'll be dead in a day."

"Not that it's important, but why didn't anyone ever say they were brothers?"

Cassie shook her head. "No one knew except the earl. Apparently, Warwick's mother was the ward of the Earl of Dartraven's grandfather. The Earl of Dartraven's father, who was engaged to a relation of royalty, seduced Warwick's mother. They set her up in a nearby manor and married her to a poor local barrister named Warwick. Had they done what was right, Warwick by all rights should have been the Earl of Dartraven. Warwick spent his whole life doing and saying everything he could to subtly ruin the earl and his family. I still can't believe what he did to Rebecca. Leaving an innocent child to fall to her death—"

"Prudence and Rebecca!" I gasped, realizing that I didn't know what had happened to them.

"They are fine and I expect will be even finer very soon. The earl has asked Prudence to marry him." Gemini clasped her hands, giving emphasis to her words.

"It's about time."

"Well, it's not official yet." Cassie smiled, as if enjoying a secret.

"What?"

"Prudence has informed the earl that she'll accept his offer shortly, but wants a wee bit of time to assure herself he can be the attentive husband and loving father she and Rebecca deserve."

I smiled, feeling all tingly that Prudence had realized her own worth as a person and wasn't going to settle for what crumbs life dished out to those not willing to grasp their own happiness when it passed them. I clasped my hands and felt the familiar curl of the golden, green-eyed serpent around my finger—Aphrodite's ring. Looking into its eyes an odd feeling of unrest niggled inside of my heart. Had I done that? Had I let happiness pass me by without even trying to grasp it?

No. How can you grasp what doesn't exist? If in those moments of absolute dire emotion Alex didn't love me, then he never would.

I met Jamie for the first time the very next day when I walked into the kitchens to pilfer a scone. I hadn't felt much like eating, but Mrs. Murphy had the entire castle smelling so strongly that my mouth watered despite my lack of interest. I'd *had* to get out of my bed.

At first Jamie's sheer size took me aback and I wondered if I'd suddenly shrunk to the Lilliputian size depicted in *Gulliver's Travels*. He stood towering above Stuart, Mrs. Frye, and Mrs. Murphy. He was very pale and trembled with every movement. It was then that I saw how baggy the clothes he wore were. He'd apparently lost a tremendous amount of weight.

"Scones, Jamie, fresh scones just for you." Tears were streaming down Mrs. Frye's cheeks.

"N-n-no," Jamie cried. "C-c-can't. S-s-sick."

It would take time for Jamie to heal. I tentatively walked farther into the kitchen.

Mrs. Frye gasped and turned away.

Jamie looked at me and I wanted to cry from the bruises on his face. "M-m-mary?"

I decided to follow Cassie's lead. There would be time enough when Jamie was well for him to learn my name. "Yes. Remember? I need you to help me. You have to eat to help me."

"Broth?" I looked at Mrs. Murphy. "Do you have some?"

She pointed to a bowl and spoon on the counter.

"Sit before you fall down, Jamie," I told him firmly as I shoved a stool behind him and tugged on his sleeve. When I touched him, I could see his thoughts. He was afraid. Food had made him sick in the prison and he thought all food would make him sick now.

"Jamie, this food won't hurt you. It is good food now. You won't get any bad food any more. Do you understand?"

"G-g-good. M-m-mary?"

"Yes."

"Hurt you," he cried. "M-m-mary hurt you."

I saw it then. How Jamie had been trying to help a wounded fox that had run into the caves. Maybe he'd seen the fox while searching the shore for Mary. He'd followed the fox and had found Mary's body in the chamber under the Circle of the Stone Virgins. He'd cried and cried. From the image in Jamie's mind, Mary had been dead for some time. If Jamie confused Cassie and Mary, no wonder Cassie's appearance had upset him.

"This is medicine, Jamie. Medicine to make Jamie well to help." I held the bowl of broth in my hands and gave Jamie the spoon.

He took a shaky spoonful, then several more.

"Thank God," Stuart said. "I'll be back shortly."

He crossed the kitchens. "Where are you going, Stuart Frye?" Mrs. Murphy asked. "I've fresh scones that need to be eaten."

"I'll be back. First, I have to speak to my father. The earl said he had some horses for sale."

"What are you going to do with horses now?" Mrs. Frye asked as she cautiously drew closer to where I stood next to Jamie.

"Haven't you heard of the Frye brothers, Mother? They're famous. They're the best horse breeders and trainers in all of Ireland." There were tears in Stuart's dark eyes.

Mrs. Frye shook her head in confusion. She started to say something else to Stuart and I touched her sleeve, drawing her attention to me. "Every man has to have a dream," I whispered. "And every woman, too."

I didn't have one.

"I stopped dreaming a very long time ago," Mrs. Frye said. "Dreams are for fools."

I blinked at her, wondering if I would be just like her forty years from now. "No. Dreams belong to those who are alive, not to fools. Fools are the ones who don't believe in them. They shrivel up and die inside." I placed the bowl in her hand. "The food in prison made Jamie sick, so now he thinks all food will make him sick. If you want him to eat, for now you have to tell him it's medicine until he gets well enough to understand."

"Who are you?" she asked.

"Cassie's sister and I hope not a fool."

The scones turned out to be the most delicious meal of my life. Later that day, when I told Cassie and Stuart what I'd seen, they'd both cried, tears of guilt and tears of relief to finally understand what had happened. But that was the only relief in the tension surrounding Killdaren's Castle. The rest of the week passed as if everyone was holding their breath. Sir Warwick died and was buried. Cassie, Gemini, Prudence, and Bridget lit a fire for him and burned all of the gruesome cards from the music room. A second week passed and we knew we were going to die if we didn't get out.

Alex's ship had docked three days before, so I knew he'd received my letter, thanking him for saving me and wishing him a happy life.

Sean, who had gone to Dragon's Cove to see him, said Alex had lost some weight, but looked well. He didn't tell me anything else, and I curled my hand into a fist, refusing to give in to the temptation to touch him and see Alex's image.

A beautiful fall morning arrived. A morning where the sea and the wind swirled briskly, let loose from the heat of the summer sun to dance excitedly amid the chill in the air. Cassie declared at breakfast that Sean could send an entire army with us, but the women were going in to town to shop. Quite frankly we were all aware of the fact that if we hadn't been forbidden to leave the castle, we wouldn't necessarily be dying to leave at the moment. But I could see Cassie's point that we couldn't spend our entire lives hidden either. Whether Constable Jack Poole had died at sea, or ever appeared again to terrorize women, we couldn't stay imprisoned by our fear.

That revelation drove home a very sore point to me, for that was exactly what I had planned to do with my life just a month ago. Having lived through the evil of Constable Jack Poole and Sir Warwick, my urgency to leave had eased a great deal. What had once seemed my only choice had now faded to an option. Did I want to live my life alone and hidden?

It wasn't until we were in the back corner of the mercantile store, admiring a section of fashion wares and looking through a number of older issues of *Godey's Lady's Book on Fashion and Patterns*, that I was reminded of the ugliness still in the world.

Two women came in the door, speaking loudly. At the time I was sure it was for me and my sister's benefit.

"I tell you, Alex Killdaren killed those women and then framed the poor constable and that sad, lonely Sir Warwick. The rich think they can do anything they want regardless."

I saw red and went steaming across the store. "You ignorant fools don't have a clue what you are talking about and how much a disservice you are doing a great and honorable man! Alex Killdaren had nothing to do with those women dying. The constable tortured women. He raped them. If they were virgins, he carved their breasts with a sacrificial symbol, and if they weren't, he tortured them. He . . . oh . . . God . . . he—"

"Andrie!"

I froze at the sound of Alex's voice and shifted my gaze. He stood across the room, looking more of a pirate than ever, sun bronzed, dark hair longer and wilder, features leaner and harsher. But his full, lush mouth was the same.

"You have to let it go," he said softly. "You can't let that monster haunt you. I hope these women will never know the horrors we've seen. I'd much rather have my incorrigible self impugned than for any woman to know what that man did. It sickens the soul. Do you understand what I'm saying?"

Tears filled my eyes and fell. He was right; my soul had been sickened and I hadn't let myself grieve or heal.

"Are you ready to marry me yet?"

"No," I whispered, and turned from the store and ran.

He caught up with me outside. "Why the bloody hell not?"

I shook my head and began walking down the street. Killdaren guards followed and everyone on the street stared.

"Andromeda!" Alex shouted. "Damn woman!" He snatched me off my feet and flung me over his shoulder. My breath flew out in a whoosh. I kicked and he grabbed my legs tighter.

"Put me down." He didn't and I couldn't read a thing in his mind.

I arched back and looked at the following guards. They were grinning, thoroughly enjoying the spectacle, obviously not seeing Alex as any threat to my well-being. "Fools," I yelled at them.

Alex marched down the street to the docks. Charging over to the planks, he carted me to his ship and crossed the gangplank, yelling at the men to make themselves scarce, quick. Everyone disappeared and the guards didn't board the ship. Once Alex reached the far end of the deck, he plopped me on my feet and grabbed my shoulders.

"Tell me!" he shouted. "Tell me why you won't marry? Why would you rather face ruin and be ostracized than be with me?"

Real pain and confusion filled him. I inhaled, trying to see past my own emotions to make him understand. "Alex. You don't *have* to marry me. Whatever the repercussions of our affair are, I am fully prepared to face them. And after last week, I know there aren't any forthcoming consequences either."

"Hell," he said, releasing me and raking his hands through his hair. "I didn't mean for it to sound as if I *had* to marry you. I want to marry you."

"No. You don't. I know. So you don't have to lie to me."

"I'm not lying."

"Yes, you are."

"Good God, woman. You must be the most exasperating person on the face of this earth." He paced the deck a minute. "Believe me, I wouldn't marry you if I didn't really want to marry you."

"You don't understand, Alex. I know you don't because . . ." I drew a bracing breath. "I can read people's thoughts."

He froze for a long moment; his sharp green gaze searched mine. "What do you mean, you can read thoughts?"

I turned and faced the sea, setting my hand on the railing, drinking in the salt and the sun. "Remember that day in town when the man on the boardwalk bumped into me? I had said more to him than I admitted to the constable. And it wasn't anything like 'Lou Tiller or Miller' as you suggested. I said, 'You killed her. You strangled her.' When he touched me I could read the thought that he currently had in his head; it was of him murdering his wife. It's that way with most people, most of the time. You're a little bit different for me. I can only read your thoughts occasionally."

He moved to stand beside me, facing out to the sea as well. "You're serious, aren't you?"

"Yes."

"So what thoughts of mine have you read?"

I drew a deep breath. "Here on the ship, the day you got Iris, you had an image of me bound naked in a ship's bunker. Another clear thought was immediately after the first time we made love. More than anything else you wanted to make love to me again, right that minute, saw yourself thrusting into me, but the hunger scared you somehow and you wanted to get me dressed and out of your home as quickly as you could. And you were very much of the opinion that I had seduced you and you weren't sure how you felt about it. When I fell into the sea and you found me, you blamed yourself for what happened. The moment I reached the surface and could speak, I—"

"You said, 'Don't you dare think that! It's not your fault.'"

"Yes. In the sheriff's office and when you . . . when you tried to free me in the dungeon, you had only one thought in your head. You—"

"I had to marry you. That thought has been consuming my every waking moment for some time now. Andrie, just because a woman ruins herself before the world to save a man, and that man walks out of jail panicked that he has to marry her before anyone causes her any harm, does not mean that the man doesn't *want* to marry her and that he doesn't love her. When a man thinks he is dying and that the woman he loves will be left unprotected, he's thinking with his whole soul that he has to marry her before he dies."

"I know," I said softy, tears gathering in my eyes. "Alex, that is your honor crying out, not your heart."

He swung me around to face him, cupping my cheeks in his hands and staring deeply into my eyes. "No, it's not. Reading a man's heart is different than reading a man's mind, Andrie. And you can't read all of a person's thoughts, therefore, you don't ever have a clear picture of who that person really is. Everyone is like the sea, different on the surface than beneath. By reading random thoughts you're always drawn beneath the surface, and you must feel like you're drowning all the time. At least those of us in complete ignorance can choose to stay on the surface and accept people for who they purport themselves to be, or delve beneath the surface and conjecture if they are vastly different. You've been saddled with a grave disability in life. It's mind-boggling."

Nobody in my entire life had ever understood me so well. I set my hands on his shoulders and searched his gaze. "How can you see that so clearly? How can you accept what I am so easily?"

"I've explored many things in this world and have discovered many mysteries. There is much that can't be explained. But more than anything else, I believe in things greater than myself and of times and people different than me. The Druid chanting can only be done by a few that are blessed with the right tone to their voice and an inner knowledge, or instinct if you will, of what a creature or person is feeling. Usually it is only when I am focused on that individual, and I have blocked everything from my mind, that I can sense emotions. When you declared you wouldn't marry me in the constable's office, I knew you needed a lot more time and space, but I'm out of patience. I so desperately need you. Will you marry me, Andrie, and share life with me?"

"What about your vow to leave Sean your title?"

"That's what my challenge in the sword fight was all about. You urged me to see for myself if he was crippled or not, and you were right. I was more hindered by the past than he was."

"And what if he'd stumbled and faltered?"

"And I still felt compelled to leave him my title to make amends for the past?"

I nodded.

He grinned. "Well, before I became involved with you I'd decided that I wanted you for my mistress. I'd never had one really, and you were it. Once you became my sister-in-law and I didn't see that as possible, I tried to stay away from you, but that was becoming impossible. Then when I became involved with you, I decided that having you for a mistress just wouldn't do. On my trip to Penzance, I began investigating just how Alexander Killdaren could disappear forever, and Captain Black could move to America. But that was going to take some planning because I couldn't leave Cornwall without my Friesians."

I frowned, then blinked. "Iris and Eros."

"Yes. Are you by any chance wondering where you fit in this grand scheme?"

I nodded.

"Maybe I can read a thought or two of yours as well," he said, making me laugh. "You were in my bunk in my cabin. Unfortunately, I've yet to imagine you there bound. It is a thought worth investigating, though, especially since it seems to be your, um, secret desire."

"What?"

"I'll lay claim to all of those other thoughts, but that one had to come from you."

"That's impossible; I've never imagined something like that, ever."

"So, you don't have imaginings about a swashbuckling pirate having his way with you?"

My cheeks burned. "No."

"What, never?"

"Not ever," I said, though I had and he knew it. He scooped me up and I wrapped my arms around his neck. "Where are you going?"

"I'm going to have my wicked way with you." Then he stopped and looked at me very seriously, his green gaze teeming with heat and deep emotion. "I love you, Andromeda. Will you marry me?"

"I love you, too. Yes, I'll marry you." I leaned up and kissed him, my heart singing.

"Tonight?"

"What?"

"Will you marry me tonight? We're on a ship in the sea and Captain Jansen is somewhere belowdeck. We can send for family and be married when the sunset paints the sky with glory."

"Yes."

"I'll marry you again, later, as well. I want the whole world to see that you are mine."

"Then I'll marry you twice." I sighed with pleasure and a bit of relief, for I think Cassie would have had my hide if I'd cheated her of the pleasure of planning a wedding.

"All right, you eavesdropping, wily sea dogs. Show yourselves or face the cat'o'nine!" Alex shouted, making me jump.

Loud grumbling voices came from behind a pile of crates.

"He heard you scratching, Davey."

"Did not, Brighty, you uppity fool. The captain's got ears in the back of his head."

"Eyes you dolt. The saying goes 'eyes in the back of his head.' His ears are on the side."

"Men!" Alex yelled.

"Aye, Captain." Half a dozen sailors popped up, hats in their hands. Brighty, wearing his best butler's suit, was among them. His wig kept flapping up in the breeze and I was sure a gull would swoop down and claim the prize for its nest.

"Swab the deck and inform Captain Jansen that we set sail an hour before sunset. Brighty, go to Killdaren's Castle and tell anyone who wants to see the wedding to be on board. We will wait for no man, nor woman, except the bride, of course." The men scattered and Alex strode to the stairs that led below the deck.

"Alex," I whispered. "Where are we going?"

"To show my new bride the captain's quarters. You'll need to inspect them very closely and give me a list of things that you'll think necessary to have with you for when we go sailing." He rambled competently down the stairs with me in his arms.

"What kind of sailing are you talking about?"

He grinned. "The kind of sailing that a pirate like me does very well." He pushed through a door, then kicked it closed with the heel of his boot. He kissed me deeply as he strode across the room to his bunk, where he gently lay me down and covered me with the warmth of his love and the heat of his passion. I slid my hand down and pressed my palm to his urgent arousal. "Does this mean you'll always be sailing with a Jolly Roger now?"

Alex laughed. "At full mast at all times."

Epilogue

"You may kiss the bride," said Captain Jansen just as the sun cast the sea and the horizon in a glorious array of golden yellows, wavy blues, and soft pinks. Looking regal with sharp blue eyes filled with haunting shadows, he appeared to be a man of many experiences, and not all of them good. He wore the military uniform of an officer, but he was no longer in the Queen's service, a mystery to be sure, but one for another day.

No bride could have had a finer sanctuary to wed than that of God's own. Nor could I ask to have better people with me. Cassie, with a peaceful hand gently pressing her stomach, stood to my left. She glanced my way and I knew we'd won, we'd slain the Dragon's Curse and conquered the evil with love. Gemini was next to Cassie, and didn't look my way. I don't think she could see anything but Captain Jansen. Sean, wearing dark glass spectacles Alex had found in his travels, braced Alex's right. They were brothers that no man or curse could split asunder. Bridget was next to Gemini, and was now known as Mrs. Bridget Frye, having married Stuart not more than ten minutes ago. She smiled brightly, her hopes and dreams shinning like stars in her eyes. Stuart stood by Sean, looking antsy. He was a man with a dream that he couldn't wait to make happen. Alex had promised Stuart Friesians to breed on his future farm.

"Has he kissed the princess yet?" Rebecca asked in a loud whisper.

"Not yet," said Alex, grinning so broadly that both his dimples danced with humor.

I smiled, turning to face the full warmth of Alex's love. "Tell him to hurry, or you'll be all grown up before it happens," I said.

"Hurry," said Rebecca. "You have to kiss the plums, Georgie Porgie." She stood between the earl and Prudence, holding their hands.

"Sugar plums, Becky," said the earl. "Remember that makes them dance, not cry."

Alex blinked. "Kiss the bride," he whispered. "A very special bride. My bride."

Lord Ashton, Mr. Drayson, Mr. and Mrs. Murphy, Mrs. Lynds, Dr. Luden, Brighty, and all of the sailors witnessed Alex declare his love for me and mine for him. The sea swayed the ship, rocking us gently. Salt flavored the air to a tangy sweetness and the wind kissed my skin like a benediction from a host of angels. I turned my face to Alex, reading his heart in his eyes as he leaned down and kissed me. Just before I closed my eyes to give myself over to feeling only Alex, the emerald eyes of the serpent's ring winked at me, as if Aphrodite sent her approval. I winked back and then felt my spirit soar. I could be all that I longed to be.

Only love could lift the weight and pain of life and fill the heart.

Alex loved me, and the cleansing wonder of it renewed my soul.

Turn the page for a special preview of
Jennifer St. Giles next novel

Silken Shadows

Coming soon from Berkley Sensation!

My hopes that the splash of Captain Jansen's bath water had drowned out the sound of my stifled sneeze sank as I heard his movements still.

It was too quiet; nothing but the rock and creak of the ship could be heard. I didn't dare breathe or move, yet my heart thundered so loudly that I knew it had to be echoing off the cabin walls.

I was a fool. I should have crawled back into my brother-in-law's sea chest the moment I'd attended to my needs. Then I, Gemini Andrews, wouldn't have been day-dreaming about the maddening Captain Deverell Jansen, the kiss he'd given me three months ago, and what further pleasures would be mine were he to find me in his bunk.

I wouldn't have been sitting on his bed, soaking up the sandalwood and spice scent from his pillow. And I wouldn't have had to dive for cover when the deckhands had barged into his cabin with bath water. And I now wouldn't be stuck under his bunk listening to him climb out of the tub while dust bunnies danced under my nose.

"What in the bloody hell?" he roared.

I must have shut my eyes in dread, because I popped them open when his hot, wet hand clamped around my arm and he dragged me from under his bunk.

He was naked. I couldn't seem to think about anything else, but that. Forget that my plan to reach Northrope before revealing my stowaway status had just gone up in smoke, threatening everything I knew I had to do.

The only thing that mattered was that he was naked and I was flat on my back staring at him, at everything about him. Any sense of modesty escaped me. I was much too interested in seeing up close what I had spent a year imagining.

I didn't even spare a glance at the amused ghosts hovering over his shoulders. I'd seen their crusty, sea salt faces on several occasions and had managed to ignore them. But I'd never seen the captain quite like this before, and couldn't have shut my eyes if my life had depended on it.

He knelt before me, tanned skin, solid muscle, and dark curly hair sluiced with water. Droplets fell from the hard edge of his shadowed jaw, splashed upon my neck, and rolled between my breasts, making me lick my lips in thirst. I hadn't eaten since last night just before I left Killdaren's Castle.

His blue gaze, flashing with anger and something intriguingly darker, felt like a brand upon my lips. The tension filling the air between us sparked almost as much heat inside me as his unrestrained kiss had last Christmas Eve. My lips parted, remembering the gentle coax of his mouth against mine. I'd had several celebratory glasses of the Killdaren's famous spiced wine, he'd had more, and that gentle-at-first kiss had become a hard demand that had awakened a deep hunger.

I sucked in air and his gaze shifted to the rise of my breasts and stayed there. Because of the tight confines of the trunk I'd hid in, I'd worn a loose gown for comfort. Being dragged from beneath the bed had displaced the bodice to the point that my gossamer chemise was the only thing keeping me somewhat decent.

The flare of heat in his sea-blue eyes, left me no doubt that he was remembering our kiss, remembering how he'd cupped my breasts and brushed his thumbs over their aching crests until I'd shuddered with need. I was still quivering with need.

Instead of covering myself, I dropped my gaze to absorb his broad chest, tapered waist, strong legs, and . . . jutting male anatomy that suddenly grew large.

"Good heavens, that's . . . amazing." I blinked several times to assure I was seeing correctly.

Releasing my wrist, he stood. "No, Miss Andrews. What is amazing is that I've refrained from throttling you within an inch of your life. Why in the bloody hell are you on my ship, in my cabin, under my bed!"

The ghosts laughed until they were rolling around in the air, making so much noise my ears hurt. I sent them an admonishing glare and tugged my bodice up.

The captain hadn't waited for an answer. He'd turned away from me, strode to the tub and wrapped a towel about his waist before facing me with a glower. "Bloody hell. What possessed you to pull such a childish prank? There's a storm chasing us and we'll now have to head into the thick of it to get you back. Hopefully, we'll reach Dartmoor's End before people learn of this idiocy and you're reputation will remain intact."

Though I wanted to gasp with outrage that he'd label my mission of duty as a childish prank, I forced myself to calmly rise from the floor and dust off my skirts, inciting another sneeze. His opinion of my venture stung my mind back in order. Naked or not the captain was proving himself to be as insufferable and stifling as the sea chest.

"I'm not returning to Dartmoor's End, Captain Jansen. Not until I help Mr. Adams," I said firmly.

He laughed, harshly incredulous. "Miss Andrews, you're barely out of the schoolroom and have thankfully had few dealings with the realities of murder. There is nothing that you can do to help Mr. Adams that the authorities aren't already doing and what Sean Killdaren will do once he secures his family and can travel north."

Whether it was his disregard of my abilities or the too many years of my life I'd spent suppressing everything about me that didn't fit into the frivolous facade I'd been forced to keep up, but something inside me snapped.

I wanted to shake Captain Jansen off his high mast. I wanted to break free and grab life with my own hands instead of watching others live . . . and love.

"Schoolroom?" He made nineteen sound as if it was a step past wearing nappies, a convenient lie to avoid having to face his feelings—both Cassie and Andrie agreed. And both had said it was up to me to show him the error of his thinking. My sisters had had a great deal of experience with the erroneous thought patterns of men lately. I sauntered to Captain Jansen, my left brow arched with doubt. I didn't stop until my breasts pressed firmly against his damp chest. Then I moved closer until the feel of his arousal pushed enticingly against me. "At least part of you can admit the truth."